THE
HA'PENNY PLACE

GEMMA JACKSON

POOLBEG

Published 2015
by Poolbeg Press Ltd.
123 Grange Hill, Baldoyle,
Dublin 13, Ireland
Email: poolbeg@poolbeg.com

A catalogue record for this book is available from the British Library.

ISBN 978178199-9455

About the author

Gemma Jackson was born in inner-city Dublin, the fifth of seven children. Educated by the nuns at Mount Sackville Convent in Castleknock, she remembers a childhood of hunger, cold and desperation. Yet, through it all, making life worth living, were wonderful people, stories, music and gales of laughter.

She left home at seventeen, desperate to see the wider world.

Gemma has worked her way around the world. As long as the job was legal, she'd do it. She has been an air hostess, advisor and writer for a TV evangelist, hand model and movie extra.

The Ha'penny Place is Gemma's third novel, following on *Through Streets Broad and Narrow* and *Ha'penny Chance*. All three novels are fictional amalgamations of the stories about 'The Lane' and its people that she grew up listening to.

Also by Gemma Jackson

Through Streets Broad and Narrow

Ha'penny Chance

Published by Poolbeg

Acknowledgements

To the people at Poolbeg, thank you so much for allowing me to realise a lifelong dream. I'm a published author – I'll be losing the run of myself. Paula Campbell and Gaye Shortland, thank you. I have heard it rumoured that you are both checking out the webpage of homes for the perpetually bewildered after having to deal with me – sorry!

I am especially grateful to the readers who take the time to visit my webpage and tell me they've enjoyed my books – thank you.

To the Dubliners I grew up around, especially the ones long gone – I remember you all with love and gratitude.

To my daughter Astrid for feeding my tea addiction – I'd get nothing done without the constant supply of tea.

For the people, real and imagined, who populated The Lane. The history of those people is kept alive by the storytellers. I'm proud to be one of them.

Dedication

The Dublin I grew up in was a place where no one locked their doors. You got a box around the ear from whichever adult caught you doing something wrong. A hob-hatcher – someone who stayed inside all day – was one of the worst things you could be. The coal, milk, vegetables were delivered by horse-drawn carts. The local farmer loaned you goats and donkeys to cut the grass. When did my past become ancient history?

Chapter 1

"I feel as if I've spent half me life standing on the Dun Laoghaire docks waving goodbye to people." Ivy Rose Murphy looked into her brother's eyes, determined to imprint his image on her memory forever.

"At least this time you'll have something to remember me by." Shay Murphy AKA Douglas Joyce, star of stage and soon to be famous on the big screen, jerked his head in the direction of the newspaper cameramen loitering around the shipping company's first-class lounge, hoping to capture an image for their papers. He had delayed his departure because of his sister – he couldn't wait any longer. He had places to go, worlds to conquer. He thought the second day of 1926 an ideal time to step out into the unknown.

"Being in the dailies might be alright for you," Ivy nudged her baby brother gently, "but for the likes of me it's mortifying." He'd left home for the first time as the penniless Shay Murphy – today he was the feted entertainer Douglas Joyce. It was far from this kind of attention both of them were raised. Ivy's ivory cheeks were stained with red. She'd never become accustomed to people looking at her and shouting questions. Had these reporter people no homes to go to?

"The state of us and the price of best butter!" Doug/Shay grinned down at his sister, his sparkling violet eyes so like hers it was easy to see the relationship between the pair. "The last time we were here I was down there," a nod of his head towards the crowds of shabbily dressed people milling around the docks, "sick to my stomach with nerves and fear of the unknown. The pair of us weren't dressed up to beat the band neither."

"You'd an arse in yer trousers aself, not like some of them poor buggers." Ivy was determined to fight off the tears that had been threatening for days. She'd cry an ocean when he was gone but she'd be deep-dipped and fried before she'd see him off on his great adventure with tears running down her face.

"You made sure of that, Ivy." Doug examined their twin images in the long glass windows that circled the upper-deck lounge. They looked like two wealthy toffs. The purple tweed suit his sister was wearing covered her from neck to ankles. It was too long to be bang-up-to-the-minute fashion-wise. He'd tried to talk her into the shorter lengths but she'd been horrified at the very thought of exposing her ankles to the world. But, over the suit, Ivy wore his gift of a beige cashmere coat and hat with elegance and style. She looked like she should be in the 'fillums' herself. The sight of his own expertly tailored clothing amused him. The good looks and talent he'd been born with had seen him this far. He wondered how much further he could climb.

"I wish you'd change your mind and come to America with me, Ivy," Doug said for what felt like the thousandth

2

time. He'd saved the money for Ivy's first-class ticket to the land of dreams. He'd had such great plans for them in their new life in America. He'd been offered the chance of a lifetime. A talent scout had approached him with an offer to star in the new 'talkies'– newfangled pictures being made with sound. He'd grabbed the chance with both hands. But the hard-headed woman in his arms had refused all suggestion that she should leave her hand-to-mouth existence in the tenements of Dublin. He'd tried to give her the money he'd saved for her but she'd insisted he'd need it more than she ever would. He'd reluctantly agreed.

"I've given yeh me opinion," Ivy stated firmly. Who knew what Shay was going to find in this place he talked about, Hollywood if yeh didn't mind, and talking pictures. What would they think of next? It would never catch on and Shay was going to need his wits about him to keep from starving. She had her own life to lead and had no wish to find herself in a strange country without a penny to her name and no way of making one. She'd stick to what she knew, thank you very much. She was making a life for herself that many a woman would envy. She'd a roof over her head, food on the table and fire in the hearth. She was wealthy in comparison to her tenement neighbours.

"Smile, Ivy!" Ann Marie Gannon shouted. She was completely unaware of the crowds around her. The expensive camera in her hands held all of her attention. She was determined to record this moment for Ivy.

"Ann Marie, I swear to God yeh sleep with that bloody camera." Ivy turned in her brother's arms and smiled at her friend.

Ann Marie had bought the camera as a Christmas present to herself. It seemed to Ivy the woman was determined to record every moment of daily life. It was a good job she was learning to develop the film herself or she'd be in the poorhouse. The woman might be loaded but she hadn't a lick of sense about saving the pennies. Ann Marie's beige silk suit was bang-up-to-the-minute, the shorter skirt-length exposing her shining silk stockings and butter-soft beige leather shoes. The hat she wore was a song to the milliner's art and framed her pretty face. She'd covered the expensive garment with the long black woollen coat that Ivy's tailor friend and neighbour Mr Solomon had made for her. The coat was covered in special pockets Ann Marie had designed for her equipment.

"It's a shame Mr Smith has gone ahead," Ann Marie said, referring to Doug's friend Johnjo Smith. The man had gone aboard the ship with the luggage. He was determined to earn his keep as Doug's 'dresser'. "I'd have liked a few more photographs of him." She was frustrated at the time it took her to set up the shots but she'd get quicker. She was determined to capture the world around her on film.

"It's almost time, Ivy," Doug said as a loud bleat from a foghorn cut through the sound of the milling crowd.

"Write to me." Ivy hugged her brother to her, her heart breaking.

"It will be weeks before I arrive in California." Doug was glad the studio was paying for his first-class ticket to America. He would have to earn his passage by allowing the studio publicity crew to follow him on the voyage. The film crew and Johnjo would be travelling third class but he would be travelling in style. He expected to be asked to sing and dance for his supper. He didn't care – for the chance he'd been offered he'd stand on his head and whistle if they asked him. "You've seen the brochure of the ship that's going to take us from Liverpool to New York." Doug was trying to distract himself from the pain of this parting.

"A floating palace, you mean." Ivy had been astonished at the sheer glamour of the ship that would carry Shay and Johnjo to the new world. The brochure was almost bald now. It had been passed from hand to hand in 'The Lane' and was the talk of the place still. "You better get going then, Shay." Ivy could hardly speak past the lump in her throat. "I want to hear from yeh regularly. You remember that." She hugged him tightly, her body shaking in his arms.

"I'll write. I promise." Doug hugged his sister close. Who knew if they would ever see each other again? But he refused to allow himself to believe this was the last time he'd see his sister. He'd make it in these new talking pictures, he swore. "I'll send for you when I've made me fortune."

"You do that and if I happen to make me fortune before you I'll come visit yeh in that heathen land." Ivy pressed a kiss into his cheek and stood back. She had to force herself to let go of him.

"Goodbye, Ann Marie." Doug bent and pressed a kiss into the woman's cheek, careful not to knock her gold-rimmed glasses askew. "Take care of my sister, please – if she's ever in need, let me know," he whispered into her ear before stepping back.

Then he waved out the window at Jem Ryan who was

standing down in the street by his gleaming black automobile.

Jem returned the wave, raising his fancy trilby from his head. He was outside the double entrance doors that led into reception and to the stairs up to the first-class lounge. He was waiting for the two women. He leaned against his automobile. He wouldn't trust anyone but himself with the new (second-hand) machine he'd bought from an Anglo-Irish family leaving the country. The vehicle, which he kept polished to a high shine, was his pride and joy.

Ivy was going to be heartbroken. He checked the pocket of his black suit for the clean handkerchief he'd put in there specially.

The first-class departure lounge exploded with the cries and last-minute instructions being given by the voyagers' families. Some of the people in the lounge were travelling for business, but some like Shay would be travelling to make a new life for themselves. These people were the lucky ones, travelling in style to their new lives. Ivy was caught up in the excitement of the crowd. She had little time to think any more about this final goodbye to her baby brother. Shay was a man now. She'd done her best by him. She'd lit so many candles and prayed so much for his success in his new life that God must be sick of listening to her.

Ann Marie followed the crowd down the stairs and out onto the docks. She snapped her camera as quickly as she could, hoping she'd capture images worth keeping. She was aware of Ivy peeling away from her brother and walking slowly in the direction of Jem and his automobile.

"You doing alright, Ivy?" Jem put his arm around Ivy, pulling her in close to his side.

"I knew this moment was coming, Jem, but, God, it hurts to let him go again." Ivy felt the strength go from her knees. She leaned against Jem thankfully, her tear-washed eyes searching the crowd for Shay's distinctive blond head and fashionable hat. She watched him walk away without looking back. "I don't know if I'm on me head or me heels."

"You'll be able to sit down and collect yourself soon," Jem promised. "That fancy hotel Ann Marie is taking us to for a cup of tea will soon put the smile back on your face." He knew Ivy was nervous at the very thought of stepping through the doors of the Royal Hotel in Dun Laoghaire, so mentioning it would take her mind off her troubles.

"I'll be losing the run of meself if we keep this up, Jem." Ivy stood upright, forcing her knees to lock into place. "What in the name of God is the likes of me doing going into fancy hotels for tea, I ask yer sacred pardon?"

"I'll be with you this time," Jem said. His life was certainly looking up since he'd started keeping company with Ivy and Ann Marie. "The hotel has a special place to leave the automobile – I checked."

"Ivy, quick – wave, there's Doug and Johnjo!" Ann Marie shouted like a hooligan as she came back in the direction of her waiting friends. She was almost skipping along. This was such an adventure. "Look! There they are, up there on the top deck – wave!"

Chapter 2

While Ivy and company were taking tea in the glamorous lobby of the Royal Hotel, Brother Theo, a Franciscan Friar who had appointed himself Ivy's friend and mentor, was in a state of agitation.

Theo had been called in to a meeting with the Abbot. He was still reeling from the tone of the interview. He'd left the meeting and walked, without speaking to anyone, into the small private chapel of the friary. He desperately needed time to think about all that the Abbot had said to him. He took a creased handwritten copy of Saint Francis' Prayer from his pocket and laid it carefully on the shelf of the prayer bench on which he knelt. He didn't need a written reminder of the prayer – he felt it was carved on his heart – but he hoped that seeing the written word would give him a small portion of the peace he so desperately needed.

"Lord, make me an instrument of your peace . . ." Theo tried to breathe the opening words of the prayer in while staring at the carved image of the Crucifixion before him. He'd been subjected to a stern lecture that had left him wrestling with his anger. The Abbot had received a

letter from the Archbishop of Dublin, strongly recommending that Brother Theo cease interfering with the workings of 'his' archdiocese.

"'*Father Leary will be returning to take up his work with the Dublin poor*,'" the Abbot had read from the letter he held in his hand.

Theo had jumped to his feet, prepared to state his opinion of this idiocy forcefully. He hadn't been given the chance to open his mouth. The Abbot had glared him into silence before reminding him of his vow of obedience.

"*Where there is hatred, let me sow love . . .*" Theo didn't believe Ivy Murphy was capable of hatred but he truly believed that the Westland Row parish priest, Father Leary, held an unnatural hated of Ivy Murphy. Theo had been instrumental in having Father Leary removed from his position. He'd requested particularly that Father Leary's mental welfare be assessed. How could the judging panel have failed to see how unsuited Father Leary was for the position of power he held?

Theo stared at the carved figure in front of him, praying fervently for guidance in handling whatever might come of this ill-advised decision on the part of the Dublin Archdiocese.

"*Where there is injury, pardon . . .*" Theo tried to find forgiveness in his heart for Father Leary. He fingered the long string of wooden rosary beads hanging from the waist of his brown habit and tried to find the peace he usually did from his prayers.

"*Where there is doubt, faith . . .*" He'd been instructing Ivy Murphy for over a year. Her inquiring young mind and the questions she raised were a source of fascination to him. He'd never told Ivy that he'd been instrumental in the removal of her tormentor. How could he inform her that the man who took an unhealthy interest in her private affairs was returning to his duties?

"*Where there is despair, hope . . .*" Theo fought the despair that threatened to sink into his very bones. One of the reasons given by the archbishop for the return of Father Leary to his parish was the decline in funds being offered to the Westland Row church. Theo had listened to his Abbot with his tongue firmly between his teeth. He'd remembered the many times he'd been subjected to Ivy Murphy ranting about Father Leary's habit of removing the last penny from the clenched fists of his parishioners.

"*Where there is darkness, light . . .*" Theo had been ordered to break off all contact with Ivy. He could not believe that the Lord he trusted in so fervently would disapprove of his relationship with Ivy. He had plans for her continued education. He had loaned her books from his private library. He enjoyed listening to her unique views and opinions when she returned one of his books. Surely he should be allowed correspond with Ivy? She was a lost soul needing his guidance.

"*Where there is sadness, joy . . .*" Theo prayed he was wrong about Father Leary, who was, after all a man of God. Surely the time the man had spent away from his parish had given him the time to pray and reflect on his actions? Theo felt someone needed to – warn – inform Ivy of the return of the man she feared.

Chapter 3

"Did Shay get away alright?" Maisie Reynolds, the skinny dishwater-blonde dynamo who rented the two rooms over Ivy's basement flat, shouted as soon as Jem's car pulled to a stop in the central courtyard.

The day was cold but the rain was holding off and the bright sharp sunlight allowed the women of The Lane to stand out on the cobbled courtyard and gossip to their hearts' content. The group of women were well wrapped up in the tenement uniform of long black skirt, and long dark shawls wrapped tightly around their heads and shoulders. They looked like crows cawing about the goings-on of their neighbours.

"He did that, Mrs. Reynolds!" Ivy shouted from the open passenger window of the automobile. "I'll see you later!"

She gave Jem a quick smile before jumping from the car. They had dropped Ann Marie off at her house.

"We saw Shay off in fine style!" Ivy shouted as she almost ran to her own basement home. "Ann Marie took a lot of photographs. We'll show them to yeh when she has them developed."

"Ivy Murphy, hold yer horses!"

The shouted order froze Ivy's hand on the gate at the head of the steel steps leading down to her rooms. She turned her head and watched Patty Grant, a neighbour of long standing, march in her direction. Patty's chin was pushed forward, her thin-lipped mouth pursed, brown eyes fixed firmly on Ivy's face.

"I want a word with you." Patty pushed open the gate and stood glaring – obviously waiting for Ivy to lead the way down the steps. "Private like."

Ivy wanted to groan but she couldn't turn a neighbour away. She took the key to her front door from her skirt pocket and meekly walked through the gate. Without a word, the two women descended to the cement area before Ivy's front door. She unlocked and pushed open the door leading into the tiny hallway off the front of her two rooms.

"What can I do for you, Mrs Grant?" Ivy turned to face her neighbour as soon as both women had stepped into her cold front room.

"I'm goin' to say to yer face what everyone is saying behind yer back." Patty Grant pushed the sleeves of her hand-knit black jumper up to her elbows while staring around at the room she stood in. She gave a displeased sniff, presumably at the state of the room.

"What's that then?" Ivy wondered what she'd done this time to bring the gossip down on her head. She fought the need to apologise for not cleaning out the fireplace and dusting the room before she'd left home.

"It's a bloody disgrace – a young single woman having all this space to herself!" Patty waved her hands around the room. "You don't need two rooms, Ivy Murphy. Me and my Boney, and he the best of husbands, have only the one room. What with me five childer that makes seven of us all told – falling over each other we are."

"My family have lived in these two rooms for over twenty years, Missus." Ivy could practically see Patty Grant measuring up the room for her own needs.

"That's true." Patty nodded her head so hard her shawl fell onto her shoulders, revealing an untidy head of dark hair streaked with grey. "But you have to face the facts, Ivy. Your family have all gone now. None of them have any notion of coming back here – they always did think too much of themselves." The woman sniffed mightily. "You won't be trying to tell me your Shay, with his fancy ways, would ever think of this place as his home. Everyone knows he's making an eejit of himself – all that talk of making it big in A-mer-ee-kay – it won't be long till he's left stranded in that foreign country – with his tail between his legs." Patty wrapped her shawl around her generous figure and gave a nod to underscore her opinion.

Ivy opened her mouth to object. "Missus –"

"You listen to me, Ivy Murphy." Patty Grant had come to have her say and this little guttersnipe wasn't going to stop her. "You can't expect to live in all this space by yourself. Anyway, you're walking out with Jem Ryan. It won't be long before you'll be churched and moving out of here. I want these two rooms for me family. Me three boys are in work. We can pay the rent."

"Your lads are old enough to be walking out with young women and moving out themselves. Maybe you should be thinking of that." Ivy didn't say 'mind your own business' but it was understood.

"Indeed they won't," Patty snapped. "My boys will be

paying back their da and me for all their years of raisin' before they can even think of stepping out with some painted trollop."

"Missus," Ivy had known people would have their eye on her two rooms but she'd never expected Patty Grant to be one of the people demanding she move, "I have no intention of giving up me rooms – not at the moment anyway. Have you tried talking to the rent man?" The rent men who visited the tenements and surrounding areas collecting the landlord's money would know of vacant rooms.

"I'll not be moving from The Lane, Ivy Murphy, are yeh mad?" Patty Grant was mentally dividing the room she stood in to make separate sleeping areas for her three sons and two daughters. They wouldn't know they were born with all this space. "My Boney and the lads have only to step out and walk to their work. The girls will soon be out of school. Father Leary has promised them work in the local factory. They'll not be paying good money they could be handing up to me to take the char-a-bang to work. The very idea." Patty liked to say her big words slowly, to show she wasn't ignorant like some people.

"Mrs Grant . . ." Ivy had had enough. They could talk all day but she wasn't going to move to please Patty Grant or anyone else. "I'm sorry for your difficulties but I'm not moving. I suggest you take a walk down to the rent office and ask them if anyone is leaving The Lane. You might ask after the two rooms the Johnsons rented – that place is still empty."

"You've got your cheek, Ivy Murphy." Patty Grant pushed her finger into Ivy's chest. "That place is diseased.

14

I'll not move me family into that place. I want these two rooms. You have the only basement that has a front and back door that can be locked by key. Yer auld man was a cute whore in that respect. He demanded this place, the way I heard it." She pushed her finger into Ivy again with some force behind it. "I want these rooms."

"It's a pity about yeh, Missus." Ivy brushed the woman's hand away from her. "I live here and I have no intention of giving up me rooms to suit you. If anything changes I'll make sure you'll be the first to know." She walked back to the hallway and opened her front door. She stood holding it open. "I'll ask you to leave as I've things I need to be getting on with."

"You think on what I've said, Ivy Murphy." Patty Grant pulled her shawl over her head and walked towards the door with her chest proudly out. "I may be the first to ask about these two rooms but I'll not be the last. You make sure you tell me first of any changes."

"I'll do that," Ivy said as the woman walked past her. She pushed the door closed with a deep sigh and stood listening to the other woman's steps on the steel steps outside. When she heard the gate at the top close she pushed away from the door.

Chapter 4

"Well, that was a kick in the teeth." Ivy hurried through the front room that she'd set up as her work space and into the back room. She made a quick mental note to herself to tidy the place. The dust was looking up at her. "Do I not have enough to be worrying about?" She removed her coat and draped it over the end of her bed. She tossed her fashionable cloche hat on top of the coat with one hand while running the other through her short black hair. Her tweed suit jacket joined the clothing on the bed. "What with one thing and another I've let everything fall by the wayside, Da." Ivy was in the habit of talking aloud to her late father when she was alone. "I've that much to do to catch up with meself, I'll be meeting meself comin' and goin'." With an experienced flick of her wrist she quickly covered herself in the sleeveless wraparound navy-blue apron she took from the nail on the back of the door separating the two rooms. The apron, tied by cloth strings at the waist, covered her from neck to ankle. "I have to get in touch with Brother Theo and tell him I'm ready to continue me studies."

She stood well away from the big black range while

using the poker to force the ashes to fall from the barely glowing embers into the grate. She used the range's special handle to remove the lid from over the fire.

"I don't want to be stupid all me life." She shook pieces of kindling and small nuggets of coal from the old biscuit box she kept by the range into the opening, directly onto the burning embers. "I have to be thinking about what I'm going to do for me business too."

She quickly had the fire stoked with extra nuggets of coal and the stub of a candle, stacked carefully for maximum effect. She left the iron plate off the top of the fire and put the freshly filled big black kettle directly over the coals, hoping it wouldn't take too long to boil.

"With the grace of God I'll have a bit of time now to catch me breath." Ivy removed her apron again and every stitch of clothing before pulling on an old vest of her da's. "I've that much to do. I'll have to write everything down so I don't forget anything." She pulled on a pair of lads' tweed trousers and tucked the vest into them. She'd discovered wearing lads' trousers under her long skirts kept the wind from freezing her private parts. She picked her coat from the bed and hung it carefully on a long nail forced into the bare whitewashed wall. The hat went on a matching nail.

The spout of the black kettle began to spit steam. She crossed to the range and made a pot of tea in her battered metal teapot, putting it on the range top to brew.

"Shay and me lit a few candles for yeh, Da, on the anniversary of yer death." Ivy grinned, thinking, not for the first time, that her da was better company dead than he ever had been alive. "I hope that pleased yeh. We talked a lot about the secrets you and our mother kept to yerselves." She resisted banging her precious dishes about. It didn't make sense to ruin the little she had by reacting to something she couldn't change. "You could have told me you had family living around the place." Her da had never expected to die so young, she knew, but would it have hurt him to tell her a few home truths?

"It's 1926 now, Da, can yeh credit it?" she continued aloud. "Are yeh up there on a cloud somewhere, looking down at your childer? Yeh'd be that proud of our Shay, Da. He's made something of himself. Did yeh see the way the ones went after him with their tongues practically hanging out of their heads? It was a bloomin' wonder to me who'd slapped his arse and wiped his nose. Scandalous, I can tell yeh."

She took one of her new yellow flower-decorated teacups and saucers from the tall old cupboard – part of the set Jem had given her for Christmas. The man knew what pleased her. She sniffed the can of milk she'd left standing in a bucket of cold water. It was still fresh. With a glow of pride she took the time to fill the matching yellow flowered milk jug. She carried her dishes over to the kitchen table parked against the wall just inside the back door.

"I'd better put me skirt and jumper on in case anyone knocks," she muttered. She'd be the talk of the place if she was seen in her da's vest and a lad's trousers. All the people who were saying Ivy Murphy was losing the run of herself would be proved right. She pulled a black woollen skirt up her long legs. She'd bought a thick knitted underskirt at the market and this too she pulled up her legs and settled under her skirt. A thick long-sleeved vest went under a hand-knit woollen jumper in moss green, completing the outfit. She pulled on her long knit stockings and boy's work-boots. Without thought she covered her clothes with the long wraparound apron.

"I'll have to be sure and check the papers, Da." Ivy poured a cup of tea and pulled one of her two wooden chairs from the table. She'd have this pot of tea sitting at the table like a human. "I suppose our Shay will be all over the papers this evening and tomorrow. I'll cut out his pictures and add them to the book I'm keeping for him." She sipped her tea slowly.

"I don't know how many times Mrs Wiggins and some of the neighbours went to see our lot up on stage at the Gaiety. They were all thrilled to see our Shay in the panto, Da."

Marcella Wiggins and her brood had been among the many that had accepted Ann Marie's offer of free theatre tickets to see the Gaiety pantomime. The people of The Lane had a lot to boast about over the holiday period. Not only had Shay Murphy been the star of the show but Liam Connelly, his sister Vera and Seán MacDonald had been another three of their own up there on the stage. The tongues had never stopped moving.

"Mrs Wiggins told me that she thought our Shay had grown up to be a very 'extinguished' looking man!" Ivy laughed at the memory. It wasn't her place to tell the older woman the word was *distinguished*. "It was a livin' wonder to me to see people I knew dancing and singing on the stage. I won't be the only one losing the run of themselves. Brian and Lily Connelly haven't stopped talking about their two – and why should they? They get their talent from their parents after all."

She sipped her tea and her thoughts grew sombre.

Patty Grant's demands had frightened her. How many more people thought she should give up her two rooms? She looked around the room with a heavy heart. These two rooms were the only home she'd ever known. She knew she had it better than most in The Lane but she hadn't thought her neighbours wanted her shifted. Well, they could want. She needed these two rooms – she wouldn't give them up before she was ready and had something better to go to.

"Jem's been after me to set a date for our wedding, Da." Was she mad for putting him off? "He seems to think we can live here after we're married – all right and tight." If Jem and Emmy moved in she'd have to start tidying away her work again. "Is it wrong of me to want more out of life than this?" She dropped her heavy head into her hands, elbows on the table. "I was born and raised in these two rooms. But I refuse to be ashamed of meself for wanting more."

Chapter 5

While Ivy was sitting contemplating her future, Jem Ryan had driven his precious automobile over the canal. Ann Marie had just offered him the use of the carriage house at the rear of her property as a place to store the vehicle. The automobile was his big investment in the future he saw coming. He didn't want to leave it out in the open to be touched by everyone who passed it. It seemed to take forever to polish all of the fingerprints off the black paint. He'd telephoned Ann Marie to tell her he was coming. When he approached the entrance to the grounds surrounding her house, he saw her standing by the open gates. She saw him coming and waved him down.

"The entrance to the carriage house is around the back." She jumped into the passenger side of Jem's automobile. "It will be easier to show you. You can get to it from this side but the entryway is a sea of mud right now. Drive around the block and I'll guide you in."

"Are you sure about this, Ann Marie?" Jem followed the directions from his passenger carefully. The way took him off the main street that bordered the Grand Canal and into a wide laneway.

"It's not a problem, Jem." Ann Marie pointed to the locked tall double doors of the carriage house that served her property. The lane had a long line of similar buildings marching along both sides. "You need somewhere safe to leave your vehicle and I have the space. Look," she held up a heavy iron key, "this is the key to these doors." She pointed with the key. "You'll need to swing out a bit to get the automobile lined up before you drive it inside. Park it here for a moment and I'll show you around." She saw him hesitate and rushed to reassure him. "We'll be able to see it the whole time, Jem." She jumped out of the car, key in hand, and hurried over to unlock the carriage house, pushing both doors open as she went inside.

"There's certainly plenty of space here." Jem stood in the open doors, staring into the cavernous space. Ann Marie's automobile didn't take up a quarter of it.

"I'm very grateful to the previous owner of this property." Ann Marie waved her arms around. "A lot of these carriage houses have been sold off separately and turned into individual dwellings. There's a cobbler's shop, an ironmonger's and even a tripe house along this lane."

"It's a handy spot for a business." Jem walked out into the laneway and looked along the cobbled length. He'd make a note of the tripe shop. Tripe and onion was a popular dish and cheap. The lads would enjoy a change from the typical menu of stew provided by the 'Penny Dinners' which were cooked for the poor in a local convent.

He turned and walked back to join Ann Marie. He noticed an indoor wooden staircase and wandered over to put his foot on the first step and look up. He couldn't see a thing.

"There's a living area up those stairs." Ann Marie

crossed to join him. She'd offered Ivy this carriage house to live in. It would be an ideal space for a married couple and she herself would enjoy having Emmy running back and forth. Ivy didn't even think about it before refusing. It seemed the thought of leaving The Lane and its familiar surroundings had been too much for her.

"Who lives there now?" Jem didn't want some unknown person around his precious vehicle.

"No one," Ann Marie said. "I'm going to turn part of it into a dark room. I need somewhere to develop my photographs and the rooms up there," she jerked her chin upwards, "have running water and indoor plumbing. I can leave my photographic equipment up there too."

"Have you grown out of that big house already?" Jem couldn't imagine what Ann Marie wanted with all the space she already had.

"I'm going to be using a lot of dangerous chemicals to develop my photographs, Jem." Ann Marie had thought to use one of the bathrooms in the main house as her studio but the constant interruptions from Sadie had inspired her to look for somewhere more convenient. If she'd had to refuse one more cup of tea or snack she'd have screamed at Sadie. "Would you like to see?"

"I'd love to," Jem grinned. He wanted to get a good look at this living space with indoor plumbing. "I'll just put my automobile inside first."

He went and reversed neatly into the open space.

"Show off!" Ann Marie grinned and thumped him gently on the shoulder. "Here, you need this key. I have others." She passed the large key to Jem, waiting while he closed and locked the double doors. She pressed a switch, illuminating the space.

"Begob, Missus," Jem stood staring around open-mouthed, "you have the electricity in here and all. I knew you had it in the house but putting it in your carriage house, that's posh."

"Yes, the previous owner seems to have been a man ahead of the times. He had the latest inventions like plumbing and electricity put into the house and grounds." Ann Marie too was fascinated by the uses of electricity.

"How do you turn it off?" Jem walked over to join Ann Marie by the light switch. He watched carefully, a wide grin of sheer delight on his face. When Ann Marie had turned the lights off and on again he raised his eyebrow in query – at her nod he experienced turning the lights on and off himself – several times. "Begob, Missus, that's mighty." He heaved a sigh of sheer satisfaction.

"Come on upstairs – I'll show you around." Ann Marie didn't think there was anything risqué about inviting Jem upstairs with her. He'd become the brother she'd never had. She led the way up the wooden staircase. "There are two bedrooms and a box room up here." She opened doors as she spoke, showing Jem the space available. There was a kitchen, bathroom and living room all carefully spaced around the large upstairs area. She wanted Jem to see what it was possible to create with careful planning.

"I asked Ivy to come live in this carriage house, Jem," she said, when they stood in the living room before the large window overlooking the manicured lawn of her property. "She refused."

"Ivy has had more shocks and sorrows in the last year than most people have to deal with in a lifetime, Ann Marie." Jem stood – hands on his hips – and simply stared around. He understood Ivy's fear of this big place. A body would rattle around all of these rooms. "I think leaving The Lane and her neighbours might have been one shock too many." Besides, he thought his Ivy would be too proud to be beholden to anyone and the rent on this place would be a shocker.

"I have a friend . . ." Ann Marie had been thinking about this ever since Ivy had told her she would be marrying Jem. She did not want her friend to start her married life in those two basement rooms. Ivy deserved better. "He has studied architecture . . ." She stopped, unsure how to continue.

"What's architecture when it's at home?" Jem knew Ann Marie had another shock to deliver him. He tightened his sinews and waited.

"The study of buildings," Ann Marie said simplistically. "Jem, with careful planning and the help of my architect friend I'm sure you could create something similar to this place at one end of your livery."

"Between you and Ivy, Ann Marie, a poor man could end up in the loony bin."

Without another word Jem began to pace the living space, his head full of plans and dreams, Ann Marie a silent shadow at his heels.

Chapter 6

"Miss Murphy, if I might have a word?"

Ivy smiled at her landlord's agent as he hurried importantly from his backroom office. Greg Norton was a decent sort but she couldn't imagine what he needed to talk to her about. With a sigh she accepted her rent book from the office clerk and moved down the long polished wooden desk to try and escape from listening ears.

"Mr Norton, I haven't seen you in ages." Ivy offered her ungloved hand.

"That is only too true, dear lady." Greg Norton took the offered hand gently and shook it quickly before releasing the contact. He only saw the tenants who fell behind in their rent or caused problems. He should have had no reason at all to bother Miss Ivy Rose Murphy, but sadly he felt the need to talk to the unfortunate woman today. "You have always been a good tenant."

"What's going on?" Ivy didn't have time to waste in chitchat. The fact that Mr Norton was making a point of seeking her out meant trouble.

"The rent collector for your area has expressed his concerns to me."

Neal Ramsey had only recently taken over the area that included The Lane. The man was conscientious and caring, unlike the blackguard he'd replaced. He had never met Ivy Murphy as she insisted on paying her rent directly into the company office.

"Yes?" Ivy needed to get on. It was late Monday afternoon and she'd spent the day collecting the discards from the homes of the wealthy on Merrion Square. It was her custom to stop into the rent office and pay her rent before she returned home.

"Mr Ramsey, the rent collector for your area, has received complaints from a number of individuals about a young single female renting what some consider a prime property." Greg Norton almost swallowed his tongue on that little snippet of exaggeration. The two basement rooms this woman rented were little better than dungeons in his personal opinion. He shrugged mentally. He supposed every eye formed its own beauty.

"My family, as you well know, Mr Norton, have rented those two rooms for over twenty years." She'd been earning and paying the rent for the last thirteen years. Mr Norton had explained to her that paying her rent weekly gave the landlord the power to evict her with only a week's notice. The fear of becoming homeless kept her awake at night. "Would it be possible for me to pay my rent monthly, Mr Norton? That would remove a great deal of weight from my shoulders."

"I'm afraid that would not be possible, Miss Murphy." Greg Norton knew the slum landlords refused to issue monthly rent agreements. The power to evict tenants with only a week's notice was a privilege they demanded. A problem tenant could be thrown out in the street with only seven days' notice. The raggedly dressed woman in front of him paid her rent in full and on time every week. That was a rarity for tenement tenants.

"I was hoping for the additional security a monthly rent book would grant me." Ivy grabbed the handle of her old pram and prepared to leave the rent office. "I suppose I should have known better." It wouldn't do her any good to kick the tall wooden counter, no matter how much she might want to.

"Perhaps you could talk to Jem Ryan about the situation," Greg Norton called softly. "I believe you two are walking out together."

"I'll do that." When Hell freezes over, Ivy thought, while pushing her pram through the office door. "See you next week, Mr Norton."

"Good day to you, Miss Murphy."

"It'll be a great day now you've frightened the life out of me," Ivy muttered under her breath.

She pushed her pram in the direction of home, feeling her bones almost shake her body apart. She was terrified. What would she do if they decided to kick her out of her rooms? Jem had only the one room over the stables. How would she keep her business going?

Putting her back into pushing the stubborn pram in front of her, she walked without seeing along the old familiar paths. She had serious thinking to be doing.

Chapter 7

The following morning, after tossing and turning half the night, Ivy was determined to go about her business. She had used the sleepless time to make plans and jumped out of bed determined to implement them. She'd give the markets a miss today. She had places to go and people to see.

"Thanks to the sale of all them dolls I've more money in the bank than I know what to do with." She prepared a pot of tea and a slice of bread to start her day. "That's the kind of problem many a one would like to claim." She wanted to think of something she could do with all of the little rubber dolls she had in stock. "I'll never give up me round, that's me bread and butter," she hurried around the room, getting herself organised for the day ahead, "but them dolls are the jam."

She gave herself a good wash before dressing in what she thought of as her business outfit. She left her rooms with a smile on her face and renewed hope in her heart.

"And where are you off to, all cocked, powdered and shaved, Miss Murphy?" Jem Ryan was standing in the courtyard, overseeing the business of hitching up carriages.

He stood surrounded by horses and men getting ready to drive the carriages around the town. His business was thriving.

"I'm surprised you were able to drag yourself away from that newfangled radio of yours," Ivy said.

"The programmes don't start until the evening." Jem had given in to the temptation to buy a radio now that Ireland had its very own radio station.

"That day would skin yeh, Ivy." John Lawless was sitting in his wheelchair, checking that this second shift of drivers had the papers and instructions they would need for the day. His daughter Clare, a trained telephonist, was in the office.

"I'm off to make me fortune, lads." Ivy laughed as she walked around the men and carriages. "I'll see yez later."

"Be sure and telephone if you need a carriage to carry your money back with you!" Conn, one of Jem's lads, shouted.

"I'll do that." Ivy exchanged a soft glance with Jem.

"I'll have the kettle on when you get back," Jem called out, while admiring Ivy's retreating figure. He stood for a moment watching and wishing they were married already. When was she going to set the date? He turned back to his business with a sigh. His Ivy was worth waiting on.

"Miss Harrington, how lovely to see you," Ivy said in the posh accent she used for such business dealings and which came to her so easily. Hand out, smile professional, she approached the owner of the upmarket Grafton Street toyshop. She was wearing her purple tweed suit under her beige cashmere coat. She didn't care what Ann Marie said about the fashion for shorter skirt length. The morning was cold and mucky and her smart beige coat and hat covered a multitude of sins.

"Miss Rose!" Geraldine Harrington grinned delightedly. This woman had added a generous amount to the money the shop had made over the Christmas period. "I'll put the kettle on. It's not a fit day out there for man nor beast." She hurried into her back room to put the kettle on the primus stove she kept for her own use. "I'll telephone across the road to Bewley's," she said over her shoulder. She could afford to be generous. She lived by the motto '*Speculate to accumulate*'. A cup of tea and a cream cake might soften Miss Rose's attitude towards her profit line. She doubted it but one never knew. "Would you prefer a cream slice or puff, Miss Rose?"

"A cream puff would be delightful," Ivy answered while checking out the work the owner had spread out around her counter top.

It seemed Miss Harrington was putting together Easter Baskets. At least that's what she thought the straw baskets with little bunny rabbits and fluffy chicks encircled by big pink silk bows were. Her mother had talked of these baskets but Ivy had never seen them. Her mouth went dry while her mind spun frantically. She looked at the discreetly placed price tag and almost passed out – in the name of Jesus – all that money for a bloody little basket?

"The kettle won't take long to boil." Geraldine came through to the shop. "I see you're admiring my Easter Baskets. Easter is a busy period for me, thank goodness – not as busy as Christmas but nevertheless I need to stock up for the occasion."

"I have my artists working on a six-inch Alice in Wonderland doll which I believe would be ideal to include

31

in your Easter Baskets," Ivy lied quickly.

The idea had just exploded into her mind. *Alice's Adventures in Wonderland* was always a favourite for story nights. She remembered the drawings of the little girl Alice on the book covers. It seemed to her that, every time someone was lucky enough to get a new Alice book, the girl on the cover was different. But one thing remained constant: Alice was always blonde. She had an abundance of the small blonde rubber dolls she'd used to make Cinderella. The outfits could be run up on the sewing machine in next to no time. It would be fiddly work but her heart sang at the thought of the profit that could be made.

"Why don't we discuss this?" Geraldine knew she could make a larger gift basket and charge a great deal more. "Do you have a sample doll with you?" She didn't see a case.

"I hadn't originally considered your store for our Alice doll," Ivy spread her hands in silent apology, "but I was passing and saw the dainty china tea sets on display in your shop window." She'd go to Hell for lying but this was business. "The window arrangement made me smile and think of the Mad Hatter's tea party."

The bell over the shop door rang and a black-and-white-garbed waitress clutching a white bakery box pushed her way into the shop. Ivy wanted to kiss the woman, she was that glad of a chance to catch her breath. This lying took it out of her. She stood back and allowed her mind to wander while Geraldine Harrington and the waitress from Bewley's café across the street took care of business.

She'd have to visit Harry Green's warehouse. She closed

her eyes trying to remember the last time Alice was read aloud on story night. A vivid image of Jenny Duncan formed behind Ivy's eyes. She was standing on the tenement stairs holding her new book up for everyone to admire the cover. Yes, the girl on the cover had been wearing a sky-blue dress with a white apron – easy enough to replicate. She would need to buy extra blue and white thread for the sewing machine. She opened her eyes, hiding a grin – Harry was still frothing at the mouth over her success with the Cinderella dolls. Every time he saw her now he had something to say about her thieving ways. She needed to catch him in a good mood and order more naked baby dolls too.

She'd come into this shop to sound out the owner concerning another consignment of baby dolls. The Lawless family needed to get started dressing dolls for the Christmas market. It seemed ridiculous to be thinking of Christmas when they hadn't even celebrated Easter.

"Shall we step in the back?" Geraldine offered when the waitress had left. She carried the white box with her and led the way. "I'm afraid talk of an Alice doll made me completely forget the kettle. It must be boiled dry."

The two women stepped into the small space at the back of the shop set aside for Geraldine's use. She could boil the kettle and have a snack while still being available to customers. It didn't do to close the shop for any length of time. It depended on passing trade.

Ivy gave only half of her mind to the discussion about business. She drank the offered tea and nibbled on the cream puff but her mind was frantically planning. She needed to make a pattern out of brown paper for the Alice dress and apron. She'd make one complete outfit herself.

She could paint little black shoes directly onto the dolls' feet. She wanted to be able to pass the pattern and instructions to anyone she asked to dress the dolls. How many could she and her crew turn out in a short space of time?

"How many Alice dolls can you let me have?"

Ivy almost jumped – for a moment she'd thought Geraldine had read her mind.

"I'll need to discuss production details with my artists." She never called them *workers*. "I'll bring a sample doll for you to examine – would Thursday suit you?" It was Tuesday now. She'd sit up all night and dress a batch of the dolls herself if she had to.

"That would be wonderful." Geraldine liked doing business with this woman. It was unusual to meet a female sales representative. She enjoyed the mild flirtation that took place between herself and the travelling salesmen who visited her shop but the chance to sit down and have a cup of tea and a cream cake with a fellow businesswoman was a rare treat.

"I'm aware you mentioned that the Baby Bundle dolls you supplied for the Christmas market were of a limited edition." Geraldine sipped her second cup of tea, hoping no stray cream decorated her face. She wanted to lick her lips but resisted the temptation. "The dolls were such a wonderful success. I was wondering if you planned to make another baby doll available this year."

Ivy opened her mouth to answer, her mind spinning.

Geraldine didn't wait for Ivy to speak. "If possible I would like to have some of your dolls available to me throughout the year. Something like those baby dolls would make an ideal birthday present." The dolls this

34

woman offered were of a superior quality, the handwork beautifully finished. The profit margin had been exceptional.

"To my knowledge there are no baby dolls in production at this moment in time." Ivy was glad she was sitting. She was getting too good at this lying to suit herself. Was it a big sin? "I'll discuss the issue with my artists and get back to you." She'd planned to create a Christmas doll and thought she'd have to work hard to sell it. Now, with this, perhaps she could come up with something they could sell year round.

"Wonderful," Geraldine beamed.

The two women settled down to discuss business. They would never be friends but they shared the burden of being females trying to make a living in a man's world, which created an intimacy that both enjoyed.

Chapter 8

Ivy walked along Grafton Street in the direction of Stephen's Green. A display in the stationary shop she was passing caught her eye. She took it as a sign from above and, without a second thought, stepped into the shop to buy one of the large illustrated editions of *Alice's Adventures in Wonderland* that were piled high in the shop window.

With the heavy book in hand, she turned down South Ann Street. She regularly passed a large haberdashery on Dawson Street. She'd buy the thread for the sample dolls there. She didn't have time to go home, change out of her good clothes and head for the market and Harry Green's warehouse.

She stood staring into the high wide glass windows of the haberdashery. She wanted to run in and buy everything she saw displayed so temptingly before her. The shop window was cleverly arranged with a mouth-watering selection of tools and threads. The shop doorway divided the two large windows and sat back from the pavement.

"Ivy Murphy!" A woman stood in the open doorway, smiling sweetly. "I haven't seen you admiring my shop window before."

"Hannah Solomon," Ivy had forgotten that Mr Solomon's youngest daughter was married to the owner of the haberdashery, "I haven't seen you in ages." They were of an age and had grown up together in The Lane.

"Was there something you needed?" Hannah waved towards the shop window. She wanted Ivy to step inside – her mother-in-law was out and about, leaving Hannah in charge of the shop. They would be able to talk in peace.

"I'm standing here hopin' me Fairy Godmother will arrive and buy that silver sewing kit for me." Ivy shrugged. "I may as well dream here as in bed."

Hannah stepped outside and looked at the kit Ivy was indicating. "We sell some of those pieces loose." She looked over her shoulder, almost expecting her husband's domineering mother to appear. The woman did like to pinch. "The implements are not so expensive when you buy them individually." She held open the heavy wood and glass door. "Step inside and see."

"I was going to go home first, Hannah." Ivy wasn't sure about going inside – the prices on the items in the window had shocked her. "I wanted to make a list of the things I'll need before I came into your shop."

"Come in, please." Hannah refused to take no for an answer. Ivy Murphy didn't know it but she was an answer to Hannah's fervent prayers. "Come in and look around. If you tell me what you need perhaps I can help you make a list."

"Alright." Ivy stepped forward, surprised at Hannah's insistence.

She stepped into a wonderland of colour. She stood in the middle of the store, slowly turning on her heel as she tried to take everything in. The selection of coloured embroidery threads and knitting yarns stretched to the ceiling. The long waist-high glass-topped cabinets sitting on the floor held silver needlecraft tools. She wanted one of everything.

"Papa tells me you're walking out with Jem Ryan." Hannah was enjoying Ivy's reaction to the shop. She had been working in this place for what sometimes felt like forever. She didn't see the beauty surrounding her any more. "Have you set a date yet?"

Ivy bent over one of the cabinets, her hands behind her back, resisting the temptation to lean on the glass top and just stare. "Don't you start, Hannah Solomon." She raised her eyes from their examination of the treasure locked in the cabinet. She knew Hannah had married Manny Felman but she would always be Hannah Solomon in her mind. "I feel as if I have the world and his mother asking me to make an honest man out of Jem Ryan. I'll make me own mind up if you don't mind." She smiled to remove the bite from her response.

"Jem Ryan is a good man." Hannah's dark eyes lit up with a smile that didn't reach her lips. "But I'll say no more on the matter." She held up delicate, blue-veined hands in defeat. "Come, tell me what it is you need."

"I need to make an Alice in Wonderland outfit for a doll. I thought to buy the stuff I need in here but, honest to God, Hannah – these prices!"

"Papa told me you were making dolls." Hannah walked slowly over to a heavily curtained alcove. She divided the curtain to reveal a hidden section of the shop. "I saw you outside the Gaiety." She hadn't been able to go over and say hello to her old friend. She'd been with her husband, his mother and four of his sons. They would

38

have fainted if she'd mentioned she knew the doll seller. "My husband bought one of your Cinderella dolls for his granddaughter." And complained all the way home about the price, she didn't add.

"Then you have an idea of what I need."

Ivy was examining Hannah from under her eyelashes. She didn't want to stare but the other woman looked like she had the weight of the world on her shoulders. She seemed a shadow of the laughing girl Ivy remembered. The black dress Hannah wore was old-fashioned and unflattering. There were dark shadows under her big brown eyes and her black hair was dull and lifeless, pulled back into a tight bun at the back of her neck. Mr Solomon boasted a great deal about the wonderful marriage he had arranged for his youngest daughter. Hannah's husband was a wealthy businessman much older than his wife.

"We have a selection of doll patterns." Hannah left the alcove exposed. They could visit that section when she had a clearer idea of Ivy's needs. "The under-nannies in the surrounding big houses sometimes enjoy dressing the nursery dolls." She walked to a tall cupboard, opened it, and withdrew a large thick pattern book. She carried the book over to the shop counter and with a wave of her hand invited Ivy over to take a look.

"These are wonderful," Ivy turned the pages of the large book carefully, "but they're all for china dolls. I was going to make the pattern myself." She planned to copy the outfit on the cover of the book she'd bought.

"I thought this book would give you some ideas." Hannah didn't want Ivy to leave.

"There are so many different illustrations of Alice." Ivy stood upright. She'd been bending over the cabinet and this counter too long – her back was kinking. "I've seen Alice drawn with a brown dress, a white dress with a red apron and even a red, white and blue outfit."

"The latest editions of the book seem to have settled on a blue dress with a white apron – look." Hannah nudged Ivy gently to one side and opened the book at a pattern of a doll's outfit that claimed to be taken from the drawings of Sir John Tenniel – the original illustrator of the Alice books. "See," her finger pointed to the printed claim, "that is the look you need for your doll."

Ivy took a notebook and a pencil from the beige handbag Ann Marie insisted she carry. With a few quick flicks of her pencil she copied the design from the pattern book. The individual pieces of the pattern would give her some ideas for cutting out her own pattern.

"Right." She put her notebook and pencil back in her handbag. "I need fabric, blue and white. I need thread. I will buy them here this once but, honestly, Hannah, your prices are way too high for me to shop here often."

"I know," Hannah smiled sadly, "but, if you will follow me, I think I can show you items that you can afford." She walked over to the curtained alcove and, with Ivy at her heels, stepped inside. "I have already mentioned the under-nannies – well, the seamstresses and housekeepers of the big houses shop here too. I have set aside this area and sell off the opened packages and returned goods for a fraction of the cost of the items in the main shop."

Ivy stepped into the alcove, looked around and with a deep breath decided not to look at the prices. She needed these articles now. She would determine the price of the doll on how much she spent in this shop. "You have a bit of everything in here. First, I want one of those fine bristle paintbrushes and a pot of black acrylic paint." Ivy began to amass the items she needed.

There was a small table with two chairs sitting in the middle of the little space. She looked back out at the ornate table and chairs in the main shop and sighed. She always seemed to be in the ha'penny place.

"I really want a pair of silver sharp-nose sewing scissors if you have any on offer in here." Ivy put a roll of blue and a roll of white fabric on the counter on one side of the alcove opening.

The two women settled down to business. They were like children in a sweetshop, pulling out articles and exclaiming over their beauty. The alcove had a tall cupboard filled with drawers that hid many delights. Hannah pulled these out to show Ivy. In the time they spent together Ivy thought Hannah stood taller and seemed to regain some of her drooping spirits. She was aware Hannah was giving her sideways looks but, if the woman didn't want to say what she was thinking, well, it was none of her business.

Ivy bought a pair of silver scissors and a silver thimble. It was ridiculous but she had decided to treat herself and to heck with the cost.

"Why has this shop been left unattended?" An imperious voice carried over the frantic ringing of the bell over the front door of the shop. "Hannah, are you in your penny-dreadful department again?"

"My mother-in-law . . . has returned," Hannah offered, the vitality and joy draining out of her so drastically it was visible. She grabbed Ivy's elbow and went on her toes to whisper in her ear. "Can I come to your back door one evening?"

"Yes," Ivy whispered back.

"I'm with a customer, Mother Felman!" Hannah picked up the roll of blue fabric and carried it into the main shop.

"A servant person, no doubt."

Ivy couldn't see the speaker but she didn't like the tone of her voice. She was a customer here and spending good money in the place.

"I realise my son married far beneath himself," the voice said just loud enough for Ivy to hear, "but after all this time I had hoped some of our polish would have rubbed off on you, Hannah." There was a world of sorrow in the domineering voice. "I am disappointed – yet again."

Ivy walked out into the shop. "I do not believe it is quite the done thing to discuss your private affairs in front of a customer." She had her chin in the air and the bit firmly between her teeth. She'd had just about enough of old goats like this one.

Ivy walked across the shop to stand on the customer side of the long counter. She tried to ignore the tall looming figure dressed from head to toe in black bombazine. The woman was huge. Her black-feathered hat almost filled the shop. She towered over poor Hannah.

"You have been extremely helpful," Ivy said to Hannah. "I had intended to open an account for future purchases. I have since changed my mind." She put her bag on the counter beside the cash register, opened it and took out the folded leather chequebook she'd never used. She was going to write her very first cheque. She'd have liked to share her joy with Hannah but not with that old bat looking down her nose at her. "I will write you a cheque for these purchases."

Hannah returned to the alcove to pick up more of Ivy's items.

Ivy saw the gleam of avarice in the older woman's eyes. "If you would be so kind as to telephone that number." She had taken one of her Ivy Rose Dolls business cards from her handbag and now pushed it across the counter towards Hannah, "and order my carriage to return for me, I would appreciate it."

"Certainly," Hannah hid the gleam in her eyes by staring at the embossed white card on the counter, "Miss Rose."

"You take care of the telephone call, Hannah," Ruth Felman barked suddenly. "I will tend to Miss Rose. You haven't offered Miss Rose any refreshment." She glanced at the bare table set up for their customer's convenience. She stripped off the heavy overcoat she wore and passed the garment to Hannah. She removed her black leather gloves and the pins from her oversized hat. She pushed everything in Hannah's direction, for her to deal with.

"I prefer to continue being served by this lady. I've found her knowledge of needlecraft superior to most that I have met in my travels." Ivy turned her back on the woman. She didn't dare catch Hannah's eye or the game would be up. She'd collapse giggling at the feet of the woman, gasping like a landed cod fish.

Hannah went into the small office to make the telephone call while Ruth Felman tried to engage Ivy in conversation. Ivy was chillingly polite. While refusing to offer any information.

"Your carriage will be here momentarily, Miss Rose,"

Hannah said, coming back into the shop. She had to bite her lips to keep the bubble of laughter from escaping. Ivy Murphy, the rag woman, had put her overbearing mother-in-law in her place. She wished she had someone to share the joke with.

"Thank you." Ivy opened the snap that held the cover of her chequebook closed and prepared to do business. She silently thanked Ann Marie for insisting she carry a good fountain pen in her handbag.

Chapter 9

"Well, well, well, Ivy Murphy." Jem stood in the open door of the livery, his hands on his hips, a big grin on his face as he watched one of his drivers assist Ivy from her carriage. "I never thought I'd see the day."

"Less of your lip, sir – pay the man." Ivy waved her hand towards the driver. She saw the look of surprise on Jem and the carriage driver's face and lost it. To hell with it, who cared who was watching? She ran into Jem's suddenly open arms and, with a smile big enough to crack her face, said, "Hello, handsome, buy a girl a cup of tea?" She giggled, thrilled with herself. Everything else could wait – she was going to sit down with her fella and tell him all about her day.

"I think you've been drinking something stronger than tea, Miss Murphy." Jem was delighted to see the joy of living practically written on his Ivy's lovely face.

"No, but do I have a story for you! Buy us a cup of tea, Mr Ryan."

"Come on then." He threw his arm around her. "Conn," he shouted for one of his lads, "come take these parcels, will you? It looks like Ivy bought the shop out."

They waited while Conn took the brown-paper-covered parcels from the grinning driver.

Jem took the work docket from the driver before releasing the man to return to his business. With the sound of horse hooves hitting the cobbles, Ivy and he turned to go into the livery.

"Leave your parcels with Conn." Jem didn't want to have his tea in the area the lads had set up as a tea room. "We'll have our tea upstairs. I know I won't get a word of sense out of you until you've a cup of tea in your hand. But, I'm warning you, this story better be good." He stood back and watched Ivy climb the ladder to his room in the loft. He knew they were tempting fate. Their canoodling sessions were getting hotter and heavier. It was getting harder and harder to let Ivy leave his arms.

"We have to stop." Jem pushed Ivy gently away from him but still held her on his lap.

In spite of his best intentions he'd been unable to resist the temptation created by having his Ivy all to himself. They had sat at the table while Ivy had her tea and chatted about her day. When she'd paused for breath he'd stood and pulled her into his arms. He wanted the right to hold her in his arms all through the night.

"I can't go on like this, Ivy," he said now, brushing his lips over her flushed cheeks. Her lips were swollen from his kisses. "We need to name the day. When are you going to marry me?"

"Oh Jem!" Ivy pushed herself off his lap and walked over to sit in one of the two wooden chairs pulled up to the small table. She avoided his eyes by checking the buttons of her blouse – Jem's hands had been busy.

"I'm only human, Ivy." Jem remained seated in his one soft chair. He pushed shaking fingers through his hair. "We're tempting fate kissing and canoodling. One of these days I won't be able to stop. We need to get churched."

"I need a little more time." She looked around Jem's room. He kept the loft space clean and tidy. She knew there were families living in The Lane that would have been delighted with a large airy room all to themselves. Why did she want something different? Why couldn't she accept what was on offer? Why did she always seem to want more – what was wrong with her? "Where would we live?"

"Your family lived in those two basement rooms." Jem had hoped to offer Ivy something better but at least they could start their married life in those two rooms. He hadn't mentioned Ann Marie's idea about converting one end of the livery into living accommodation. He was worried about the cost of the alterations. He didn't want to start his married life deep in debt.

"It seems everyone and his mother has their eye on them two rooms."

"It would only be to start off, Ivy." Jem resisted the temptation to pull her back into his arms. He wanted to kiss her worries away. "Your doll business is taking off and I can't keep up with the demands that are pouring in for carriages and movers. We can start in those two rooms and work towards something better – together."

"I'll –" Ivy opened her mouth with no idea of what she was going to say. A loud shout from downstairs saved her from having to come up with an answer at that moment. Jem was needed in the livery. "We can talk later." She jumped at the chance to escape. She had things to think about.

"Emmy will be home soon," he said. "Are you going to eat with us?"

"I won't, Jem, thanks. I have so much to do."

"I'm not letting this go, Ivy." Jem held the door open. "We need to set a date for the wedding – the sooner the better."

"I'll think on it," Ivy promised, hurrying from the loft room.

As if she'd be able to think of anything else.

Chapter 10

"Think about it, the man says." Ivy had pushed her sewing machine into the back room. She had a wash basin of hot soapy water on the kitchen table and was scrubbing twenty of the little rubber dolls before laying each one on a nearby towel. "I've nothing else to be doing with me time. The dirt of the place is looking up at me. I haven't a minute to draw a deep breath and there's yer man asking me to rearrange me life. Think about it? *Aagh*!"

A knock on her back door had her stopping her rant.

"I can't even be left alone with me thoughts," she muttered, heading for the door. "If that's Jem Ryan at the door I'm going to scalp the man."

She headed for the door and opened it.

Hannah Solomon-Felman, a black shawl wrapped around her shivering figure, stood in the doorway.

"Twice in one day, Hannah." Ivy didn't know what else to say. She stood back and silently invited Hannah into her rooms.

She busied herself putting the kettle on to boil. Hannah wanted something from her but she couldn't begin to guess what.

"You've started the dolls?" Hannah sat at the kitchen table, examining the little dolls and trying to think how she could say what she needed to say.

"You didn't come here to talk about dolls, Hannah – spit it out. I want to get this first batch of dolls finished. See what I have." She put the kettle to the side of the range. For once the tea could wait.

"I am a bad wife," Hannah whispered. "I am a bad mother to my husband's sons – all of whom are older than me. I am a bad daughter to a father who loves me and wants only the best for me – his idea of what's best, of course." She picked up one of the little dolls and began combing its hair with the small comb Ivy had left to hand. "I am a bad sister who will bring shame to her siblings." There was a moment of silence while she continued combing the doll's hair. "But I am not a bad woman."

Ivy didn't know what she was supposed to say to all that, so she said nothing. The other woman seemed to need to get a load off her chest. She'd just tend to her own business. She picked up one of the dolls and dried it carefully, preparatory to painting black shoes onto its feet.

"Are you listening to me, Ivy Murphy?"

"I'm listening." Ivy didn't take her eyes off the work she was doing. "Shouldn't you be getting home to your husband and family?"

"My husband," Hannah almost spat the word, "is entertaining his wife's family this evening."

"You are his wife."

"No, I'm not. His wife is dead. I'm just the girl who runs his shop and keeps his home running efficiently. He went through a wedding service with me to reduce the cost and inconvenience to him."

There was a silence while Ivy waited to see if Hannah had anything else to say. It didn't do to come between a husband and wife.

"If you've no one waiting for you to come home I have onion-and-potato soup made. There's plenty for you if you'd care to join me."

"I thank you, Ivy Murphy. No, no one will miss me." Hannah slept over the shop when her husband entertained his first wife's family. It was a pleasure not to have to lie beneath his sweating, grunting, heavy body.

"What do you think I can do for you, Hannah?" Ivy stood to put the pot of soup on the black range to heat.

"I have running-away money." Hannah waited to see if God would strike her down. "I've been hiding away money for all of the seven years I've been married." Sometimes when her husband was beating her or rutting over her, she wished for death. "If my husband should die before me his sons would see me in the street."

"You are married to the man, Hannah." Ivy began to clear her work from the table. She didn't pass comment on a wife running from her husband – hadn't her own mother done the same thing? Hannah at least was leaving no child motherless. "I believe that gives you certain rights." What did she know about the rights of a wife?

"I know what I know, Ivy Murphy. I must get away."

"Where will you go?" As far as Ivy understood it, the Jewish community in Dublin was extremely close-knit. She couldn't imagine anywhere Hannah could go that she would not be caught.

"I have dreamed of America." Hannah watched Ivy set the table for their meal.

"What about your father?" Mr Solomon was a good

man if a bit old-fashioned.

"I cannot tell my father." There were tears in Hannah's eyes. Her father had thought he was doing his best by her but his attitude of 'you've made your bed, you must lie in it' was not for her.

"You know our Shay has gone to America?" It wasn't Ivy's place to pass judgement. If the son was anything like the mother she'd met in the shop that day she'd be tempted to do a runner herself.

"Aah, your Shay," Hannah sighed. "I saw him on the stage. I was so proud of him. Prince Charming, no less."

"He hated it." Ivy ladled two bowls of soup from the pot on the range. "He said he only accepted the role because they were desperate and offered him an obscene amount of money." She put the soup bowls on the table. She had a loaf of crusty bread she added to the feast.

She sat down opposite Hannah.

"The cost of a ticket to America is very high, Hannah," she said when the two women were spooning the rich soup from the bowls.

"I thought to seek work as a seamstress on one of the sailing ships." Hannah had been dreaming of her escape for years. "I do not wish to arrive in the new world penniless. I have worked hard for my husband and his family from our first day of marriage. I set up the little shop in the alcove. My husband's mother will not step into the place, believing it beneath her dignity. This works in my favour as she has no idea how much money I take behind those curtains. I have been stashing coins like a squirrel stocking nuts for winter. It is strange. I was content to drift along, always planning my escape." She looked into Ivy's eyes. "Seeing you today broke something inside of me. I can no longer waste my youth waiting for my moment."

Neither woman mentioned the fact that it was illegal to meddle in the affairs of a married man. His wife was his chattel. Anyone caught helping his wife escape his clutches was breaking the law of the land.

"What do you think I can do for you?"

"I need your help to remove all of the money I've saved from the shop." She reached across the table and covered Ivy's hand with her own. "I know I am asking a great deal of you. But I have no one else I can turn to. The money is in coin, yes, but it is not as heavy as you might believe. I have managed to change a great deal of it into crowns. My mother-in-law's cronies seem to spend a vast amount of crowns in the shop." She'd asked a question about that once. She knew never to ask again. Some lessons were unforgettable. "The mice would eat paper. I do not know exactly how much I have managed to save but I know I will need every penny."

"Are you sure about this, Hannah? It's a big step to take and if you're caught you'll be in a worse state."

"I can't continue to live my life." Hannah tried not to sob.

"I'll put the kettle on." Ivy took her empty bowl from the table. She could take Hannah's money to the post office and open an account. That shouldn't be a problem. "Leaving your husband will take a lot of careful planning on your part, Hannah."

Hannah felt almost faint with relief. She hadn't been able to think of a way she could smuggle the coins out from under her mother-in-law's nose and change them into bank notes. Her husband's mother watched every move she made. The woman even had her cronies spy on Hannah whenever she had to be away from the shop.

"It would be best, I think, if I'm not seen to be helping you," said Ivy. "Too many people know me – know I do business with your father." She ignored Hannah's gasp. "I may know someone better able to help you plan your escape." Ivy was thinking of Betty Armstrong. Her da's long-lost sister was a woman who knew a lot more than she let on. She'd be willing to bet that woman would know how to get someone away from a bad situation. She hated to be beholden to the woman but Betty had friends in America who might be able to help Hannah.

Hannah didn't answer. She couldn't. She put her head on her arms, folded on the kitchen table, and wailed.

Chapter 11

Ivy walked along Baggot Street, checking the numbers on the houses. It wouldn't do to knock on the wrong door on this street. There were a number of very busy abortionists plying their trade along here.

She shoved her hands in the pockets of her beige cashmere coat. She had asked young Seán McDonald to set up this meeting. That lad seemed to run back and forth to Betty's whenever he felt like it.

The door to the house she was looking for opened as she neared. A slender grey-haired figure dressed all in black stood framed in the opening. The woman didn't say a word, simply stared at Ivy with the scariest eyes she'd ever seen.

"I'm here to see Miss Armstrong." Ivy offered a weak smile.

The woman, who was much younger than she appeared from a distance, stepped back.

"Ivy!" Betty Armstrong appeared in the opening to the first door on the left of the long elegant entrance hall. "Dolly, we'll have tea and biscuits, please." She looked at Ivy, wondering what had brought her brother's child to her door. "Unless you're hungry. I'm sure Dolly wouldn't mind making a snack."

"Tea would be fine, thank you." Ivy didn't want to visit politely. She passed her coat and hat to the woman who stood by her side, hands out, waiting.

"We can talk in here." Betty turned to enter the room at her back. She knew Ivy would prefer the kitchen. She didn't care.

"Thank you for agreeing to see me." Ivy looked around. The room was elegantly furnished with soft beige chairs arranged around a roaring fire. A glass-topped occasional table supported a mountainous display of fresh flowers. She looked at the roll-front desk with envy.

"Sit down, Ivy." Betty waved to the chair across the fire from where she sat. "We can discuss why you wanted to see me after Dolly has served the tea." She waited until Ivy sat stiffly facing her. "How have you been?"

"I didn't come here for polite chitchat."

"It won't kill you to indulge me." Betty was determined to form a positive relationship with Ivy. "For example, we could talk about what you've been up to today."

"Friday is my day for visiting the markets." She'd run around the markets and even bought supplies from Harry Green's warehouse.

"You appear to be making a success of your business." Betty felt she had to almost drag every word out of the stubborn woman's mouth.

Dolly entered the room silently carrying a tray which she placed on an occasional table in front of the fire.

"We will serve ourselves, Dolly, thank you," Betty said when everything was in place.

The woman left the room.

"Why have you come to me?" Betty poured tea into two cups and with silent gestures offered milk and sugar – at Ivy's nod she added milk only to her cup. She passed the prepared tea served in a delicate china cup and saucer across the small table.

"Someone came to me for help." Ivy was glad the cup didn't rattle in the saucer as she took it. She waved away the offered plate of biscuits. "I don't know how to help her. I hoped you might know something I could tell her."

"How well do you know this woman?" Sometimes holding out a helping hand was a trap.

"We grew up together." Ivy almost inhaled the tea in the delicate cup – nervousness seemed to have drained all of the moisture out of her mouth. She held the cup out for a refill.

"Tell me everything." Betty turned the handle of the silver teapot in Ivy's direction. If she was going to drink tea at that speed she could serve herself.

"Hannah is married to Manny Felman." Ivy was filling her cup and didn't notice Betty stiffen. She served herself and then told Betty everything that had happened since she'd set foot inside the Dawson Street haberdashery.

Betty wondered if Ivy had any clue what she was actually telling her. The shop took a lot of crowns. Mrs Felman's cronies visited the shop regularly – he was using old biddies as runners. The bloody man was using the shop to bank the money he took from gambling and intimidation. Entertaining his late wife's family – nonsense!

"Do you trust this woman?" Betty needed to get this information to her brother. She would do nothing that might endanger him. They had both been active in the rebellion to free their country – a fact it didn't pay to advertise. Manny Felman had been on the other side – a known enemy.

"I have no reason not to trust her."

"Did she seem unhappy to you – abused?" Was this a trap for her brother? Manny Felman's wife – dear Lord, the woman would be a mine of information if asked the right questions.

"I didn't see bruises and cuts if that's what you're asking." Ivy saw enough women around The Lane bearing the proof of their husbands' loving fists. "What I did see were her eyes, the stiff way she held herself." She looked at Betty. "I saw the change in her. Hannah was the . . ." she searched for a word, "the sunniest young girl I've ever known. She always had a smile, a greeting, a joke. The woman who came to my house is a shadow of that girl."

"You need to leave this with me." Betty knew Manny Felman's reputation. A British officer lover of hers – an informant had he known it – had talked of the man paid to extract information from prisoners. He'd remarked Manny enjoyed himself a little too much when questioning female prisoners. "Miss Ivy Rose may be needed to pass information along." Betty hated to think of Ivy involved in this but no one else could be seen to approach Hannah. "You need to think long and hard about this, Ivy. Manny Felman has a very bad reputation in this town. The kind of reputation that makes most sane people steer well clear of him. He and his henchmen play for keeps."

"Tell me what I should do." Ivy couldn't turn her back on Hannah. She'd heard the whispers going around town about Manny Felman. She planned to keep well out of his way.

"I need time to put a plan together." Betty leaned forward slightly to stare into Ivy's eyes. "What you are planning to do is not only against the law, it is bloody dangerous. Don't go near Hannah or that shop until I talk to you again. Don't come back to this door. I'll telephone you at the livery. I'll help you in this, Ivy, but for God's sake watch your back."

Chapter 12

"In the name of God, Ivy Murphy, are yeh feeding the five thousand?" Porky Donnelly, a well-known Dublin pork butcher, stared at the list of items Ivy had passed to him. He pushed his glasses on top of his bald head, put his bloodstained hands on his sackcloth-covered hips and waited.

"Now, Mr Donnelly, you shouldn't be complaining when a customer comes to your door." Ivy had made a note of her requirements because she didn't want to forget anything. "Besides, wasn't it loaves and fishes that fed the five thousand in the Bible? I don't remember any mention of ham hocks."

"I'd want to get up early in the morning to catch you out, Ivy." Porky Donnelly was standing in the back room of his two-up two-down house, cutting chunks from the pig he'd slaughtered that morning. Porky, his wife and children lived in the two top rooms, keeping the downstairs for business. The front-room shop was closed today. Friday was a black fast day for Catholics everywhere.

"The missus must have put the word out that I was butchering."

Mrs Donnelly had a stall in the Thomas Street Market.

"I'm not looking for fresh pork, Mr Donnelly." Ivy had been out and about from early morning, selling her wares to the stallholders of the Dublin street markets.

"You're not thinking of eating meat today, are you, Ivy?"

"No, of course not." She shoved her hands into her coat pocket so he wouldn't see her crossed fingers. "I'm going to slow-cook the meat overnight."

"Have yeh a pot big enough for all of this meat?" Porky stood over one of the big barrels standing against the wall of the room. The barrels were filled with brine and portions of pig.

"I haven't but I know someone who has."

"Fair enough." Porky got busy pulling the legs he had soaking in brine out of the barrels. He carried the ones that needed trimming over to the big block table in the middle of the room. He'd trim the hanging meat off and cube it. He'd strings of sausages hanging from the ceiling. "I've cooked and smoked ham hanging if you're interested?" He panted while using his cleaver to chop through the meat.

"No, thanks – I want the ham hocks, ham chunks and sausages today. I'll take half a ring of your black pudding though." She could fry the pudding up with a tomato and a slice of bread as soon as she returned home. No need to mention her sinful ways here. She needed something hot and fast to eat. A cheese sandwich wasn't very appealing when you'd been walking the streets in the cold and rain all day. "That should do me." She pulled back the covering of her pram and began making a space for the meat packages.

"That pram is on its last legs, Ivy." Porky placed the first big package of meat into the depths of the pram. He gave an experimental push to the pram, shaking his head in sorrow as he stared at his customer. "It would be easier to carry the bloody stuff home, Ivy." He looked at the big bag of potatoes and another of large Spanish onions sitting in the bottom of the pram. "That pram won't be able for all the weight."

"I'll make it." Ivy knew she needed a new pram but where was she going to get one? She had put the word out around the markets but no-one had a second-hand pram that would suit Ivy. Jem had replaced the leather straps that held the body of the pram to the springs but the old pram was on its last legs. It was exhausting work pushing it around the place.

"I've a few ham bones with a bit of meat left on them," Porky said when he'd put the second of Ivy's packages in her pram. "I'll wrap a couple up for yeh, Ivy. They give a grand flavour to the stockpot, so I'm told." He told her the total cost of her purchases with a smile.

"Thanks, Mr Donnelly."

Ivy had to almost force her own fingers to release the money from her hand. The amount she was passing over to the pork butcher would make her weak if she thought about it. It seemed to her the more money she made the more she spent.

"I'll be off," she said as soon as the exchange of money had been made.

"The blessings of God on yeh, Ivy." Porky was thrilled with the money he'd made from Ivy. He hadn't expected to take any cash today. If he was fast he could be around to the bookies before his missus got back from the market.

What the eyes don't see, the heart will never grieve over, Porky believed, and, besides, if he made a few bob on the horses sure he'd share it with her.

Ivy put the weight of her body behind the pram as she pushed it through the back streets of Dublin. Her flesh was crawling. She felt as if someone was watching her. She'd been so nervous that she'd made a deposit of most of the money she'd taken that day. She was aware of every sound around her.

She had a lot to think about as she walked the streets. The Alice dolls were on sale in the Grafton Street shop. She was glad she didn't have to stand out in the street selling them. She made less profit in the shop but it was easy money as far as she was concerned.

Maybe there would be a letter from Shay for her when she got back. She was trying to be patient. Who knew how long it would take her brother to reach this place he'd talked about – this Hollywood.

Chapter 13

"Ivy!" Jem had been calling Ivy's name for ages. If she turned down the street she was heading for he'd never be able to get his horse and small flatbed cart down there after her. He clicked his tongue at his old horse. "Ivy Murphy, will you wait up!"

"Jem Ryan," Ivy leaned against her pram, her hand to her heart, "are you trying to give me a heart attack?" She straightened and, pulling her pram along with her, crossed to the edge of the pavement. "What are you doing out and about? I thought you were getting too big for driving around the streets." She gave Rosie, Jem's longest-serving horse, a pat on her glossy black neck.

"I had a delivery to make to Old Man Muskoff, the apothecary." Jem applied the brake and tied the reins to the iron leg of his seat before jumping down to join Ivy on the pavement.

Just then he noticed a dark figure sneaking back into the shadows. He began to follow but the sound of running feet echoed down the lane. He'd never catch whoever it was now. Some young thug obviously didn't know Ivy was under the protection of Billy Flint – that worried him.

"I wish I'd known that," Ivy said. "I'd have given you a list of things I need from the apothecary." A lot of the herbs and things she used in Granny Grunt's cures were items she could pick up from parks and hedgerows but there were some items she had to buy.

"Old Man Muskoff has been a good customer of mine for years. He's having difficulty trusting the young lads who make the deliveries for me. I thought I'd take old Rosie here," he gave the mare a hearty pat, "out for a run and have a chat with the man." He would have to keep a closer eye on Ivy himself. He was travelling around the familiar streets today making a study of them with his automobile in mind. There were a lot of streets the cart could travel that would never suit his machine.

"I haven't seen you with a sack around your head for a long time." Ivy smiled. Jem Ryan had been a fixture in her life for years, driving out in all weathers to pick up fares around Dublin. "Are you on your way home?"

"I am. I thought I'd give you a carriage ride home." He walked over to her pram, preparing to hoist it up onto the empty bed of the cart. He grunted as he picked it up. "This thing weighs a ton, Ivy. I hope there's nothing breakable in it." He slid the pram onto its side and with the rope he kept attached to the cart began to tie it down, being careful not to let anything spill out.

"You have no idea how glad I am to see you, Jem." Ivy watched her pram being loaded with a sigh of relief. She'd been afraid she'd never make it back to The Lane. "I still have a few stops to make along the way – would you mind?" She might as well make use of having this private horse and cart at her disposal. "I need to stop at the creamery and the bakery."

"I'd be delighted to serve you, m'lady." Jem held his bent elbow out from his body and gave an elaborate bow.

"Get along with you, my good man." Ivy put her nose in the air and with a sway to her hips walked towards the waiting cart.

"Far from it you were raised, Ivy Murphy." Jem bent his knees, took a firm grip on her waist and almost threw her up onto the high seat right behind the horse's rump. Rosie turned her head and gave a startled neigh in his direction. "Sorry about that, old girl." He slapped his open hand on the horse's rump before walking to her head and giving her a gentle pat. He was enjoying this trip out and about. He'd have to get out of the livery more often now that he had the choice. He strolled towards the driver's seat where Ivy sat proudly waiting for him.

"That aul' pram of yours is giving up the ghost, Ivy." He joined her on the seat. He took the reins in his hand and clicked his tongue, giving the horse her off.

"I know." Ivy loved being up high like this, driving through the streets of Dublin. Her aching feet appreciated the rest. "I've the word out that I need a replacement. I've even been checking out the scrap yards for bits but so far no luck."

"If I'd known I was picking up a lady I'd have taken the time to put the top over this seat." Jem was paying close attention to the traffic on the streets. The latest fashion for rapid transit was becoming dangerous. It broke his heart to see the horses injured in the accidents that happened when some young hothead offered extra money to the jarvey for a speedy ride.

"That's okay, Jem." Ivy pulled her damp black shawl out slightly from her head, making a peak. "I come with a guarantee not to melt. It's stamped on me back, right beside *Made in Ireland*."

"Glad to hear it," Jem said absentmindedly. "What have you got in your pram that made it so heavy?" He knew that Ivy sold her goods around the markets on a Friday and usually returned to The Lane with a practically empty pram.

"I'm planning to make a really big pot of coddle tonight." Ivy leaned into his side when they turned a corner onto George's Street and headed south. The horse travelled along the wide street framed on both sides by tenement buildings. Barefoot children ran alongside the horse, calling out greetings. "I need to check on old Nanny Grace tomorrow. I haven't been in a while and I worry about the old girl. And I thought I'd drop off some of me coddle to Sadie. She could serve it up to her family – save her cooking. It seemed the thing to do since we'll be eating at Ann Marie's on Sunday. Sadie has herself worn to a frazzle worrying about the Sunday menu, if you can believe it."

"I thought Sadie was beginning to calm down a bit." Jem knew Sadie Lawless was trying to prove she could run Ann Marie's big house without a problem. The poor woman was afraid of letting her family down.

"I've a pain in me face telling her to take each day as it comes." Ivy leaned in to Jem's side again when they made the turn onto Stephen's Street, the road that would lead them past Stephen's Green and towards The Lane.

Jem slowed the horse as they approached the creamery. "If you'll give me a shout when you're ready to head off in the morning, I'll take you about in this rig," he offered to her delight while pulling on the reins.

"I'll feel like one of them ladies of leisure you read about," Ivy said, laughing.

Chapter 14

"When are you going to marry my Uncle Jem, Aunty Ivy?" Emmy was sitting between the two adults she loved – delighted with life. She cuddled under the heavy blanket draped over their laps. Her Uncle Jem had pulled two jacket potatoes from the fire and put them into her coat pockets so she was snug and warm. "Only my friend Biddy said if you don't do it soon it will be ages and ages before you can get around to it." She leaned forward to stare into Ivy's eyes. She wanted an answer to her question.

"Does she indeed?" Ivy felt as if someone had punched her. It seemed lately that every man and his dog wanted to stick their nose into her private business.

"Yes." Emmy nodded her head frantically. "Biddy says it will soon be Lent and you're not allowed to do anything in Lent. Biddy says we'll have a big, big, street party in The Lane on the Tuesday before Lent and then it will be all beating your chest and wailing."

"Really, Biddy said 'beating your chest and wailing'?" Jem asked, amused. He'd been wanting to move Ivy along on a date for their wedding but now it seemed the two little girls were also becoming impatient.

"Yes," Emmy cuddled closer to Ivy, "like the people in the story told at story time last night. Only those people were pulling their hair out as well. We won't have to pull our hair out for Lent, will we, Aunty Ivy?" She didn't wait for a reply but continued, "You looked so funny with that bucket of potatoes at your feet, Aunty Ivy. So, when are you going to marry my Uncle Jem? Biddy and me want to know."

"I thought the month of May?" Ivy glanced over Emmy's head. She smiled at Jem's look of surprise. It was time and past it she put the man out of his misery. She ignored the comment about her bucket of potatoes. She'd been able to peel what felt like a small mountain of potatoes while listening fascinated to the stories being told in the vestibule of one of the tenement houses. It had made the tedious chore seem so much easier, her hands moving almost in time to the cadence of the bible story being told.

Story nights were a social occasion for the people of The Lane. A lot of the women took needlework, darning or knitting along with them and sat listening to the stories. Last night Ivy had decided to peel potatoes. It wasn't an unusual sight and she'd have missed the story if she'd decided to peel the vegetables in her own place.

"The month of May sounds perfect to me." Jem grinned widely. Emmy had achieved something he couldn't. He didn't intend to let Ivy change her mind. "And there will be no chest-beating and hair-pulling in Lent, Missus." He nudged Emmy gently with his shoulder.

"But May is such a long, long, way away," Emmy objected just as the horse turned into Fitzwilliam Square.

"It will be here before you know it," Ivy said with a sinking feeling in her stomach. She pointed out the entrance she wanted to go through. "Now give me a minute to think. Jem, I want to drop off the second pot of coddle to Curly and Moocher." She'd already dropped off a pot of food to Sadie.

"Who are they?" Emmy looked around, fascinated. "I don't know them – do I?"

"Shush," Ivy whispered as the horse came within sight of the three-sided hut the two men called home. "Curly, are you about?"

"Sure where else would I be?" Curly's bald head, covered with old sacking, appeared in the hut's opening. "The Moocher is out and about. I wasn't expecting to see you today, Ivy. It's not Wednesday, is it?"

"No!" Ivy laughed at the old man who'd been a part of her life for years. "I'm making a special visit to see old Nanny Grace."

"Howayeh, Curly." Jem pulled the horse to a stop in front of the hut. The horse and cart would help cut the wind whistling around the hut and give the old man a bit of extra warmth.

"Jem Ryan, I'd doff me hat to yeh but then me poor head would freeze." Curly showed his gums in a wide grin. "Who's this little beauty you've brought to meet me?" He stepped out of the hut to stare up at the trio sitting so high up. "Begob, if you mixed the two of yeh – you'd make one of her." He stared from Ivy with her black hair to Jem's green eyes – both seemed to be replicated in the small girl sitting between them. "Something you never told me, young Ivy?"

"Mind your manners, Curly." Ivy jumped down from the high seat to stand beside the old man. "This is Miss Emmy Ryan, niece to the man sitting beside her grinning like a fool." She climbed up on the back of the cart and opened the tied-down chest Jem had placed there to store her pots of coddle. "Have yeh a good fire going, Curly?" She took out a pot, closed the chest and put the pot on the chest lid before jumping off the cart again.

"We had a bit of luck there." Curly was watching Ivy, wondering what the devil the girl was up to. "Sure, there were a few deliveries yesterday and them coalmen are that careless me and Moocher were able to pick up so many pieces of coal they let fall we'll have big fires for days. The horses made a few deposits for our fire as well." Curly chuckled, thinking of the manure they had drying behind the hut.

"Good for you." Jem reached behind Emmy, picked up the pot by the handle and passed it down to Ivy.

"I made a pot of coddle for you and Moocher, Curly." Ivy didn't ask if they had a pot she could empty the food into. The men would have to use a bucket to heat the coddle if she didn't leave the pot with them. "I put plenty of potatoes and onions in so it's good and thick."

"The blessings of God on yeh, Ivy Murphy." Curly almost closed his eyes and he did smack his lips at the thought of the promised treat. "I couldn't name the day nor the hour when I last had a taste of a good Dublin coddle. Me and Moocher will say a special prayer for yeh when we eat it, that I can promise."

Jem and Emmy sat silently watching the two people standing on the bare earth below them. Emmy opened her mouth to ask a question but a quick shake of her Uncle Jem's head made her keep her lips closed. She cuddled close to his side, content to wait. She'd ask her questions later.

"I'll leave the pot with yeh." Ivy carried the well-filled tightly covered pot into the hut. The pot was one of two she'd bought at the market. It had a screw-on lid and a half-moon handle that went over the top, the kind of pot that was popular for carrying food from the Penny Dinners. It was heavy and Curly's hands were bent and twisted with age. She didn't want him to drop it. His companion Moocher looked after the older man and he'd take care of heating and serving the food.

"Open the pot for us, will yeh, Ivy?" Curly couldn't wait until Moocher returned from wherever he was rambling. The very thought of a coddle had him salivating. He groaned when Ivy unscrewed the tight lid of the pot. "There's a smell that would raise the dead." He rubbed his hurting hands together. "I'm going to sit over me fire and watch that pot carefully. The smell of that coddle will have Moocher running back here like a shot." His empty stomach rumbled. He turned to shout out the opening of the shed. "I'll say me goodbyes to yeh now, Jem Ryan! I'll not be moving from this spot for a while. Be a good girl, Emmy – it was nice meeting yeh." He took his seat, with the metal bucket of embers between his knees, and watched as Ivy carefully balanced the pot over the coals in his bucket. He noticed she was careful to leave the handle of the pot standing up so he wouldn't burn himself.

"It will be really thick for the first feed, Curly," Ivy whispered from her crouched position. "If you have a bit left, add a drop of water and you should be able to get a few meals out of it. I'll pick the pot up on Wednesday when I'm doing me round."

"Your blood should be bottled, Ivy, thanks." Curly's eyes filled with tears as the aroma of ham and onion filled the hut. "Get about your business now. I hear that old woman is not doing too good."

Chapter 15

"Mr Cusack," Ivy said to the elderly man who answered her knock on the back door of the house that had been Nanny Grace's home for years, "I hope you don't mind but I'd like to pay Nanny Grace a visit."

"Ivy, by the mercy of God, come in." Paddy Cusack slowly stepped back and opened the door wider. "It's Ivy Murphy, Meg," he shouted over his shoulder.

"Thanks be to God," came from the direction of the kitchen as the two made their way down the long dark hallway towards the kitchen. "I'll put the kettle on."

"What's going on?" Ivy had left Jem walking his horse along the back lane. Emmy was happy to sit in the high seat holding the reins.

"There's that much going on, I don't know if I'm on me head or me heels," Paddy Cusack said as they entered the kitchen.

Meg, his wife, was putting a big black kettle on the range. Paddy walked over and put his arm around her shoulders as she turned around. They were a matched pair, short and plump with scraggly grey hair and pale blue eyes.

"We're not able for all this malarkey, Ivy." Meg rubbed her hands on her wraparound apron. They had been lucky to get this job – she knew that – but it was only supposed to be keeping an eye on the place. No one said anything about fetching and carrying up all them stairs.

"What's been happening?" Ivy knew the old couple were having a hard time catering to Nanny Grace. She had tried to talk the woman into coming down to the kitchen where there was always a fire in the grate. The pair standing in front of her couldn't be expected to run up and down stairs. Nanny refused to leave her third-floor room, spending most of her time in bed. The Cusacks had been willing to put up with the old woman for the few bob Ivy passed them every week.

"The old woman must be nearly blue with the cold," Paddy whispered. "What with the way me old bones locked up I couldn't get up all them stairs this morning to light her fire. While the kettle's boiling, Ivy, would you carry up a bucket of coal and light the fire?"

"Thank God there's a water closet up them stairs. Paddy would never be fit to empty a slop bucket. The place would be stinking." Meg Cusack gave her husband's hand a pat before moving away towards the cupboard that held all of their kitchen needs.

"Jem Ryan is outside waiting for me." Ivy didn't want to leave Jem and Emmy waiting out in the cold for her and this looked like it might take some time to sort out. "If you'll allow it I'll run out and tell him to tie up his horse. Jem can carry the coal upstairs and light the fire. He has his niece with him. Emmy will be company for the old woman while we talk."

"Alright . . ." Paddy said.

The pair exchanged concerned glances. This wasn't their house and they didn't feel comfortable inviting people in, but this was an emergency.

"Right, tell us what's going on."

Rosie was tied up in the back yard. The fire in the nursery was blazing and Emmy was upstairs riding the big grey rocking horse. Nanny Grace was out of her bed and dressed. Ivy had carried up a tea tray and something to eat for Nanny Grace, and now the Cusacks, Jem and Ivy were sitting around the big kitchen work table, cups of tea in front of them.

"A man came to see us yesterday," Meg said, her apple-dumpling face creasing in dislike.

"He said he'd been employed by the owners of these houses to inspect their premises in their absence." Paddy grimaced. He hadn't liked the man, not one little bit. "This fella showed us papers and everything."

He opened the drawer under the kitchen table and pulled out a sheaf of papers, passing them across the table to Ivy and Jem. He waited while they put their heads together and read what was typed on the pages.

"This seems to be all above board." Jem lifted his green eyes and stared across the table at the worried couple. "What's the problem?"

"Yer man said –" Meg hiccupped violently.

"He said . . ." Paddy put his teacup down gently and patted his wife's hand while staring at the table-top. "He said as how Nanny Grace would have to make other living arrangements or he'd make them for her."

"He said he'd call the poorhouse." Meg pulled up her apron, buried her face in its folds and wailed. "He's going

75

to send that old woman to the poorhouse. It'll finish her off." The old woman was demanding, living in the past, but she'd never wish that on her.

Chapter 16

"I thought I'd find you here" Betty Armstrong took a seat beside Ivy on one of the straw bales grouped around Hop-a-long's tea stall. She was dressed as an old tramp, clutching a walking-stick tree-limb in shaking hands. "Close your mouth girl, you'll catch flies." An elbow in the ribs knocked Ivy out of her stunned surprise at the woman's odd appearance. "Jump up and get me a mug of tea – pretend I'm old Granny Grunt." She waited until Ivy was standing in front of her making certain the 'old dear' had a good grasp of the mug before saying: "Ivy, you are being followed."

"Declan Johnson?" Ivy named a man who had threatened her life. She didn't question the woman's sudden appearance. It seemed everyone and his dog knew her days for visiting the markets.

"I thought you knew." Betty visually checked out the people surrounding them. She was taking a risk meeting Ivy in the open, but nobody should be able to see through her disguise. She'd learned her craft from the best. "Declan Johnson died in an institution for the diseased."

"Jesus!" Ivy blessed herself. She'd been keeping one

eye over her shoulder for that blackguard forever, it seemed.

"One of Manny Felman's neckless wonders has been following you around."

Hannah Solomon had been living in Betty's Baggot Street house for ten days. The change in her appearance was remarkable. It would take longer for her to stop jumping at shadows. "You didn't tell me you paid for your purchases from the haberdashery with a cheque."

"I didn't think it was important."

"Everything is important." Betty allowed her hands to shake. Ivy reacted by moving closer to put her hand under the mug. "Manny Felman was able to question a bank clerk. A man who, for a small fee, was willing and able to supply Felman with information concerning Miss Ivy Rose and her thriving doll business. Success makes enemies, Ivy. You need to learn that."

"I'm sorry." Ivy had passed the problem of Hannah over to Betty, but 'Miss Rose' had made several visits to the haberdashery to pass notes and instructions before Hannah left.

"Hannah's husband enjoys inflicting pain." Betty had been obliged to bathe and spoon-feed Hannah that first night. She'd arrived shaking and shivering at the back door. The woman was frightened almost out of her mind. The old and fresh cigar burns covering her skin – revealed when Betty removed Hannah's old-fashioned clothing – had been weeping pus. They had needed immediate treatment. Betty's knowledge of wise-woman cures was extensive but it was taking all of her skill to heal Hannah's physical and mental injuries.

"The word on the street is that Hannah is in a

sanatorium," Ivy whispered. "She's had some kind of crisis of the nerves according to her distraught husband."

"Felman's own arrogance is working against him." Betty allowed tea to spill from her mouth. "He doesn't believe Hannah capable of escaping on her own. He is searching for a man – a lover." How any man could believe that a woman would run from one abusive man into the arms of another never failed to amaze her. Ivy continued to support the mug of tea. "He is keeping an eye on you but doesn't expect to find anything. After all, you are female."

"The Garda were called to the shop." Ivy leaned over to remove an old pair of black knitted gloves from her pram. They had holes and were unravelling – she was going to mend them. Whatever Betty had used to age her hands was cracking. They staged a small drama with Ivy offering the gloves and Betty refusing.

"You can't really blame Hannah for helping herself to a lot of the most expensive items in the shop." Betty had been surprised at the woman's daring. She'd wondered how she'd managed to walk with the weight of the goods stashed around her person. Still, the goods could be sold in America and provide a nice little nest egg. "One more reason apparently to look for a man. Manny figures Hannah isn't bright enough to know which stock would bring the most money – rather insulting since the woman ran the darn shop from what I understand."

She'd taken the precaution of asking Ann Marie Gannon to photograph Hannah's injuries. It was a risk involving another person but they needed a record of the cuts and scars on the woman. If ever they needed to seek legal advice for Hannah those photographs would speak louder than any words. She hoped the courts in America were more understanding than the Irish legal system.

"What about my Alice dolls?"

Hannah had taken over almost all of the production of the Alice dolls. The woman had inherited her father's tailoring skill. She could turn out those dolls as if she had twenty hands, Ivy sometimes thought.

"The system we've set up of getting the dolls to and from you to Hannah is safe." Betty's housekeeper was the soul of discretion. The task of carrying dolls and material about the place was not a problem for Dolly. "The work keeps her hands busy and her mind occupied. She needs that right now." Betty allowed Ivy to force her fingers into the black gloves.

"I have to get on. We've been sitting here long enough. If you need to tell me anything, Seán can give me a time and I'll be waiting by the telephone in the livery." Ivy stood and replaced the enamel mugs on the wooden plinth that formed the tea counter.

No one would think twice about seeing Seán McDonald run back and forth between The Lane and Baggot Street.

"Or you could telephone me." Betty allowed Ivy to help her to her feet. "You can't write the number down. How good is your memory?"

"Excellent." Ivy laughed, remembering when she had to remember reams of facts and figures. She could still do it but life was so much easier now that she could read and write. She made a mental note of the telephone number Betty whispered. "Tell Hannah I said hello."

Ivy grabbed the handle of her old pram and with a grunt of effort got it moving.

Betty watched her niece push the dilapidated pram

across the cobbles. The girl's pride would choke her. She refused to allow Betty or William to help her in any way. She had her mother's stiff-necked pride although Betty knew better than to say that aloud.

Chapter 17

"I give up," Ivy shouted aloud to the empty room. "Who made me responsible for the rest of the world? Who died and made me God I'd like to know." She'd been tossing and turning in her bed, trying to return to sleep. It was Saturday. She punched her pillow in frustration. She wanted to stay in bed. She didn't have to jump out of her warm nest at the crack of dawn. She wished she had a switch to turn off her brain. Whenever she closed her eyes, the problems she faced kept appearing. It was impossible to drag her mind away from its rotating list of worries.

"I may as well be up and doing."

She pushed the bedclothes away and, groaning, put her feet on the cold floor. She took care of her bodily functions and changed out of her 'poor man's pajamas' – two men's jumpers – one pulled over her head, the other on her bottom half, her legs pushed into the arms. Shivering, she quickly dressed in the outfit of black skirt and warm blue jumper she'd worn to the market the day before. When she was fully dressed she lit the two gas lamps attached to the wall separating her room from next door's basement. She raked the fire, added fresh fuel and put the kettle on the range top directly over the fire.

"There's not a sinner out and about." She'd pulled the thick tablecloth she'd turned into a curtain from the single window in the room to check the back yard. "I'll empty the slop and get fresh water. I'll be out and back before anyone's stirring." She emptied the last of her fresh water into the reservoir of the range and with the two galvanised buckets in hand hurried into the gas-lamp-lit back yard. She had refilled the water container in her range and had two full buckets of water sitting on her floor before she stopped running back and forth. She made herself a pot of tea and used the top of the range to sear two slices of bread. She had homemade blackberry jam to go on the bread.

Ivy sat at her kitchen table, a cup of tea close to her hand. She entered figures into her account book, dipping the nib of her pen into the bottle of ink sitting open on the table. She didn't use her fountain pen for book work, nervous about breaking the nib by using it too much. "I never thought I'd see the day I'd have money in the bank." She used a sheet of blotting paper to dry the ink on the page. "What's a body supposed to do with money? Do the rich just put it in the bank and count it?"

A sharp rap of knuckles on her back door made her jump in fright. She barely managed to rescue the ink from spilling all over her work. Shaking in fright at the near miss, she put the top back on the bottle of ink and tightened it before standing to see who had the cheek to knock on her door so early on a Saturday morning.

It took her a moment to recognise the two men standing before her door. To her knowledge she'd never seen them outside of Fitzwilliam Square before.

"Curly, Moocher, what in the name of God are you two doing at my door?" She opened the door wider. "Step in and welcome." She watched the two men enter her home. She hadn't even realised they knew where she lived.

"Thanks, Ivy." Moocher gave a jerky bow of his head as he passed.

"Morning, Ivy." Curly, his bald head well wrapped in sackcloth, followed on Moocher's heels.

"Sit down before the fire and get a heat." She gestured to the two soft chairs sitting before the range. "Give me a minute to gather me thoughts." She put the kettle on and with quick movements tidied up her paperwork, pushing the articles on the table to one side. "Right," she pulled one of the kitchen chairs over to the fire and joined the two men, "tell me what brings you to my door."

"We got a couple of nights' work." Curly was looking around the room. He'd been here before, many times, when Éamonn Murphy had used this back room. "At that warehouse that caught fire – down on the docks – have yeh heard about it?"

"I have," Ivy nodded. "We watched the flames roar into the sky from here." The Dublin docks weren't far from The Lane.

"Some say it's in retaliation for the accident," Moocher muttered into his chest.

"Be that as it may be." Curly didn't want to go into the politics of the thing.

"The accident that killed David Rattigan and that other fella?" Ivy had been to David Rattigan's funeral. The man had been from The Lane – he'd left a widow and five children destitute.

"That's the one." Curly held his hands out to the

flames, thrilled with the heat. "Poor aul' Mousey Rattigan, squashed flat as a pancake." He shook his head in sorrow for the passing of a man much younger than himself. The men who worked the docks were angry. There had been no money passed along for the widows and children of the dead men. The dock workers had had a whip-around but the ship owners and the warehouse owners had kept their hands in their pockets. Talk around the docks was that the fire was set in retaliation. It didn't make sense to Curly – setting the place on fire didn't do a blind bit of good for the widows and childer.

"Have you two eaten?" Ivy knew it was silly to ask but she had to say something to break the silence that had fallen. The two men were obviously here for a reason. It would be easier to get it, whatever it was, out of them over a bite to eat. She jumped to her feet. "I got a dozen cracked eggs at the market yesterday." She made the tea she'd ignored until now. "Sit down at the table and I'll make yez a bite to eat."

The two men moved quickly, eager to get treated to a hot meal sitting inside at a table. It was many a day since they had known such luxury. The room was silent as Ivy busied herself breaking the eggs into a bowl. She made scrambled eggs and fried bread. When the meal and two big enamel mugs of tea were put in front of the two men she joined them at the table, pulling one of her orange boxes over to sit on. The wooden crates used to ship oranges were the furniture of choice for the people of The Lane.

"Ivy . . ." Curly took a big gulp of tea from his tin mug. He'd half the meal inside him already. "Me and Moocher were working at that warehouse these last few nights." He pointed his fork at Ivy to make his point. "I wouldn't normally think of this but since I saw yeh with Jem Ryan and his horse and cart I got to thinking. Didn't I get to thinking?" He stared at his friend sitting across the table from him, shovelling food into his mouth.

"He did, Ivy." Moocher nodded his head in agreement. He didn't stop eating but he made the response he knew his aul' mate expected. "A fierce one for thinking, is aul' Curly." He returned his attention to his meal, satisfied he'd done all that was required of him.

"They had them big electric lights at that warehouse." Curly shook his head at the thought of the big machines that had been dragged in to light the warehouse. "They're enough to blind a man." Another big gulp of tea emptied his mug. He waited as Ivy jumped to her feet to fetch the teapot from the range.

"That warehouse is full of stuff," Curly continued when Ivy returned to her seat after refilling both mugs. "I never seen such colours in me life. There were no browns or blacks, no!' He shook his head. "Cloth the colour of the rainbow – fabric, they called it, and skeins of yarn from the floor to the ceiling. Honest to God, Ivy, the colours would take the eye out of yer head!"

"It's the truth he's telling yeh." Moocher picked up his fresh mug of tea and slurped the hot liquid into his mouth.

"The stuff is ruined, I heard them say." Curly looked at Ivy to see if she'd cottoned on to what he was talking about yet. He gave a deep sigh at her blank stare and continued. "I thought – with you being friends with Jem Ryan and all – well, I thought you could maybe visit that warehouse and make a deal for some of that cloth and wool. You'd never be able to shift the stuff with that aul'

86

wreck of a pram of yours but if Jem Ryan were to go with you," he spread his arms wide, "well, you see where I'm going with this."

"Curly . . ." Ivy didn't know what to say. She'd never bought in bulk from one of the warehouses down the docks.

"Listen to me, girl." Curly pushed his empty plate to one side and leaned over the table. "I heard them say they are going to have a fire-sale and invite all the nobs what own factories around the place to buy the stuff. That lot will be able to buy the stuff cheap and fix it up. The warehouse owner will get the insurance money plus whatever he makes from this fire-sale." He thumped his clenched fist on the table, making the articles on the table-top jump. "It's like this, Ivy." He slurped tea like a dying camel. "I know the fella that's the night manager at the warehouse. He's been put in charge of shifting the stuff under the cover of darkness." He touched the tip of one finger off the side of his nose. "The same fella was a drinkin' crony of yer da's – maybe you know him – Skinny McInerny?"

"Little fat fella with tiny eyes placed too close together?" Ivy said.

"That's him." Curly held out his empty mug for a refill. "He owes yer da, Ivy. Eamonn often loaned Skinny a few bob or put a bet on for him. I never heard that he paid the money back. The man is in yer aul' man's debt and you can call him on it."

Ivy's mind was whirling. She'd seen her da do business. She didn't know if she was capable of doing the same thing. To her eyes it appeared that the men her da hung around with spoke a language she didn't understand. It was all nods and winks – her da would tap the side of his nose and it seemed to her the person he was dealing with understood without a word being spoken. She didn't know how to do that. She refilled Moocher's mug while she was up, sliced and buttered more bread and carried it and a pot of her home-made blackberry jam over to the table.

With her head spinning she sat down again.

"I thought you could make a few bob on the stuff that's going." Curly slathered jam on a thick slice of white bread. He didn't make any mention of Ivy paying him a finder's fee but he'd make sure that was understood.

"I don't know how to do business like that, Curly." Ivy conducted her business out in the open – bartering and haggling she understood, but this was outside her field of experience.

"That uncle of yours, Billy Flint, knows all about it." Curly nodded when the colour almost drained from Ivy's face. "I'm old enough to know where the bodies are buried, Ivy."

"Curly –"

"Moocher, yeh need to turn deaf now," Curly barked.

"I can't hear a thing." Moocher was enjoying the good food and warm room. He didn't care what was said.

"Billy Flint knows all about doing business under cover of darkness." Curly shook his finger in Ivy's face. "Yeh can't be too proud to take advice. I know the word is out on the street that yer under the protection of Billy Flint and I was right glad to hear it too."

"I've never met the man," Ivy said. "I had someone else act as a go-between."

"Betty Armstrong – Billy's sister and your aunt – I

know about that and all." Curly watched Ivy stiffen. The world of Dublin was a small one and the whispers that went around the streets and pubs were heard and understood by a select few. Curly had his own sources for information. He kept most of what he heard to himself. "You knock on yer uncle's back door every Monday morning, Ivy Murphy."

"Billy Flint lives in Mount Street?" Ivy squealed. What was a man like that doing living amongst the nobs?

"No, he lives high on the hog in Merrion Square." Curly shoved the last piece of bread and jam into his toothless mouth and grinned. "If you'll give me a piece of that paper," he pointed to where Ivy had pushed her bookkeeping supplies, "I'll give you his name and address."

He took the blank page that Ivy tore from her book. He uncapped the bottle of ink, dipped the nib and without further ado wrote down the name and address of a man who was considered very dangerous and passed the page over the table to Ivy.

"If you feel you need lessons in getting the best of a deal," Curly finished the tea in his mug, "you go see Billy Flint, my girl. He'll set yeh right."

Chapter 18

"God, Jem," Ivy's whisper carried over the gentle clip-clop of Rosie's hooves on the cobbled street, "this doesn't feel right. The streets haven't even been aired yet."

The well-wrapped-up pair were walking on either side of the horse's head along the dark backstreets leading down to the Dublin docks.

"Don't be fretting, Ivy." Jem was holding a lantern in one hand to light their way. "You're going to a warehouse sale. You'll pay for the stuff we take out of that place." He'd no doubt someone was receiving an underhand payment to turn a blind eye to these goings-on – that was none of their business.

"Still and all, it doesn't feel very honest to be creeping through the streets on a Sunday morning."

Jem had been insulted when she'd talked about needing to find someone to teach her the art of double dealing, as she doubted her ability to do business in what she thought of as a 'man's way'. He insisted he came from a family of horse traders. He'd be her guide during their visit to the fire-damaged warehouse.

"We won't be the only ones there, Ivy."

He'd hitched Rosie to one of his large wagons. He had tied a hand-held cart onto the long flat bed of the wagon. They'd never be able to shift the bulky packages without the cart. He had put two of Ivy's precious tea chests, empty for the moment, onto the cart. Conn Connelly and one of his brothers were asleep under a tarpaulin on the flat bed. He had brought a load of rope as well. They didn't know what they'd find when they reached the warehouse so best to come prepared. The Connelly brothers would protect the horse and cart, keeping an eye on anything Ivy might buy. Jem thought it likely that the word was already out on the street about the warehouse. He wanted to be one of the first there – so Ivy could have her pick of the damaged merchandise.

"The place will be packed with people looking to make a few coppers from whatever's on offer," he said.

"You're a man of mystery, Jem Ryan." She'd been amazed to discover Jem knew the ins and outs of trading in bulk. Why had she thought she knew everything there was to know about Jem?

"I got to hear a lot when I was out and about picking up fares." He'd often made a few extra pence by passing along the things he'd heard in his travels around Dublin. He'd bought and sold too when he was sure he could pass the merchandise along. His lads were carrying on that tradition, bringing him the items of gossip they heard on their travels.

This morning he was keeping a close eye on the streets they passed. A warehouse sale drew the attention of people hoping to help themselves to the goods others had paid for. He wouldn't be returning by this route but it didn't pay to be careless. The street rats knew that if people were going to buy goods from a warehouse sale they would have cash in their pocket – that was a temptation to some.

"Merciful Heavens!" Ivy stopped abruptly, staring at the very bright light breaking through the darkness. Was that the electric lights Curly had talked about? The things would blind yeh! She stood staring open-mouthed at the bright beams of light shooting up into the sky – then had to run to catch up with the horse and cart that had continued on without her.

"Is that them electric lights?" she asked when she'd caught up with the horse.

"The lights are battery-operated," Jem answered without really thinking. He was aware of the press of bodies along the road leading out onto the docks. Without stopping he reached up and removed the whip from its place by the side of the driver's seat on the cart. He nudged the Connelly lads awake.

"Still and all, Jem, them lights are a wonder." Ivy too was aware of the people closing in around them.

"Come for the sale, have yeh?" Two tall broad-shouldered men suddenly appeared on the pathway. They had the bearing of military men. At their approach the flyboys disappeared back into the alleys and laneways that opened onto the road.

"Billy Flint must be providing security for this sale," Jem whispered to Ivy, his voice not showing the relief he felt. He didn't enjoy getting into street fights. He'd do it if he had to but he preferred to pass along peacefully.

"Yeh better hurry along," one of the men said, his eyes moving constantly, searching the shadows. "The stuff is walkin' out of the place."

The dock was alive with people – there were men pushing hand-held carts and women with the familiar three-wheeled rattan barrows, sleepy children popping their heads over the side from time to time – everyone was hurrying along the dock in the direction of the brightly lit warehouse.

"This is a world I never knew existed," Ivy gasped, her eyes taking everything in.

"We'll leave Rosie close by and get in there." Jem walked the horse to one of the bollards. "Conn," he passed the whip to a sleepy Conn who had come up front to take the reins, "keep your eyes open. There's help at hand if anyone causes problems but you need your wits about you."

He removed the handcart from the wagon and set it on the cobbles. Taking Ivy's elbow and pushing the handcart with his free hand, he drew her towards the open warehouse.

The smell of smoke lingered and puddles of water splashed under their feet when they walked into the well-stocked warehouse. They had to push their way through the people milling about.

Ivy tried to keep her jaw locked shut. She'd never seen anything like this before. She'd expected the place to be like Harry Green's warehouse where she bought goods wholesale. This was an Aladdin's Cave. The place was lined with shelving running the length of each aisle, the shelves stretching up to the damaged roof. How could you tell what was wrapped in all of them packages or locked in them crates?

"How can you tell what's for sale?" she whispered to Jem.

"See them fellas up there?" He pointed to a man standing on top of a crate. Two other men stood on either side of him, their hands full of papers.

"Yes." Ivy hadn't noticed the little man but she knew him: Skinny McInerny.

"Each package usually has a label and a number." Jem was looking around at the packages. "You take the label number up to him and he'll tell you what's inside and give you a price. You never pay what they're asking – just like when you bargain at the market, only for a lot more money. That fella over there," he pointed to a man sitting at a table, two big bruisers standing behind him, "he takes the money."

"There's method in this madness then. Yeh learn something new every day." Ivy began to examine the packages she could reach. She noticed men sending young lads scurrying up the shelving to tip the bulky damp packages down onto the wet floor.

"We can guess some of this stuff, Ivy." Jem stood at her shoulder, keeping careful watch for pickpockets. "Them big square-type packages must be the wool Curly told you about and the long sausage-shaped ones would be the material, don't you think?"

"You're more than just a pretty face, Jem Ryan," Ivy agreed. It was buying a pig in a poke but she knew she could make good money from the wrapping alone. The thick strong sacking cloth could be used for a lot of different purposes. The men of The Lane used the material cut into strips to make beds and support for soft chairs.

"Ooh . . ." A moan went around the warehouse when one of the bundles being tossed down exploded open and soft *báinín* – pure white wool – spilled over the dirty floor.

"Who did that?" Skinny McInerny jumped down from his crate and crossed the floor in mincing steps that travelled a lot faster than you would think, his henchmen followed along at his shoulders. "You there," he pointed to one of his men, "wrap that up." He gave a nod of his head to Jem – a quick jerk of his head – and without another word returned to standing on his crate.

"Where do you want it?" The man who'd finished wrapping the burst package with twine muttered to Jem.

"Black horse and long wagon by the third bollard," Jem murmured, seemingly without moving his lips. The man picked up the spoiled package and carried it towards the warehouse doors.

Ivy began to poke and feel at the packages as she'd seen others do. She removed a loose covering from a bolt of material and fell in love. The exposed material, while water-stained and smelling of smoke, was of a soft yellow cotton printed with colours that dazzled her eyes. There were birds the likes of which she'd never seen and butterflies flittering around brown sticks she thought might be bamboo. The sticks had big green leaves shooting out of them. She put the bolt of material on the handcart. She didn't know what she was going to do with it – she only knew she wanted it with all of her heart. It would be like wearing sunshine.

"Have yeh only bright colours?" a big man growled and flung a cut-off of scarlet material into the air.

Ivy caught the bright material and added it to her cart. Easter was near and the people of The Lane liked to celebrate with something bright and cheerful to wear. She watched the boys and men shoving and throwing the bulky packages around the warehouse. They were doing the work for her and she was going to let them. She and Jem grabbed packages of soft pink wool and one of yellow. The bright cottons the men cursed went onto the cart.

"Jem," Ivy leaned in close to whisper, "I want everything in here. The money I could make. The work I could give to the women in The Lane – me head is spinning with ideas."

"Then why the frown?" Jem began to push the cart in the direction of the warehouse manager.

"Where am I going to put all of this stuff?" Ivy followed on Jem's heels, her hand rooting around in the skirt pocket she'd pinned shut to protect her money.

"We'll worry about that later."

Jem prepared to barter.

Chapter 19

"Hurry up, lads." Ivy watched the goods she'd bought being carried through her back room into the front room. "The knocker-upper will be about soon, knocking up the Holy Marys for first Mass."

"Conn, put Rosie up – I'll be over in a minute," Jem grunted from one end of the last of the heavy bundles they carried between them.

"What was I thinking, Jem?" Ivy didn't notice the Connelly lads leaving. She stood in the open doorway between her two rooms and stared at her work room. She wouldn't be able to move. It was packed with parcels and bags almost to the roof. "How in the name of God are we going to live here if I keep filling the place with stuff?"

Jem closed the back door behind his lads before walking over to join Ivy. He put his arm around her shoulders and pulled her close to his body in a one-armed hug. The place was a mess and a lingering smell of smoke drifted around the room. "How much of this stuff do you reckon you can shift?" He pressed a kiss into her hair.

"With Easter comin' people love something bright and cheerful to wear. They'll be making and knitting for the childer. I'll keep some stuff back and use it to dress me baby dolls. But I'll move a lot of the rest along at a good profit when I figure out me costs." She leaned into him with a tired sigh. She wasn't accustomed to being up all night. She'd think about it when she'd had a bit of sleep. "That doesn't answer the question of how in the name of God we're going to live here, Jem." Her eyes filled with tired tears. She had to get the smell of smoke out of the stuff she bought – then wash what needed washing.

"Now is not the time to be thinking about that." Jem turned her into his arms, pulling her close to his body. "You're tired. You need a good long sleep. You'll hop out of bed full of the joys of spring and full of new ideas." He pressed a kiss onto her lips, forcing himself to keep the kiss short and sweet. There was nothing he'd like more than to crawl into that big bed with his Ivy and sleep the sleep of the just. "Something you could be thinking of . . ." He leaned in to sneak another kiss.

"What's that?" Ivy rose onto her toes, following his lips to deepen the kiss.

They were both tired. Their defences were down. The kiss deepened. The sound of their heavy breathing filled the room. Jem's fingers drifted to her bosom. He pulled her shawl away, pushing to get at the buttons of her old army coat.

"Whoa, whoa!" Jem jerked his head back. He stood, taking deep breaths, trying to get control of his emotions. Ivy pressing herself against him didn't help at all. He pressed his forehead into hers, using his arms to put distance between their bodies. "You stay right there, woman." He pushed away and walked towards the back door. "Don't follow me." He pointed his hand at her, to stop her joining him. "I'm only human, woman." He stood with his head bowed, fighting to get control. "We need to get churched, Ivy. The month of May can't come soon enough for me."

"Jem . . ." Ivy started to walk over to him. She wanted more of his kisses.

"Stay where you are, woman." He put his hand on the doorknob. He didn't open the door but looked at his sleepy-eyed Ivy. "I want you to give some thought to something." He closed his eyes, trying to gather his thoughts. She waited for him to say what he was thinking. "When Emmy and me move in here my room over the livery will be empty. We can put shelves up for you and move your work over there." He pulled the door open. He had to get away from temptation. "Think about that while you're getting your beauty sleep." He stepped out into the back yard. "Lock this door behind me," he ordered before pulling the door shut.

"I'm too tired to know me own name," Ivy muttered, walking over to lock the door. "I'll be more able to sort meself out when I've had a night's sleep. This staying up all night is hard work."

Chapter 20

"'Oh, Mrs McGrath,' the sergeant said, 'Would you like to make a soldier out of your son, Ted?'"

Ivy scrubbed the soft rose-scented soap over her arms as she sang lustily, delighted with the acoustics in Ann Marie's bathroom. She'd spent the morning running around the Dublin markets shifting her goods.

Ivy carefully sat up in the bath. She didn't want to disturb the towel she'd wrapped around her wet hair. She took a deep nervous breath and, almost shaking at her own daring, picked up the silvered razor she'd left on the floor by the bathtub.

"Well, here goes," she muttered, kicking one long slim leg out of the water. She lavishly applied the soap – just like Jem had shown her, using his own face as an example. She muffled her laughter at the memory of the pair of them blushing and stuttering while he gave her instructions on shaving her legs. He'd mumbled he could do it for her – after they were married, of course.

She'd never get used to the luxury of having hot and cold water on demand – running into your very own private bathtub. The Tara Street Baths would never seem the same again. There was no bath attendant here to hurry you on.

"Ivy Murphy, did yeh fall down the bath hole?" Sadie Lawless rapped her knuckles on the bathroom door. "You've been in that bath so long your bloody skin will be floatin' away with the dirty water. Get out now and get dressed."

"Sadie, did anyone ever tell you you're a spoilsport? I was having the time of my life in here. You don't know you're born with this indoor plumbing."

"Get out of there – now!" Sadie shouted.

"Go away!"

Ivy finished shaving her legs before carefully standing up. She stood out on the bath mat. She gave a sharp yank on the metal chain attached to the big black plug. She removed the thick towelling bathrobe Ann Marie had put on the back of the bathroom door for her. "A bathrobe, I ask your sacred pardon." Ivy shoved her arms into the loose sleeves, pulled the robe around her and fastened the long belt. "Some people don't know they're born." She raised the long collar around her head and face and stood enjoying the experience for a moment. "It's a livin' wonder to me that the priests don't call bathrooms dens of iniquity and order their congregation to avoid them. All this luxury and pleasure has to be an occasion of sin, to their mind." She shrugged out of the bathrobe, letting it fall around her feet. She ignored the blush that went from her toes to her hairline. With a defiant sniff she put her foot on the side of the bathtub and began to apply the body cream she'd made, following the recipe she'd found in one of old Granny's many 'healing cures' books, to her newly shaved leg. Ann Marie had warned her that it would sting but the motto of upper-crust women seemed to be 'Suffer for Beauty'.

Ivy pulled the underwear she'd brought with her from home on over her damp skin. She couldn't walk around the place naked under a robe. She covered her fine bodice and panties – a gift from her brother Shay – with a slip that covered her from her bosom to her knees and covered everything up with the robe.

She crossed to the bathroom mirror – well clear now from any steam that might have lingered. With quick movements she applied the fine cream she'd made to her face and neck. "That aul' Granny knew a thing or two about making cures," she whispered, watching the cream sink into her skin. "There must be money in the making of these things but sure I've only two hands and enough on me plate at the minute. Pity though."

"Ivy, you need to get a move on!" Sadie was back.

Ivy opened the bathroom door, tightening the belt of the robe around her. "Where is Ann Marie?"

"I think I've run the poor woman out of her own home," Sadie admitted. "She's over at the carriage house working on her photographs."

"Shout down and ask Dora to knock on the carriage-house door. She can tell Ann Marie I'm almost ready. I mean it, Sadie – shout – don't run down them bloody stairs again. Ann Marie wants to live without servants under her feet. Well, we haven't an upstairs maid to carry a message to the footman to pass to the butler – so just shout down the bloody stairs. Ann Marie will never forgive us if she misses me big unveiling."

Ivy sat on the edge of Ann Marie's big bed and prepared to pull the silk stockings up her legs. She was nervous –

she didn't want to ladder the things. She put her foot into the marked toe, pulled gently till the thick heel settled into place and prepared to pull the stocking up her raised leg.

"Ivy Murphy, the state of you and the price of best butter!" Sadie said, returning to the room after shouting down the stairs like a hooligan.

"Don't make me laugh." Ivy got one sheer stocking up her leg and attached it to the first of two suspenders per leg that were attached to the garter belt she wore around her waist. She started on the second leg while Sadie watched – fascinated. Ivy slipped her feet into the black leather T-strap shoes she'd placed by her feet. When she'd fastened the buckles on the shoes, she stood up, shaking the robe down around her.

"Ann Marie, I swear to God I'm going to go blind if you flash that light in my eyes one more time," Ivy complained.

"You look stunning, Ivy." Ann Marie lowered the camera and the long stick with its flashlight head that she'd held aloft to light the hall.

Ivy wore a narrow black skirt with a line of large white leather buttons running down the left side. The skirt was shorter than anything she'd ever worn, inches above her ankles. A black leather belt accentuated her waist. The sparkle of silk stockings flattered her ankles. The white blouse had a matching line of black leather buttons. The dainty black hat, with its long trail of white feathers draped along the side of Ivy's face, was the perfect finishing touch.

"Jem Ryan is driving his vehicle up the way." Dora carried over Ivy's beige cashmere coat. She held the coat while Ivy slipped her arms into the sleeves.

Ivy picked up the black leather clutch purse and gloves from the hallstand. She was as ready as she was ever going to be. With a deep breath, she plastered a smile on her face.

"Open the door, Dora." Ann Marie put her camera equipment on the nearby hallstand.

The two women stood in the open doorway and watched Jem settle Ivy into his car before driving away.

Chapter 21

"We're there." Jem stopped the vehicle. "Sit tight."

"It seems ridiculous to drive such a short way. I'd have nearly walked it faster." Ivy watched Jem run up the steps. She checked to be sure there were no wrinkles in her leather gloves. A quick glance downward reassured her that the silk stockings were behaving themselves, with no unsightly wrinkles around her ankles.

"Miss Ivy Rose," Jem passed the white embossed card to the butler when the man opened the door to his knock, "to see Mr William Armstrong." He returned down the steps and opened the back door of his vehicle. He held out his hand to assist Ivy in stepping out onto the kerb in front of the row of Merrion Square houses. "That's the first step," he muttered under his breath as Ivy pulled her beige cashmere coat firmly around her. "You're on your own now. Good luck."

"I'll see you later," Ivy whispered through lips that felt numb.

She climbed the steps slowly and, with barely a glance at the butler, stepped into the black-and-white marble foyer. She fought back a nervous giggle – her outfit matched the foyer. She waited with an outward appearance of calm while the butler closed the door.

The man clicked his fingers at a waiting footman.

"If you would follow me," the butler said as the footman draped the coat he'd removed from Ivy over his arm.

The butler led the way through the open door of the nearby withdrawing room.

"I will inform the master of your arrival."

Ivy walked into the room as if she owned the place. Ann Marie had told her to find something to focus on while she waited. She was so nervous she only had time to get an impression of skinny-legged chairs and tall urns with some kind of tall leaf thing sticking up. The carpet on the floor was the most beautiful item in the room. She stood before the glowing fire in the massive white marble grate. She was not allowed to sit down as that would put her at a disadvantage. Ivy didn't understand why but Ann Marie was the expert.

"Mr Armstrong will see you now." He didn't approve of a young single female visiting a man in his own home – without a chaperone to protect her virtue.

"Thank you." Ivy slowly walked over to join the butler. She remembered to push the top of her head towards the sky as she walked – something Ann Marie had made her practise. While following after the stiff-backed butler she slowly drew her black-leather gloves from her hands.

"Miss Rose, sir," the butler called as he stepped through the door he'd just opened.

"Miss Rose, a pleasure." The man behind the desk stood and walked around the impressive-looking piece of furniture.

"Mr Armstrong, thank you for agreeing to see me."
Ivy walked into the room. She had called ahead to make
this appointment.

"Tea, I think, Chiles." William Armstrong – aka Billy
Flint – was impressed in spite of himself. The girl cleaned
up well. He was curious to know what had made her seek
him out – but he could wait.

"Not for me, thank you." Ivy was afraid she'd shake
so much she'd drop the bloody thing.

"No tea." William couldn't care less. "That will be all,
Chiles."

"Very good, sir."

"I believe I've caused your butler some discomfort."
Ivy was conducting a detailed examination of the man in
front of her. She could see her father in his features but
this man gave off almost visible emanations of power. Her
uncle was a power to be reckoned with. His beautifully
tailored suit of gunmetal grey was accentuated by a
blindingly white silk shirt and a blue silk tie that sported
a diamond-and-gold stickpin.

"I pay him to do his job," William snapped. "I don't ask
for his opinion." He gestured towards the chair placed in
front of his desk. "Take a seat and tell me why you're here."

Ivy sat down carefully with elegant ease – this too
she'd been practising. She placed her clutch and gloves on
the desk in front of her and sat back in the chair with her
knees together and feet folded off to one side. "I have a
business proposition for you, Mr Armstrong." Ivy
dropped her hands into her lap. She was careful not to
twine her fingers in a knot.

"I don't make investments without the advice of my
financial advisors."

"I'm not seeking investors – what I am offering is a straightforward business deal."

"What is it you think you can offer me, Miss Rose?" William's blue eyes almost blazed as he dared her to offer him anything he didn't already have or could get himself.

"I'm selling social class, Mr Armstrong," Ivy said. "I'm selling the kind of class you and I were born without, and a family tree to boast about."

"Are you indeed?"

"I believe your eldest son's wife has just announced a happy event." Ivy had spent weeks thinking about this meeting – recent events had forced her to step up her plans. She had prepared as much as she could, gathering every piece of information from servants' gossip and the loose lips of this man's male servants at the local pub. Jem's lads seemed to be able to pick up an amazing amount of information sitting over a pint in the pub.

"What a mealy-mouth way of saying my first grandchild is expected."

"Your son married rather high up the social ladder." Ivy wanted to lick her dry lips. "A situation which hasn't had such happy results for your family in the past." She was thinking of her own parents. This man's wife was from a socially elite family fallen on hard times. They had been glad to accept his money.

"What goes on in my family is none of your business. I will accept no interference in my affairs." He'd kept a close watch on his brother and his offspring over the years. He didn't need or want any problems from that direction. It was smarter to anticipate trouble and head it off. The death of his brother appeared to have allowed this young woman to emerge from her grey little world.

She'd be worth watching in the future.

"I am not here to bamboozle or amuse you. I am here to offer you something that will help ensure your grandchild's future and impress your daughter-in-law – a woman, I believe, who is very aware of her family's social standing – and astound her snobby family." His son and said snobby wife lived in this house – under this man's roof.

"Indeed?" If the bloody woman could pull that off she was a magician.

Ivy took a deep breath, preparing to dare the devil. "I'd like you to take me upstairs and show me the nursery you are preparing for the expected child."

She stood and leaned over the desk, staring into the eyes that were the same shape and colour as her da's but had much more awareness and almost an animal magnetism within them. She had a deal to offer and wanted to get her terms and conditions settled. But first, she needed to see if any effort had been made to set up a nursery – according to the servants the place was a mess but she needed to see it for herself. She straightened and stood waiting for him to make a decision.

"I'll have one of the upstairs maids take you up."

"No." Ivy waited for the counteroffer.

"I do not take spinster ladies upstairs in my home." William leaned back in his chair.

"Live dangerously. I don't believe that's a foreign concept to you." Ivy walked over to the door and put her hand on the doorknob. She wanted to lean against the door because her knees didn't feel like they wanted to hold her up. "I wouldn't ask if it wasn't of vital importance. I need to see the nursery."

"Vitally important to whom, Miss Ivy Rose?" William stood. She obviously thought she'd an ace up her sleeve. He'd see what cards she had to play in this game and then he'd throw her out. He had no intention of playing happy families with this urchin.

"My offer will be important to both of us." She remained standing with her back to the door, her white-knuckled hand clenched around the doorknob. "It will cost you nothing to accompany me upstairs and listen to my proposal."

"You've piqued my interest at least." Which was a rare event these days. He walked over to the door and put his hand over hers on the doorknob. "Allow me."

She jerked her hand away and waited for him to open the door.

"Here we are." William stood on the nursery landing, his hands shoved into his pockets. He waited to see what would happen next.

Without asking permission Ivy began opening doors. According to her sources the previous owner of this house left Ireland in a hurry. It was rumoured the man staring after her with feigned patience had bought the house for a peppercorn price – he'd paid in cash.

The cluttered rooms she stepped into were damp and neglected. They smelled musty. The area gave off an air of long neglect. She walked into each room, mentally comparing them to the space Nanny Grace inhabited. The rooms were a mirror image of that space. She returned to join the man who stood like an oak in the long corridor. She crossed her fingers, said a quick prayer and began.

"The baby's room." Ivy waved her hand towards one

of the doors she'd deliberately left standing open. "I see a cradle craved by a master craftsman, a matching chest of drawers and two cedar-wood trunks filled with the most exquisite baby clothing. A symphony of silk, satin and lace embroidered with love and kept for generations to come."

"You apparently have an active imagination." William took his hands out of his pockets. "I have given you more of my time than most people get." He stood looking around an area that he was going to have to fill. He'd been avoiding furnishing it, waiting for an actual baby to appear. "You are trying my patience."

"A boy's room." Ivy had seen the interest in his eyes – she waved her hand towards another dusty room nearby, "with a carved child's bed – a much-loved globe that has been handled by generations of your family, sitting on a desk carved to fit his small figure – a child's bookcase filled with the much-thumbed books you loved as a child." She was praising the Lord for her excellent memory, the images of the well-stocked rooms surrounding Nanny Grace coming vividly to life behind her eyes. "I can fill all of these rooms with wonders."

"I'm listening." He could practically see the rooms she described. Could she deliver on her promise?

"If you would follow me, please?" Ivy knew this man would walk all over her if she allowed it. Time to reveal her cards.

She stepped into the largest of the rooms, waiting for him to follow and close the door at his back. They didn't need any passing servant listening to their conversation. When he did she turned to stare at him, surprised she'd succeeded in getting him into this position. "You need to have your staff begin clearing and decorating these rooms."

"Indeed, I'd never have thought of that on my own."

"No need for sarcasm." She took a deep breath, preparing to dive in. "I'm offering you the chance to create an impressive family background," She held up her hand when he opened his mouth to answer. "I can make an entire nursery suite available to you. The items are used but in the best way possible. The touch of generations of tiny hands can be seen on the articles I'm offering – plus decades of polishing by skilled servants."

"Go on."

"This room will be an Aladdin's cave of treasure." Ivy walked around, pointing out places for the items she mentioned. "A dappled-grey rocking horse with flowing white mane and tail, red-lined nostrils flaring – a miniature saddle and stirrups." She waved towards the empty shelf. "A collection of hand-carved doll's houses." She whirled around and then, standing still, shrugged. "Books of pressed flowers, paintings and everything you could possibly imagine for a generation to come."

"You believe yourself a magician?"

"I suggest you tell your family – in front of your son's family by marriage – that you are having your own nursery taken out of storage and moved into these rooms."

"I don't give a tinker's curse for the opinion of a crowd of snobby twits." William walked over to stand almost toe to toe with her, glaring down at the cheeky upstart.

"That is patently not true." Ivy wished she was wearing her old black skirt so she could shove her hands into the deep pockets and pinch herself. She needed something to hold onto, to steady her nerves. It seemed obvious to her – when she was planning this visit – that this man intended to establish himself as a leading member of Ireland's new ruling class. What she had to offer would be of value to him. She just had to hold on to her nerve. "You have established your own power base, certainly. What I'm offering will simply 'gild the lily' of your family background. Your son will benefit greatly, as will the expected child and any children that follow." Ivy raised her chin and stared up at the man trying to intimidate her with his height and power.

"What exactly are you offering me, young woman?" William demanded. "In basic terms, it's time to piss or get off the pot." He was being deliberately vulgar – he didn't like feeling at a disadvantage.

"I have at my disposal not only enough furniture, books, toys and musical instruments to furnish these rooms completely but also a lovely old English nanny." She hadn't asked the old woman but Nanny Grace had been abandoned by the family she'd served for almost sixty years. The old woman could not survive on her pitiful savings. "I am sure Nanny Grace will be thrilled to tell delightful little tales about her beloved Master William as a child." Ivy had played all of her cards.

"And if I should be fool enough to take up this offer, how much will it cost me?" William asked after what, to Ivy, had been a prolonged pause.

Ivy mentioned a figure that had William gaping at her. It was an astronomical price.

"That is robbery, young woman. I could purchase a bloody house with that amount."

"Yes, you could." Just voicing the amount of money she wanted made Ivy feel weak. The money would set Nanny Grace up for the rest of her days. Ivy's share would make a nice addition to her bank account. "A two-up two-down in a bad area of town but a house none the less." She took a deep breath and continued. "However, we both know to completely furnish these rooms would cost you twice that amount. Besides, what I am offering is the kind of roots you want for your family. You've bought yourself respectability. What I'm offering will add to your mystique around this town."

"We need to talk further – in more comfort than can be found here. Let us get out of this cold room." William was willing to listen. "I want to hear the whole story behind your offer." It would be worth it to him to pay the outrageous price she was asking. If – and it was a big if – she could deliver what she offered.

"The price you're asking is ridiculous." William stood and walked over to the modern bar unit he'd recently had built into his study. He served himself a whiskey.

"I won't argue about the price," Ivy stood and, without asking permission, used the bar tap she'd noticed to wash the dust from her hands. "That is non-negotiable." She glared into his eyes to underscore her determination to get the best price possible. "You can well afford it and what I'm offering is beyond price and we both know it."

"I'll need to meet this Nanny Grace and see these wonders you're trying to sell me." He returned to the fireside and stood waiting until she joined him in the chair facing his. He sipped his whiskey. She'd refused his offer of something to drink. "Unlike you, apparently, I never fly by the seat of my pants."

"All appearances to the contrary," Ivy mumbled under her breath.

"Let us not descend into insult." William's mind was whirling with the possibilities – if this woman could supply what she offered he had to plan on the presentation carefully.

"There is nothing worth keeping in those rooms upstairs, I think you'll agree. With your permission I can send a team to clear out the rooms and haul the rubbish away." Ivy had everything at hand to make this move work quickly and efficiently. "If the clutter of years is removed before your staff begin cleaning it will speed the process of preparing the rooms for decoration." That didn't mean she couldn't make a few pennies from some of the stuff they removed.

"I haven't agreed to anything yet," William snapped.

"I'll explain the situation to Nanny Grace." She ignored his words. They both knew he was going to accept what she offered. Tomorrow was her day for visiting Fitzwilliam Square – she'd talk to Nanny Grace. She couldn't see the old girl refusing to play along. The woman desperately needed somewhere to live out the rest of her days. "You will need to employ at least two young women as nannies for your grandchild. Nanny Grace can train them and instruct them in organising the rooms. In Nanny Grace you will also have at your disposal a woman who has decades of knowledge of the private lives of the gentry." The servants' gossip Nanny Grace had accumulated over the years would be an invaluable source of insider information for this man and they both knew it.

"I'll agree to your team clearing the space." That was work that needed to be done anyway. "We can discuss the matter further when you've shown me what it is exactly that you are offering." William was becoming more

115

intrigued by the minute. He could afford the price she asked but he wasn't a fool. He needed to see the items with his own eyes, meet the woman who would claim knowledge of his own childhood.

"I've been here longer than I intended." She stood up and stepped away from the fire. She'd achieved what she'd wanted and it was time to leave. "My telephone number is on my business card. If you'd be good enough to telephone and provide a time convenient to you I'll arrange a showing."

William too stood and stared down at her, almost as if trying to see inside her head. "You had better be as good as your word. I do not like wasting my time."

"I'm confident you'll appreciate everything I've spoken of." She wanted to get away from this man. She'd made her offer and now felt the need to lie down in a darkened room and have a nervous breakdown. She'd secured a home for Nanny Grace – she'd done it. "I'll have a team in to clear those rooms tomorrow." He would see the quality of what she offered himself. Time was of the essence. She needed to get Nanny settled into her new home. The old woman's health was going downhill since she'd been abandoned. "As soon as you agree to my terms and inform me the rooms upstairs are ready, I will have a team deliver and place the furniture. The team are mine – they will not speak of anything they have seen and done." She could guarantee that. Jem's teams were being well trained and discretion was head of a long list of instructions they received.

"You talk a good game, young woman," William said just as a knock sounded on the study door.

"Come in." He stepped away, leaving a space between them.

"The young lady's car is here, sir." Chiles stepped into the room. He had been frustrated in his efforts to find out what was going on under his roof – an intolerable situation.

"Thank you, Chiles." Ivy picked up her bag and gloves from the desk and turned to walk out of the room.

"Well?" Jem couldn't wait any longer.

"Give us a minute, Jem – me nerves are shot." Ivy was trying to stop the shaking that had attacked her body. "Where's Emmy? Is she with Ann Marie?"

"I'm here, Aunty Ivy." The blanket on the floor between the front and back seats moved. A pair of dazzling green eyes gleamed up from the dark space. A gleaming grin soon joined them. "Can I get up now, Uncle Jem?"

"I should have known you'd be in the middle of this." Ivy grinned as Emmy Ryan, with permission from her adoptive uncle, climbed up to join her on the back seat.

"John Lawless said Uncle Jem was going to walk a trough into the livery floor." Emmy covered her mouth with her hands and giggled with sheer delight at the adventure.

"If you two ladies wouldn't mind," Jem said from the front seat, "I want to know what happened before I have to sign myself into a padded room somewhere."

"Armstrong was too cagey to agree to everything at this first meeting but I'm almost positive Nanny Grace is set for the rest of her life." Ivy had seen Armstrong's hunger for what she was offering. Nanny Grace and her treasured possessions would seal the deal.

"I'm sure the poor man never knew what hit him."

Jem was learning not to underestimate his future bride. Ivy was a force to be reckoned with when she put her mind to something.

"Getting Nanny Grace settled safely will be a load off my mind." Ivy sat back against the leather seat and closed her eyes. She was only now beginning to relax. "Why don't you take us back to Ann Marie's place, Jem?" She'd left her work clothes there and, besides, everyone in the house would be waiting to hear how her meeting had gone.

"But you're all dressed up, Auntie Ivy," Emmy objected. "Mr Lawless told Uncle Jem that his Sadie said you went out of the house looking like a film star. He said Uncle Jem should take you out to trip the light fantastic." She turned to stare at Ivy. "What is the light fantastic? It sounds too wonderful for words."

"You hear too much, Miss Sugar-lugs." Ivy put her arm around the little girl and hugged her. "I'm afraid what I want to do would be very boring for a film star. I want to change out of these fancy clothes, sit in the kitchen, drink a pot of tea and talk to my friends. Does that disappoint you?" She leaned over to whisper in Emmy's ear – loud enough for Jem to hear, "Besides, then your Uncle Jem can put his baby to bed in her warm carriage house." The two females tittered while Jem drove through the dark Dublin streets.

Chapter 22

Jem Ryan stood on the long wide stretch of cobble road running between the Stephen's Lane tunnel that he used on a daily basis and the opposite tunnel leading out to the Grand Canal. He was standing hands on hips, head bent back, staring at the blank wall that formed the gable end of his livery building. He was trying to mentally compare Ann Marie's carriage house and this space at one end of his livery. He could build something similar to that carriage house here – if he dared spend that kind of money.

"You'll take root if you stand there much longer." A grumpy voice almost barked in his ear.

"Good morning, Mr Wilson."

"What's good about it?" Frank Wilson almost pushed Jem out of his way on his route from his own front door to the Stephen's Lane exit.

"Miserable bloody way to live," Jem muttered under his breath, watching the old man march towards the tunnel exit. He returned to his daydreaming – putting the image of the carriage house and its three-bedroom flat in his head. What would it be like to have all that space to live in? The mere idea of having the luxury of such modern conveniences as indoor plumbing and electricity – right in your own home – was breathtaking. He'd be a proud man to be able to promise his Ivy a luxury home like that.

He caught sight of Ivy and her overburdened pram out of the corner of his eye. "Ivy, where are you off to?"

"She is heading straight for Hell, Jem Ryan." Sheila Purcell had been going to pass the beggar and her pram with her head in the air. She was too good to notice the likes of her. But she changed her mind when she heard Jem Ryan's shout. Who did he think he was making that kind of commotion around decent people? The Lane was going to Hell since Father Leary had been away. She'd seen it with her own eyes and wouldn't she have a lot to say to anyone who cared to listen! She put her hands on her skinny hips, covered by a threadbare coat, and glared at Ivy with sheer malice in her eyes.

Jem hurried over to stand by Ivy's side. He was aware of the people of The Lane watching and listening. The children who usually ran between the two tunnel exits, shouting and playing, had disappeared. The young children didn't stay around when they saw Mrs Purcell out and about. The people of The Lane left Sheila Purcell alone – the woman's tongue could be vicious. She hadn't a good word to say about anyone except her sainted Father Leary.

"You'll be joining her in the burning fires of Hell, Jem Ryan, if you don't change your wicked ways. I've seen you, walking out – kissing and canoodling – with no view to matrimony. The pair of you sinners are doomed." Sheila loved the sound of that word. She wished she had her holy water and cross with her. She'd soon show these godless creatures the error of their ways. "It will soon be the Holy Season of Lent. That will put a halt to your gallop, Ivy Murphy."

Ivy glanced at Jem before rolling her eyes up to Heaven. Had she not enough problems to be dealing with this morning? She had been struggling to push her pram – with an empty tea chest sitting up high on it – towards the exit. She'd have to stand here and listen to Sheila Purcell shouting her religious fervour to the sky – she'd been raised to respect her elders.

"Our parish priest, that sainted man Father Leary, is returning to guide his flock – any day now he will be back among us and not a minute too soon. They offered me extra money to get his room ready for him." Shelia looked around to see who was listening. She cleaned the parish priest's house and never let anyone forget it.

Jem reached for Ivy's hand. He didn't want her to let this woman see what a shock this news was to her.

"I wouldn't accept any extra money of course. I offered up me work to the good Lord – as a good Catholic should." Sheila gave her head such a fierce nod her battered hat almost slipped off her thin grey hair. "Father Leary will soon put an end to your sinful ways, Ivy Murphy. I'll be watching you." Having delivered her mini-sermon, Sheila continued walking towards the exit tunnel leading out of The Lane onto the Grand Canal.

"Jesus, it's worse she's getting, Jem." Ivy had to keep her reaction to the news of Father Leary's return locked firmly behind her teeth. It wouldn't do to voice her opinion aloud – not out here where anyone could hear. She watched her neighbour march stiff-backed towards the exit, She was grateful for Jem's silent support. "I hear tell she made a show of herself in the shops the other day."

"What did she do now?" Jem put his free hand on Ivy's pram, trying to push it. The thing wouldn't move. He released Ivy's hand and tried again, using both hands to shift the stubborn pram. It wouldn't budge.

"The bawld Mrs Purcell told the Ivors that they would have to close their creamery for the season of Lent, it being a sin to indulge in any luxury for the forty days. Then she took herself in to the butcher and gave him the same lecture. Still, it could be worse. We might have to live with the woman." She wasn't the only one who pitied Sheila's husband and children.

She wouldn't think about Father Leary coming back to take up his post as their parish priest. That was one problem too many for her right at this minute. She wondered why she hadn't seen Brother Theo lately. It wasn't like the man to allow her to neglect her education. The friary was only a step away from Smithfield market. She'd drop in to see him on Friday. She had a book to return to him and the homework he'd given her finished.

"Ivy, if Father Leary is going to take up his duties again he might well be the one to marry us." Jem was on his knees by the side of Ivy's pram, trying to see what was blocking the wheels.

"Devil a bit of it," Ivy snapped. "I won't be standing before that man with me head bowed."

"Ivy, where were you heading?" Jem stood up and used his hands to brush the dust from the knees of his trousers. He eyed the tea chest sitting on the pram. He let the subject of the priest drop. His Ivy and Father Leary

122

had been locking horns for years – here and now wasn't the time to pursue the issue.

"I'm taking this tea chest to Nanny Grace."

"You won't be able to get that pram out of the tunnel." Jem put his hand on the pram's handle. He knew Ivy would kill herself trying to move the thing. "I'm sorry but this pram is finished. It's going nowhere, Ivy. The wheels are buckled."

"What am I going to do?" Jem kept fixing the old pram up, trying to keep it working. She could tell by the look on his face that he was telling the truth and the pram was past fixing this time.

"I could always teach you to hitch old Rosie up to a cart," Jem said, grinning.

"Jem Ryan, this is not the time for jesting." She tried not to wail like a banshee. She needed her pram. It was a vital piece of equipment.

"Come on." He began to drag the pram behind him in the direction of the entrance to the livery. "If we put our heads together we can come up with something. Come along, we'll go up to my place and have a talk in peace. I'll put the kettle on."

Ivy, fighting tears, followed along.

"There are days when it's not worth me while getting out of bed." Ivy sipped at the tea Jem had put in front of her. They were sitting at the small table Jem kept in his living space tucked under the eaves of the livery. She didn't want to think about Father Leary returning. She refused to worry or wonder about that aul' goat.

"Why are you taking Nanny Grace an empty tea chest?"

"It's for the old woman's personal bits and bobs." Ivy put her elbows on the table and buried her head in her hands for a moment. She closed her eyes and took a deep, deep breath to settle her nerves before sitting back in her chair. "I've never seen anyone move as fast as that man Armstrong."

"I thought he was a bit of a force of nature." Jem's curiosity had tempted him into leading the work crew sent into the Merrion Square house to clear the nursery floor of all rubbish. "He was standing over the painting and decorating crew shouting instructions while we were still clearing those rooms out."

"He and Nanny Grace got on like a house on fire when they met." Ivy finished the tea in her cup. "I think Armstrong's genuine appreciation of everything Nanny Grace had treasured and protected for years was what did the trick. He spent ages listening to her telling him stories about her years in service." Ivy had a feeling the man was filing away the stories to be brought out later when he wanted to impress someone. "He is sending Nanny for a two-week stay in a hotel he owns on the seafront in Bray. He wants the old woman to be petted and pampered to restore her health."

"Go 'way!" Jem stood to refill Ivy's empty cup from the teapot sitting on top of his cast-iron fireplace.

"I thought Nanny Grace would faint when he suggested the holiday." Ivy accepted the refilled cup and saucer from Jem's hand and grinned. "She isn't used to being treated so well. I've a feeling the old woman would lie down and let Armstrong wipe his feet in her ribs now."

"Still and all, Ivy, it's good of him." Jem shrugged.

"Truthfully," she leaned forward to whisper, "I think

he's going to bribe the old couple looking after the house, the Cusacks, to let him have free run of the place." She sat back, pleased with the look on Jem's face.

"Why?"

"I've been thinking about it . . ."

"Hey up! Trouble."

"Oh you, Jem Ryan," Ivy said, grinning. "I think Armstrong wants to wander around that house and get a feel for how the 'real' quality live. I saw how he looked around the place. Then too, if Nanny Grace is out of the nursery he can familiarise himself with the stuff in those rooms. He won't be caught on the hop when the stuff is unpacked in his place. That's what I'd do anyway." She sipped her tea.

"Ivy," Jem put his empty mug on the table, pushed his chair back with his knees and stood, "there are times when you take my breath away. You sit there and finish that pot of tea. I'll hitch up Rosie and we'll take the tea chest over to Nanny's place together."

"Are you going to keep that automobile of yours locked up and throw sugar at it?" Ivy asked before he could leave.

"I'm going to leave it at Ann Marie's place for the minute," Jem said with his hand on the doorknob. "I won't be long." He walked out into the loft space of the livery.

He didn't want to take the automobile out and about until he had finished making a mental note of the roads and lanes around and about. He'd been driving the streets of Dublin for years but that was in a horse and carriage – the automobile was a different kettle of fish altogether and he was not willing to damage it through ignorance.

Chapter 23

"I'm all aflutter." Nanny Grace, for all her years in Ireland, had never lost her English accent. She was directing Ivy in the packing away of her own personal knick-knacks. It was a paltry enough amount for her years of life. "Mr Armstrong suggested I ask you about hiring a vehicle to take me to Bray, Ivy. I've never been to County Wicklow – is it a great distance?"

"It's a good piece of road." Jem came back into the main room just as Nanny was asking the question. He had been checking out the area, doing a mental inventory of the nursery contents which he'd been hired to cart over to the Merrion Square house when the rooms there were ready. "But it might suit you better to take the train." It was going to take more than a few trips to move all of this stuff. "There's a locked room near the staircase, Nanny Grace." The woman had asked him to address her as 'Nanny Grace' but it felt strange on his lips. "Does that need to be cleared as well?"

"Oh for heaven's sake!" Nanny Grace slapped her own forehead. "The box room. I didn't mean to lock it – habit, I suppose. I've been in and out of that room, dragging empty trunks," she waved her hands around the room, indicating the packed leather trunks sitting in the middle of the floor, "in here so I could pack the smaller items away."

"Do you have the key?" Jem needed to see everything that was to be shifted. He'd have a better idea then of the number of wagons and crew needed for the job.

"The key is over the lintel of the door."

"Thank you." Jem turned on his heel and left the room.

"Ivy." Nanny Grace put her hand on the younger woman's shoulder. Ivy was kneeling on the floor, carefully wrapping a Dresden shepherdess in newspaper. She seemed peculiarly frozen to Nanny Grace but she continued, "I'd like you to come with me. There is something I wish to show you." She'd rediscovered an outfit she thought would fit the adorable Emmy. The navy velvet coat and matching hat, along with the white fur muff and collar, were in excellent condition. The outfit was old but of a classic design that would not date. The little black button boots she'd unearthed would finish the outfit off and should suit young Emmy down to the ground. It was the only way she had of showing her gratitude to this young couple who had been so helpful to her.

"Certainly." Ivy used her body to hide what her fingers were doing. She had brought a load of newspapers with her to wrap delicate items. She quickly checked the date on the top of the paper – it was only a few days old. She tore a section of paper away from the body of the newspaper and surreptitiously stuffed it into the pocket of her skirt. She stood and, hiding her shock to the best of her ability, followed the older woman out into the corridor.

Jem was standing in the open door of the box room. He turned with a smile when he heard them coming. "Ivy, I think you'll want to see this."

"What?" Ivy hurried to join him and simply stood with her mouth open, staring into a room that was stacked to the rafters. What held her fascinated gaze was the two prams parked side by side right inside the doorway. "Talk about an answer to prayer," she whispered.

Chapter 24

"Have yeh any lemons, Tony?" Ivy was thrilled with how her day had gone so far. She'd sold everything she'd brought to the market with her this morning. The new pram was a pleasure to push. She didn't know herself with the easy way this new pram ran over the ground.

"I'd be a right kind of greengrocer if I didn't have lemons for the pancakes on Pancake Tuesday, Ivy Murphy."

"How much are they?" Ivy wasn't sure how many lemons she'd need for the pancakes she planned to make as soon as she returned to The Lane. She wanted to be able to bring a load of pancakes to the street party being organised for The Lane tonight. She ordered a dozen lemons and hoped for the best. She wouldn't be the only one bringing out pancakes for the crowd.

"Tony, will yeh let Ann Marie take your photograph?" She'd asked that question so many times today she'd be saying it in her sleep. "Me friend has promised a free copy of the photograph for everyone who agrees to have their picture took. You could put the photograph out on your stall. Let your customers have a look."

"What about me?" a nearby stallholder shouted. "Yez

got them boots the pair of yez are wearing from my stall."

"I'm sure you'll not be missed out on, Bobby!" Ivy shouted back. "Just wait your turn."

"I'm in me dirt, Ivy." Tony looked over to the lace stall where Ann Marie could be seen taking photographs of the stallholder, a crowd of curious people gathered around watching the excitement.

"Ann Marie's wantin' to take photographs of everyone in their natural environment." Ivy laughed at the look on Tony's face. She knew how he felt but she was becoming accustomed to her friend dogging her heels with her camera in hand.

"Like them reels they show at the Pally?" Tony and his family were regular cinemagoers. "I never thought of meself as a lion or a tiger, Ivy."

"You could come out here and stand by your blackboard." Ivy, from watching Ann Marie work, was learning to set up a picture ahead of time. If it didn't suit her friend she could change it. Tony had a tall blackboard in front of his stall with his prices clearly written in white chalk.

"I've customers waiting." Tony passed Ivy's goods over his counter. He took the coins from her hand, checking the amount before dropping the money into the money-belt he wore at his waist over his apron. He began brushing down his leather apron even as he made his objections.

"I'm sure they won't mind waiting." Ivy looked over the gathered crowd and received a mumble of good-natured agreement.

"I don't want me picture took with an aul' rag on me head." Tony allowed himself to be persuaded. He came around his vegetable stall to stand beside Ivy. He removed the sacking from his head, displaying a fine head of brown hair. He took a comb from the back pocket of his trousers and applied himself to restoring order to his locks.

Ivy checked her pram and its contents against a list she took from her pocket. She had everything she needed. "I'm going to have a cup of tea and a sit-down at Hop-a-long's stall," she told Ann Marie when her friend reached her side. "Do you need anything from me pram?"

"No, I'm fine, thank you." Ann Marie used Ivy's pram to store heavy items while they walked through the Dublin streets.

"Right, I'm away." Ivy grabbed the handles of her pram. "Don't forget to smile, Tony," she shouted over her shoulder, hurrying away in the direction of the food stall. Ann Marie could be at this for hours, she knew. The woman forgot everything when she had that camera in her hands.

Ivy sat on a straw bale with a metal mug of tea in her hand, glad of the chance to sit. She was normally in such a rush to get everything done that she never took time to simply sit and enjoy herself when she came to the market. It amused her to note the crowd that gathered around Ann Marie. In a few minutes mothers were going to start pushing their childer forward to get their pictures took.

She spent time admiring her new pram. She was sorely tempted to keep the second pram for her own children. It was a Rolls Royce of a pram bought for the five-year-old twin boys that had been Nanny Grace's last charges. She'd thought long and hard about keeping that pram for her own use. She'd finally accepted the fact that it was too fancy for the likes of her. She planned to sell that pram to your man Armstrong for a small fortune and split the money with Nanny Grace. The pram Ivy was using was a much older model but in great condition.

"Ann Marie, I'm not going to sit here all day!" Ivy shouted as a crowd pulled in around her friend. She stood to return the empty mug to the stallholder. The winter sunshine was a delight to sit in but she'd things to do and shouting at Ann Marie would shift the crowd along.

"Coming!" Ann Marie yelled back. She pushed her way through the crowd, apologising as she went. She couldn't wait to get back to her darkroom and develop the photographs she'd taken today. She was paying Milo Norton, a neighbour of Ivy's, for photography lessons. The man was a mine of useful information about the use of the camera.

Ivy stood waiting while Ann Marie removed her packing cases from the pram – her friend took excellent care of her equipment.

"I'm ready," Ann Marie said when she had everything packed away to her satisfaction.

"Not before time." Ivy grinned as she said it, showing there were no hard feelings.

The two women shouted a loud general goodbye to the people in the market, waved and with a spring in their step set out to make the return walk to The Lane.

"Are you coming to the street party tonight?"

"Yes," Ann Marie almost skipped along, "we will all be there. Sadie is bringing pancakes and we have put together a basket of food to bring along."

The women walked along the busy streets, each lost in her own thoughts.

"Ivy," Ann Marie broke the comfortable silence, "do

you think anyone would mind . . ."

"*If* I took some photographs," the two women finished the sentence together and laughed aloud.

Chapter 25

"Aunty Ivy," Emmy ran up to throw herself on a bale of hay – one of many Jem and his lads had pulled out onto the cobbled courtyard, "am I going to do my party piece?" Her big green eyes were gleaming. She was having a lovely time running wild with her friends. She'd eaten so many thin pancakes sprinkled with lots of sugar and fresh lemon juice she felt almost ill.

The street party was well under way with tables and chairs dragged out of homes and parked on the cobbled courtyard. The big party fires were burning brightly in their tin bins, adding to the glow of the gas street lamps. The people of The Lane were standing about laughing, talking, eating and drinking. Everyone was determined to enjoy this last day of gaiety before the greyness of the season of Lent. The Catholic Church frowned upon people enjoying themselves in the days leading up to Easter. Pancake Tuesday was always a knees-up, bang-out party.

"Not yet." Ivy had taught Emmy the old nursery rhyme 'Who Killed Cock Robin?'.

Emmy didn't have much of a singing voice but she'd

learned the words and actions to go with the rhyme and couldn't wait to stand up on one of the tables and perform.

"Where's my Uncle Jem?" Emmy looked around. "I hope he isn't inside listening to his radio."

"No, it's too early yet for the radio," Ivy assured the little girl. "Jem is around somewhere." He'd been with her a few minutes ago.

"Ivy!" two voices called out at once.

She turned to see who was calling her. Ann Marie and Mrs Wiggins were making their separate ways in her direction.

She sent Emmy off to play, promising to call her as soon as it was time for her to do her party piece. "Give yourself time before you eat any more pancakes!" she yelled at the little girl as she ran away to join her friends.

"Ivy!" Marcella Wiggins hurried over, wanting to reach Ivy before her friend. Marcella worked as washerwoman three days a week at Ann Marie Gannon's house but that didn't make her feel in any way inferior to the other woman. Ann Marie could wait a minute. Marcella had things to get done.

"Mrs Wiggins." Ivy smiled at her neighbour as Ann Marie stepped to her side. She gave her friend a smile and waited to find out what Mrs Wiggins wanted her to do. The woman couldn't bear to see anyone standing around idle.

"It's about the Johnson lads," Marcella leaned in to say. She searched in the deep pockets of her skirt for her notes. "I heard that if we can find homes to take them they'll be allowed out of the Artane Boys' Home for the Easter holiday." The Johnson family had been removed from their home in The Lane and separated.

"I couldn't put up one of those lads," Ivy said quickly. It wasn't that she wasn't willing to help out an old neighbour but she was a single woman and couldn't have a pimply-faced youth staying with her.

"I wasn't expecting you to take one of the lads, Ivy." Marcella consulted her notes importantly. She shook the pages. "I have homes set up for all seven of them but," she shrugged and gave Ivy a stern glare, "there will be the question of money. Lord knows young lads take feedin'."

"I'll gladly put in a few pence a week to help out," Ivy offered.

"I'd like to help too, Mrs Wiggins," Ann Marie said softly. The generosity of these people who had so little never failed to astonish her. "I'll add a florin a week to the costs if that is acceptable."

"A florin." Marcella tried to hide how impressed she was with the amount offered. With careful handling the lads could eat like kings on that amount a week. "That would be very kind of yeh, Ann Marie, and gratefully accepted." She took the stub of a pencil from behind her ear and made a note on one of her pages. "I'll be about me business now. I'll get back to yeh about the money, Ivy, Ann Marie." The woman bustled away to accost more of the people gathered around. She knew who could and couldn't afford to help out the less fortunate.

"That woman is a marvel," Ann Marie said softly.

"She is something special all right," Ivy agreed. "What were you shouting about earlier?"

"When?" Ann Marie had forgotten for a moment why she'd come over to Ivy's side. "Oh yes, I've been talking to Milo Norton and he has informed me that my next photography lesson will be in studio work." She gave a little hop of joy. She loved learning new ways of using her camera. Milo Norton rented two rooms from Mr Wilson – he used one room to develop the photographs he took of the passing crowd on O'Connell Bridge. That was his day job. Ann Marie was paying him to teach her everything he knew about photography. The man had an amazing amount of knowledge he was willing to pass along – at a price. What had started as a hobby for her was quickly becoming an obsession. "I'm going to set up a studio in one of the rooms over the carriage house. Mr Norton is going to instruct me in setting up the space."

"What has that to do with me and the price of eggs?" Ivy asked.

"I wondered if you thought Jem would object to me making Emmy my first subject." Ann Marie held her breath. There was something different about the little girl who called Ivy and Jem aunt and uncle.

"You had better ask him yourself," Ivy was glad to be able to say. "Here he comes now."

Chapter 26

Wanted
Information leading to the whereabouts of
Miss Mary Rose Donnelly

"Dear Lord above, how could I have forgotten I pushed that into my pocket?" Ivy stood at her kitchen table staring in horror at the tattered stub of newspaper sitting on the table top.

The rain was coming down in sheets, the wind lashing around the back yard. A perfect time for hanging out heavy woollen clothing as the wind and rain cleaned and freshened the thick fabric. She'd cleared out the deep pockets of the skirt she was wearing, planning to put the skirt onto a clothesline she'd erect outside her back door.

She continued to read the black-rimmed announcement she'd torn from the newspaper when packing away Nanny Grace's knick-knacks, and shoved into her pocket. The notice gave a fairly accurate description of Emmy's aunt, Miss Mary Rose Donnelly, but the announcement made no mention of the child. Ivy stood dripping onto the black slate slabs of her back-room floor. She'd just returned home after spending the day visiting Fitzwilliam Square. She'd removed her coat and shawl – those two articles were draped over a kitchen chair in front of the black range that she'd stoked to a blaze.

"I was that thrilled with finding a pram I could use I forgot all about this bloody notice." She wanted to kick herself for not making note of which paper had run the announcement. "It says here," she put her finger on the notice and bent forward to make sure she got the details right, "all information to Bishop Troy at an address in Galway – her own family doesn't seem to be looking for the aul' besom."

Emmy and her aunt, the Miss Mary Rose Donnelly mentioned in the newspaper, had been passengers in Jem's carriage when the aunt suffered a fatal accident. Jem had made the decision to keep Miss Emerald O'Connor of Galway – as Emmy was then – with him. The aunt had made no secret of her intention to leave her niece with the nuns at Goldenbridge. The place was supposed to be a trade school but the people of Dublin knew it for something else. It was a place you wouldn't put a dog if you had the option. Jem and Ivy together had disposed of the aunt's body.

"This is a fine howdeedo." Ivy wanted to run into the courtyard screaming Jem's name. What should she do? She couldn't leave this piece of paper sitting around. It was too dangerous. If anyone found out what she and Jem had done they'd be lynched.

She picked up the piece of newspaper and, shaking, walked over to the range and shoved the scrap of newspaper into the open grate. She stood watching until the paper crumbled and blackened, then with the poker

139

shook the coal in the fire until the paper had disappeared completely.

"There's shag all we can do about the situation." Ivy stood with her hands on her hips, glaring at the fire. "I'll hold me whist until we see what happens. No point in rushing to meet trouble. I'll keep me eyes open and, if I see another one of them notices, then I'll tell Jem – least said soonest mended."

Weeks passed with Ivy checking every paper that crossed her path. She didn't see another notice that concerned her. She was glad she'd decided to keep the notice to herself. Jem had enough to worry about.

Chapter 27

"It's nice to be able to step out like the nobs," Jem said as they strolled down the gas-lamp-lit Grafton Street. The lack of red-coated soldiers marching along the street was still new enough to be remarkable. The poor of Dublin had feared showing their faces on the streets after dark. The wealthy had walked out without encountering problems.

"I've never really thought about the evening strollers as a business opportunity," Ivy said as Jem waved away a flower seller. "I sold me dolls in the afternoon and missed out on the evening trade. Still and all, I didn't do too badly."

"Let's not talk business this evening, Ivy."

"Alright." She could think about the situation later. For now she'd enjoy the time with Jem – she was surprised she'd managed to drag him away from his beloved radio.

"Is Emmy over at Ann Marie's again?"

"She is," Jem sighed. "Emmy runs in, throws her schoolbag into the office, and disappears over to Ann Marie's place. Do you know what they're getting up to over there?" He'd suggested an evening stroll because lately the snatched moments of time he and Ivy managed were spent in dangerous proximity. They couldn't continue to tempt fate.

"I've had the whole thing explained to me until my head spins but I still don't understand what Ann Marie is trying to do with these 'sepia' photographs she's trying to produce."

"It's a lovely evening. March might have come in like a lion but today was lovely." The first two weeks of the month had been miserable but today had held a promise of spring. "I thought I'd go over and talk to the priest at St. Andrew's." Jem gave the church on Westland Row its official name for once. "We need to find out what date in May they can marry us."

"I don't want to get married in church, Jem." Ivy held her breath, waiting for the sky to fall on her head at her words. She had tried to speak to Brother Theo about this but every time she went by the friary he wasn't there. Brother Roderick would take her homework and give her the lessons Brother Theo had prepared for her. It was strange how she kept missing him.

"What!"

"I want to marry you, Jem," Ivy almost whispered. They'd come to a stop outside West the jeweller's. She stared blindly into the window backlit by the nearby gas lamp. "I thought, when you paid for the licence and whatever else . . . we could marry at the registry office."

"Ivy," Jem wasn't sure how he felt about this latest idea of Ivy's, "we wouldn't be married in the eyes of God."

"No, we wouldn't be married in the eyes of the Catholic Church – there is a difference." Ivy used the arm she had linked through his to pull him along towards Exchequer Street, out of the main thoroughfare.

"Jesus, Ivy," Jem allowed his feet to follow along, "you've fair taken my breath away."

"I know." She did but she would not participate in a church ceremony. She had no intention of following the rule of the Church that dictated she must produce and multiply, and she couldn't stand before the altar of God with a lie in her heart.

"Do you want to tell me why?" Jem himself feared the stranglehold the Catholic Church was trying to establish over this new Ireland they were living in, but the idea of marrying in a registry office was too much for him.

"We should have had this conversation before." Ivy was glad they were walking along, surrounded by people out taking the air. She had been trying to find the time to talk to Jem about her worries but, whenever they had a moment together, they got lost in kissing and cuddling. She blushed red at the memory of the temptation she'd barely been able to resist. "I want a modern marriage, Jem." She began to release his arm, thinking he'd be disgusted by her words.

"You better explain this 'modern marriage' to me." He took her hand in his, stopping her from stepping away, then pulled her arm through his again and they continued walking in the direction of George's Street.

"I won't follow the teachings of the Church about having babies, Jem." She felt tears flood her eyes – could he possibly understand how she felt?

"Are you trying to tell me you don't want my baby?" He couldn't agree to that. He wanted children. He loved having Emmy around the place. With the increased revenue from his business he could afford a wife and children. But, on the other hand, he worried about Ivy being constantly pregnant like some of the women of The Lane. He wouldn't allow one of his horses to be used in that way, let alone the woman he married.

"I want your children, Jem." Ivy could feel the embarrassed flush burning her cheeks. What kind of conversation was this to be having with a man you were walking out with? What kind of a woman was she? Still, if she didn't talk to Jem about her worries, who else could she talk to? "I'd like, if it's possible, to wait a while before we have the first one. I'm twenty-two years old – that's considered old to be having a first baby but I don't care. I still want to wait. I want to spend time with you – time learning to be a married woman. Am I a terrible person?"

"No, I don't think you're terrible." Jem patted the hand of the arm linked through his. "I knew what I was getting when I asked you to marry me. Ivy Murphy, always thinking of a way to do things differently – that's the woman I want to marry." Lord above but this woman challenged him at every turn. It would take a strong man to handle a woman like Ivy. Jem pushed out his chest, pleased with himself – no better man.

"I won't agree to discussing our private life with a priest." It was her opinion that if Father Leary the parish priest had kept his nose out of her parents' private affairs her mother would never have left Ireland. "I want to be able to talk to you about my fears and concerns without worrying that you'll drag me before the priest." She had seen too many of her neighbours being browbeaten by the parish priest whenever they tried to disagree with their husbands.

"I have no problem keeping our private life to ourselves, Ivy," Jem fought his body's reaction to just the thought of having a 'private life' with his Ivy, "but I don't know how to stop the babbies coming." He hated to confess his ignorance. "Not and live as man and wife anyway." He couldn't promise to keep his hands off her after they were married. He'd never be able to keep his word.

"There has to be a way, Jem." Ivy shook the arm she held slightly. "I've been giving this a lot of thought. The rich have only one or two children. How do they manage that? You tell me – what do they know that we don't?"

"Ivy . . ." He thought he'd choke over the words but she wanted them to have candid talks – so, on her own head be it. "The rich make one or two babbies with the women they marry. For slap and tickle they visit the Monto or have a 'bit' on the side." His face felt on fire, he was that embarrassed.

"They can't all of them be wandering dogs, Jem." She was convinced the rich knew something the poor didn't.

"I might have heard of something." Jem was thinking of a news item he'd heard on the radio. He'd inadvertently tuned in to the British Broadcasting Channel when he was tuning his radio. The words coming out of the radio had shocked him – all about some woman who was lecturing other women about controlling the number of children born. "I heard about some woman preaching about something she called birth control. She's in an awful lot of trouble, Ivy. They're saying she's going against the laws of God and man." The woman was some class of an Irish American . . . he tried to remember her name . . . Margaret Sanger – that was it, he was sure of it. How would he go about knowing more?

"Well," she punched his shoulder with her free hand, "see – there is something they know that we don't. That thing you heard on the radio – that's all about them not wanting the rest of us to know all about it."

"You'll have to give me a bit of time to find out about this." He hadn't a clue how to go about finding out about this Margaret Sanger.

"We can't let anyone know what we're doing, Jem," she whispered. "We'd have The Lane down around our ears. We'll never be able to go to Confession and Communion again if we do this. You know the aul' biddies make a note of who attends the sacraments. It won't be only Sheila Purcell calling us sinners. I've made me decision but you have to think long and hard about it, Jem. What I'm suggesting could get us excommunicated."

"I'm not a religious man, Ivy." He went to Mass more out of habit than anything else. "I'll look into the matter of stopping babbies but I don't see any reason we need to shout our business to the world." Trust his Ivy to give him something new to worry about. Still, with Ivy in his life he'd never be bored. "So, Ivy Murphy, will you be marrying me in six weeks' time?"

"Yes, please," she whispered, almost weak with relief. She'd keep trying to discover the secrets of the rich herself but having Jem's help would be a godsend. Ann Marie was a devil for research – she'd get the woman's name from Jem and ask Ann Marie to find out everything she could about her. If this woman was teaching all about – what had Jem called it, birth control? – well, she, Ivy Rose Murphy, wanted to know all about it. She'd like one or two children, what woman wouldn't? But she didn't want twenty like some families in The Lane.

146

"You know we'll have to have a street party on the day or The Lane will never forgive us?" Jem was frantically trying to figure out how they could sneak away to marry at the registry office. If he had to pretend they were travelling to Sligo to have his family at their wedding, he would.

"That's fine with me, Jem." The neighbours wouldn't expect to be invited to the church. A wedding was not the social event a funeral was. A street party, however, was essential. One would be organised with or without her participation. "If we're lucky we'll have a nice day for it."

They turned back in the direction of Grafton Street, lost in their own thoughts.

Chapter 28

Ivy dropped the locked leather bank bag holding the money she'd taken at the Friday markets into the night safe of the bank on College Green. She'd taken a lot of money today. The news of her wedding had relieved some of the pressure from neighbours wanting her rooms. She hoped that would stay that way for a while. She didn't want any more neighbours knocking on her door demanding her two rooms.

She locked the fat-bellied door of the night safe before carefully putting the big steel key in her skirt pocket. She grabbed the handle of her pram and with a contented sigh set off. She walked the familiar streets towards home with her mind fully occupied with thoughts and plans.

She'd seen and heard nothing of Father Leary. She was keeping well out of the man's way. She kept her wits about her and her eyes open when she was out and about. The Good Lord knew Father Leary had made his opinion of visiting places like The Lane well known. It was beneath his dignity to visit the tenements himself. He sent a junior for any and all duties. He did, however, make exceptions and she'd hate to be caught on the hop.

She walked along Kildare Street, trying to imagine how her married life would work out. It was impossible to move in her work room now, though the goods she'd bought from the warehouse were in great demand. She'd shifted a lot of the wool and materials to the women of The Lane and down the markets. None the less the remaining stock seemed to take up every inch of available space. She'd tried to plan out the living arrangements for her new family but failed miserably. Jem was talking about clearing out the two rooms and whitewashing the walls. He wanted everything to be fresh and clean. She'd decided to just take each day as it came. There wasn't much else she could do.

It had been a long hard day but the longer evenings made being out and about a joy. She had been to visit an old contact, Pa Landers – a man known for his superior second-hand clothing – looking for an outfit suitable for a long journey and a wedding. It seemed everyone and his brother had an opinion about what Ivy should wear on her wedding day. Jem had let it be known they would be travelling to Sligo for the actual wedding which, while removing one set of problems, created more.

Mr Clancy would be coming to the livery tonight. She had her homework ready and what felt like a million questions to ask the man about business bookkeeping. Mr Clancy was a retired professor of mathematics, if you wouldn't be minding. Brother Theo had recommended the man. He came by the livery twice a week to teach Ivy, Jem, John Lawless and anyone else interested about finance. That's what he called it anyway – to Ivy's mind it was bookkeeping and sums but the man was a mine of useful information.

Ivy sighed with pleasure at the easy way her pram travelled over the cobbled streets. She walked on, a familiar dark shape pushing her pram around the Dublin streets. Her feet moved automatically but her mind was making and discarding ideas and plans. She had more than just herself to be thinking about these days. How had she become involved in so many people's lives? She'd been minding her own business keeping herself to herself and now look at her. She was a business woman for heaven's sake – with money in the bank. How had that happened?

"Jem, are yeh about?"

Ivy had dropped her pram into her own rooms, stoked up the fire and put fresh damp nuggets on to smoulder. She'd taken the time to give herself a quick wash and changed her old jumper for a white cashmere one she'd been given on her round. The jumper had been badly stained but Ivy had used her handcraft skills and prettied the plain jumper up with a lace border and white on white embroidery. She was proud of the end result. She remembered to put her homework under her arm before leaving her place by the front door and hurrying across the cobbled courtyard to the livery.

"Auntie Ivy, Auntie Ivy!" Emmy Ryan, black curls bouncing on her back, big green eyes gleaming, ran out of the room the lads were calling their tea room to greet one of her favourite people.

"Miss Emmy!" Ivy caught the young girl up in her arms. She put the child on her hip and smiled into the beautiful face. "How are you doing?"

"I'm fine, thank you," Emmy said impatiently. "Uncle Jem has your dinner on a pot over the fire." She took Ivy's face in her two little hands and stared deeply into her eyes. "Have you done your homework for Mr Clancy?" she demanded seriously. "Do you need me to check your sums?"

"Would you let the woman breathe, Miss News of the World?"

Jem stood in the open doorway of the tea room, a huge grin on his handsome face. His green eyes, so like those of his adopted niece, sparkled, his white teeth gleamed.

"John!" he shouted, stepping forward to take Ivy by the arm. "I'll be upstairs if I'm needed."

"Fair enough." John Lawless shoved his wheelchair away from the large central telephone-exchange board to push his head with the attached earphones and mouthpiece into view.

"Evening, Ivy!" he called cheerfully before disappearing back into the office. John was working hard to get back on his own two feet after a work accident but for the long hours he spent in the office he found his wheelchair handy for getting himself around the place.

"Evening, John." Ivy put Emmy down and the little girl scampered away.

Emmy went up the heavy wooden ladder leading to the loft like a monkey, skimming up the steps at speed. Ivy followed more carefully, with Jem bringing up the rear.

"Are you coming?" Jem turned and looked back over his shoulder to where Ivy stood on the lip of the loft, staring down into the main body of the livery building.

"So many changes, Jem." Ivy liked standing here – it gave her a bird's-eye view out over all the changes Jem and his lads had made to the main floor of the building, "In such a short space of time." She sometimes wished she could just stop the world and take note of everything that had happened or was being planned. She couldn't of course and it never did to stand still. She had to keep pushing forward and it seemed to her Jem Ryan was a man on the road to success. Who knew where the pair of them were going to end up?

"Are the two of you coming?" Emmy Ryan stood in the open doorway of Jem's room, glaring crossly out at the two adults standing there like statues. "Your dinner will be burned dry, Auntie Ivy."

"Coming," the two said together and turned to join her in the large room Jem called home.

"Sit yourself down, Ivy." Jem gestured to the small table and two chairs sitting close to the wall of his room. A lone place setting sat waiting on the small table. "I'll put the kettle on while you have a bite to eat. Emmy, get the cups out."

He grabbed the linen cloth hanging on the door of the closed cast-iron fire that warmed his room and served as a stove. With the cloth to protect his hands, he carefully lifted the covered plate sitting over a pot of gently boiling water.

"Get that inta yeh." He dropped the hot plate on top of the cold plate on the table before Ivy. With careful fingers he removed the lid from Ivy's meal.

"Jem, your blood should be bottled." Ivy expressed her gratitude while her mouth watered. "I'll be getting spoiled with this kind of service – one of me favourite dinners." She almost smacked her lips as the aroma of the smoked fish cooked in milk and onions assaulted her senses. She'd make short work of the mashed potatoes sitting under the fish.

"It's as easy to cook for three as for two."

Ivy concentrated on her meal and didn't speak again until she had made serious inroads into it. "Have you talked to the Widow Rattigan?" she asked then.

Jem carried the teapot over to the table. He poured tea into the cups Emmy had set on the table, before dropping into the chair across from Ivy. Emmy carried a handy orange crate over to use as a seat.

"I –" Jem began to answer.

"Do we have any biscuits, Uncle Jem?" Emmy searched the table top for her favourite treat.

"There's a few mixed biscuits in the cupboard," Jem remarked absently. "Get yourself two."

Emmy jumped from her perch and hurried towards the free-standing cupboard. She'd seen the brown-paper bag of biscuits earlier but it was polite to ask.

"Well, Jem – the Widow Rattigan," Ivy prompted.

The Rattigans rented the back rooms in Mr Wilson's house. Ivy had the widow knitting for her. The money the woman made wasn't much but every little helped. The rent on their rooms was high. The rooms had a private toilet out back and a garden where they kept chickens, a few geese, a pig and even a nanny goat. One of the rooms held a big black range and the unheard-of luxury – for The Lane anyway – of a water pipe right inside the room. The woman worked wonders with that range. When she could get the ingredients she produced food that Ivy thought would shame a French chef. Sadly she also had five young sons to look after and was in real danger of being evicted.

"I talked to her." Jem watched Emmy while sipping his tea. "I have Conn doing a cost analysis for me."

"Cheeky devil – I suppose Conn will be using that for his homework for Mr Clancy."

"Two birds with one stone."

"What are you two talking about?" Emmy returned to the table, a biscuit clutched in each fist.

"Your uncle is thinking of having the Widow Rattigan cook for the lads." Ivy sighed with pleasure – why did food prepared by someone else taste so much better than anything you made yourself?

"Why?" Emmy's big green eyes examined the two adults.

"None of your business, Miss." Jem removed the empty plate from in front of Ivy.

"Why?" Emmy waited, knowing if they didn't answer she'd still learn something if she listened carefully.

"Mrs Rattigan," Jem ignored one of Emmy's many whys as he returned to the table with the teapot, "reckons if we send one of the lads down to the Smithfield market first thing every morning we can buy bruised vegetables and cracked eggs cheap. She reckons we can get bones from the butchering at the same time. The woman had all kinds of plans when I mentioned what we needed." He emptied the slops and refilled the teacups.

"The Widow Rattigan is in need." Ivy nudged Jem's leg with her toe when he rejoined her at the table. "You're a big softie, Jem Ryan."

"Ivy, I'm spending money on the Penny Dinners every day. With the number of lads in and out of this place that soon mounts up. If I can help a neighbour by putting a bit of work in front of her all the better. The nuns don't need the money and we'll maybe have something besides stew for the lads now and again."

"Do you want me to keep me eye open for big pots

going cheap?" The lads had been taking their food directly from the buckets of dinners Jem kept over the fire in the 'tea room'. That would have to change if the Widow Rattigan was going to take over keeping the lads fed.

"It couldn't hurt." Jem shrugged.

"So Conn is going to work out the logistics of the thing, is he?"

"My God we're certainly learning big words these days." Jem laughed and nudged Emmy. "We won't be able to keep up with your woman if she gets any smarter."

"I will, Uncle Jem. I'm very smart," Emmy said in all seriousness. "I'll explain things to you, promise."

"That's a comfort to me." Jem grinned. "Ginie MacDonald is paying Mrs Rattigan a few coppers to teach her how to keep house and cook." He was referring to a young woman from the tenements who had recently rented a room for herself and her son.

"That can only do the girl good." Ivy thought of the young woman sold into prostitution by her own brother. "I haven't seen much of her since she and Seán moved into their own place."

"She should be doing alright, what with Seán earning a few bob from his work on the stage and the money her brother Johnjo promised to send her from America. I haven't seen much of Ginie myself but you know how The Lane is – everybody knows everyone else's business." Jem could feel his face flush scarlet. He didn't even want to think about what John Lawless had told him about Ginie's job. He found it hard to believe that men actually paid to be spanked. According to John, Ginie was getting paid good money to slap sense into the idle rich. "About your aunt . . ." Jem knew Ivy's aunt, Betty Armstrong, had been the one to get Ginie her job in a 'fancy' house.

"I would prefer it if we didn't refer to the woman as my aunt." Ivy didn't want to think about what she was calling 'the Christmas revelations'. It had been a shock to find out that Betty Armstrong was her da's sister. "I admit the woman has been a help to me and the other women of The Lane but that does not give her the right to call herself my aunt." The woman seemed to be trying to make a place for herself in Ivy's life. Well, it was too little too late as far as she was concerned. Ivy had never known the woman when she was growing up. It was a bit late in the day now for them to play at happy families.

"Ivy –"

"No, Jem, I mean it. I got along fine with no relatives. They didn't want to have anything to do with me. Well, I'm doing fine on my own, thank you."

"If that's the way you want it." Jem was conscious of Emmy taking in everything said. Now wasn't the time to discuss Ivy's family.

"I'll put little Miss Big Ears to bed while you finish up here, Ivy." Jem stood to begin the nightly preparations. He needed to put his place in order and get Emmy into bed before he went downstairs to his lesson with Mr Clancy.

"We'll need to move my bed over to Ivy's place when you get married, Uncle Jem." Emmy loved the tall wide cupboard bed her Uncle Jem had made for her. She felt safe and secure tucked up in her soft bed knowing her Uncle Jem was snoring softly a few paces away from where she slept.

"All in good time, Missy." Jem couldn't wait to move into Ivy's place himself.

Chapter 29

Ivy rolled over in her bed, slowly awakening to a bright new day – it was the 4th of April, Easter Sunday. This time last year she'd been alone, confused and hurting from too many shocks and upsets. What a difference a year made. She snuggled beneath her bed covering, her fingers pulling the luxury of a sheet and blankets up around her ears. The fire in the black range was nearly out but she didn't care. Sunday was supposed to be a day of rest. She was darn well going to learn how to rest.

Unlike many of her neighbours she didn't have to jump out of bed to get a large family ready for Mass. She had no need of the services of Eddie Baldwin, the knocker-upper. She had her very own chiming mantel clock. She smiled, thinking of the old woman who had been waking The Lane up for decades. She'd earn herself a few farthings this morning, using her long stick to knock on windows and shift the lazy. Eddie had bought brightly coloured material from Ivy to make a blouse for herself. The priest would be blinded this morning if everyone turned up in the clothes they'd made from all of the material she'd shifted.

The women of The Lane would have a bit of a rest this morning as no breakfast would be served – the entire family would fast before going to receive Holy Communion.

The children would have nice outfits to wear to Mass today. Ivy couldn't wait to see what the women of The Lane had managed to create from the wool and fabric they'd bought from her. She'd have a chance to see everything when people gathered in the courtyard before Mass. Some of the outfits would be passed down from older children but a lucky few would have new clothes from the skin out. The new outfits might well end up in the pawnshop on Tuesday but Easter Sunday and Monday the little ones could step out proudly.

The state of the Johnson lads had her tossing and turning in the bed, trying to force the image of the seven poor souls out of her mind's eye. They seemed so happy to be allowed visit The Lane over the Easter holidays. Not a one of them said a word against the Artane Boys' Home. They were in a terrible condition – broken was the only word she could think of to describe the change in the lads. "I don't want to think about this right now, God. I can do nothing about it. I'm sorry for them. Of course I am and I'll help where I can but I am only human, God. Can I please be allowed think about myself for once?"

The words echoed around the dark room.

"I can't do it." Ivy jumped out of bed. "I'll drive meself mad thinking about things I don't want to think about. I'm obviously not cut out to be a lady of leisure." She simply could not remain in bed and do nothing.

She took care of her bodily needs before raking the barely glowing embers of the range and adding fresh fuel.

She included a stub of candle to make the fire burn quicker. She needed the first pot of tea of the day.

She removed her poor man's pajamas, and replaced them with a black skirt and green jumper. She'd set out her new dress outfit last night. Mr Solomon had made a very fashionable hip-length blouse from the yellow cotton material. Ivy loved the long-waist fashions and had knit a white jacket to cover the blouse. She'd closed her eyes, taken a deep breath and dared to spend money on a brand-new fashionably narrow black skirt in the shorter style for herself. The outfit was draped over one of her kitchen chairs, ready for her to step into. She'd cleaned the black T-strap leather pumps with the two-inch heel to wear with the outfit. The shoes had been in the suitcase her brother Shay left with her. She hoped to God she could manage to walk around in them for the day. She'd wait to put her good clothes on until it was nearer the time to meet Jem and Emmy. They were going to Mass in St. John's Lane. Now that Father Leary was back at Westland Row she had no intention of darkening that doorstep. She wouldn't be going up to Communion so she could have a cup of tea and something to eat before leaving the house.

"Well, well, well, Ivy Murphy, would you say you're indulging in the sin of vanity?" She addressed her own image in the tall mirror propped against one wall of her room. She was wearing her new outfit – silk stockings and all. "I'm really losing the run of meself but I don't care. I like looking nice. I love being able to walk out with me head held high."

She'd scrubbed herself to within an inch of her life before getting dressed although she'd taken a bath at Ann

Marie's house the evening before. They all had – Jem, Emmy and Ivy. It was so much easier than having to haul water. Jem had examined the plumbing with great satisfaction, promising Ivy that they would have the self-same luxury some day.

She walked closer to the mirror and examined her face. She'd followed all of the instructions Betty Armstrong had given her about the care of her skin and such. She looked good if she did say so herself.

"Aunty Ivy!" A sharp rap of knuckles on the outside front door sounded. Emmy had become impatient.

"Miss Emmy, good morning." Ivy opened her door and smiled down at the little girl dancing in place. "Where is your new coat?"

Emmy was wearing a green dress that Ivy had run up on the machine, the colour exactly matching her eyes. Ivy had knit the white cardigan the little girl was wearing and embroidered it with a border of forget-me-not flowers and green vines.

"My friend Biddy says I can't wear blue and green together." Emmy stared up at Ivy, worry in her eyes. "Biddy says it's wrong."

"Come in a minute while I finish getting ready." Ivy was heartily sick of hearing 'Biddy says'.

"Why is it wrong, Aunty Ivy?" Emmy followed at Ivy's heels, sure her aunt would have the answer to her problem. She loved her new velvet coat and hat and wanted to wear them today.

"It's not wrong." Ivy was standing at her kitchen table checking that she had a clean handkerchief in her black leather handbag. She was more accustomed to shoving everything she might need into her coat pockets. It was a worry to make sure the darn handbag was packed with everything she might need through the day but Ann Marie insisted she carry one. "Biddy is probably thinking of the rhyme '*Blue and green should never be seen except on a gypsy or a fairy queen*'." Ivy chanted the old rhyme. She dropped the bag on the table, took Emmy by the shoulders and smiled into her eyes. "If Biddy isn't happy with your green dress and blue coat you can tell her I said you, Miss Emmy Ryan, are a fairy queen."

"I think I might like being a fairy queen." The young girl had known her Aunty Ivy would have the answer to her problem. Then she whispered, "But, Aunty Ivy, Uncle Jem is worried about something I don't understand."

"Today is a holiday, Emmy. We're going to have a lovely day and leave all our troubles behind us – your Uncle Jem will too." Ivy knew Jem was worried – so was she but there was nothing anyone could do at the moment.

It was Easter Sunday, a very important day in the Irish calendar. There was to be a march and gathering in the Phoenix Park that afternoon. Jem had orders for every carriage he could find to carry people to the Park. Tempers were still running high since the rebellion of 1916 – today was the ten-year anniversary. Jem thought there was going to be trouble. He was worried for the safety of his drivers and horses. He'd ordered the men to drop their fares at the Phoenix Park and retreat to the nearby Kingsbridge railway station. He was leaving it up to each man to judge for himself how safe it was to wait around to pick up fares. At the first sign of trouble all of the men were ordered to return to the livery.

161

Ivy kissed Emmy on the nose and stood to fetch her good beige cashmere coat from the nail on the wall. She pushed her arms into the coat sleeves, picked her beige cloche hat from another nail and walked over to the mirror to finish dressing. She hated to cover her new outfit completely but it was too early in the year to walk out in her figure.

"Right." She stood for a moment, checking to make sure she'd remembered everything she needed to do before leaving the house. She'd banked the fire, emptied the slop from the po and basin, locked the back door and given the room a quick clean. If she'd forgotten anything she couldn't think of it right now. "Let's be about our business, Miss Ryan." She took Emmy's hand and with a spring in her step prepared to enjoy her day off.

The courtyard, when they reached it, was a mass of families getting ready to walk to Mass. Greetings were shouted, new outfits admired and women's voices echoed around, shouting dire warnings to children not to get their new clothes dirty. The Lane courtyard was a hive of happy smiling people – bright colours were in evidence for this special day.

"Morning, Ivy, don't you look nice!" Maisie Reynolds was standing on the steps leading up to the main door of their tenement. She was wearing the blouse and matching turban she'd made from the material she'd bought from Ivy – her yellow knitted jacket was beautifully made. Maisie was checking the appearance of her husband and two tall sons. "Emmy, petal, where's your coat? The sun might be shining but never forget '*Ne'er cast a clout till May be out*' – it's a wise old saying for a reason. Are yez off to Mass?"

"Take a breath, Maisie." Pete Reynolds looked down at his wife. She was brushing invisible dirt off the shoulders of his good suit while making sure her neighbours noticed her men had new second-hand outfits for the day that was in it. She'd fluttered like a young girl when he'd told her she looked a treat in her new outfit.

"We'll see yez later," Ivy said. There was no point in answering Maisie – the woman was talking to hear herself speak. Ivy grabbed Emmy's hand in hers and, after checking the gate leading down to her basement was firmly closed, they fought their way through the crowd towards the livery.

"Don't forget the party later, Ivy." Marcella Wiggins voice could be heard but Ivy couldn't see the woman in the crowd.

"I'll be there." Ivy didn't stop. She was almost pulling Emmy along behind her. She'd have a chance to admire her neighbours' new outfits at the street party.

"Sadie Lawless," Ivy was surprised to see the other woman standing by her pram off to one side of the open livery doors, "I didn't expect to see you here – give us a minute." She released Emmy's hand and with a gentle shove sent the girl into the livery to fetch her coat and hat.

Emmy ran forward, eager to fetch her blue coat. She couldn't wait to be a fairy queen.

"I thought, if you don't mind, Ivy, I thought me and John could walk to Mass with yez." Sadie clenched the handle of her pram with white-knuckled hands. The big navy-blue pram was moving frantically up and down in reaction to Sadie's rocking. In spite of that the baby was peacefully asleep inside.

"What's up?" Ivy gently removed Sadie's hands from the pram. The frantic rocking would make the baby sick if Sadie didn't let up.

"I don't know what to do with time off," Sadie almost wailed.

Ivy looked around. It would take them ages to get through the crowd with this big pram. She wished she could push it through the livery and out the other side but the centre aisle of the livery was busy with some horses being groomed, and others being hitched up to carriages. She'd gladly walk through the hubbub but not while pushing a baby.

Ivy took Sadie by the shoulders and shook her gently. There was more to this than met the eye. "You make your way to the tunnel leading out to Stephen's Lane." It was nice to have a choice of exits now since the previously blocked-up tunnels had been opened up. "I'll get Emmy and meet you there. I'll tell Jem and John that we're going ahead of them." She gave Sadie a gentle push in the right direction before hurrying into the livery – stepping carefully. She didn't want to dirty her good shoes.

"Ivy, is Emmy not with you?" Jem was overseeing his workers.

John Lawless, wearing one of Mr Solomon's beautifully tailored suits stood at his side, his crutches resting on the earth floor. An empty wheelchair was off to one side.

"I'm here, Uncle Jem." Emmy appeared, her blue coat flying open, the matching hat swinging from her hand.

She ran over to join the three adults and waited while Ivy fussed over getting her dressed properly. Jem pulled a comb from the back pocket of his trousers and quickly restored order to Emmy's long black hair.

"You're not dressed, Jem Ryan." Ivy hadn't thought of Jem's business when she'd suggested going to an early Mass. The demand for carriages to carry people about the city this morning was obviously high. Jem was wearing his work clothes.

"I'll have you know, Miss Murphy," Jem struck a pose, "that I am not standing here in my birthday suit. I'm decently covered. It won't take me long to change into my good suit."

"No," Ivy looked around at the mayhem surrounding them, "we can go to a later Mass. You stay here and take care of business. John, you sit down in your chair. I'm going to take Sadie for a long walk by the canal. We'll be back later. Come along, Emmy." Ivy grabbed the child's hand and hurried through the livery and out the far door. She'd avoid the crowd in the courtyard.

"By God, Jem," John Lawless made his way over to his wheelchair and sat down slowly and carefully, glad of the chance to rest, "I think we've been given our orders."

"What's really wrong with you, Sadie?" Ivy asked when they were walking along the bald pathway in the grass verge cut from the driving hooves of the horses that pulled the barges along the canal. Emmy was in front of them, concentrating mightily on pushing the pram with the sleeping baby inside. It was a pleasant walk with the swan-covered canal on one side, the occasional barge boat with its occupants waving gaily as they passed and the clip-clop of horses' hooves on the cobbled street on the other. She promised herself to take more time to enjoy the simple pleasures available to her.

"It's that couple that Ann Marie got in." Sadie was

165

blind to the beauty around her. "They are taking over me kitchen. I feel like I'm in the way."

"Honest to God, Sadie, there's times I feel like boxing your ears." Ivy stopped walking. She kept a careful eye on Emmy who continued to walk along the path. The little girl got to hear too much of what went on. She'd prefer to keep this conversation private. "I know Ann Marie sat you down and talked about this."

Ivy had been there when Ann Marie explained – in detail – why she was employing the couple over the Easter holidays. Eleanor and Martin Skelly had been removed from their positions of cook and footman when they had fallen in love and requested their employers' permission to marry. Ann Marie heard of their problems and employed the pair to give Sadie a break from the constant demands of her home and family. The couple were being tried out by Ann Marie for permanent positions in her Dalkey home. She was planning to re-open her Dalkey Estate with a minimum of staff on hand.

"Why can't you just look and learn, Sadie?" Ivy asked. "You have the chance to ask the pair about life in a big house. They are doing you no harm and I for one can't wait to have the Easter meal Eleanor is preparing for us. We'll be served like the nobs and everything. Would you for feck's sake just relax and enjoy yourself?" Emmy was too far ahead by now. "Emmy, that's far enough! Turn around now." She watched the little girl turn the big pram carefully and begin to walk back in their direction.

"Them two lost their home from one day to the next." Sadie was terrified of the same thing happening to her and her family. No one seemed to understand her fear no matter how many times she said it.

"Sadie, the same thing could happen to any of us." Ivy too was very conscious of the fact that she could be evicted from her rooms with very little notice. It was a fact of life for people who rented their homes. "You were in danger of losing your rooms when John had his accident. You're in a better state now. I know you and John have money saved. You make a good amount from all the work your family does on my dolls. You won't be homeless." She shook the other woman gently. "You can't keep worrying about stuff that hasn't happened yet. You're making everyone bloody miserable and that's not you." She snapped her lips shut – Emmy had almost reached them.

Chapter 30

"I'm looking forward to this fancy meal we've been promised." John Lawless was inching along slowly on his crutches.

Dora, his daughter, was pushing the wheelchair along Grafton Street with her sister Clare and Emmy aboard. The three girls were having a lot of fun, bringing smiles to the faces of the people they passed.

"There's times, John, when I have to stop and check I'm still standing because the world's spinning that fast around me." Jem was walking beside John, ready to grab his friend if the walk became too much for him. They had been to Mass and were now making their way back to Ann Marie's place. "What's the likes of us doing getting ready to have Sunday lunch like the nobs?"

"Jem, since the moment Ivy Murphy marched into my hospital room I haven't known what's going to happen next. I was lying there minding me own business when that woman," he gave a nod of his head to where Ivy and Sadie walked at the front of the group with the pram, "demanded I pick up me bed and walk like something out of the Bible. Honest to God, nothing's been the same since. I'm proud of myself and my family for grabbing at the chance of a better life. So, anything that comes my way – well, I'm just going to grin and enjoy it."

"That's a good attitude to have." Jem was worried about the men driving his carriages out and about. The people on the radio were talking about the trouble the march to the Phoenix Park might bring to their doors. He wished there was something he could do. He'd taken every precaution with his men – all he could do now was hope and pray.

"That woman Eleanor knows what she's about in the kitchen." John's arms and back were aching, but he didn't want to give up the feeling of standing on his own two feet, surrounded by family and friends. The girls were having the best of time using his wheelchair as a toy. He wouldn't take it away from them just yet. "She went down to that fancy market on Stephen's Green and stocked up with all kinds of things me and Sadie never heard of." John wished Sadie would allow the woman to teach her what she knew. "Had the stuff delivered to the door if you wouldn't be minding. She doesn't haul the stuff about herself like my Sadie and your Ivy."

"She'd be used to a different way of doing things," Jem answered with his mind on other things. Was it just his imagination or were there more men hanging about the streets than usual? He had to stop thinking like this or he was going to drive himself mad.

The group continued to make their way slowly back to the Grand Canal, exchanging Easter greetings with those they passed. They were working up an appetite for the promised feast. John and his family had been fasting to receive Communion so they were particularly hungry.

"Jem, would you carve, please?" Ann Marie was keeping

a careful eye on Martin Skelly, the man serving the meal. She was judging his attitude towards her guests. She could not employ a couple who would look down their nose or in any way make her less fortunate friends uncomfortable. She didn't see anything she could object to in the man's attitude.

"A leg of lamb, Ann Marie!" Jem stood and took the offered utensils from the silver salver in Martin's white-gloved hand. "You're spoiling us." He pulled the platter holding the beautifully presented meat towards him and began to carve, carefully placing the thin slices of lamb onto the serving plate Martin had put close to his hand.

"If you and Martin would be so kind, Ann Marie," Ivy dared to say what she believed everyone else was thinking, "you could perhaps offer us ignorant peasants instructions on how to serve ourselves this wonderful meal before we start gnawing on the legs of the table." They were gathered around the long table in the dining room. The silence was deadly as each person sat afraid to make a wrong move. The food was beautifully presented on salvers and in glass and china – most of the people at the table had never seen the like – the food they and their friends served usually came from the pot on the fire to the plate.

"You will never find a more snobby individual than an upper-house servant, Miss Murphy." Martin Skelly knew how he reacted to this unusual situation was important. The lady he prayed would employ him and his new wife had explained the situation to him when he'd come to the first meeting at this house. He and the missus had discussed the matter. They would learn to live with this motley crowd and make the most of the chance offered. "I believe you should count your blessings that you don't have a crowd of servants breathing over your shoulder. I don't imagine it makes the food go down very pleasantly." He'd taken a chance and now he'd see if he'd read the situation correctly. He waited for the ceiling to fall in on him for speaking out of turn.

"Very true, Martin," Ann Marie smiled. "We cannot expect Martin to serve all of us so we shall dine en-famille. The food shall be passed from my hand to Ivy on my right and she will pass it on to the next person and so on." She picked up a flowered china bowl almost overflowing with creamy white mashed potatoes. She passed the bowl to Ivy after serving herself a small portion – aware all the time of every eye at the table fixed on her every move.

"I'll serve the meat and gravy." Martin watched the goings-on with fascinated eyes. He couldn't wait to get back to the kitchen and tell his Eleanor about it all. The dishes were passed, the meat and gravy served and Martin left the room.

The meal progressed quickly after that with everyone serving themselves from the many dishes available. For a while the only sound in the dining room was that of utensils tapping plates as everyone dug in to one of the best meals they had ever tasted. Some of the spices and herbs were strange on the tongue but after a moment the sensation was delightful.

"No offense to anyone here," Jem patted his lips with his linen napkin, "but that's some of the best food I've ever tasted."

"The woman is an artist in the kitchen," Ann Marie agreed.

"I'm glad you didn't expect us to sit here while you took photographs of the food, Ann Marie," Ivy laughed.

Dora, Clare and Emmy exchanged grins while continuing to enjoy the food.

"Oh, I never thought," Ann Marie almost wailed.

"You can't be hiding behind that camera all of the time, Ann Marie," Sadie said. "You would miss all the fun of living if you did that."

"Very true, Sadie," Ivy nodded, "and besides she'd have had a mutiny on her hands. My stomach thought my throat was slit I was that hungry."

"I asked Mrs Skelly to teach me how to cook," Dora Lawless offered softly. "I don't want to go into service." She hadn't mentioned the matter to her parents. She looked at them now, scared she'd done something wrong. "I would like to learn from Mrs Skelly – I thought cooking might be a skill that would be useful to me. I don't want to work in an office and answer telephones like our Clare."

"We'll talk about this later," John said with a smile.

"What a marvellous idea!" Ann Marie was delighted to note that Dora's English was improving due to the elocution lessons both sisters were attending.

The conversation around the table became general. The food disappeared at a great rate. Ann Marie had to ring down to the kitchen for a refill of several dishes much to the delight of Eleanor Skelly.

"I thought, if everyone agrees," Ann Marie said as people sat back from the table with softly contented sighs, "that we could sit in the lounge and allow our meal to settle before being served Easter cake and tea. Does that suit everyone?"

"I'm going to check on the baby, then the girls and I will help wash these dishes and clean the kitchen," Sadie said. "We can't expect the woman who's been working all morning to clean up as well. It wouldn't be fair."

"I want to show you two my photographs of Emmy," Ann Marie said. Only Jem, Ivy and Emmy had joined her in the lounge. The Lawless family had chosen to tend to their own wants and needs. Everyone would meet up again later for cake and tea or coffee.

"Yippee!" Emmy clapped her hands.

"We'd love that." Jem sat on a small sofa, Ivy at his side.

"I put everything here in preparation." Ann Marie crossed to a mirror-decorated sideboard and began riffling through the photographs she'd stacked there.

"Let's see all of them," Ivy suggested. "I love looking at the photographs you take, Ann Marie."

"I have a great many here that I took out at the new airport that has recently opened outside Glasnevin," Ann Marie said as she checked the first stack of photographs. "I spent one day there trying to capture the airplanes coming and going. It was exhilarating, I can tell you. I was even offered a ride in one of the airplanes."

"You got a chance to go up in one of those flying machines?" Jem moved to the edge of his seat. He couldn't imagine anything more exciting.

"Ann Marie, did you really get into one of them air-o-planes?" Ivy felt dizzy just at the thought of it. What would it be like to fly high in the sky?

"I did." She whirled around, her face shining with joy at the memory, her hands full of photographs. One large print slipped from the bundle and fell to the floor. She didn't notice, too intent on thinking about her magical experience. She was giving serious thought to taking flying lessons. She passed half of the photographs in her hand to Ivy and the other half to Jem.

Emmy crossed the floor to pick up the fallen photograph. She wanted to see. She turned over the large black-and-white shiny photograph and froze. She stared at the image. Her green eyes, glistening with tears and dark with worry, travelled over to where Jem and Ivy were exclaiming with delight at each new image revealed in Ann Marie's photographs.

"Emmy, come look." Ivy never removed her eyes from the images she was holding in her hand. Ann Marie had captured Emmy beautifully. In some of the photographs Emmy was a modern young girl but in some Ann Marie had somehow aged the image and made it look as if Emmy had lived long, long, ago. They were magical.

"I hope you plan to give me some of these photographs, Ann Marie?" Jem was astonished at the images in front of him. His little Emmy captured for all time. He'd frame these pictures and put them on the wall of the home he planned to create for his family.

Emmy walked slowly over to stand at Jem's shoulder. She didn't express any interest in the photographs of herself. Her stomach felt sick, she wanted to cry, she wanted to run away. She held the photograph she'd picked up from the floor so tightly the heavy paper Ann Marie used for her prints crackled.

Jem turned to caution the child to treat the photographs carefully. One look at Emmy's face froze the words on his lips. He raised his eyebrows, silently asking the child what was wrong.

Emmy passed the picture over reluctantly. The image was of a handsome man with a strong serious face framed by his flying helmet. He was standing with his hand on an airplane. She said one word softly but it echoed around the room like a shout.

"Papa."

"Emmy?"

The little girl crawled up on Jem's lap, ignoring the photographs that fell to the carpet-covered floor. Ivy and Ann Marie were frozen in place, unable to understand the situation.

"I don't want to go back." Emmy slipped her arms around Jem's neck in a stranglehold, her green eyes overflowing, a silver trail of tears running down her ashen cheeks. She stared into Jem's eyes, her lips trembling. "Please don't send me away. I don't want to go back."

Jem put his arms around the little girl and held on tight, his own eyes damp.

Ivy finally unlocked her limbs enough to move. She fell to her knees on the carpet and slowly picked up the photographs. She put those photographs plus the ones she held onto a nearby coffee table. She reached out shaking fingers to pick up the one crushed photograph – then, returning to her seat at Jem's side, she stared down at the image in her hand.

"Ivy?" Ann Marie stood with one hand pressed against her chest.

"Who is this?" Ivy passed the abused photograph to her friend with shaking hands.

"My goodness," Ann Marie stared at the image, "that is the gentleman who took me up in his flying machine."

She stared at the tableau before her, knowing more was needed. She'd liked this man very much. He was educated and entertaining, had travelled the world. She'd wanted to know more about him but their time together had been short. "I captured this image of Mr Edward O'Connor standing by his airplane whilst I visited the new airport I was telling you about."

"Is the man staying in Dublin?" Jem croaked. He'd known this day would come and had thought himself prepared. He tightened his arms around the little girl who had come to mean so much to him. Could he hand her back to the family who had neglected her?

"What is going on here?" Ann Marie stared at the little family group sitting so close together on her sofa – Jem with the child held close to his heart, Ivy leaning in close and rubbing gently at the little girl's delicate back. They were a picture of dejection.

"Ann Marie, is that man staying in Dublin?" Jem repeated.

"Yes." It was obvious she wasn't going to get an answer until she'd explained what she knew. "I received the impression that Mr O'Connor is entering into talks concerning investing in the new airport. I didn't feel it was my place to ask for details."

"Did you exchange cards?" Ivy said.

"We did of course," Ann Marie replied, "but the card I received from Mr O'Connor was one from his business. The card is embossed with the address of his London head office. He explained he travels extensively." She'd felt quite breathless when Edward O'Connor had stared down at her with intense green eyes while pressing his card into her hand.

Ivy stared at the delicate colour staining Ann Marie's cheeks. "Do you have reason to believe that Mr O'Connor will contact you again?" What a kettle of fish that would be – Ann Marie walking out with the man who could send her two friends to the gallows.

"I really couldn't say."

"I need to know where that man is staying in Dublin," Jem said softly.

"*Nooo*," Emmy wailed. "You'll get into trouble for helping me! *Noooo*!" She sobbed so hard her little body was trembling in his arms.

"Emmy, I have to do this. Mr O'Connor needs to know." He stood up with the child clinging to his neck. Her sobbing tears were soaking his collar. "Ann Marie, now is not the time for this conversation. I know you've been wondering about Emmy. I thank you for not questioning me about her presence in my life." Jem was conscious of the fact that the Lawless family could return at any time. He did not want them involved in this matter. His mind spun with frantic plans. He needed to contact this O'Connor.

Ann Marie could hear the other members of her strange household approaching the room. She didn't know what was going on. She had the feeling the less people involved the better. It was obvious Jem loved Emmy and the child was happy – for the moment that would have to suffice. "Ivy, take Jem and Emmy up to my suite until the little one calms down. I believe the Lawless family are about to join us for the promised tea and cake."

"Right." Ivy jumped to her feet. She tried to pull Jem along but he and Emmy were lost in a whispered conversation. They couldn't stand here like statues. She pulled Emmy from his arms and turned towards the door.

Ann Marie was standing with her hand on the doorknob.

"Jem," Ivy hissed, "pull yourself together and follow me." She went through the door being held open for her without a backward glance.

Ann Marie watched her friends almost run from the room. She intended to get to the bottom of this but now wasn't the time. They had Easter tea to get through. She sighed deeply. Then there was the street party in The Lane. They couldn't miss that without causing comment and questions. She smiled at the Lawless family entering the room.

"The others will join us presently. Emmy had a slight mishap." She said no more, leaving it to each person to imagine what they liked.

Ivy went up the wooden staircase at speed, Emmy clutched close to her chest. She was fighting her own fear for the child's sake. She heard Jem taking the stairs two at a time to catch up with her. They hurried into Ann Marie's large bedroom at the front of the house, slamming the door at their back as if they were being followed by the hounds of Hell.

"We all need to calm our nerves." Ivy, still holding Emmy, collapsed onto the flowered settee placed under the bow window.

"That's easy for you to say." Jem pulled Emmy from Ivy's arms and, with the little girl clasped tight, began to pace across the Persian carpet that covered the wooden floor.

"Jem," Ivy jumped to her feet and grabbed at Jem's

elbow as he passed her, "you have to calm down – *now*." She stared into his green eyes – eyes that were almost crazed. "You pacing up and down like a madman is doing no-one any good." She shook the arm she held. It had little effect but it made her feel better.

"We have to tell Papa I killed my aunt," Emmy raised her head from Jem's chest to whisper.

"In the name of God," Jem groaned.

"Will the pair of you stop it?" Ivy was frazzled enough for all of them but meeting trouble halfway didn't make a lick of sense. They needed to catch a hold of themselves. "I feel as if I'm in the theatre watching actors work themselves up into a frenzy. Stop it right now." She grabbed Emmy from Jem's arms. The poor child must feel like the package in a pass-the-parcel game.

"I'm taking Emmy into the bathroom to wash her face and comb her hair. While I'm away, Jem Ryan, you catch a hold of your nerves and calm bloody well down." So saying, she marched into the en-suite bathroom.

"Calm down, she says!" Jem looked at the delicate settee – the strength was going from his legs. He hoped the feminine piece of furniture would hold his weight. He dropped down, put his elbows on his spread knees and buried his shaking hands in his hair. "I'm on me way to the gallows and the bloody woman is telling me to calm down. How am I supposed to do that, I'd like to know?"

His mind whirled. He had to let that man O'Connor know he had his daughter. The man must be going out of his mind wondering where his little girl was – he had to be told she was safe and well. Then there was all that cash and jewels the aunt had had about her person. The sparkles were in a bank box but he'd been using the cash to improve his business and provide a better standard of living for little Emmy. He needed to check his books to see how much he owed the man. He'd been paying the money back. He was no thief but the sums involved made his head spin.

While Jem was wrestling with his conscience, Ivy was trying to calm down a distraught little girl.

"You need to stop this crying, Emmy." Ivy washed away the fresh burst of tears with a warm flannel. The tears kept coming. "You're going to make yourself sick, petal."

"Uncle Jem will be in so much trouble for helping me," the little girl sobbed, as if her heart would break.

"Listen to me." Ivy gave up attempting to wipe the tears away. She sat down on the closed wooden seat of the toilet and pulled the shaking girl into her arms. Emmy leaned against her as if all the strength had left her body. "I don't know your papa," the word 'papa' felt weird on her lips but that was what the child had called the man, "but I do know that if I lost you I'd go out of my mind." She tipped up the little chin and stared into the child's eyes. "Are you listening to me?" She got a little nod for her trouble. "We have to let your papa know that you are safe and well. You know that, Emmy."

"I'm afraid," Emmy whispered.

"There's no need to be afraid." Ivy was scared enough for both of them. "You are just a little girl, Miss Emerald O'Connor of Galway."

"I like being Emmy Ryan."

"Be that as it may, you are both Emerald and Emmy, but your uncle and me want you to enjoy being a child. We'll do the worrying and fretting if we have to."

"I don't want anyone to hurt my Uncle Jem."

"I know, petal, but we can do nothing right now." Ivy sighed and pulled the little girl close. "We have to go back down those stairs with a smile and have tea and cake. Leave the worrying to me and your Uncle Jem – can you do that?"

"I'll try."

"Good girl. Now let's get you cleaned up. It's a holiday and we are going to enjoy ourselves." She pressed a kiss into Emmy's damp forehead. "I can't wait to see what kind of fancy cake Ann Marie's cook has made for us. Me mouth is watering at the very thought." She knew cake wasn't the answer but she had nothing else to offer right now. The little girl needed something to take her mind off this shocking new development.

She opened the bathroom door and gently nudged Emmy before her.

"Jem, we're going to have to bring the date of our wedding forward," she said with her chin in the air as soon as she emerged from the bathroom.

"In the name of God, Ivy Murphy," Jem jumped to his feet, "what are you talking about now?"

"I can't be made to speak out against yeh if we're married." Ivy took Emmy's hand in hers and made for the bedroom door. "I read that somewhere."

Chapter 31

"I was half joking, whole in earnest, about bringing forward the date of our wedding, Jem."

It was the evening of Easter Sunday. The sound of the die-hard partygoers still echoing around the courtyard. Jem held a sleeping Emmy against his chest as they hurried around the tenement block to Ivy's back door. With the goods all over the place they couldn't enter her front room without some kind of light.

"They'll be expecting us to go back out to the party," Jem whispered while Ivy fumbled to get the key in the lock.

"Pity about them." Ivy got the door unlocked and hurried over to light the gas lamps. It was black as pitch. "Put Emmy in my bed," she said when the soft gas light illuminated the room. "I'll make some tea." She threw her coat and hat on the foot of the bed.

"Have you anything stronger to put in it?" Jem's coat and hat joined hers.

"Jem Ryan, don't you be taking to strong drink now," she said over her shoulder while raking the fire out. She'd banked it before going outside to attend the street party.

Jem removed Emmy's outside clothes without disturbing the sleeping child. She'd been a little wonder to him today. She'd preformed her party piece standing on one of the tables pulled out into the courtyard. The child had been better at hiding her worries than the adults.

"The only thing I have to hand is some of me da's poitín." She turned into his arms when he walked over to join her in front of the range. "That will do neither of us any good." They stood for a moment in silence. "Jesus, Jem, what are we going to do?"

"What can we do, love?" He took comfort from holding Ivy tight to his body. He felt as if his bones were going to rattle apart he was that scared.

"You did what you thought was best for her." She turned her head to look at the little dark head peeking over the bedclothes. "Surely to God any father should fall to his knees and thank you for keeping his child safe?"

"We both know the rich are different, love." He pressed a kiss into her hair. "Where the heck has he been all this time? What kind of man is he that doesn't come looking for his child? I'm that afraid of what he'll do that me bones are rattling. At the same time I want to punch him in the face for not protecting his child." He loved the little girl he'd taken into his heart and home. It was going to break his heart to give her up. "It's what happened to the aunt that's going to be the biggest problem." He released her from his hold, knowing his Ivy thought better with a cup of tea in her hand.

"Ann Marie says yer man is staying in Dublin." Ivy began to make the tea while Jem dropped into one of her easy chairs.

"Do you think we should tell her what happened?" He

let his head fall onto the back of the chair. "Would she understand?"

"We need advice." Ivy passed Jem a mug of tea and, with her own cup and saucer in hand, sat into the chair across the range from him. "We need to understand how much trouble we are in."

"I don't want you to have anything to do with this." He put the mug on the floor beside him. "I was the one who took the law into my own hands."

"Jem Ryan, talk like that will get yeh lynched." Ivy bent forward and slapped his knee. "We'll have to tell Ann Marie everything. We need her help. She'll have the name of some expert who can advise us I've no doubt."

They fell silent for a while, brooding as they drank their tea. Then Ivy stood to refill her cup. She leaned and pressed a kiss into his hair. He reached up, took the cup and saucer from her hands and placed them on the floor. He put his hands around her slim waist and pulled her onto his knees.

"I'm sorry for getting you involved in this."

"Don't talk so daft." Ivy sank into his body. "Where would we be now if you hadn't asked for my help that night?" She put her arms around him, her head on his shoulder.

"It's a bloody mess."

"You need to get them books out of the bank." She was referring to the diaries kept by Emmy's aunt. They had found them in the woman's luggage. The books were lodged, along with a fortune in precious metals, in a safe-deposit box at the bank. "You should let Ann Marie read them. The woman's own words will speak in your defence."

"You never stop thinking, love." Jem fought the temptation to bury his problems in her arms. "I've been spending all of that cash money the woman had too, don't forget."

"You can show the man your account books." Ivy pushed back to look into his worried green eyes. "Explain to him that you've been treating that money as a loan, that you were building up your business in order to provide Emmy with a secure future." Jem had been making regular payments into an account to pay back the loan.

"What will happen to the business if I have to go to gaol?"

"Would you whist!" She pressed a kiss into his lips. "We are going to get out of this mess – somehow – or my name isn't Ivy Rose Murphy."

They held each other tight – each with thoughts and worries scurrying through their heads.

Chapter 32

Ivy stared at the flickering flames of the candles she'd lit. The church was cool and silent around her. She remained standing before the altar of St. Francis.

'You'd say it was vanity, wouldn't you, Da?' she thought. 'I don't want to kneel down and ladder me silk stockings.' She was wearing her Easter outfit. She felt the burning behind her eyes. She was so scared. What was going to happen to Jem? He had done nothing wrong. He'd protected an innocent child. Surely he wouldn't be punished for that?

'I tried telephoning Brother Theo this morning. That's why I'm lighting candles to St. Francis. I haven't seen the man in ages. I hope he's alright.' She wished she knew what to say. Her thoughts were so muddled she didn't know how to be going on. She needed advice but couldn't voice her worries aloud. She'd brought them here to soak up the peace of the church. Even here she couldn't voice her worries aloud.

It was Tuesday, the Easter weekend behind them. She felt as if she hadn't had time to take a deep breath since looking at the captured image of Edward O'Connor. She'd had to hide her fear and worry. Jem was worried enough for both of them.

'Granny, them books of cures and potions you left me were worth their weight in gold this weekend.'

Jem had been called back to the street party as his men had returned to the livery. You could see some of the tension drain from him as each man brought his carriage back safely, but some of his drivers had been caught up in the trouble that exploded in the Phoenix Park in spite of all of his precautions. Ivy sighed now, thinking of the battered and bruised men sitting around the cobbled courtyard telling their tales of woe to a fascinated audience. 'I had to brew up a big batch of those herbal remedies of yours, Granny, to relieve pain. I owe Jem a block of lanolin. I had to borrow it to make your nettle and dandelion cream. At least the men had the sense to leave the horses and their carriages at a safe distance from the trouble in the Park.'

She blessed herself and turned to leave the church. Once out of the lane that ran alongside Grafton Street she turned in the direction of home.

She wanted to talk to Jem. He had gone to the bank to retrieve those journals of the aunt's. He must be back by now. They had spent Easter Monday trying to snatch a moment to discuss the urgent matter of Emmy's future but it seemed everyone needed to have a word with one or the other of them. It had been impossible to find a moment of peace. Emmy had turned clingy and tearful. It had taken both of them to reassure the little girl.

Then this morning Geraldine Harrington had telephoned, looking for Ivy. The Grafton Street toy shop had sold all of the Alice dolls. The baby dolls had sold out too. Ivy had packed up the few Alice dolls she had on hand and delivered them to the shop. She'd deposited the cheque she received. The longing to light a few candles had tempted her into the church off Grafton Street. She walked along now, thinking of all she needed to get done. She had to talk to Hannah and the Lawless family – more dressed dolls were needed. Ivy's sigh almost shook her body. It seemed no matter where she went she took her worries with her.

She walked past the Park and towards the Stephen's Lane entrance into The Lane. With her mind busy she strolled into the tunnel, blinking at the absence of light for a moment. It was a quick walk through to the other side and into The Lane. She was surprised to hear what sounded like Liam's dogs barking wildly – the animals were usually better behaved than that. She couldn't see into the courtyard of The Lane from this angle so she hurried her steps, anxious to see what was going on.

"Miss Murphy!" the postman, standing on the pavement outside Wilson's house, shouted as soon as he saw her. He began searching in his big canvas bag.

"Have you something for me?" Ivy called out. Her heart began to beat double time, all thoughts of the barking dogs going out of her head. She'd been expecting a letter from her brother Shay. Was this the day?

"I have, Miss Murphy." The door opened at the postman's back and Old Man Wilson stood in the opening, responding to the postman's knock.

Ivy didn't notice him as she hurried over to stand in front of the postman, almost dancing with impatience.

"Miss Murphy, is it?"

The sound of her name was accompanied by a burning pain across her back.

"*Harlot is more like! Sinner, showing her legs to the world, cutting her hair, shameless!*"

Another blinding pain pushed Ivy off her feet. She dropped her handbag, falling forward against the postman and pushing him back into Frank Wilson who was forced back a step into his own hallway.

"*I didn't see you taking Communion in the Holy Season of Lent!*"

Another flash of pain almost brought Ivy to her knees but she was determined not to collapse. She would not kneel before her tormentor.

"*You weren't at the Stations of the Cross either, you spawn of the devil!*" Father Leary raised his walking stick to administer another blow to Ivy's back.

"Enough." Frank Wilson stepped around the postman and Ivy. Strong workworn hands grabbed onto the priest's wrist in mid-air, stopping the man from administering another of his wicked blows.

"Unhand me!" Father Leary couldn't believe that anyone dared to lay hands on him. He was a man of God. "I will beat the devil out of that sinner. She should not be allowed to go about in the company of God's children."

"If there is a sinner here," Frank Wilson whispered into the priest's sweating face, "I know who it is and it's not that poor innocent woman." He gave the hand he was holding a shake before forcing it down to the parish priest's side. "You had better be on your way now before I parade a few of your sins to the fascinated listeners."

The people of The Lane had disappeared at the first shout from their parish priest, none of them wishing to run afoul of the man. They were watching and listening though. Ivy had one hand on the lintel of Wilson's front door, determined to remain on her feet and appear unaffected by the pain burning her back. Tim Allen the postman was leaning on the opposite lintel in a state of shock.

"How dare you – you a failed Catholic dare to lay hands on me – a man of God?"

"I don't know what God would choose you to represent him." Frank Wilson was walking the priest out of The Lane by the powerful grip he had on the man's elbow. "You think no-one noticed the way you looked at that little girl's mother – brushing up against the woman – panting after her like a dirty dog." Frank shook the priest's obese body. "It wasn't as a man of God you looked and lusted after her." He squeezed the elbow he held with enough force to cause pain. "It's your own sin you see when you look at Ivy Murphy. You lusted after Violet Burton – everyone knew it except her poor fool of a husband. Well, you won't abuse her daughter – not in front of me."

They had reached the tunnel exit leading onto the Grand Canal. Frank snapped his mouth closed. He didn't want his words echoing around the place. He marched Father Leary out of The Lane and barely resisted putting the toe of his boot to the man's arse.

Ivy was having a hard time believing her eyes. Frank Wilson was marching Father Leary out of The Lane and there wasn't a one objecting. She was shivering with delayed shock. The priest would not take this insult lying down. He'd find a way of making Ivy pay.

"I'd think twice about spreading any of your poison in here again," Frank shook his finger in the priest's face. Out of the corner of his eye he saw the heavy wooden walking stick being raised. "I dare yeh," he spat and waited. He wasn't a girl standing with her back to him.

"You are going straight to Hell, Frank Wilson, for daring to lay hands on a man of God." Father Leary was shaking. It was that harlot's fault. Ivy Murphy, she was the cause of this trouble.

"I'll be sure to save you a seat if I get there before you." Frank Wilson turned his back on the other man half hoping he'd try and hit him. He'd like an excuse to punch him in his sanctimonious face. When nothing happened he sighed and continued walking back to his own home.

"Are you alright?" Tim Allen, the postman, asked Ivy. He was still shaking. He had never seen anything like it in his life. That priest had appeared out of nowhere and attacked without warning. He hadn't known what to do.

"I'm fine," Ivy replied as she picked up her handbag, still watching her neighbour. She'd never expected help from that quarter. Her back and shoulders were burning. "You called my name, Tim?" She had no wish to discuss the priest's actions. "Do you have post for me?"

"My Lord!" The postman hit his own forehead and returned to rooting in his large sack. "I've a big envelope for you, Miss Murphy." He pulled a large well-stuffed brown envelope from his sack with a grin. "This here has come all the way from America."

At the word 'America' Ivy turned her full attention to the postman. "Oh!" She grabbed at the envelope but the postman pulled it back.

"You have to sign for it," Tim Allen said. "I can't give it to you until you sign for it."

"You had better come inside and do that very thing."

Frank Wilson had come to stand behind them. "You knocked on my door, postman. I'm assuming you have something in your sack for my attention?" He didn't want to think about the trouble that was going to fall on his head for manhandling a priest. He'd do it again. He wouldn't stand by and see a man abuse a woman no matter what kind of collar he wore.

Jem Ryan turned his automobile onto Kildare Street. It was a beautiful bright spring day. He'd been to the bank and removed the journals from the safe-deposit box. He hadn't bothered rereading any of the vitriol written within the pages. He remembered well the words written in those books. While he was out and about he'd taken the time to visit the registry office. He had a crisp new marriage licence in his pocket. He was going to carry that licence next to his heart like a good luck charm.

He'd take his vehicle to the carriage house and leave it there. He could walk back over to The Lane. He planned to tell Ann Marie the truth about Emmy. He needed to know where O'Connor was staying. He was sure Ann Marie's aunt would know the whereabouts of an eligible gentleman. The Dublin social scene was a small closed club. It shouldn't be too difficult to find out the man's whereabouts. His mind was spinning with worry and doubts while his eyes kept close watch on the wide road. The stretch of road always seemed to be full of school children and college students visiting the museums.

"In the name of God, what now?" Jem moved the car carefully towards the pavement. He opened the driver's door and stepped out into the street without looking. He ignored the angry bleats of horns and the shouted abuse from carriage drivers. All of his attention was focused on the bike-rider peddling frantically along the pavement in his direction. A little dark-haired girl clung to the bike-rider's back, screaming madly.

He stepped up onto the pavement and stood with his hands in the air, shouting, "*Stop!*"

The pair on the bike almost tumbled to the ground, their shock was so great. Jem caught the bike in one hand and with the other removed his white-faced, sweating niece from the pillion seat. Emmy almost climbed up his body. She got such a tight hold around his neck he was in danger of suffocating.

"What in the name of God do you think you are up to, Conn Connelly?" Jem barked while trying to loosen Emmy's grip. How dare this young man endanger his niece – what was he doing taking Emmy out with him anyway?

"Ivy . . ." Conn couldn't believe they had actually found Jem. He hadn't been thinking clearly when he'd grabbed the bike from its stand outside the livery. What he'd witnessed the priest do to Ivy had panicked him completely. All he could think about was getting to Jem. Ivy needed him. Emmy had seen him take the bike – she'd demanded to come with him. He had pulled her up on the bike without really thinking about it. He couldn't believe they had bumped into Jem minutes away from The Lane.

"He was hitting her with a big walking stick, Uncle Jem!" Emmy pushed her head away from Jem's chest to say.

"Who? What are you talking about?"

"Father Leary." Conn watched Jem turn back to his car at the mention of the priest's name. "Wait! He's gone."

He grabbed at Jem's arm. The man could have an accident if he drove off in a fury.

"Where is Ivy now?"

"In Old Man Wilson's place," Conn said.

"She's where?" Jem couldn't get his mind around this. "Never mind. Conn, take the bike back. I'll take Emmy with me. No doubt she can fill me in on what's been happening."

Jem put Emmy in the passenger seat and hurried to get behind the wheel. He had to get back to The Lane and see Ivy with his own eyes. They drove off.

"Tell me what happened, love," said Jem.

"The priest was shouting at the sad boy." Emmy never called Liam Connelly by name. He was always 'the sad boy' to her. "I heard him, Uncle Jem – everyone could hear him shouting. The sad boy just stood there with his head down." Emmy hadn't liked to see that. "Conn let the dogs out." She hunched down in the seat. It was important to get the story just right. She had to tell her Uncle Jem what had happened. The dogs appeared on the stage with Liam. They were part of his act and they loved him. They hadn't liked the priest and started to bark and yap at him, running around his legs. "The priest tried to hit the dogs with his stick but they ran away."

"Yes . . . and then what happened?" Jem urged her.

"Then Aunty Ivy came home," Emmy whispered, her voice shaking.

"What happened?" Jem had a white-knuckled grip on the steering wheel.

"The priest heard the postman calling to Aunty Ivy. He held up his stick and ran up behind her." She had thought it was funny watching the fat man run at first. "He hit

Aunty Ivy, Uncle Jem, real hard, with his big stick."

Jem was concentrating on driving his car through the tunnel leading from Stephen's Lane. The tunnel opened up onto a wild area of green growth that led to the gable end of his livery and Old Man Wilson's house. He pulled the car to a stop before Wilson's door, jumped out of the vehicle and began banging with his fist against the closed wooden door.

"That will be your knight in shining armour," Frank Wilson remarked.

Ivy hadn't yet recovered from the parish priest's vicious attack. Mr Wilson had made her a pot of tea to help settle her nerves. She was sitting in a deep wooden chair clutching the unopened envelope from Shay to her chest. The soft cushion of the chair at her back was a blessing. The area Father Leary had beaten was throbbing and had begun to sting something awful.

"You drink your tea." Frank Wilson wanted a word with Jem Ryan. "I'll open the door to him."

Ivy was glad the old man had left the room. She needed to stand up. Her back and the tops of her arms were on fire. She slid her precious envelope in beside her and then used the wooden arms of the chair to push herself painfully to her feet. The furniture in this room was beautiful and all hand-carved. The walls were covered in cupboards from floor to ceiling. Each cupboard had a carved double door over it. There were fairies and unicorns in magical landscapes carved into each door. Stifling groans of pain, she admired the room.

On one side of the chimney breast there was a sink with taps and running water. On the other side there was a freestanding gas cooker. She'd never seen one before. She'd watched carefully as Mr Wilson put the kettle on over the blue flames to boil. The water seemed to come to the boil with a speed that left her gasping. She'd been able to use the indoor toilet when Mr Wilson pointed it out to her. She could never have imagined wonders like this behind Old Man Wilson's door.

"You need to get that woman of yours before the altar of God," Frank Wilson was telling Jem. "That priest needs to have his horns pulled in – I can't think of anything that would work as well as having a man at her back to protect her."

"I want to see Ivy." Jem's big hands were clenched into white-knuckled fists. He wanted to punch something.

"You can leave your automobile there for a minute." Frank was looking around the courtyard. The neighbours had come back out. There were groups of women standing around the courtyard gossiping. "Send the little one away to play with the dogs," he suggested. The dogs were running wild with excited children chasing them. "Give Ivy a few more minutes to recover." He turned back into his home, leaving the door open at his back. He expected to be obeyed.

Jem went around to the passenger side of his vehicle. "Emmy, I want you to run into the livery."

"No, I'm staying with you."

"Emmy, listen to me." Jem bent at the knee. "I need your help now." He stared into her eyes, willing her to agree. He did not want her around while he questioned Ivy.

"What do you want me to do?" Emmy could tell she

wasn't going to win this argument.

"I want you to run into the livery and get one of the lads to watch my automobile. I don't want anyone putting their fingers all over it. Can you do that?"

"Yes."

"Then I think you should help Conn gather up all of those dogs before someone gets hurt. Can you do that?"

"Yes."

"Good girl." Jem ignored the shouts of his name from the women gathered around. "Go on now. I'm going to have a cup of tea and I'll see you in a little while." He stood and waited while Emmy ran off before making his way to Wilson's door. He stepped inside, closing the door at his back.

"We're in here," Frank Wilson came to stand in the door of his living room. He kept two rooms in the house for his own use. The rest of the house he'd set up into rental units.

"Ivy!" Jem dropped to his knees by the side of the chair Ivy was sitting in. She leaned forward slowly and without saying a word dropped her head onto his shoulder. He didn't know what to do. He moved to pat her back.

"Don't." Frank Wilson had seen what Jem was about to do. He grabbed hold of Jem's wrist and stopped him. "I would imagine her back is burning like the fires of Hell for all she keeps telling me she's fine." Frank let go and turned away to make tea.

"Ivy, is it true? Emmy says Father Leary hit you with his walking stick – did he?"

"It's true right enough," Frank Wilson answered when Ivy made no attempt to answer, "and more than once."

"Sweet Jesus!" Jem stood upright when Ivy leaned away from him. He didn't know what to do with his hands. He was afraid to touch her in case he hurt her. "He can't be allowed to get away with something like this."

"Who's going to stop him?" Frank Wilson was taking dishes out of one of his hand-carved cupboards.

"There must be something we can do." Jem wanted to call the Garda on the man. He had no right to go around beating up innocent people.

"Jem," Ivy eased her back into the soft cushion of her chair, "leave it. There is nothing anyone can do."

"Ivy –" Jem started to protest.

"Jem, the man is a priest. It would be me against him and we both know how that would turn out. We can do nothing." Ivy had thought about it while sitting here. She had no intention of taking off her clothes to a group of hairy-knuckled men to show them her bruises. Father Leary hadn't hit her anywhere that could be seen in public.

"I can't just do nothing, Ivy," Jem protested.

"Sadly," Frank Wilson pulled a shelf from one of his cupboards and with a twist legs appeared, to create a table, "she is right. There is nothing you can do about that man, Jem – other men have tried and come to grief. Let it go."

Ivy was watching the man's every move. She knew Mr Wilson was a ship's carpenter. The man had obviously learned clever ways of keeping his place tidy. She wished he was the kind of man she could question. She'd love to have a good look around this room – explore all the nooks and crannies.

"You need to get Ivy past all them gossiping biddies

standing out there, waiting to put their tuppence-worth in." Frank set the table. He felt all fingers and thumbs. He wasn't used to company. "You will have to ask one of them to take care of Ivy's back. She can't do it herself."

"No." Ivy wouldn't ask any of her neighbours for help. That would get them into trouble with the parish priest – someone was sure to tell him who had helped her.

"Right." Frank passed the cups and saucers around, leaving the milk jug and sugar bowl on the table. That was as fancy as he got. "You'll have to take care of it, Jem." He almost smiled when the two in front of him started blushing. "It needs tending. I doubt the skin is broken but you need to check." He left it at that. It was between the two of them now.

"You are going to get into a lot of trouble for helping me, Mr Wilson." Ivy sipped the tea and stared at the man who had saved her. "Father Leary isn't one for turning the other cheek for all it says so in the Bible."

"I know." Frank had opened a can of worms today but if he had it to do over he would have still done the same thing. He had very little in his life now that he would mind losing. Besides, there were some things a man had to do to be able to sleep at night.

Chapter 33

Jem insisted on driving Ivy the short distance to her home. She shouldn't have to deal with nosey neighbours right now. She was obviously in a great deal of pain but, being Ivy, was denying it.

"It never rains but it pours." Ivy wanted to see what was inside her brother's envelope – still clutched unopened to her chest. Was that too much to ask? "What's she doing here?" she barked when she spotted Betty Armstrong standing outside her door.

"Looks like young Seán ran and got her." Jem brought his vehicle to a stop outside Ivy's back door under the fascinated gaze of everyone standing in line for the tap. "It's a good thing too," Jem exchanged glances with Betty. "That woman can take care of your back for you. You can't do it yourself, Miss Hardhead."

"I suppose." She waited while Jem walked around to open the passenger door for her. Truth be told, her back was aching. She watched Jem stop to have a quick word with the woman.

Jem held out his hand to assist Ivy from the automobile. "Betty will be glad to see to your back. I'll take my automobile over to Ann Marie's. I'm going to stop for a chat." He gazed meaningfully at Ivy. She gave a nod, showing she understood. He was going to talk to Ann Marie about Emmy and how she'd come into their lives. "I'll be back this evening to check on you."

"You're getting very bossy in your old age, Mr Ryan." Ivy allowed Jem to practically pull her from the car. She was still feeling shaky. She wanted to get behind closed doors where she could scream and cry in peace. "I'll see you later – go about your business."

"Talk about bossy!" Jem touched his fingers to her face. Then with a half-smile and a raised hat took his leave.

"Seán McDonald, shouldn't you be on the stage?" Ivy began to search in her pockets for the door key before remembering she'd had her handbag with her.

"Is this what you need?" Betty held the handbag Jem had passed to her.

"There's no matinee on a Tuesday." Seán hadn't known what to do when he'd seen the priest go for Ivy. He'd taken to his heels, going for the one woman he thought might be able to help.

"Thanks." Ivy took the handbag from Betty and removed her keys. "I suppose you'd better come in."

"I'm going into my own place." Seán lived with his mother Ginie in the basement room next door. He stepped away with a wave over his shoulder.

"He was worried about you." Betty waited while Ivy unlocked the back door. "Do you want to tell me what happened?"

"No."

"Jem said your back needs tending."

"Look, I don't mean to be rude." She looked over her shoulder as she stepped into her room. "Well, maybe I do." She offered a half smile. "Come in, sit down and let me get me bearings." She put Shay's envelope in one of the drawers under the kitchen table. She wouldn't open it until she was alone. She then removed her cashmere coat. She examined the back carefully before giving a big sigh – the coat hadn't been damaged, thank God. She could see the impressions of the stick on it but she'd be able to ease them out. The heavy material had added protection from the priest's blows. She put her coat and hat on the nails in the wall. She turned to find her visitor standing staring at her.

"Sit down at the table." Ivy pulled her wraparound apron on. "I need to get organised before I can sit down." She didn't wait to see if the woman sat. She began to rake out the ashes from the banked fire in the range, biting back groans behind clenched teeth. She didn't turn back to her visitor until she had the fire roaring in the grate and the kettle on.

"I'll do your back now." Betty, sitting at the kitchen table, had been watching Ivy. She could see the stiff way she moved. "I'm sure you want to change your clothes anyway," she added when Ivy opened her mouth to object.

"Okay." Ivy was hurting too much to argue. She'd let the woman see her back and then maybe she'd leave. "I made up a fresh batch of ointment we can use." She took the can of ointment she'd made to relieve the pain of Jem's injured men from one of the lower cupboards of her tall unit. "It's a bit fresh – it's better if you can leave it to set for a while but beggars can't be choosers."

202

"Let me help you." Betty stood and, without waiting for the objection she was sure was coming, began to help Ivy out of her clothes.

"I can't remember the last time someone helped me out of me clothes." Ivy was too sore to blush.

Betty bit back the bawdy comment on the tip of her tongue. "What are you going to put on?" She knew Ivy kept most of her worldly goods under the big black ugly bed. If she had to fall to her knees and search for something soft for Ivy to wear she would.

"There's a soft shirt of me da's under me pillow." Ivy kept the shirt close and sometimes in the dark of night she took it out to sniff at it. The strong smell of her da was gone but she still imagined she could smell him on the shirt. The soft white shirt would cover her to her knees.

"Sweet Divine Jesus!" Betty prayed when she got a look at Ivy's bare back. There were ugly red welts running across it and onto the back of her arms above the elbow. "My brother should have gelded that bloody priest years ago."

"I put a wooden tongue-depressor in the can to use to put the ointment on," Ivy said, ignoring Betty's remarks. There was nothing she could do about the parish priest. She refused to dwell on the man.

"I'll use my hands." Betty let the matter drop. "They're clean."

"The ointment will burn you. Use the depressor." Ivy wanted to get this done. She couldn't stand here naked from the waist up.

"Bend over the table." Betty picked up the can of ointment and sniffed. "Are you sure this is the right thing to be using on those welts?"

"Positive." Ivy bent over her kitchen table, clenching her teeth in anticipation of the coming pain. The ointment would burn for a minute, she knew, before it began to draw the pain out of the bruises.

"At least we don't have to get your hair out of the way." Betty began to use the thick wooden tongue-depressor to coat the marks in ointment. "I'm sorry, did I hurt you?" she asked when Ivy stiffened under her hand.

"It's okay."

"I'm going back to America." Betty was trying to take Ivy's mind off the pain. "I've done what I came here to do."

There was no reply. Ivy's jaw was clenched tight against the moan of pain that wanted to escape.

"I have a business in New York. I left a manager in my place but I'm ready to go back and take up my own life again." She had hoped to talk Ivy into going back to New York with her. She had dreamed of showing her the wonders of the city. It wasn't to be. Ivy had a life of her own she was making here. If her brother Shay couldn't talk her into going to Hollywood with him, what chance had she? "I haven't booked my passage yet." She had been putting off buying her tickets, hoping to form a closer bond with her stubborn niece. It seemed to her Ivy fought her every step of the way. "I plan on taking Hannah Solomon back with me." Betty stared at Ivy's back. Was it her imagination or was the first welt she'd covered in the ointment fading slightly? "Where did you say you got this cream?"

"Made it," was all Ivy was capable of saying at the moment. The burning pain in her back and upper arms held her almost rigid.

"How? Never mind, you can tell me later – I've almost finished." Betty continued to apply a thick coat of the ointment. When she had finished she walked over to the bed and pulled the shirt from beneath the pillow. Ivy hadn't moved. She dropped the shirt on Ivy's bare back and helped her stand upright.

"I'll need to soak Granny's pain-relief brew – it's a tisane." Ivy wiped the tears of pain from her face. She wanted to fall onto the bed and scream. Instead she shoved her arms into the shirt sleeves and fastened the buttons. "I'll make a pot of tea while I'm at it." She stepped out of her short black skirt, pulling her old skirt from the bed and up her legs. She sat on the bed and slowly began to roll one of the silk stockings down her leg. She removed her shoe and pushed the stocking into the toe of the shoe. She repeated the movements for the other leg before kicking the shoes under the bed. She stood and shimmied to remove the suspender belt that had held the stockings in place.

In her bare feet she walked over to take the boiling water from the stove. She pinched a handful of dried twigs into a mug and covered it with boiling water. She put it to one side to brew. She crossed the room to take the can of milk from the water-filled bucket. She sniffed – it was fine.

She began to set the table for tea, glad of something to do.

When she had finished, she put cold water into the mug of tisane and with a grimace gulped the horrible-tasting brew until the mug was empty.

"I need more Alice dolls dressed," Ivy said when the two women were sitting at the kitchen table. She had put the kitchen chair with its back against the table and was straddling the seat. The position protected her back. The two women had cups of steaming tea before them. "Would you take some of the naked dolls I have over to Hannah?"

"I'll be glad to." Betty couldn't understand it – the strain and pain seemed to be draining from Ivy as she watched. She knew her niece was addicted to tea but it wasn't a miracle brew. What was in that ointment? Could that tisane really account for the improvement in Ivy? "I think having those dolls has saved Hannah's sanity. Have you seen any more of her husband's men around the town?"

"I've seen them talking to the Jewish dealers in the markets." Ivy stood carefully. "A few of them have been in and out of The Lane visiting Mr Solomon. I don't think he suspects anything. The men come to order suits and shirts. If they take a good look around the place nobody thinks anything of it." She refilled both cups before sitting back down.

"Ivy, may I please look at your back again?" Betty stood and was picking up the back of Ivy's loose shirt before she could answer. She stared at the marks she'd just painted with ointment. They were fading slightly and Ivy was moving better. It hadn't been her imagination. "You said you made that ointment? And what was in that tisane?"

"Just some of Granny's recipes I made up," Ivy looked over her shoulder to say.

"How?"

"I just followed old Granny Grunt's written instructions."

"Ivy," Betty was almost breathless when she returned

to her seat at the table, "was this Granny Grunt a 'wise woman'?"

"Yes, she was."

A wise woman was a much-respected member of any community. They were the people you went to when you had an illness or injury. The poor couldn't afford to go to doctors. They consulted the wise woman or the apothecary for their woes.

"My Lord!" Betty buried her face in her hands and laughed uproariously. "A wise woman!" she hiccupped, "And you have her recipes?"

"Yes, Granny was a devil for writing down her 'cures'. I have books and books of hers."

"Ivy," Betty gulped the tea in front of her until the cup was empty, "give us another cup of this magic elixir. I have something I want to talk to you about."

Ivy stood to fetch the tea, wondering if insanity ran in her family. She hoped to God it didn't. She'd enough to cope with.

"Do you know what a percentage is?" Betty asked.

"Of course." Ivy poured the tea.

"I told you I have a business in New York," Betty said as Ivy sat. "I didn't tell you what kind." She laughed gaily. "I have a factory that produces creams, potions and lotions that I sell in my shops." She had been one of the lucky ones. She'd arrived in New York after surviving the sinking of the *Titanic* without a stitch or a penny to her name. A wealthy gent had taken a shine to her when he'd come to offer his assistance to the survivors. She owed everything she was to that man.

"Go 'way!"

"Ivy," Betty clapped her hands, "if the other recipes

207

Granny left you are as good as the two you just used – you and I are going to be very, very, wealthy women." Betty couldn't believe it. She had hoped to help the niece she had never met and instead Ivy was going to help her.

"I won't give you Granny's books." Ivy's mind was working frantically. She had no idea how business was run in New York but the recipes she had on hand were very useful to her. She wouldn't give them away. But if she could make money from the recipes – well, she'd have to think about that.

"I wouldn't expect you to," Betty agreed. "What I'd like you to do is allow me to copy the books for my own use."

"Let's talk terms." Ivy was no one's fool. If she had something worth money she wasn't willing to give it away.

The two women discussed business and drank tea. Betty Armstrong talked in sums of money that seemed more of a fairy tale to Ivy than the stories told on story night. If there was any possibility that she could make the kind of money this woman talked about – well, no better woman. Ivy Rose Murphy would jump on that bandwagon.

"I'd want papers drawn up by a man of letters," Ivy said when the talk seemed to be winding down.

"You don't trust me." Betty grinned, delighted with the woman her niece had become without any help from her.

"This is business, trust doesn't come into it." Ivy planned to discuss everything with Ann Marie and get her advice. That woman had a head on her shoulders for money that was a wonder.

Chapter 34

"*Dear Sir –*"

"That's a bit formal."

"We can't put 'Howayeh, Eddy' on the bloody thing." Ivy was again straddling a kitchen chair, the dull ache in her back a reminder of the day's events. She and Jem were attempting to compose a letter to Emmy's father. "'Dear Sir' is how you start a letter. Brother Theo taught me that."

"Ann Marie suggested we make it a short message asking for a meeting to discuss a financial opportunity." Jem remembered the look of horror on Ann Marie's face when he'd told her about Emmy's aunt. She'd insisted they not contact a member of the legal profession until they knew how much trouble they were in. "She's gone to talk to her aunt. Just as you thought, she said if anyone would know where an eligible bachelor was staying in Dublin, it would be her. She'll let us know what she finds out."

"Jesus, Jem, what's the likes of us doing writing about financial opportunities?" Ivy pushed the paper and pencil away. "I ask yer sacred pardon."

"Well, we sure as shite can't say 'Here, Eddy, we have

your daughter – where the fuck have you been?'" he almost yelled, pushing to his feet. "I'm going to check on Emmy." He almost ran through the obstacle course in the front room. Emmy was playing with her friends in the courtyard.

Ivy pushed the paper and pencil away from her. It was obvious neither of them was in the mood to write such an important letter tonight. She pushed her chair back from the kitchen table slightly, opened the drawer underneath the rim of the table and removed the big brown envelope from Shay.

Jem returned. "I'm sorry, love. I shouldn't take out my frustrations on you." He was trying to keep his eyes away from Ivy's top half covered only by a man's shirt. What kind of man was he that he had to fight the urges of his own body at a time like this? When he knew the poor woman was injured? He gritted his teeth and removed his eyes from temptation.

"This is hard for everyone." Ivy's head was reeling from the shocks of the day and her body ached. They both needed something to distract them and she had the very thing. The photographs and letter in the envelope – photographs of her Shay standing beside the likes of Lillian Gish and Mary Pickford – women she'd only ever seen at the fillums. She'd come over all funny when she'd seen them.

Jem joined her at the table.

"I got a letter from Shay today," she told him. She pushed one of the large black-and-white photographs across the table.

"Are me eyes deceiving me?" Jem lifted his eyes from the photograph to stare across the table at Ivy. "Is that

210

who I think it is?" He returned his eyes to the photograph.

"Me baby brother consorting with fillum stars." Ivy was glad to see the shadows leave Jem's face. "Would you credit it?"

"It looks like he landed in the gravy."

"He says in his letter that the place, Hollywood, is a wonder to behold. Everyone has their own private swimming pool if you wouldn't be minding."

"Go 'way!" Jem took the second photograph she passed him – right enough Shay was standing grinning by the side of a pool. "Them women aren't wearing very much, are they?"

"Them's the latest in swimwear, I'll have you know." Ivy was delighted with Jem's reaction. She'd almost had to pick her own chin up from the floor. "Shay says the whole place is in an uproar because of these new talking pictures. He says some of those famous people we've looked at over the years have voices that would peel paint."

"Go 'way!" Jem took the next picture – it showed Shay on the ship that had carried him to America. "What's the world coming to?" He accepted another photograph. The glamour of Shay's surroundings aboard ship was breathtaking. "You and me, Ivy, we're only in the ha'penny place."

"I don't know, Jem," Ivy said slowly. "Them photographs are lovely. I was thrilled to get them – see what me baby brother is up to – but in his letter Shay says his nerves are shot because he's afraid to say a word out of place. I wouldn't like to live like that."

"Still and all, Ivy, it's far from it we were raised." Jem was still looking at the photographs on the table in front of him, wondering if he should have encouraged her to go

211

with her brother. Lord knew what was going to happen after he met with O'Connor.

"That's the truth." Ivy picked up the photographs and put them back in the envelope. "I'll put the kettle on." She was looking down at the drawer she'd opened.

"Do you have a jumper or something you can put on over that shirt, Ivy?" He couldn't take Ivy walking around the place like that.

Ivy looked down at her chest. Merciful Jesus, she'd been sitting here half naked. You could nearly see through the old shirt she was wearing. "Close your eyes, Jem Ryan." She jumped away from the table like a scalded cat, ignoring the pain that stabbed through her back and upper arms.

She went and dropped to her knees beside her bed. She pulled the first jumper she felt out from underneath. Without checking she pushed her head and arms into the garment. She looked down at her chest – wonderful – it was one of the jumpers she used for sleeping in. It would have to do. She was covered at least. "I'm decent," she said.

"Ivy," Jem turned to watch her put the kettle on, "you know we talked about turning the end of the livery into something like the carriage house?"

"Yes." She filled her black kettle from the reservoir in her range. She gritted her teeth at the stab of pain at her movements. She'd need to brew up another batch of that tisane.

"I don't think we can do it," Jem said very softly. It broke his heart that he couldn't offer her the best of everything. Look what she would have had if she'd gone with her brother.

"Why not?" Ivy stood with her hand on the tall handle of the black kettle. She was feeling too hot and bothered to walk over and join him at the table. Besides, sitting hurt a lot more than standing at the moment.

"Well, with the sudden appearance of Emmy's father," Jem struggled to explain the fears that kept him awake at night, "I've been doing me sums. I've paid back a lot of the money I spent and with the way the business is going I'll be able to pay the rest back. But I'd have to use O'Connor's money to pay for the work on the livery. I don't want to spend any more of that money, Ivy."

"That makes sense to me." The idea of living in a fancy place had never seemed real to Ivy. But it would have been lovely to have indoor plumbing. "It won't kill us to start our married life in these two rooms. It's more than a lot of people have to start off." She didn't turn to face him. She didn't want him to see the disappointment on her face. He was a good man and she certainly had more than most.

"I bought the marriage licence this morning," Jem said softly.

"You what!" She did turn to look at him then.

"I bought the licence," Jem repeated. "With everything that went on today I wasn't going to tell you. Do you still want to marry me?"

"Of –" she started to answer just as a frantic rapping sounded on her back door.

"Aunty Ivy!" Emmy's voice carried into the room. "Uncle Jem! I'm hungry!"

"Of course I want to marry you," Ivy snapped while walking carefully over to let the little girl in.

"I could be in a lot of trouble, love. And I won't be

able to offer you the kind of home I hoped for. It's not exactly high romance."

Emmy ran towards him and crawled up onto his lap.

"It's us," Ivy closed her back door and looked down at the man and child, "in me kitchen with the kettle on and a hungry child to feed. It suits us, Jem. We don't need swimming pools."

"Can you feed a hungry man as well?" He looked into her pale face and changed his mind. She didn't need to be feeding other people right now. She was in pain and it showed.

"Well . . ." Ivy looked around, frantically trying to think what she had on hand. She hadn't planned on feeding anyone this evening.

"I'll tell you what," Jem jumped up with Emmy in his arms, "I'll pull the kettle off the fire. You might want to change out of that jumper. We'll all go for an evening stroll and buy thruppence worth of fish and chips." He didn't care what jumper Ivy wore but he knew she would. "Do you feel up to doing that, love?"

"Yeah!" Emmy clapped.

"I'll change me jumper and get me coat," Ivy said. She'd be glad of the chance to walk out in the evening air. Maybe that would relieve some of the pain in her back and arms. She'd drink the tisane before she went to bed. "See, Jem, this is us – fish and chips in newspaper and back here for a pot of tea. Yeh can't beat it."

Chapter 35

"Mr O'Connor." Jem shook the hand of the man standing in front of him. He could see Emmy in the man's face. "Thank you for agreeing to meet with me." There was a slight resemblance between the two men. They were both tall with green eyes. O'Connor had the blue-black hair of the Irish while Jem's hair was burnished with mahogany fire. They were both dressed in dark-grey suits and brilliantly white shirts. Jem wore the green silk tie Ann Marie had given him while O'Connor's tie was blue with a diamond pin embedded into the silk. Jem had passed his overcoat, hat and gloves to the valet manning the cloakroom. He'd held on to his leather briefcase.

"I'm always ready to discuss financial opportunities." Edward O'Connor examined the man in front of him. His letter had aroused his curiosity but it was the mention of Miss Ann Marie Gannon that had secured this interview. The woman intrigued him. "Come, we can discuss business over a whiskey." Edward led the way into the lounge of his club.

Jem followed, knowing Ivy and Ann Marie would want a description of everything about this elite men's club. The Hibernian Club was a well-known Dublin landmark. O'Connor was staying at his family suite. Jem was going to disappoint the ladies. He couldn't describe his surroundings to save his life. All he could see was O'Connor, the man with the power to destroy his life. He sank into the deep button-back dark-green leather Chesterfield chair across a table from O'Connor, glad to get his weight off his shaking knees. He put his briefcase on the floor by his chair and watched while the man ordered whiskey from the uniformed servant who'd rushed to his side.

"That is not a Dublin accent," Edward said while they waited for their drinks to be served.

"I'm from Sligo." Jem felt sweat trickle down his back when they started to chit-chat about the prominent families of Galway and Sligo. They knew some of the same people. He didn't mention he knew them from pulling his forelock when the gentry passed his family farm in their carriages. He could keep up his end of the conversation, remembering the gossip his mother loved to share about the local gentry.

"I haven't been back home in so long." Edward stared around the woodlined room, his thoughts miles away. "I hadn't intended to stay away this long," he muttered practically under his breath.

The arrival of the servant with a silver salver bearing a whiskey decanter and glasses broke the silence that had fallen.

"We will serve ourselves."

The servant withdrew.

"Right, to business," Edward said when both men had glasses of fine Irish whiskey in hand. "What was it you wanted to discuss with me?"

Jem gulped the whiskey, trying to find his courage. He had tried to plan what he would say to the man. Sitting here in the lounge of a club he'd never dreamed to enter, with the man himself examining him with cool green eyes, his mouth dried up. The man across from him waited patiently, seeming to have all the time in the world.

"Mr O'Connor . . ."

"Edward, please."

Jesus, could it get any worse, Jem thought. "Edward, I'm afraid I asked to see you under false pretences." That sounded about right to his ears.

Edward said nothing while he watched the man across from him place his glass on the table with shaking hands. There was a bloom of sweat on his face. It wasn't that warm in this room.

"Mr O'Connor . . ." Jem tried again.

"What is it you want from me, Ryan?" Edward didn't have all day to wait for this man to make his appeal. It wasn't the first time he'd been approached for money. He was surprised and disappointed that Ann Marie Gannon would have a part in this situation.

"I want to talk about your daughter Emerald," Jem managed to blurt out.

"How dare you, sir!" Edward slammed his glass down. He stood to lean over the table, glaring at the man who dared to mention his beloved Emerald. "My daughter is dead and no concern of yours."

"Wait!" Jem stood and faced the man. "Please, sit down, please." He was shaking. Dear Sweet Jesus, the man believed his child had died.

"I –"

217

"I'm begging you, sir, sit down." Jem became aware of the glances they were attracting. What in the name of God was he going to do now?

"You have two minutes." Edward also was aware of the attention they were attracting. He took his seat again.

"You have no reason in the world to trust me." Jem refilled their whiskey glasses. They were going to need another drink. "I'm asking you as Emerald's father to listen. I swear to you that I am not trying to deceive or con you."

"Speak."

"Your daughter, Emerald, is not dead."

Jem had been expecting the punch in the face. He'd allow the man one free shot. He pushed O'Connor back into his seat with one hand while struggling to open his briefcase with the other. He was aware of the outraged gasps around the room but didn't care. The servant hurried over to their table, calming agitated club members along the way.

"We really cannot allow fisticuffs in this club," the servant stated when he reached their table.

"Leave us!" O'Connor waved the man away.

Jem slapped the photograph of Emmy he'd taken from his briefcase down on the table. He was glad he'd asked Ann Marie for copies. The photograph showed Emmy on a flower-bedecked swing, a smile almost splitting her face. "We need to talk."

"How . . .?" Edward caressed the face in the photograph with shaking fingers.

"If Mary Rose Donnelly were not dead I'd kill her myself," Edward O'Connor bit out.

"I didn't kill her." Jem wanted to get that very important point across. He'd talked till he was hoarse.

"I received a letter from a Bishop Troy informing me of my daughter's sudden tragic death from meningitis –" He had to stop. He couldn't believe what this man was telling him. "My father, the letter continued, had a seizure at the news." He bit back the rest of the words. No need to tell this man of his family's problems. "It was too late for me to do anything. My daughter was gone." He'd accepted the news, feeling it was God's judgement on him.

"You have no reason to take the word of a stranger." Jem took the journal he'd marked from his briefcase. He pushed it across the table in O'Connor's direction. He might be the one who had taken a punch to the jaw but O'Connor looked like a man reeling from one too many punches at the moment. "I've marked the passages that mention Emerald and yourself." He held the book open at the place he'd marked. "I believe you need to read this for yourself."

O'Connor leaned over the table, reading from the open page. "My God, the woman hated me and mine."

"No," Jem too leaned in, "she wanted what you had offered her younger sister." He'd read all of the journal.

"How did she think to get away with this?" Edward waved a hand at the page that described her plans for Emerald.

"It would appear she did get away with it."

"I returned home. I closed up my house, put a black ribbon on the door and haven't been back since. I visit my family estate of course." He rarely made the time to visit his family. Seeing his father so reduced and his eldest brother happy in his life of the landed gentry with his

219

young family around him hurt too much.

Edward continued to read the vitriol that bled over the pages.

"I have a great deal of precious jewels and metal that belong to you," Jem said when O'Connor finally slammed the journal shut. He went on to describe the goods they had removed from the aunt's luggage.

"Dear God above!" Edward recognised the goods being mentioned. He'd inherited the snuff boxes from his maternal grandfather. "The woman cleaned out my vault. How on earth did she get the combination to the safe?"

"The items are in a safe-deposit box at the bank." Jem took a deep breath. "The cash money, however . . ." His mouth dried as he thought of the amount of this man's money he'd spent.

"I don't care." Edward couldn't talk about money right now. "I want to know about my daughter, my Emerald. Where is she?"

"At school at the moment."

"You have had her all of this time?"

"Yes, I couldn't allow her to be placed in a home." Jem stared at the other man. He knew everything now. Jem's fate was in his hands. "I didn't know what to do for the best. I'm sorry. I never thought you might be told that she had died." He didn't mention how many times he'd cursed the man for his neglect of his child.

"Who could think something so monstrous?" Edward wanted to run to this school and snatch his child up. But what could he do with her? "I need to find a nanny and rooms to rent." He looked around with unseeing eyes. "This is a gentlemen's establishment. There is no place for a child here."

Jem felt his heart break. This man had found his child but Jem was about to lose his.

"Let us go to this school and get my daughter." Edward was consumed with the need to see his child, touch her, watch her breathe. He was a man released from a living nightmare.

"Emmy won't thank you for removing her early from class," Jem said sadly. "She takes her education very seriously."

"Emmy?" Edward queried.

"Miss Emmy Ryan." Jem packed the items he'd removed back into his briefcase. "I let it be known she was my niece. I had to call her something."

"It doesn't matter." Edward stood. "Come, man. I want to see my child."

The two men, dressed in their overcoats, hats and gloves, stepped out of the club. They walked in the direction of Stephen's Green.

Jem felt his heart was bleeding with every step. "I haven't been able to offer Emmy luxury," he said as they walked, long strides matching. "I appreciate I have no rights where the child is concerned but would you consider leaving her in my care until you have settled the matter of her future?" He prayed the man would at least consider leaving Emmy with him for a while longer. After all, he couldn't take the child to his club – he'd said so himself.

"I want my child." Edward matched Jem's quick strides through the streets of Dublin, not really seeing anything of his surroundings.

"Of course you do," Jem was quick to agree. "I have no intention of keeping her from you. I only ask that you allow her to stay with me while you settle on a home for her." They were making good time. They'd be at the little school Emmy attended soon.

"I find I am unable to think beyond the thought of seeing Emerald." Edward couldn't make plans for his future at this moment in time. He had to see Emerald, touch her, to truly believe that what this man had told him could possibly be true.

"We're here." Jem felt his eyes water. "I'll ask the teacher to release Emmy early. I'll be right back." He stepped through the school doors.

Edward stood in the street, staring at the nearby biscuit factory. His eyes examined the rough area around him. What was his child doing in a place like this? What kind of effect had all of this had on his little girl?

"*Papa!*" The joyous shriek broke through the noise of the passing traffic.

He opened his arms to the little hooligan running towards him, her black hair streaming behind her.

Chapter 36

"This is where I play ball." Emmy pulled her father by the hand. "My friend Biddy is at school. You can meet her later, Papa." She continued to charge all around The Lane, determined to show her papa her new world. "Those are my friends," she pointed him in the direction of the sad boy and his dogs. They were in the back yard of the tenement block, practising new routines. "They appear on the stage. The dogs are very clever."

"Emerald . . ." Edward wanted to pull his child into his arms and run from this place. He gave generously to charity but this place was beyond his experience. He wanted to express his horror but his daughter was obviously extremely proud of this world.

"You don't like it." Emmy stared up at her father.

"I'm a little confused." That was all he was willing to say to his child. He had noticed that Ryan spoke to the child as an adult.

"I love my new life, Papa." Emmy could see that something was very wrong. She didn't understand. Her papa and Uncle Jem didn't laugh and joke with each other when they went to lunch at Bewley's restaurant. They were cold and polite and she didn't like that. "I have loads of friends. I'm never alone. No one pinches or punishes me here, Papa."

"You are my daughter, Emerald." Edward tried to explain what should be perfectly obvious. "Your place is with me."

"But you go away all the time, Papa," Emmy said. "You leave me alone with staff. Uncle Jem doesn't leave me with anyone. I love my Uncle Jem and Aunty Ivy, Papa. I don't want to go away and leave them."

She didn't want to show her papa any more wonders. He didn't understand. She began to walk sedately back in the direction of the livery, her papa's hand holding hers tightly. It was as if he was afraid she was going to disappear. He was the one who always disappeared and left her alone.

"Is my Uncle Jem going to be in trouble because he helped me?" She stared up into his face. She would be able to tell if he told an adult lie.

"How could I be anything but thankful to Mr Ryan?" Edward wasn't accustomed to having his emotions in such a turmoil. There was a correct way to do things and he prided himself on always behaving correctly. He could not believe that he was walking around this den of poverty, his daughter's hand in his. He should have insisted on booking a suite at the Shelbourne Hotel. He wanted to remove his daughter from this place but how could he do that? Emerald was happier than he had ever seen her. She had been full of news and stories about the many wonderful people in her new life. She'd insisted on performing her 'party piece' for him over lunch.

Perhaps he was dreaming. He had fallen ill and was in

a world where his Emerald was alive but everything else around him had changed.

"I want to show you where I live."

Edward followed meekly along as he was towed through the livery. The working lads shouted greetings at 'Emmy' as his daughter was called here. Everyone seemed to have something to say to his little girl. The men and young lads working around the place were examining him carefully, he noted.

"Everything okay?" Jem stood in the aisle of his livery. He'd changed out of his business suit and was now wearing his work clothes.

"No," Edward understated.

"You are confused and lost, aren't you?" Jem thought the other man looked as if he needed to lie down in a darkened room.

"I'm completely at sea."

"Might I make a suggestion?"

"Please."

"Return to your club." He held up his hand when the other man looked like objecting. "You have a great deal to think about. I can't imagine how you must be thinking or feeling. Today has been one shock after another." He picked Emmy up when she ran over to his side with her arms in the air. With the child on his hip he faced this stranger who had the power to change all of their lives. "You can see that your daughter is safe here. Give yourself time to reflect on all that has happened to you. I promise Emerald will be here when you are ready."

"I want my daughter with me."

"I appreciate that but, until you can arrange something for her, she is safe here with me." He held out his hand. "I promise I will take very good care of your child until you can rethink your life."

"I don't know what to do."

"Come," Jem put Emmy on the ground, "if you are not too proud to be seen with a working man, Emmy and I will walk you back to your club. I've given you my card. As soon as you are clearer about what you want to do, telephone me here."

"I don't want to let her out of my sight."

"You look like you need a nap, Papa," Emmy said.

Chapter 37

"Miss Gannon," Edward raised his hat. "Thank you for offering the use of your home for this meeting. I'm very grateful."

"Mr O'Connor, do come in. You are the first to arrive." Ann Marie stared at the man standing on her doorstep. He looked nothing like the debonair airman she'd photographed. His eyes were haunted.

"I'm afraid this must be a great imposition." Edward, when he'd telephoned the livery after hours of heart-searching, had almost been ordered to present himself at this house by Ryan.

"Please." Ann Marie stepped back, silently inviting him inside.

She waited while he removed his hat and coat, hanging them on the stand she pointed out. She walked to her study, conscious of him at her back.

"I know a little of what has been happening but not all," she said over her shoulder as she pushed the door of her study open. She'd set up the large front-of-house withdrawing room as her own personal study. The big green leather chairs and heavy furniture gave the appearance of a men's club. The delicate feminine touches and tall containers filled with fresh flowers dotted around the room offset the severity of the space.

"I feel as if I'm lost in one of those 'penny dreadful' novels." Edward almost fell into the chair placed in front of a gently glowing fire. He took a deep breath. "I wondered if I might ask your advice."

"I'll help in any way I can." Ann Marie didn't offer the man a drink. It seemed what he needed was someone to listen. She wasn't surprised. What Jem had to tell must have come as an enormous shock to him.

"I've learned so much in such a short space of time." Edward quickly filled her in on the details of the injustice perpetrated against him.

"How dreadful!" She had believed as soon as she'd heard Jem's story that there must be more to be revealed. Edward was not a man who would neglect his duties or those under his care.

"I spent the most astounding period of time with my daughter," Edward said. "I wanted to hold her close and never let her out of my sight." He shrugged. "Emmy Ryan, as she is called now, let it be known that she had obligations. She had friends to play with and places to be. A father appearing out of the blue did not appear to bother her at all." He'd been horrified to learn that his child lived over a livery – sleeping in a cupboard bed, for goodness' sake. Emerald had pointed all of this out to him with enormous joy. "In point of fact my child practically ordered me to go away and take a nap."

"She is a delightful child," Ann Marie said.

"How well do you know this chap, this Jem Ryan?" He didn't know what to do for the best. How could he leave his only child living in what he considered dire poverty? He looked around the well-furnished room he sat in. Surely this woman shared his opinion of the living conditions in that place Emerald called The Lane.

"I was introduced to Jem by my friend, Miss Ivy Rose Murphy." Ann Marie felt she knew how he was feeling. "Yes, the people of The Lane are not in our social class. I can quite see how that would concern you. I have to say, however, that Ivy Murphy and Jem Ryan are two of the finest people I know."

"Steady on . . ." Edward stared to see if she really meant that statement.

"I would imagine that you and I were raised in the same fashion." Ann Marie didn't smile but she wanted to. "I would never allow my uncle or his family to visit The Lane. I would be mortified by their reaction. But I have come to know these people and I find them fascinating."

Edward didn't want to get into a discussion on social standards. He was having difficulty putting his thoughts in order. "Jem Ryan has asked that I leave my child with him while I sort out my own situation."

"I would not hesitate to agree," Ann Marie said, since he appeared to be waiting for her opinion. "Emmy is one of the most loved, bright, articulate young ladies that I've encountered. She has had the opportunity to see a side of life that you and I were never aware of. She has been cosseted and loved by Ivy and Jem. You can surely see that at first glance. Did she appear distressed to you?"

"I am her father," Edward stated. "I want her with me."

"Forgive me." She understood, but Emmy was happy where she was. She knew it was going to break Ivy and

Jem's hearts when the child left their care. "I understand that you are staying at the Hibernian Club. You have nowhere to take a young girl. Why not leave Emmy where she is for the moment? I am sure you could see her as often as you wished. You would have the freedom to plan what you want to do. Surely that makes the most sense."

"You truly believe that my child is safe where she is?"

"A lot safer than where you left her." She was being cruel to be kind.

"Touché," Edward was forced to agree. He'd believed he'd left his child with someone who cared for her. Look how that had turned out. Emerald appeared to love the life she had at this moment in time. How could he tear her away and put her under the control of a strange nanny in a hotel room? That was all he had to offer at the moment. "I need to return to Galway and speak with some people."

Ann Marie leaned forward. "If you will forgive me for being presumptuous –"

"I came here seeking advice," Edward cut in.

"Today's events have come as the most appalling shock to you. Why not give yourself time to think before making plans that affect the rest of your life. Emerald is safe and close to your hand. Get to know the people who have had the care of her. See the kind of young lady she has become. The decisions you make now are vitally important. I advise you step back and consider what you want for both you and your child."

"I was presented as 'Emmy's da'," he offered helplessly.

Ann Marie's laughter pealed around the room. "It is somewhat off-putting, I'm sure." She tried to keep the broad grin off her face.

"You have no objections to Ryan using your home as

a meeting place?" He was vastly more comfortable in this room than standing in the walkway of a livery.

"My friends thought you would be more at ease in these surroundings." She gestured around the room with her hand. "Relax," she advised. "We all want what is best for your child. She has stolen our hearts. Now, what would you like to drink?"

Emmy was standing on one of the kitchen chairs in Ivy's back room while Ivy tried to get her ready to go out. She was scared – her Uncle Jem had told her that her papa would take her home with him. She didn't want to go. She loved her papa but why couldn't he leave her here with her new family and friends? Papa travelled all the time. She was lonely and frightened when he was away. She wanted to stay here with the people who loved her and took care of her. Was that wrong? Was she a naughty girl?

"Bend your arm, love."

Ivy gently pushed Emmy's arm into the sleeve of her white broderie anglaise dress. The little girl had eaten a hearty meal before her bath. Jem and Ivy hadn't managed to eat a bite. Their emotions were choking them. It took a great deal of effort to wash Emmy's hair but, with the help of the special soap they all now used, she'd succeeded. Ivy had spent time towelling dry and combing Emmy's mane of glossy black hair. It was past the child's bedtime but the upcoming confrontation could not be delayed – not if she and Jem wanted to retain their sanity anyway.

"I feel like one of the toffs today, I've changed my clothes that many times." Jem came into the back room. He was attired once more in the suit he'd worn to his meeting with O'Connor. "I'll finish up here." He walked over to join his little family, his heart breaking. "It's your turn to put on your glad rags."

"I left the green ribbon on the table." Ivy stepped back, away from the chair. She brushed her hand softly against his and gave a half smile. They were both miserable. "I gave the ribbon a belt of an iron."

"She's a thing of beauty," Jem said, staring at Emmy. He reached for Ivy's fingers, desperately trying to hold onto his composure. "It won't take a minute and we'll be cocked, powdered and shaved. I'll take the little one over to the livery – give you a chance to wash yourself down." He released her fingers, stepping over to pick up the long green ribbon that went around the waist of the white dress.

Ivy prepared an enamel bowl of water for her use while watching Jem and the child out of the corner of her eye. She smiled and promised not to be long when the other two were ready to leave. She had to fight the tears she wanted to shed. She wasn't going to meet Emmy's papa, the man with the power to ruin their lives, with red eyes. Time enough for tears later when it would just be the two of them. The pain in her heart at that thought was almost crippling.

She'd asked Ann Marie's advice about the clothes she should wear for this first meeting with Emmy's papa. Ann Marie had suggested she wear the blue dress she'd worn to the theatre. The dress was drop waist in the current fashion and the bugle beads that covered the top of her arms would cover her fading bruises. It felt a bit naked to Ivy but Ann Marie was the expert. Her matching blue fabric T-strap shoes would complete her outfit.

The adults stood around Ann Marie's study, staring at

each other, unsure of what to say or do. Jem had Emmy in his arms, unwilling to release the child.

"This is ridiculous," Ann Marie said suddenly. "Sit down and I'll pour each of us a stiff drink."

Edward wanted to grab his child and leave but the way Emerald was clinging to Ryan's chest showed more than anything that he needed to understand this situation.

Ivy was desperately trying to hide her emotions. Jem and Emmy were breaking her heart.

"Jem, I can fetch a rug to go over Emmy," Ann Marie said. "She can have a nap on one of my settees."

"No!" Emmy had a stranglehold on Jem and at this suggestion she tightened her little arms, almost choking him. What if she went to sleep and when she woke up her Uncle Jem and Aunty Ivy were gone?

"We're fine," Jem took a seat, arranging Emmy on his lap, "but I'll take that drink and thanks."

"Ivy, I know you would rather have a pot of tea but just this once I think you might have a drop of the demon drink." Ann Marie was glad she had something to occupy herself with. The misery on her friends' faces was enough to break her heart. "I have blackcurrant cordial for Emmy. I must say you all look very attractive this evening." Ann Marie passed a sweating glass of gin and tonic to Ivy. The green grin of a lime slice bobbed within the ice pieces.

"You don't look so bad yourself." Ivy accepted the glass and sipped. She admired Ann Marie's silk dress.

"Emerald!" Edward couldn't bear to watch his child settle into the other man's arms.

He stood and pulled the child into his arms. Jem and Ivy jumped to their feet as if the child were being threatened. He was her father!

"Papa, I'm Emmy now." The little girl returned her parent's fervent embrace. She wanted everyone to be friends. She loved her papa but she loved her Uncle Jem too.

"Please, we should all sit down," Ann Marie said into the awkward silence. "There is a great deal to discuss."

They sat.

"If I might make a suggestion?" Ivy said. "I believe we should hear what Emmy has to say."

"Emerald is a child." Edward had been raised to believe that children should be seen and not heard. It was ludicrous to suggest a child could be capable of forming an opinion about anything.

"A very bright child."

"I want to understand what happened to Emerald. Jem tells me that my child had been abused." Edward was having a great deal of difficulty processing all of the information he'd been given today. He kept hoping to discover that what these people were telling him was untrue. He couldn't bear to think of his child in danger. How could everything change in such a short space of time? He had his daughter back in his life – everything he'd believed for so long was a lie.

"She was," Ivy said. "I removed Emerald's clothes when Jem rescued her from her aunt's evil clutches." It was easy to think of the sad little child she'd first met as Emerald. The wild child that ran around The Lane with a permanent smile was Emmy. "The clothes she wore were made for a much younger child and were difficult to remove." Ivy wanted him to understand what Emerald had been subjected to. She needed this man to appreciate why Jem had decided to take the law into his own hands.

"Her back was covered in fresh and ageing lash marks. Her toes and heels were bleeding from being forced to wear boots much too small for her growing feet."

"I killed my aunt, Papa," Emmy whispered.

"What!"

"Shhh, love." Jem leaned forward and brushed his hand over her hair. "You did no such thing."

"I believe I need to hear this story again." Edward accepted the glass Ann Marie passed him. He gulped the liquid without stopping to notice what it was he was drinking.

"Would you like to go down to the kitchen, Emerald?" Ann Marie didn't think the child should be present.

"No!" Emmy jumped from her father's arms and onto Jem's lap. "You'll go away and leave me, Uncle Jem! I don't want you to leave me."

"Emerald, this is none of your concern." Edward felt almost betrayed by his daughter's desertion.

"On the contrary," Jem said softly, "this concerns her more than any other."

Ann Marie felt a twinge of sympathy for Edward O'Connor. Her parents had been considered liberal but the freedom that Emmy enjoyed was outside of her experience too. They had never run wild without adult supervision.

"We are getting off track." Jem pressed the trembling little girl to his chest. The story he was about to tell was nothing new to her. She had lived through it. "Let me tell you in more detail of my own part in our present circumstances."

Ivy felt her heart swell with pride as her future husband faced down the toff glaring at him.

"In the first weeks of last year I was sitting waiting for

235

a fare outside Kingsbridge train station . . ."

Jem told of his first impression of Mary Rose Donnelly and the child she had persecuted. There was no other sound but his voice as he took them through his first dealings with the woman and child. Jem winced to remember the woman's abusive tone to the poor child. When she'd ordered him to take her to Goldenbridge his heart had almost stopped.

"I knew old Rosie would only take minutes to trot from Kingsbridge to Goldenbridge." He looked around at his fascinated audience. "I decided to take the long way around. I was hoping to think of some way to help the little girl." He shook his head. "There was nothing I could do but it didn't sit right just to deliver the child to Goldenbridge trade school. The place doesn't have the best of reputations around Dublin." He paused and looked at Edward. "If Miss Donnelly had remained sitting in the cab the accident would never have happened."

"She was never a woman to sit back and wait," Edward said when Jem seemed to be struggling.

"We were passing Kilmainham Gaol – there was some kind of protest going on – anyhow," he pushed his fingers through his hair, "yer woman almost crawled out of the cab shouting abuse and instructions. A stone thrown by someone in the crowd hit her head. I had my hands full trying to control the horse." He closed his eyes and took a deep breath. "I'll remember the sound that stone made when it connected with her forehead for the rest of my days. Emmy managed somehow to pull the woman back into the cab and I got us out of there."

"You were helping me, Uncle Jem." Emmy tightened her arms around his neck.

Jem noticed her eyelids were beginning to droop. Despite all the tension, she would soon be asleep.

"I didn't know what to do." He pressed a kiss into Emmy's hair and continued. "I drove around for what felt like days, trying to think of a way to protect the little girl who had stolen my heart."

"My daughter was in the cab with a dead woman!" Edward, without taking his eyes from Jem, passed his empty glass to Ann Marie for a refill.

"No, of course not!" Jem patted the sleepy child's back, trying to calm his nerves. "I stopped as soon as I had cleared the crowd and took the little one up on the driver's seat with me."

"You –" Edward took the freshened drink from Ann Marie.

"Will yeh let him tell the story!" Ivy snapped. "This isn't easy for him."

"I went to ask Ivy for help." Jem looked down at the little girl. A soft snoring snuffle assured him she was out of it, thank God. She didn't need to hear all of this. He continued telling the story of their disposal of the dead woman and his decision to claim Emerald O'Connor as his niece Emmy Ryan.

"You have reason to believe that the woman's remains would not have been buried?" Edward thought his voice sounded far calmer than it had any right to be. He was shocked to the roots of his hair by the plans the woman had made for his only child.

"Mary Rose Donnelly was what we would call a horse of a woman." Jem remembered trying to move the woman who had been almost as big around as she was tall. He'd pushed the body in a wheelbarrow the short distance between The Lane and the place where he knew the 'death wagon' would be. He'd been relieved to get rid of the body. He had flashed Ivy's father's death certificate at the men but, as he had known they would, they'd paid no attention to the document. "My uncle and I used to drive one of our wagons around the city picking up the dead." He shivered at the thought. He'd been glad to get rid of that part of the business as soon as his uncle died. The grisly nightly ride through the dark streets picking up the dead, people who couldn't afford a decent burial, still haunted him. "I believe the men who took over that job will have sold the body for study. You don't often see a well-fed body on that round."

Edward gulped his drink, unsure of what to say or do. If the woman had succeeded with her plans he would never have known what happened to his Emerald. His child would have been lost to him forever.

"It is a great deal for you to take in, Edward." Ann Marie had joined him on the two-seater settee. She pressed her shoulder against his in silent support.

"While I grieved and wandered the world my daughter was living in a stable." Edward stared at the sleeping child.

"Jesus Christ was born in a stable," Ivy snapped. "If it was good enough for him it's good enough for anyone."

"I mean no discourtesy," Edward offered.

"I did what I did to protect the child." Jem didn't think it would be a good idea to say he'd do it again in a heartbeat. "Emmy has been with me from that moment to this." He longed to ask this man his plans for the little girl he loved. Did he have that right? Emmy gave a soft little snore, almost breaking his control.

"You have been placed in a dreadful position, Edward," Ann Marie said softly into the uncomfortable silence that had fallen over the group. They could not remain seated staring at each other with distrust. "But it is getting very late, well past Emerald's bedtime. Would you consider leaving your child with Mr Ryan while you make arrangements?"

"But . . ." He couldn't let his daughter return to a stable for heaven's sake!

"It must be obvious to you that your child has come to no harm in Jem's care. Quite the contrary." Ann Marie understood his concern but she knew Emmy loved her life.

"Emerald is old enough to attend boarding school," Edward mused aloud.

Jem bit back the 'No' that wanted to explode from behind his teeth.

"You do not need to make plans at this moment," Ann Marie broke in before her two friends could give their opinion of that idea. She had seen the shock on their faces. "You can't have made any plans yet for Emerald's care?"

"The Shelbourne offers trained staff." He had asked after he discovered Emerald. It would not be difficult to find a member of staff willing to sit with the child.

Jem and Ivy remained silent, each praying that Ann Marie could make the man see sense. They appeared to speak the same language.

"Why not leave the situation as it stands?" Ann Marie waved at the child sleeping so trustingly against Jem's chest. "You can see for yourself that your child is in the best of hands. It may not be what you or I would consider ideal but I believe Emerald will thank you for not removing her abruptly from people she loves. You will then be free to take time to consider the ramifications of this situation." The poor man had received so many shocks in such a short space of time. She intended to offer him her assistance. She planned to be by his side to help in any way she could. Time enough to mention that.

"I do have a great deal of thinking to do." Edward had never been totally satisfied with the life he led but this day's happenings seemed to have completely knocked his world off its axis.

"Ivy and I will guard your child with our lives," Jem said.

"That is not the point." Edward hoped no-one asked him what the point was. He simply did not know. Was leaving his child with these strangers really any different than leaving her with staff? "I'm sorry. I don't mean to be ungracious. Perhaps it would be best for Emerald to remain in your care while I return to my club."

Ann Marie stood up. "Take Ivy and Emmy home, Jem," she said. She didn't want Edward to change his mind. "Edward and I will have another drink and chat."

Chapter 38

"Is this not one of your days for the market?" Jem called when he noticed Ivy making her way towards him. He was keeping an eye on the last of his street carriages pulling out.

"If this keeps up, Jem, I'm going to have to make two of meself." Ivy strolled over to join him.

"Where are you off to then?"

"I told you last night." She couldn't blame him for forgetting. There was so much going on. "I'm meeting Betty Armstrong at that lawyer friend of Ann Marie's. We are going to draw up papers about this business deal yer woman Betty thinks is going to make us rich as kings."

"Jesus, Ivy, I'll be able to say I knew you when you hadn't a sole on your shoes."

"I wouldn't be holding me breath for that if I were you." She tightened her grip on her handbag, came up on her toes and gave him a buss on the cheek for luck. "I'm off. I'll see you later."

"Mr Flint sent me to fetch yeh."

Jem felt the hair rise on the back of his neck at those

softly spoken words. He turned to stare into the eyes of a hulking mountain of a man. He knew who he was. He'd seen him around town. He was Flint's enforcer.

"What does Flint want with me?" Jem was only now starting to breathe easier after his meeting with O'Connor. Ann Marie was keeping the man busy while Emmy went on with her life as usual. That would change, he knew, but in the meantime he'd been enjoying having his life back.

"You don't ask Mr Flint what he wants. You just give it to him." A tap to his shoulder that felt like being hit by cement underlined the sentiment.

"I'll get my coat." He'd go see the man but he was going to make sure John Lawless knew where he was going.

"Information, as I'm sure you are aware, is my stock in trade." William Armstrong aka Billy Flint stared across his desk, in his Baggot Street house, at the man who would marry his niece. He had investigated this man and been impressed with his vision and ambition.

"You do have something of a reputation."

"I hear tell you plan to marry my niece." William thought there was no point hiding the connection. The man in front of him had driven Ivy to his Merrion Square home after all.

"I didn't know you had a niece." Jem glared. This man had refused to acknowledge Ivy when she had nothing. It was a bit late now to step in and play the concerned uncle.

"Let's not play these games." William refused to apologise for his actions. "It has come to my attention that you have been making enquiries around town."

"I'm naturally curious." Jem hadn't a clue what the

242

man was talking about. He'd wait to see where this conversation was going.

"I'm given to understand that your line of enquiry is about the kind of conversation that usually takes place between a father and his spotty-faced youngster." William Armstrong wasn't enjoying this conversation. "I've had this talk with both my sons." He intended to be a part of Ivy's wedding celebration. He was going to use Ivy to establish a relationship with the socially prominent, wealthy and much-admired Miss Ann Marie Gannon. The man seen escorting Miss Gannon around Dublin was some class of a titled gent from Galway. William wanted an introduction.

Jem squirmed in one of the two leather chairs sitting before the desk. They were in a room that had been described to him as Billy Flint's office.

"I can help you out there, Jem Ryan." William was disgusted at his own cowardice. He needed to get this done. "I've heard good reports of you through the years. I've been impressed with the changes you're making in your life. You just might be good enough to marry my niece."

Jem didn't say a word. He was angry hearing this man claim a relationship to Ivy. Where the hell was he when Ivy was being treated like a slave by her own family? He had more sense than to state his opinion aloud. He could never forget the reputation this man had earned.

"I can't believe how fucking hard this is." Armstrong opened a desk drawer. He removed an item and almost flung whatever it was across the desk in Jem's direction.

Jem grabbed at the object before it fell on the floor at his feet.

"That's called an English Hat or a French Letter or a load of other names." William Armstrong could feel the heat burning his face. He was fucking blushing like a callow youth. When he'd heard this man had been asking the apothecary for a means to control the number of children he might breed, he'd been impressed. He'd thought it would be a simple matter to supply the answer to the man's questions. He wanted an invitation to the wedding and this seemed a good way of going about it. "The important thing is – it will prevent pregnancy if used properly."

"What!" Jem felt his jaw drop. He'd suffered true mortification as he'd tried to discover how to avoid Ivy becoming pregnant in the marriage bed but this was the last straw.

"Look," Armstrong pointed his finger at Jem, "this kind of thing is usually discussed when you are drunk as a skunk and can indulge in nudge, nudge, wink, wink, but it's too fucking important to be messing around with." He shoved back his chair and stood. "I don't care how early it is, I need a strong drink – you want one?"

Jem wondered if it would be rude to ask for the bottle. "Yes."

There was silence in the room until Armstrong returned with two well-filled crystal glasses of whiskey. He passed one to Jem before sitting down again.

"I know which one of you decided to marry before a judge." Armstrong found he couldn't meet the other man's eyes. "I know more about the parish priest than I want to. Better men than I have tried and failed to get that man removed from his position." His teeth snapped closed. "If you are man enough to listen to your woman's opinion, you are man enough to control your own body."

"Tell me about this." Jem had unrolled the heavy thick rubber item Armstrong had thrown at him. He crossed his legs in reaction to the shape of the thing. "The two of us can't sit here all morning blushing like virgins. I don't want Ivy to be pregnant every ten months." He gulped the whiskey until the glass was empty. He put the empty glass on the desk.

"That thing," Armstrong turned the bottom of his own glass up before meeting Jem's eyes, "will interfere with your pleasure." He passed over a pamphlet with instructions on the care and use of an article that had been constructed for the troops going to war. "You have to be extra careful that no cracks develop in the rubber – if that happens Ivy will be pregnant. Come to me when you think you need a new one."

"Right." Jem raised his hip and shoved the precious rubber item and instructions deep into the pocket of his work trousers. "I thank you for this but you're not known as a man who does something for nothing. What do you want?"

"An invitation to the wedding."

"Talk to Ivy." Jem almost felt his jaw drop. This was all about an invitation to a registry-office ceremony? He didn't think so.

"I want to arrange the ceremony." William had no intention of attending a little hole-in-the-wall affair. "I have a friend who is willing to marry you in his chambers."

"Talk to Ivy." Jem stood. He was ready to leave. He wasn't getting in the middle of these two strong-willed people. He'd end up battered and bruised.

"Are you a man or a mouse?" Armstrong stood too.

"A smart man. Talk to Ivy." Jem wouldn't take offense. He started walking towards the door. "It's up to her."

"I'll do that." He'd just have to find the best way to convince her to let him and Betty take control of the ceremony. He walked to his office door. "I hope you've had Old Man Solomon make you a suit for the wedding?" Armstrong too wanted to put this room and this conversation behind him. "That old man is a master tailor. You lot in The Lane don't know how lucky you are to have him."

"Thanks for this." Jem ignored his comments, patting the pocket holding the item he'd searched the city for. "I appreciate it."

He almost ran from the house. He had the answer to one of his problems but he'd a feeling he'd just acquired a lot more. Ivy's uncle wanted something and he wasn't a man known for taking no for an answer.

Chapter 39

Ivy pushed her pram along the railings that surrounded Stephen's Green Park. She was almost home. She'd be glad to sit by the fire and think. The date of her wedding seemed to be galloping towards her. Everyone and his mother had an opinion about what she should, do, wear or say. She wished they'd all just leave her and Jem alone to get on with it. She approached Stephen's Lane with a slight shiver. Ever since Father Leary had attacked her she'd been nervous about stepping into this tunnel. She refused to allow that man to scare her to that extent. She took a deep breath and, grabbing her courage in both hands, marched towards the entrance. She stood inside the lip of the tunnel for a moment, waiting for her eyes to adjust to the light.

"Ivy, there you are!" The Widow Rattigan stepped out of Wilson's house where she rented the back rooms. The countrywoman's long black widow's dress was hanging on her frame, she'd lost that much weight since her husband died. "I'm getting ready to carry over the grub for that lot." She waved her hand in the direction of the livery. "I haven't the time to stop for a word." She didn't wait for a response but shouted, "Jem, I'll need some of the lads to give me a hand! Tell them to come around the back and mind me animals." Without waiting, the woman stepped back into Wilson's house, closing the door at her back.

"That woman moves like lightning." Jem had walked over to join Ivy. "I have my orders, it seems." He turned and shouted for two of the lads who were washing down the horses. "Bill, Tiny, give Mrs Rattigan a hand – don't let any of her animals out again." Mrs Rattigan had one of the best-kept little farmyards Jem had ever seen, in the back yard of Mr Wilson's house. It had taken them ages to get the geese and pig back inside their runs the last time the lads had been careless opening the back gate.

The two lads jumped to obey the order, anxious for their food. Some of them had been working since early morning without bit, bite nor hot sup – cold water didn't fill an empty belly.

"Wait a minute, love," Jem said to Ivy. "Ann Marie telephoned – we have orders to present ourselves at her house this evening." He pressed a quick kiss into her hair, knowing what he was about to say would upset her. "It seems she wants a meeting with us to discuss our wedding."

"Jem!" Ivy wanted to kick something.

"Nothing to do with me, love." He stepped out of reach of her boots. "I'm passing on the message."

"Where's Emmy?" The child was usually to be found after school playing ball against the wall of the Stephen's Lane tunnel with her friends.

"She's with her da." Jem shrugged. Edward O'Connor had permission to use Ann Marie's house as his base. He slept at his club but seemed to be spending a great deal of time with Ann Marie. The child was running between her father and Jem, seeming to have no trouble adjusting to the changes in her life. He was dreading the time when O'Connor would remove Emmy from his care altogether.

"I better get about my business. I'll need to have a wash and change me clothes if we're going out." Ivy had learned the importance of appearance. She wouldn't turn up at her friend's house looking like a rag bag. "You need to get cocked, powdered and shaved yourself, Mr Jem Ryan."

"Right, you lads!" He clapped his hands to attract the attention of the young people working around the livery. He was aware of Ivy hurrying away with her pram. "We need to get ourselves organised."

With shouted instructions the horses were returned to their stalls.

Ivy examined her image in the mirror from head to toe. She was wearing her black skirt with the big white buttons decorating one side and the matching white blouse with black buttons. She turned to check that the seams in her silk stockings were straight. The fashionable outfit would create the right impression for a visit to the home of Miss Ann Marie Gannon – she hoped.

"You look like something out of the films," Jem said when she opened her door to his knock. They had each taken a quick swill to freshen up before changing their clothes. He was wearing his good grey suit and a blazingly white cotton shirt under his dark overcoat.

"You're looking very dapper yourself, Mr Ryan." He was a fine figure of a man and no doubting, she thought.

"Give us a minute to put me hat on."

He followed her over to stand at her shoulder in front of the mirror. Jem's hat was a trilby while Ivy's was a confection of black with trailing white feathers.

"Bejesus, Jem, the state of us and the price of best butter!" Ivy grinned, delighted with the image they portrayed.

"I'll hold your coat." He took her beige cashmere coat from its peg and stood holding it open while she slipped her arms into the sleeves. She stepped to the mirror to check her appearance.

"Come on, Missus." Jem took her elbow in his hand and drew her towards the back door. "Ann Marie didn't tell me who was going to be at this meeting."

"I'm getting really fed up with people dipping their noses into our business."

Ann Marie did a final visual check of her study. She dreaded thinking of Ivy's reaction to the upcoming gathering. She examined the area she liked to think of as a meeting area. She had arranged three dark-green two-seater Chesterfield sofas with the fire on the fourth side. A glass-topped coffee table took centre place.

The sound of the doorbell rang through the house. She was ready. The room looked inviting and charming to her eyes. She hoped the first caller was Edward with good news.

"Mr O'Connor has come a-calling – again." Sadie opened the door and stepped back to allow Edward enter. She closed the door at his back as he stepped into the room.

"Have I ever mentioned, Ann Marie, how fascinating I

find your household staff?" Edward said with a laugh.

"No, I don't believe you have." Ann Marie fought a grin. She hurried over to press her cheeks against his in greeting.

"Emerald has elected to remain downstairs and lend a hand with the 'babby'," Edward said. "My daughter appears to have acquired a unique way of employing the English language."

"She is a delight." Ann Marie began to prepare a gin and tonic. She no longer needed to ask his preference. "How went the hunt this morning?" She hated to think of this man touring the places around Dublin that could have purchased a cadaver.

"We found her." He needed that drink. The grisly appearance of a body preserved for the study of the human anatomy would stay with him for the rest of his days. The scientist who had purchased the cadaver had been reluctant to lose such an unusual study subject.

"Dear Lord," she said, his words freezing her in her tracks for a moment. "You are sure?" With a deep breath she turned back to assemble their drinks. "How?"

"The embalming procedure used was excellent." He crossed to stand at her shoulder. "I identified the body myself." There was no need for him to mention the state of the body. When she turned and passed him the glass he rather rudely grabbed the drink from her hand and gulped the liquid. He needed it. "That man Armstrong you introduced me to is frighteningly efficient."

Ann Marie had been helping Edward in the search for Mary Rose Donnelly's body. Through her work at the hospital morgue Ann Marie had many useful contacts around the city. She had hoped it would be a simple matter to discover the person who had purchased the body. They had not discussed the matter with Ivy and Jem, not wanting to disappoint them if they should fail in their endeavours. They had spent weeks searching the Dublin area without success. Ann Marie had approached Betty Armstrong for advice. The woman was a mine of very useful information. She'd introduced them to her brother William. That man had contacts in some very high places.

"I telephoned the Donnelly home from my club. I informed them of her death." Edward, with Ann Marie's prompting, hoped to prevent trouble from coming to the door of the people who had protected and cared for his child.

"That must have been difficult for you." Ann Marie carried her own drink over to the Chesterfields by the fire. She sat in one and with a wave of her hand towards the sofa across from hers invited him to join her. She was unaware that the elegant copper-silk drop-waist dress she wore was complemented by the dark leather of the chair.

Edward sat. "At the time that I was informed of Emerald's death . . ." He had to stop for a moment at the memory of that horror. He had a white-knuckled grip on the glass in his hand as he fought for control. "I'm sorry," he pinched the bridge of his nose, "give me a moment, please."

Ann Marie stared into the glowing flames of the fire, giving the strong man facing her a semblance of privacy to fight his overwhelming emotions.

"I was informed," he continued when he again had control, "that Mary Rose Donnelly had taken the veil. Such was her horror at the loss of her niece that she had

252

turned to God." He intended to investigate the true happenings surrounding the deception practised on him – but that would have to wait.

"I don't know what to say," Ann Marie murmured.

"From reading the journals Jem Ryan gave to me it is obvious to me that Mary Rose Donnelly was an evil woman. I do not believe I'm being dramatic when I say that."

Ann Marie agreed but didn't say so aloud. Jem and Ivy had both told her of the condition little Emerald O'Connor had been in emotionally and physically when she'd arrived into their care.

"Do the family wish the body returned to them for burial?" Ann Marie asked.

"No." Edward looked over at the woman who was coming to mean a great deal to him. She had stood beside him through this difficult time. "When I advised them that she had died in an accident over a year ago they stated they were content to leave her where she lay. They asked only that I furnish them with a death certificate."

"Oh dear." Ann Marie didn't know what the legal situation would be after all this time.

"There is an inheritance involved apparently." Edward shrugged. It had intrigued him to learn that the Bishop Troy who seemingly wrote the letter concerning Emerald's sad demise had been enquiring after Mary Rose Donnelly. Apparently the woman had promised a large donation to the church funds. Sadly it seemed that Mary Rose Donnelly would not be mourned by her family.

"What on earth are we going to do?"

"No problem, my dear." Edward shook his head at the memory. "Armstrong is also a member of my club. He was present when I made the call. I had an official death certificate in my hand in hours – cause of death 'accidental'. I sent the document by registered post from the GPO."

"My dear, you have been busy!" Ann Marie almost wilted on the sofa. She had only had that worry for weeks. Jem and Ivy had lived with the fear of discovery for over a year. "Is that really an end to my friends' involvement in this matter?"

"I could not allow Jem Ryan to suffer for saving my daughter's life." Edward leaned forward, putting his empty glass on the table. "The man had a fortune in gold and jewels fall into his hands. Did you know that?"

"He mentioned something about 'sparklies'," Ann Marie said.

"Those 'sparklies' could set him up in a mansion and remove his need to work for the rest of his life."

"I had no idea of the financial worth, I must admit."

"I have the impression Ivy Murphy could tell you the worth down to the penny." Edward smiled. He'd been impressed by Ivy and her knowledge of antiques. "None the less, both of them decided to secure a bank box and save everything for my daughter to use in the future. It is rare to meet one completely honest person let alone two. I simply could not allow them to be punished."

"I'm very glad."

They sat for a time in silence, both wondering what the future held for them. Lost in their thoughts, they waited for the rest of Ann Marie's guests to arrive.

"My friend Ivy is not going to be happy at Armstrong's presence here this evening," Ann Marie said when the clock over the mantel chimed the time. "She'll be here soon."

"I understood the man to be her uncle?"

"It is a long story and not mine to tell." As she spoke the doorbell sounded. "That will be Ivy and Jem now."

"Stand up straight, Jem," Ivy hissed while using her elbow to nudge him in the ribs. "You look like you have the worries of the world on your shoulders." They were standing on top of the steps leading up to Ann Marie's door. "You look like you'd be better off discussing a funeral instead of our wedding."

"That's how I feel," Jem said. "I bet that fella O'Connor will be here. I can almost feel the noose around my neck every time I see the man."

"You can't show you're nervous." She knew they had to figure out a way of escaping from the trouble that was following them but it didn't do to let the world and his mother know your business. "Put your chin up, Jem, and stick your chest out." She nudged him again.

"But –"

"But me no buts, Jem Ryan – we are in this together."

"Sorry, Missus." He gently brushed his shoulder against hers. "I don't know what I'd do without you, Ivy."

"If I have my way you'll never have to find out."

"Well, are you two going to stand out there until the cows come home?" Sadie Lawless stood in the open doorway, a smile on her face. Emmy stood at her side, grinning.

"Uncle Jem, Aunty Ivy, I'm helping mind the babby." Emmy jumped into Jem's open arms.

"I'm sure you're a great help." He stepped into the hallway with the child clinging to him like a monkey.

"I hope you have the kettle on, Sadie Lawless?" Ivy

was removing her coat and hat and hanging them on the hallstand. She ignored Sadie's muttered "Cheeky madam!" and took Emmy from Jem's arms while he removed his hat and coat. "Well, Miss Emmy, did you have a fine time today with your father?"

"We had tea and cream cakes at Bewley's," Emmy said.

"Did you think to get me a cream cake?" She rubbed her nose against the little girl's, trying not to think of the heartbreak in store. She'd miss this little one so, when her father took her away.

"I didn't think!" Emmy slapped her two hands to her cheeks.

"It's not a cream cake she's needing." Jem turned to join the women. "We are supposed to be meeting Ann Marie and some other people."

"My papa is with Ann Marie in her study," Emmy informed them importantly. "I don't think there are any other people, are there, Mrs Lawless?"

"They haven't arrived yet," Sadie said. "Now hop down and come help me. Ivy wants tea – you can help me get it ready when she rings down for it." She held out her hand to the little girl. "You two know the way."

"Right." Jem offered his arm to Ivy. She put her arm through his and they walked down the hallway towards Ann Marie's study. Jem gave a quick rap of his knuckles against the door before pushing it open.

"Jem, Ivy, come on in." Ann Marie stood. She picked up Edward's empty glass. "Jem, may I offer you something to drink? I know there is no point offering Ivy anything but tea." She grinned at her two friends, delighted with the news Edward was going to give them.

"You two sit down over there. Edward has something to tell you."

"Ann Marie and I have been busy over the last few weeks," Edward said when they were sitting side by side on one of the Chesterfields. He went on to tell them about his handling of the situation regarding the woman they called 'the aunt'.

"Jem!" Ivy collapsed against Jem's side when Edward O'Connor told them what he had done. They were safe. Dear God, her Jem was safe.

"I don't know what to say." Jem took the offered whiskey from Ann Marie with a visibly trembling hand. He gulped some of the liquid and passed the glass to Ivy, insisting she take a sip to settle her nerves. He hadn't been expecting this news.

"I could not allow you to pay for my error in judgement." Edward took Ann Marie's hand when she sat by his side after placing their drinks on the table. He had spent these weeks mentally kicking himself. How had he ever imagined that Mary Rose Donnelly would be a suitable guardian to his only child? He wasn't the first man to lose his wife to childbirth. What kind of parent was he that he'd taken to his heels at the first sign of adversity, leaving his child behind?

"I don't know if I'm on my head or my heels." Jem could feel the worry draining out of him. He could marry his Ivy now with no shadow over their heads.

"That will be Betty and William Armstrong," Ann Marie said when the doorbell sounded through the house.

"Have yeh lost the run of yourself, Ann Marie?" Ivy yelped. "What are they doing here?"

Chapter 40

"Ivy, are you awake?" a soft voice whispered.

"I am now." Ivy rolled over in the big sweet-smelling bed. It took her a minute to remember where she was – in Ann Marie's house in one of the guest bedrooms. The fire in the grate burned brightly – someone had crept in while she slept and tended the fire. She wasn't sure how she felt about that.

"May I go in, now she's awake?" Emmy obviously didn't wait for permission. She bounced up onto the bed and grinned widely at Ivy. "Today is the day you marry my Uncle Jem." Emmy's long black hair was wrapped in rags Ivy had put in the night before to shape the hair into big fat ringlets. The little girl shook her head now, delighted with the fuss.

"Is that a fact?" Ivy pushed herself up in the bed. Ann Marie rushed forward to arrange the pillows at Ivy's back. Sadie entered the room with a well-filled tea tray. Betty Armstrong brought up the rear.

"What time is it?" Ivy looked around at the smiling faces. How were you supposed to handle opening your eyes to so much company first thing in the morning?

"It's only just gone eight," Betty Armstrong answered. "We have plenty of time to get you ready."

"No point in asking you if you want a cup of tea, Ivy," Sadie Lawless, her rag-wrapped hair bouncing, said.

They'd had a ladies' evening in Ann Marie's house the night before. Hair was curled, brows plucked, facials and manicures were given – all under Betty's supervision. It had been a celebration of femininity.

"I'm not going to drink tea in this bed." Ivy was terrified of spilling tea on the pure Irish linen bedclothes. She had never slept in anything so beautiful.

"While you go into the bathroom, me and my Clare are going to set up an occasional table here to put the tea things on. I told this lot," Sadie gave a jerk of her head at the other two women, "that you would never agree to coming down to the morning room in your new lingerie."

"I'm not running around the house in me scanties!" Ivy yelped. "The very idea!"

"Told yez," Sadie grinned.

"Your new negligee set is perfectly respectable," Ann Marie said without much hope of shifting Ivy. She had bought the set as a wedding gift. It was in no way scanty. "And apart from one baby boy we are a totally female household at the moment."

"Give us a cup of that tea to take with me, please, Sadie." Ivy waited to see if anyone would look away when she threw back the bedcovers. Every eye in the place was on her. With silent thanks for the cover of the long white nightdress she pushed her feet towards the floor. A quick shake of her body had the nightdress covering her from neck to ankle.

"Wet your hair well and I'll put the pin curls in now,

Ivy," Betty Armstrong instructed. She had washed and conditioned Ivy's hair the previous evening but if she'd put the pin curls in then sleep would have been impossible. She was thrilled to be one of the bride's attendants.

Ivy took the tea from Sadie's hand and hurried into the en-suite bathroom. She needed to relieve her bladder before she did anything else. She pulled the chain on the toilet with a wide grin. The luxury! She drank the tea, then bent at the waist to put her head under the hot-water tap. The water was only warm but that was fine. She wrapped a white towel around her head and with a deep breath stepped back into the fray.

"Ivy," Sadie said as soon as Ivy walked through the door, "have you the stomach for a full Irish breakfast?"

"Surely not!" Betty Armstrong stared. "We don't want the bride throwing up on her groom."

"Perhaps something delicate like a poached egg and a thin slice of toast?" Ann Marie suggested.

"Would the lot of you relax, please?" Ivy tried not to snarl.

They were enjoying themselves.

"Something light before the service then back here for the wedding breakfast." Ann Marie had arranged for the Skellys to be on hand to cater the wedding breakfast.

"Sit down here." Betty pulled the delicate white wrought-iron chair away from the matching dressing table. "I'll put the pin curls in your hair now. The curls will be the finishing touch. Sadie, you better pour her another cup of tea or we'll get nothing done."

"Ivy," Clare Lawless, her hair in rags and a baby on her hip, entered the room, "Jem telephoned – he wanted to know if you had a bag packed. He sounded very nervous."

Dora Lawless had chosen to remain in the kitchen with Eleanor Skelly.

"I have, thank you." Ivy and Jem were going to spend the first days of their marriage at Ann Marie's Dalkey estate.

"I told him that if there were any problems I'd let him know," Betty Armstrong said through a mouthful of hairgrips.

Ivy looked and listened to the fuss going on around her. The quiet, private wedding ceremony she imagined had grown into a major event. Her wedding day seemed to have taken on a life of its own. She felt powerless to stop what sometimes felt like a runaway train.

William Armstrong insisted he should be allowed give the bride away. She wasn't fooled into thinking he gave two hoots about her. He was out to impress Ann Marie and, through her, her social circle. Still, with all the help he'd been settling the matter of the aunt's body how could she refuse? He'd organised for a judge, a personal friend of his, to conduct the ceremony in his chambers. John and Jem had spent the night at the Baggot Street house with William Armstrong having a 'gentlemen's evening'.

"Will you miss me?" Emmy came over to stand by the dressing table and watch.

"We won't be away for long." Ivy smiled at the young girl's image in the mirror.

"I'll miss you." Emmy didn't want to be left behind.

"We'll have a big street party when we come back," Ivy promised. "Perhaps Ann Marie could teach you a new party piece?" Emmy had taken to performing like a duck to water.

The morning passed in a rush with everyone getting in on the act. Ivy was punched and poked until she wanted to scream. Everyone seemed to have set ideas on what was needed.

She stood before the mirror with a crowd of beautifully dressed, tearful females at her back. Ann Marie had insisted that a new dress for the bride was essential. Ivy had thought to buy a second-hand suit. She stood before the mirror in her dress, admiring her own image. The dress was the shortest she had ever worn. It was a dropped-waist, violet underdress covered by an overdress of gleaming white broderie anglaise. The white fabric was artfully gathered inches above the hem of the violet underdress. The sleeves were broderie anglaise, revealing her arms underneath. Her white lace cloche hat framed her face.

"Well," Betty Armstrong stood back from Ivy and admired her own handiwork, "you have something blue in the violet of your dress, I suppose. The new of course is everything else. For something borrowed I have some pearl earrings."

"Oh, that would be perfect." Ann Marie took her hand from the pocket of her own coffee-coloured silk suit. She pulled out a string of pearls. "I had thought to offer these, but they can be considered something old."

Ivy could only stare openmouthed. Pearls – I ask your sacred pardon. Who did they think she was – the Queen of the May?

"You put these on, Betty." Ann Marie passed the pearls into Betty's hands. "I'm going to go set up my camera." She almost ran from the room. Ivy looked so beautiful. She wanted to record every precious minute of this day.

"Me, Papa, me, me, me!" Emmy ran between the newly

married couple. She stood grinning broadly while the photograph was taken. Edward had been drafted in as Ann Marie's assistant.

"Am I the world's worst because I want to wrap the bloody camera around Ann Marie's neck?" Ivy hissed from behind clenched teeth and a forced smile.

"Just grin and bear it." Jem too was fed up. He wanted Ivy to himself. They were married. He wanted to act like it.

"I don't know these people." Ivy continued to smile, glassy-eyed. The reception felt like a punishment. "I notice the Lawless family left as soon as they could. Everyone else seems to be having a great time impressing each other."

"Armstrong is having the time of his life, glad-handing Ann Marie's relations." Jem obeyed the order to put his arm around Ivy's waist.

Ivy had been surprised to see Ann Marie's uncle and his family here.

The dining room was being cleared of the remains of the bridal breakfast. The group were gathered in the festively decorated second withdrawing room. People were standing about sipping champagne and chatting.

Ivy felt as if the walls were closing in on her. She obeyed the order to stand with her hand on Jem's shoulder when someone had produced a chair for him to sit in. She'd seen stiff wedding photographs like this in many of the homes around The Lane. She was surprised Ann Marie would want something so formal.

"That group Armstrong is leading over to Charles Gannon must be his wife and children, don't you think?" Jem stood up when ordered.

"Just a few more." Ann Marie could see the storm-clouds in Ivy's eyes. Her friend didn't like all of this attention. But this was an important day in a woman's life. She wanted Ivy to have a record of the occasion. She was determined to get a family picture involving Ivy and all of the Armstrongs. It was past time that connection was recognised. If Ivy's family were going to use her to their own ends then they could claim her as a blood relation. She'd explained the situation to Edward. He was organising the group picture at this moment. It only needed the bride and groom.

"No." Ivy dug in her heels when she saw where she was being led.

"Ivy!" Ann Marie urged.

"No."

"Ivy," Jem bent to whisper in her ear, "Betty will be going back to America soon. Let her have this picture to take with her." He saw the refusal on her lips. "Think of the explanations Armstrong will be forced to make to his family after this. Besides, love, you can send a copy to your Shay over in America. I'm sure he'd enjoy seeing everyone together."

"Can we leave soon?" She could feel people staring at her. It was making her skin itch.

"Just as soon as Ann Marie has her family photographs we will run out of here," he promised.

"I'm starving," Ivy whispered.

"Sadie packed a basket for us." He'd known Ivy wouldn't be able to eat with all of these people looking at her. "It's in the back of my automobile."

"Let's be doing this then." She put her chin in the air and with her head held high walked over to join her father's relations.

"Oh, oh!" Jem recognised that light in her eyes.

"Ann Marie, shouldn't you introduce me to these people?" Her smile could have cut glass.

Ann Marie, a polite smile on her face, performed the introduction with style. It gave her great pleasure to see the shock on the faces of Armstrong's family when she included the family connection in the introductions. Let him talk himself out of that!

Ivy allowed herself to be pushed into position – well aware of the cat that had just been put among the pigeons.

Betty Armstrong stood by her brother's side, delighted with life. She planned to have a copy of this photograph framed on her New York mantelpiece.

"That is it." Ivy had had enough. Ann Marie had run out of film. She wasn't going to wait until the camera had been reloaded.

"Time for the bride and groom to leave!" Jem said loudly, grabbing Ivy to his side before she could say more. "I hope you all enjoy yourself. Thank you for coming." Without another word he pulled her from the room. "I don't know if that is how the thing is done," he whispered to his glaring bride. "I don't care though. Let's get out of here."

Chapter 41

"We should visit Dalkey Island while we're here." Jem didn't take his eyes off the road in front of him. "Ann Marie said that the fishermen will take people out to the island for a few pence."

Ivy kept her eyes focused on the sea that ran along one side of the road in a stormy grey path that seemed to stretch into infinity.

An uncomfortable silence settled over the pair.

Ivy was scared. She'd never found it difficult to talk to Jem. Why was she feeling tongue-tied now?

"Did I tell you that you looked lovely today?" He wished he'd taken the time to remove his suit jacket.

"You didn't look so bad yerself, Mr Ryan." She wanted to scream. They were acting like strangers.

The whole day had been strange. She'd wanted to walk into the registry office, get the words said and leave. Was that so wrong? The reaction of her friends to her plans had seemed extreme to her. She'd finally stepped back and allowed them to take the matter out of her hands. Their wedding guests had been mostly strangers. Now look at them. They were acting like polite strangers who had been forced to spend time together.

"Do you think Ann Marie got enough photographs?" Jem said slyly, his eyes still on the road stretching in front of them.

"It was lucky you pulled me out of there." Ivy looked over at the man who was now her husband and grinned. "I was thinking of making her eat her infernal camera."

"I thought I saw smoke coming out your ears." He moved one hand from the steering wheel to pat her thigh.

"Still and all, everyone seemed to be enjoying themselves." A wedding breakfast. I ask your scared pardon, she thought. Who had come up with that nonsense? They'd been standing around like shop dummies. She preferred a good funeral herself.

"They'll have more fun now that we've left." He took her hand in his and returned their joined hands to the wheel. "I believe that's how it's supposed to be anyway."

"More power to them." She stared at their joined hands for a moment. "It's been a funny aul day. I don't know if I'm on me head or me heels." She gave herself a silent lecture about relaxing and enjoying herself before turning her attention to the passing scenery.

"We'll stop for a picnic on the way," he said. "I've a blanket and the basket of food Sadie packed in the back."

"Jesus, Jem," Ivy stood in the open doorway of the bedroom Ann Marie had prepared for them, "this room is nearly the size of the bloody livery!"

She exaggerated. The long wide room had beautiful bevelled windows directly across from the entrance. Yellow embroidered Chinese silk curtains opened onto a view of the sea. A small table with two dainty chairs sat in the nook formed by the bend of the window.

"Not quite." Jem too was overcome with the luxury of their surroundings. When they had visited the estate to see where they would be staying he'd been gobsmacked. The place intimidated him.

"I feel like the country cousin even though we're city people." Ivy tried to take everything in.

A four-poster bed draped in yellow silk stood proudly inches away from the wall that stretched from the doorway to the window. A huge black marble fireplace, a turf fire set ready for a match in the grate, was to the left of where they stood in the open doorway.

"Well, we can't stand here like statues." He took her elbow and led her into the luxurious room, closing the door at their backs.

"It was good of Ann Marie to loan us her house." Ivy wanted to laugh hysterically. She walked over to the dressing table. Standing in front of the high mirror, she began to remove the hat pins from her lace-covered white cloche hat.

"It's been quite a day." Jem slowly walked to the wide window. He put his hat and cashmere overcoat onto the small table. He stared out the window at the white-capped grey waves that raced towards the house. There wasn't another house in sight. A soft whisper of sound had him glancing back over his shoulder. Ivy had removed her shoes and was reaching under her dress to remove her silk stockings. He stared at the unexpected intimacy for a moment before returning his eyes to the view outside.

"I don't know what to do with meself." Ivy's naked feet were tickled by the rich Persian carpet under her feet. She joined Jem at the window, both staring out at the sea view.

"There's neither of us accustomed to having time on our hands. I'll put a light to the fire." He went to take care of putting a match to the kindling in the grate. "I suppose you want a pot of tea," he said over his shoulder.

"I can wait." She picked up Jem's coat and hat, carrying them over to the freestanding wardrobe. She turned the key in the lock and opened the door. A whiff of some kind of perfume wafted out of the hidden depths of the wardrobe. She didn't know what it was, never having smelled sandalwood before in her life. "Me head is still a bit off from all that champagne Ann Marie poured down us at the wedding breakfast."

"Fair enough."

Jem picked their cases up from the floor just inside the door. Ivy's he put on the dresser. He wasn't touching her things. He put his own case on the blanket-box at the end of the bed. He hadn't known what to pack. What did anyone else wear on their honeymoon? He knew the nobs seemed to change their clothes every two minutes but he and Ivy wouldn't have enough clothes for that kind of malarkey. Was he supposed to put his unmentionables beside hers in the dresser of drawers? He wouldn't be having these problems if they'd stayed in their own place.

The knock on the bedroom door frightened the life out of Ivy. She looked around frantically, almost tempted to jump into the wardrobe. She wouldn't think of allowing a man not her husband to see her naked legs – she pulled open a door she'd only just noticed and almost jumped into the open space.

She stood with her ear pressed to the door, listening to Jem tell Martin Skelly that they would tend to themselves. More power to him – she wouldn't want to do it. She turned her attention to the space around her. "In the name of all that's good and holy!" She stared in openmouthed surprise at the most decadent bathroom she'd ever seen in her life.

"Ivy!" Jem's yell carried from the other room.

"In here!" She opened the door and peeked out. Jem was alone. "Come in here and have a gander," she invited, opening the door wide.

"Sweet Lord . . ." Jem stared around him.

"That toilet seat is fit for the arse of the King of England." Ivy pointed to the square toilet cabinet framed in mahogany. "Have yeh ever seen anything like all them mirrors? You'd see yourself coming and going." She eyed the claw-foot bathtub sitting proudly in the middle of the room. She'd be having a dip in that – mirrors or no mirrors.

"Martin Skelly told me this is a guest bedroom," Jem almost whispered, overawed by his surroundings. "If the guest room is this fancy, I wonder what the family rooms are like?"

"We'll have a nosy." Ivy promised herself a tour of the mansion house. "I'm going to change." She almost ran over to grab her case from the dresser. "I'll feel more comfortable in a skirt that reaches me ankles even if it is old-fashioned." She'd packed her white summer suit into the case. It would do for sitting around this fancy guest room. "I'll only be a minute." She pushed Jem from the bathroom.

"That's better." Ivy came out of the bathroom wearing the long white skirt Mr Solomon had made for her, using one of a pair of fine Irish linen sheets. She'd matched it with a high-neck lace blouse.

270

Jem had removed his suit jacket and waistcoat. He was standing before the long windows in his suit pants and fine white shirt. "I was wondering if you would like to go for a walk along the sand in a little while." He was nervous now that it was just the two of them in a bedroom.

"Jem," Ivy began as she walked towards him, an uncertain smile on her face. "Jem," she said again, "can we go to bed now?" She wanted to get that out of the way. She had a case of the collywobbles that was going to send her running to hide in the bathroom if they didn't get down to it soon.

"It's a bit early." Jem's ears burned.

"Let's just get it over with."

"Is that how you think of it? Something to get over?"

"I'm that nervous me knees are knocking together." Ivy grabbed for his hands, needing to touch him. "I'm surprised you can't hear them. I want to go to bed with you. Lord knows it was all I could do sometimes to call a halt to our kissing and hugging. I want to go to bed and lie in your arms and see where it takes us. Am I a shameless woman, Jem?"

"Come here then." Jem pulled her into his arms.

They stood before the wide window, kissing and caressing each other, each shyly uncertain of the next move. The familiar passion between them burned hot and bright, taking them to a world of their own making, their seeking hands becoming trapped in the unfamiliar task of removing each other's clothing.

"Well," Ivy put her head on Jem's naked shoulder and smiled, "I won't be jumping out of this bed to write sonnets to yer eyebrows, Jem Ryan."

"Is that a fact?" He laughed softly.

"I wasn't '*transported to an Isle of Delight*'," Ivy whispered into his naked flesh. She'd read that in a book she'd picked up at the market. "Were you?"

"In the name of Jesus, Ivy Murphy, what are you talking about now?" He stared at the pleated material that formed a ceiling over the four-poster bed and waited for her explanation.

"I read it in a book," she tittered. "This fella kissed a girl and she was instantly transported to an Isle of Delight."

"Brother Theo never gave you a book like that."

"That's a fact." Ivy stretched her body. She cuddled into his side, throwing one leg over his thighs, delighting in the feel of his long naked muscled body against her own.

She must remember to thank Betty Armstrong for her words of advice. Although, maybe not . . . she'd almost burned up she'd blushed that much when the woman was telling her what to do and how to do it. It was strange to think it was an unmarried woman who had taken the time to sit Ivy down and advise her on the intimacy to be found in the marriage bed. The woman certainly seemed to know her onions.

"Are you all right, Ivy?" Jem raised his head from the soft feather pillow to look down at the woman tucked into his side. He could only see the top of her head.

"I don't know." She moved her head slightly to meet his concerned green eyes. "You're the expert in this bed, Jem Ryan." She didn't think this was the first time Jem had indulged in bed sport. "Shouldn't you be the one telling me if it was alright?"

"Woman, you'll be the death of me." He moved his body, setting her gently off to one side. He pushed his body to the side of the big bed.

"Where are you going?" Ivy rose up on her elbow to watch the show as her new husband slid out from underneath the bedclothes.

"I'll be right back." He hurried towards the bathroom door. The rubber thing he'd put on before making love to Ivy was beginning to pinch, hurting him in a most delicate area.

Ivy fell back onto the pillows with a sigh. Betty Armstrong said enjoying bed sport with your husband wasn't a sin. That was more than anyone else had told her. She was grateful for the advice – left to herself she'd have made a right mess of the whole thing. She'd enjoyed herself well enough with what they had done here in this bed. She supposed it was like riding one of them big heavy bicycles of Jem's. The more you practised, the better you got.

She nestled further into the soft bed, her eyes examining the room around her. It was far from it she was raised. She wondered idly if there was something wrong with her because she'd have preferred to be in her own home. This would be the second time in her life she'd spent a night away from The Lane. It was different from last night. She'd had old friends around her then, everyone fussing about the wedding. Here she was in a strange house run by people she didn't know and to top it all off she was far away from everything she knew.

Ivy's sigh almost shook the bed. She didn't know what to do with herself. It was still early – was she supposed to spend the evening in bed? What the heck were the rules?

"I've started running a bath for you." Jem was standing in the open doorway of the bathroom, a white towel wrapped around his waist. "Or are you planning on spending the rest of the day in that bed?"

"You might be a useful man to have around, Jem Ryan." Ivy turned in the bed, coming up on her elbow again. She was careful to insure the dazzlingly white linen top sheet covered her private bits. "I was lying here wondering what I was going to do with meself."

"Well," he said, looking over his shoulder to check the running taps, "hop out of your nest, little bird. This bath won't be long filling."

"Give us your shirt." She pointed to his white shirt thrown on the floor. "I'm not wanton enough to run around the place in me birthday suit."

"Shame." He went to pick the shirt off the floor. It wasn't like him to throw his good clothes around the place.

"Jem," Ivy turned to look into his eyes as he sat and held the shirt open for her, "what was that thing you put on . . . ?" Her eyes travelling to his towel-wrapped lap supplied the words she felt incapable of uttering aloud.

"Your –" he started and stopped. He knew better than to refer to William Armstrong as her uncle – his Ivy believed titles of respect like uncle and aunt had to be earned. "Billy Flint gave it to me. According to him it's a thing they developed for the young lads going off to war." He felt more comfortable for some reason thinking of the man who gave him the rubber sheath as Billy Flint.

"What's it for?" She didn't want to guess and get it wrong. She hid her blush by lowering her head to button the shirt.

"It's to stop a woman getting pregnant." Jem slid off the bed. He hadn't enjoyed wearing the thing. He was going to put it to soak in the bathroom – perhaps hot water would soften the rubber. He wanted to try and stretch it. Perhaps they made them in a bigger size?

"Oh." She joined him on the bedroom floor without another word. Together they crossed to the bathroom.

"Which one of us gets the end with the taps?" Ivy was determined to enter this new world of married women with an open mind and heart. Betty Armstrong had advised her to 'start as she meant to go on'. She wanted to explore every new experience with Jem – even if she did feel like her body was on fire with the blush that travelled from her hair to her toes.

"Neither of us." Jem felt like the luckiest man in the world. His Ivy was not a shy young miss having to be cajoled every inch of the way. He should have known she'd surprise him even here. "I'll get in first." He dropped the towel after shutting off the running water and checking the temperature of the bath. He stepped in, settling his back comfortably into the curved rim. "You'll have to drop that shirt." He grinned at the sight of Ivy clutching onto the shirt for dear life. "Unless you're planning to wash the thing?"

"You're full of yourself, Mr Ryan." She released her death grip on the shirt front and, before her nerves could get to her, pulled it off, giving her new husband a view of her in all her naked glory.

"I am that, Mrs Ryan." He slapped the water. "Now climb in here."

"How?"

"With your back to me." He held up his arms, taking

275

hold of her hips when she obeyed his instruction. He helped her settle between his spread legs.

"You didn't learn this at the Tara Street Public Baths," She was glad her back was plastered to his chest because she didn't know where to put her eyes.

"You'd be surprised." He didn't intend to tell her about the bath attendants that would join a man in his bath for a few pence extra.

"Did Billy Flint really give you that thingy?" She could talk about this now that her back was to him. She settled down in the warm water, more content than she could remember being before in her life.

"Yes." He moved his hips slightly, settling more comfortably into the bath. "Most embarrassing conversation I've ever had with another man in my life."

"Stop moving, you'll drown the floor."

"No, I won't." He used his foot to point at the overflow in the bathtub. "The water runs out there."

"You'll never get me out of here."

"When you make all that money from old Granny's potions that Betty Armstrong talks about – then you can have a bath like this for yourself."

"I won't be holding me breath for that. That woman – she talks pounds when we haven't pennies." The bathroom was silent for a moment before she asked, "Jem, you were only joking before when you said it," she stopped to gather her courage, "but would you teach me to drive out with old Rosie hitched to that little cart?"

"What are you thinking of now, Ivy Murphy?" He leaned forward to try and see her face.

"That's Mrs Ryan to you, Mister." She pushed back against him with a grin.

"You didn't answer the question, Mrs Ryan." He bit gently at the pale white flesh of her shoulder.

"It was seeing all those fancy houses we passed on the way out here to Dalkey," She turned her head slightly to meet his eyes. "I wouldn't mind paying a visit to the back door of some of those fancy houses. But it would be a bit of a march to take with me pram."

"I'll teach you how to hitch up old Rosie and drive her if that's what you want." He'd promise her anything when she called herself Mrs Ryan. "Don't you think you might be taking on a bit much though?"

"I'll never know until I try." She quite fancied the thought of herself trotting out in her own pony and cart like one of the nobs.

The bathroom was silent while they both became lost in their thoughts. Ivy had visions of herself driving around country lanes behind Rosie. Who knew what she could score from some of the mansions dotted around the country?

They settled into the bath. There was no thought of soap or scrubbing – they simply enjoyed the new experience. The bathroom echoed to heavy breathing as they explored each other. With gentle brushes from fingertips they explored the differences between them.

Chapter 42

"There yeh are, Ivy – it's fresh and well yer looking."

"Morning, Sam," Ivy said to the back of the man hurrying past her to reach Hop-a-long's refreshment stall at the Smithfield Market. She didn't take her eyes from her notebook. She was checking off the items on her list, one by one, making sure she'd done everything she'd planned for that morning.

"Time yeh put that pram of yours to a better use, Ivy."

She ignored the comment about her pram. God knows it wasn't the first time she'd heard it.

"Do you have someone to fetch a mug of tea for yeh, Sally?" Eleven o'clock in the morning, she knew, most stallholders stopped to have a mug of tea with whatever packed lunch they had brought to the market with them. Some had families that brought their meals down to them at the market stall – they too needed to buy a mug of Hop-a-long's tea. Some like Sam who had just walked past her paid a lad to watch their stall while they took a well-earned break.

"Me youngest will be here soon, love, thanks." Sally gave the customer fingering the items on her stall a glare.

"Marriage suits yeh, love," another stallholder shouted as she pushed her pram past his stall.

"It does, thanks." She was learning how to live with someone else around the place. It wasn't always easy. But there were advantages. This morning had started with a kiss. A fine way to start any day. Then she'd crawled from the bed and made a pot of tea for herself and Jem on the Primus stove he'd bought. The muggy weather made using the black range a miserable experience. The little paraffin-filled stove boiled the water for her tea without heating the room.

"E'er a whisper?" She didn't know which of the stallholders had shouted that question.

Ivy thought if she had a penny for every time she'd heard the same remarks she'd be a wealthy woman. She'd been married for six full weeks now and people were beginning to check out her figure in a way that she secretly found very offensive. She didn't pass any remark though – it was the Irish way, she supposed.

"Did yer mate not come with yeh today? I washed me face special, like, for the photos." A stallholder in the crowd gathered around the refreshment stall nudged her as she parked her pram out of the way.

Ann Marie had become such a familiar figure around the Dublin markets that people were beginning to look behind Ivy as if expecting her friend to be standing at her shoulder. Ann Marie was in Galway with Edward O'Connor and Emmy. They had been away ten days. She hoped they would be returning soon.

Hop-a-long held an enormous teapot aloft while he poured tea in a continuous stream into the closely packed enamel mugs on his counter. He ignored the good-natured

279

ribbing his customers were giving Ivy. While they were chatting to her they were giving someone else a rest.

"I saw that, Mikey Miles!" Hop-a-long shouted. "Put yer money on me counter before yeh take a mug of tea. Yeh know the rules as well as the next man, yeh bloody chancer!"

"I'll fix yeh up later, Hop-a-long." Mikey tried to shuffle back out of the crowd around Hop-a-long's market stall. The dealers packed tightly in front of the stall refused to move and let him through. They all had experience of Mikey helping himself to what didn't belong to him. "I'm a bit short, don't yeh know? I'll be flush later when I get a bit more business under me belt."

"Come back then." Quick as a flash Hop-a-long pulled the mug out of Mikey's hand.

"I started drinking that," Mikey shouted. "Yeh won't be able to sell it to someone else."

"I'll make the same amount of money from it any way you look at it." Hop-a-long emptied the mug of tea onto the cobbles under his feet. "I'm not standing here for the good of me health. Come back when you have money to pay for yer tea like everyone else. I'm not runnin' a bleedin' charity house."

Ivy stood sipping tea from an enamel mug. The routine of the market was as familiar to her as her own face. She hid her face in her mug, content to stand and watch, a silent figure among the noisy stallholders and market shoppers.

"I'm off." She returned her mug to the counter. "See yez all next week if God spares us." She didn't wait to hear the response. She wanted to get on her way. This spell of muggy weather was taking the energy out of her. She felt very daring in her brightly coloured drop-waist dress. The short cap sleeves and open neck of the dress allowed what little breeze there was to cool her damp skin. They needed a storm – something to break this weather that felt to her like walking along covered by a damp blanket.

"Miss Rose, isn't it?"

Ivy felt the hair rise on the back of her neck. Who in the market would know to call her by that name? She turned slowly to face the woman who had called her name aloud – her mind frantically working at possible outcomes of this unexpected encounter.

"Mrs Felman, isn't it?" She wondered what the woman – Hannah Solomon's mother-in-law – was doing in the market. She'd never seen her here before. There was no use in pretending she didn't recognise the woman. She'd just have to brazen it out. She thanked God that Hannah and Betty Armstrong had set sail for America a little over two weeks ago.

"I thought I recognised you." Mrs Felman examined Ivy with eagle eyes. "I believe I saw you in our shop – with my daughter-in-law, wasn't it?"

"I stopped in from time to time, yes." Ivy was aware of the dark-clothed men closing in on where they stood. Manny Felman was not giving up hope of grabbing his errant wife off the streets. She'd been aware of his men searching the streets and markets but this was the first time anyone had approached her. "I generally buy my supplies in bulk." She left it at that, not wanting to babble and appear nervous.

"Mr Solomon, a relation by marriage, mentioned you in passing last Shabbath." She searched Ivy's eyes intently as two of her son's men came to stand at her shoulder.

"I know Mr Solomon well." Ivy knew Shabbath was a

Jewish day of rest. A lot of Jewish families came together Friday evening to celebrate. She hadn't known Mr Solomon joined Hannah's in-laws. "He is a neighbour of mine." She waited to see what would happen next. She didn't want to turn her back on these people.

"Yes, he mentioned a neighbour who made use of skilled needlewomen."

So that was it. Ivy felt her heart thumping against her ribcage. They thought Hannah might be working for her. Well, they were too late. Hannah was safely away. Billy Flint had lent his expertise to spiriting Hannah away without anyone being any the wiser.

"That is correct." Ivy put one hand on the handle of her pram and smiled sweetly – she hoped. "Do you know of some women who might be interested in making dolls' clothing? I must admit I never thought of your store as a source of skilled needlewomen – remiss of me." She waited with raised eyebrows.

"Certainly not." Mrs Felman's many chins waggled in outrage. To think that she might know women who sought menial labour – the cheek of the woman!

"That is a shame. I can always use additional skilled needlewomen." Ivy took a firm grip on the handle of her pram and with an abrupt nod stepped away from the woman and her cronies. "Good day to you, Mrs Felman." She didn't take a decent breath until she'd walked several steps away and no hairy-knuckled hand had been put to her shoulder.

Ivy pushed her pram easily along the Dublin streets. She was aware of the people around her but this time alone – one among many – gave her a chance to think. She missed Emmy running around the place. Would they get to spend more time with the little one? She knew Jem was heartbroken but they didn't talk about it. What would be the point?

"Howayeh, Missus, fancy a dip?" a cheeky child shouted as she approached one of the many street water fountains. The little boy ran naked around the cement basin of the fountain.

"I'd love one," Ivy laughed at the children splashing and screaming about in the water, "but I think I'd be arrested if I tried."

She stopped her pram, took a large man's handkerchief from her dress pocket and dipped the fabric in the fresh water splashing from the mouth of the fountain. She gave into temptation and held both hands out to the rushing water, glad of the chill.

"Enjoy yourselves!" she shouted, turning away.

"Ivy!"

"Brother Theo." She'd been aware this fountain was situated at the end of the street that housed the Friary but she hadn't expected to see any of the friars out and about – not in this heat. "Are you not cooked in that heavy habit?" She hadn't seen this man in ages. She'd been dropping off her homework and picking up fresh lessons and books from the friary door.

"This weather is trying." Theo took a handkerchief from one of the pockets of his long brown woollen habit. "I thought to do as you have just done and cool myself down a little." He stepped past her to wet the cloth, striking the street kids dumb. "How have you been, Ivy?" He turned away from the fountain, knowing his presence inhibited the street children. He took several steps away, expecting Ivy to follow.

"I've been getting along fine." She'd missed seeing him

around The Lane – missed their talks. Brother Theo insisted Ivy learn to think for herself and question the world around her.

"I'm sorry I haven't had time to visit The Lane lately." He ran the chilled cloth over his sweating face and neck.

In fact he'd been ordered to keep away from The Lane by his Abbot. Father Leary appeared to have many powerful friends. The parish priest had begun a campaign of whispers against Brother Theo that was causing him some level of discomfort.

"It is too hot to stand out here." Theo was aware of the curious eyes upon them. "I will be returning to my home for a short break but I will leave some prepared lessons for you at the friary." Theo pushed the damp cloth into one of his deep pockets. He'd love to pull up his habit and step into the water with the children.

"Thanks, Brother." Ivy wished she felt confident enough to question him about his absence from her life. She appreciated the education she continued to receive but she missed his teaching skill.

"I'll correct your work when I return. I'll telephone you when I have done so. God go with you, Ivy."

"See yeh, Brother."

Theo gave her a quick nod of his head and turned away. He felt better in himself. He would find a way to deal with Leary. The man would not be allowed to dictate his actions. Besides, he liked Ivy's totally irreverent attitude towards him – it kept him humble.

Ivy grabbed the handle of her pram and prepared to continue her journey home. The people of The Lane had set out for the seaside early that morning. The women pushed their prams packed with children and supplies to the nearby Sandymount Strand. She thought she'd join them as soon as she'd dropped off her pram and changed her clothes. Maybe Jem would like to come along with her. He could take some of the stable lads and horses along.

A dip in the cold sea water would do everyone a world of good. This weather was giving man and beast a hard time. Some people had taken to sleeping in the entry tunnels to The Lane. The muggy heat made the overpacked tenement rooms miserable.

Thinking of visiting Sandymount Strand put a kick in her step. A cool paddle in the sea was practically calling her name. She slowed her steps approaching the O'Connell Street ice-cream parlour. Burton Moriarty, a man who thought a lot of himself, had bought her an ice cream from that parlour once upon a time.

"Well, think of the devil and he'll appear." She stopped her pram, not wishing the man to see her.

Burton Moriarty, wearing tennis whites just as he had when she'd met him, was holding the door of the ice-cream shop open. Two fancy vehicles sat waiting in the street close to the shop. Ivy was on the opposite side of the street. She leaned her weight against the base of the new Daniel O'Connell statue. She'd watch a minute and catch her breath.

"That's not his wife his fingers are rushing all over," Ivy muttered. The shadow cast by the statue at her back was welcome. She watched Burton kiss the hand of a laughing young woman. The two ran to the vehicle parked behind the other. Still laughing, they jumped into the open-topped vehicle. "They must be what the papers are calling 'bright young things' – well for them."

She continued to watch.

"God!" The air left her lungs.

Two of her brothers, wearing whites, each with a laughing girl on his arm, rushed out of the ice-cream parlour. Eamo and Petey. What were they doing here? Did they know Moriarty was their cousin? She collapsed against the wall at her back, her hand to her mouth. She must have made a noise because her brother Eamo looked directly at her. She waited for him to call her name. There was only a year in age between the two of them. He'd been gone for years. He looked so much like their father. She felt tears fill her eyes. The pain of his glance almost crippled her. Eamo, her own brother, visually examined her from hair to toes and dismissed her.

"Let us away, cousin!" the man once known as Eamo Murphy shouted to Burton, leaping into the driver's seat of the front vehicle.

His younger brother seated the two ladies and cranked both cars before jumping into the back seat. "I intend to beat you soundly at tennis," Eamo said. "I give you fair warning." He turned the key and without a glance in Ivy's direction drove away.

"God!" The pain was physical. She wanted to throw up. She was icy cold, trembling. "Shay warned me you'd become a pompous hypocrite, Eamo. But seeing is believing."

She watched the vehicles head in the direction of Grafton Street. She'd walk along the Liffey. She didn't want to chance bumping into them again. He'd called Moriarty 'cousin'. It seemed they were all one big happy family.

"The two of them looked well." Ivy pushed her body

away from the shadows. She could stop worrying about them. They had made a new life for themselves. Wasn't she doing the self-same thing? "I won't be giving you a second thought, Eamo Murphy." With her pram firmly in hand, she began the walk home. She had a husband waiting for her. If her face was wet with tears as she travelled the sweltering streets no one noticed.

Chapter 43

"Well, isn't it well for yez?" she exclaimed, catching sight of Jem and some of his lads, naked from the waist up, trousers rolled up, feet bare, as they used a pump hose to wet the horses and themselves down. They were working in the newly opened yard that led directly to the Stephen's Lane tunnel. The hulking shape of the livery at their backs cast a long shadow over the yard.

She wouldn't allow the insult offered her by her two brothers to spoil her day. She could tell Jem later in the privacy of their bed.

"Ivy," the Widow Rattigan stepped out of Wilson's house, "yeh better get that pram of yours parked before this lot eat everything in front of them." She stepped closer to Ivy and whispered. "I want a word in private with you. When you have the time." She stopped speaking at Jem's approach.

"You go do what you have to do, love." Jem joined Ivy. "I've the water hot for tea." He pressed a quick kiss into her hair before turning away with a smile. "I'll throw me body over the sandwiches if I have ta. I'll not let me mot starve," he offered in a fair copy of a Dublin accent.

"Right, you lads!" He clapped his hands to attract the attention of the young people working around the livery. He was aware of Ivy hurrying away with her pram. "We need to get ourselves organised."

With shouted instructions the horses were returned to their stalls, a table and a few chairs carried out and put on the damp cobbles of the yard. He had used some of the bricks taken from the walls that had hidden the tunnels for years to build a safe wall surround for a bucket fire. It was his habit in this warm weather to have a big black kettle sitting over the red coals in that fire. He never knew when his Ivy might need a cup of tea.

"This is the life." Ivy sat on a chair in the yard, a cup of tea in her hand, an egg and tomato sandwich on the table in front of her. "I was thinking we could take some of the lads and horses to the seaside later. We all need to cool down." She'd changed her leather sandals for a pair of white plimsolls, the canvas shoes the children of The Lane wore all through the summer. When the shoes were worn through they made a grand addition to the fire in winter.

"We might do that some day – but I want to stay close to home for the minute." Jem didn't like to leave his business for too long. "We're getting a lot of orders for taxis in this weather. It seems people don't want to walk anywhere. It's hard on the horses. I have the men changing horses more frequently. The radio mentioned thunder and lightning that might be coming our way. I'll need all the hands I can get to keep the horses calm."

"Fair enough."

Ivy looked around at the crowded yard. The lads Jem employed were sitting on the bare cobbles stuffing their faces with the sandwiches Mrs Rattigan had provided. There were long wooden boards piled high with sandwiches, covered with damp tea towels, sitting off to one side of the table. The lads knew they could have two sandwiches each – if they were still hungry there was plain bread to go with their mugs of tea. It was more than most of them would get at home. Mrs Rattigan made her own bread which was delicious and cheap. Ivy didn't envy the woman the heat of her kitchen in this weather.

"Isn't it well for some?" John Lawless stood in the open door of the livery, leaning unsteadily on his crutches. "I suppose you never thought to ask me if I had a mouth?"

"Come on out and join us, John." Jem stood to fetch an enamel mug of tea for his friend.

Ivy stood to fetch a chair and carry it over to their table. They had been left alone to enjoy their meal. The lads preferred to sit on the ground, their backs to the nearest wall.

"My Clare is at the telephone switchboard," John said. "Someone needs to carry a mug of tea and a sandwich in to her."

"I'll take care of that." Conn Connelly followed John from the livery building. He took careful note of the lads sitting around the yard. It wouldn't be beyond some of them to try and get served twice. He'd lads working away inside the livery building who needed to get their turn at the tea and sandwiches.

"Good lad." John accepted Ivy's help in lowering his body onto the wooden chair. She took his crutches and leaned them against the livery wall, well out of the way.

"Here you go." Jem put a mug of tea and a sandwich

on the table in front of John.

"That's what I like to see, service with a smile." John too took note of the lads sitting around laughing, joking and stuffing their faces. He'd shift them soon enough and let the next lot out.

The three friends sat sipping tea, nibbling on sandwiches and talking about nothing important. Ivy allowed the peace and familiarity of the scene to soothe her emotional injury.

"I can't make them Alice dolls for you any more." The Widow Rattigan had her back to Ivy, washing the dishes at her indoor sink.

"I'm sorry to hear that." Ivy looked around at the gang of boys picking up their belongings. For some reason they were piling them into a heap in one corner of the kitchen – she didn't like to ask why. She'd come to see the Widow Rattigan after the woman had put her head out the door half a dozen times to see if she'd finished eating.

"I'll have to tell Jem as well." The woman turned from her washing, drying her hands on her apron. She leaned against the sink at her back, staring across the room at Ivy who was still standing inside the door that separated the Rattigan rooms from the rest of the house. "Father Leary, that sainted man, has found me a job as a housekeeper."

"Has he?" Ivy kept her teeth firmly clenched around what she might want to say. A good deed done with bad intentions was still a good deed.

"You know how hard I've been having it since me husband died." The woman was practically rubbing her hands raw on her apron.

"I do." Ivy walked across the room. She took the

woman's hands in hers. "Sit down and tell me everything." She led the woman to the well-scrubbed kitchen table and sat down with her.

"Father Leary," she blessed herself with tears flowing down her ashen face, "I don't know how to thank him. He found me a job. In a big house close to my parents' home in Mayo." She fought the sobs that shook her body. "I don't know if I'm on me head or me heels. Father Leary found apprentice jobs for my two eldest boys. The three youngest can live with my parents. I'll be able to help out with the money. The job is live-in but I'll have Wednesday evening and Sunday afternoons off. I'll be able to walk home and see my family." She covered her face with her hands and sobbed as if her heart were breaking.

"Have you told Mr Wilson you're leaving?" Ivy asked when the other woman had calmed down slightly.

"He's been so good. He told me not to worry. He's glad I'll be well fixed."

"Jimjo!" Ivy shouted at the nearest Rattigan boy. "Ask Mr Wilson to make a pot of tea for us, will you?" She didn't know where anything was in this kitchen. Besides, that gas cooker of Wilson's would heat the water in no time.

"Oh, I couldn't," Mrs Rattigan gasped.

"You're not asking, I am," Ivy insisted. "Go on, Jimjo, get the tea." The lad looked as if he wanted to cry. Mrs Rattigan might be returning home but this was the only home her children had ever known. She doubted they'd even met their grandparents.

"I have a basket with all of the doll stuff in it," Mrs Rattigan sniffed. "I'll give it to you before you go. I'm sorry to be letting you down. I hope you know I was grateful for the work you put my way."

"Don't worry about it." She could make the Alice dolls herself until she found someone else to take over the backbreaking work. "How are you getting home?"

"Father Leary got a voucher from the Saint Vincent de Paul to pay for train tickets for all of us – with a little left over. That man will be in my prayers for the rest of my life. He's been so good to us."

"Ivy Murphy, you have a cheek ordering me to serve up a pot of tea to you." Frank Wilson opened the door that divided the long hallway of his house. The door served as a private entrance to the Rattigans' back rooms. Jimjo stood at the old man's side, sniffling.

"Devil a bit of it." Ivy smiled over at the cranky old man. His bark was a lot worse than his bite. "Did you make it?"

"It's brewing." Frank Wilson stared at Ivy. It seemed his helping her out was bringing good to someone. Leary was depriving him of rent and Ivy of a worker but the Rattigan family were being given a chance. So some good would come out of it. "I made a big pot if the lads would like a mug." He turned to go back to his own rooms, Jimjo at his heels.

"He's been that good to us," Mrs Rattigan said. "I know he has a bad reputation in The Lane but he's never been anything but kind to me and mine." She looked across the room and out the window over the sink that opened onto her small backyard farm and the animal enclosure her husband had built for her animals. The geese, chickens, pig and goat that she'd reared wandered about the mud enclosure. "The lads are broken hearted about leaving the animals. I promised them there would be plenty of animals at my parents' place but it's not the same, is it?"

Ivy hadn't an opinion either way. She'd never had an animal. "Have you cups about?" She wanted to give the woman something to think about that didn't make her cry. "I can help you make a list of everything you need to get done before you leave, if you like."

"That would be great." Mrs Rattigan stood to root out the cups. "I'm that afraid of forgetting something important. A list is the very thing."

Ivy looked around her back room. She had the range lit, the water reservoir full to the top and the kettle filled. The people of The Lane were still away taking advantage of the nearby Sandymount Strand. There had been hardly anyone around while she'd been running back and forth with brimming buckets of water. The promised storm was rolling in – thunder rumbling over their heads.

"I'm going over to the livery – keep Jem and his horses company."

She put more coal on the range fire. The heat in the room was unbearable. The water could heat while she was out and about. There was no need for her to stay here sweating. She checked the room quickly before grabbing her keys from the kitchen table. She locked the back door. She stood for a moment looking at her front room. They hadn't touched that space yet. The two of them were living in the back room. The place was an awful mess – still, there was little she could do about it. With a shrug of her shoulders she hurried out the front door, locked the door at her back and ran up the metal steps to ground level.

"He's upstairs," Conn Connelly shouted as soon as Ivy

stepped into the open doors of the livery. Conn was standing in the central aisle of the livery, a hose in his hand. He and a group of helpers were trying to give the sweating horses a cool-down.

"Thanks, Conn." Ivy walked swiftly towards the wooden ladder leading up to the eaves. She was tempted to run through the water and cool herself down. With a sigh she resisted the temptation. She was a married woman now. She had to behave herself. Before she stepped onto the ladder she pulled the loose folds of her dress between her legs and held it in place while she climbed using one hand. She was not giving anyone a free view of her bloomers.

"Jem Ryan!" she shouted when she was almost to the top of the ladder.

"Ivy Ryan." Jem appeared in the open door of the room that had been his home before he'd moved in with Ivy. He smiled and walked over to take her hand and pull her up onto the lip of the storage area that ran around the livery. He'd been trying to cool down – his work shirt was open, sleeves rolled back to the elbow.

"Put the kettle on." She didn't care how hot it was, she wanted tea.

"I lit the Primus and put the kettle on as soon as I heard Conn shout out at you."

"Yer blood should be bottled."

"I thought we could talk in private up here." They walked into the room tucked under the eaves. He left the door open at their back. It was muggy up here. "I don't want to go far from the horses."

"Mrs Rattigan is leaving us." She'd promised the woman she'd tell Jem.

"Is that a fact?" He carried two enamel mugs of tea over to the table they had left up here for such occasions. They had carried all of the good china across the way to Ivy's place.

"Father Leary has found the answer to her prayers apparently." She filled him in on all the woman had told her.

"More power to her!" He lifted his mug in a toast.

"Have you ever been in those rooms at the back of Wilson's house?" Ivy remembered the sink with running water, the window overlooking the little private garden and farmyard. "It's a gem of a place." She wanted to think a little deeper about the idea that had come to her. It was a big step to take.

"I've only been in Wilson's once in my life." He didn't like to remember Ivy hunched in pain from being beaten by the parish priest.

"That wasn't all that happened today." She couldn't keep the pain in her heart to herself any longer. "I saw our Eamo and Petey." She'd been determined not to cry but could feel the tears rolling down her face.

"Ah Jaysus!" Jem stood quickly and pulled her from her seat into his arms. "Tell me." He held her close while she stuttered over her words, trying to explain the inexplicable.

"When I think of all the times I went hungry so they could eat, all of the things I did without so they would never have to, I could spit."

"Fuck them."

"Jem!"

"I don't care, Ivy. I apologise for swearing but none the less it's how I feel. Fuck them." He held her while she cried. Shay had warned him that their two brothers might turn up in Ireland now they knew Eamonn Murphy was dead. If the two lads were here then so was Ivy's mother. Had she thought of that?

"They seemed to be in very thick with that Burton Moriarty." Ivy accepted the handkerchief Jem pressed into her hand. "That man is our landlord though he doesn't seem to know it." She'd thought to use their connection to secure her two rooms. The fear of being evicted was still very real. The room they stood in was always available to them, she knew, but she didn't want to live here. It would make running her business practically impossible.

"You should talk to your uncle." Jem released her from his arms and turned to freshen the tea, giving her time to pull herself together. His Ivy didn't like to be seen crying.

"Why?" She decided to ignore his reference to her 'uncle'. She'd troubles enough.

"That man will know the minute your brothers stepped foot in Dublin." Jem joined her at the table. "It's better to know what's going on, Ivy. You won't have any unpleasant surprises if you know what they plan to do. This could be a quick visit to Dublin, you never know." He didn't think so. If what Shay had told him was true, Violet Burton had a score to settle with the family who had all but deserted her. The woman would want to rub their noses in her improved circumstances.

"I don't know how to get in touch with the man now that Betty's gone back to America," Ivy hedged. She didn't want to telephone William Armstrong's home. She had no intention of becoming familiar with that family. Having them turn up at her wedding was bad enough.

"There is always the telephone."

"I suppose." She hunched over her cup.

"Ivy, you need to use the contacts you have. Armstrong used your connections to push his way into Ann Marie's social circle. Tell him its payback time."

A clap of thunder and a flash of lightning had them both jumping to their feet. They were needed in the stables. The sound of frightened horses deafened them.

Chapter 44

"Walk on!" Ivy slapped the reins against Rosie's rump. She was feeling very pleased with herself. She trotted the horse and small carriage around the outside of Stephen's Green Park, Jem sitting tall beside her.

"You're doing really well," Jem offered without taking his eyes off the people strolling out on this fine day.

"Thanks." She was afraid to take her eyes off the road and the horse. The street children chasing each other around the park never seemed to look where they were going. She thanked Heaven for Rosie's placid nature. Of course the nannies walking the upper-crust children had a firm grip on their young charges.

"That's enough for today, love," Jem said softly. It was a beautiful August Saturday, almost time for the shop assistants to take their lunch in the park. The crowds would soon be too much for a novice driver to handle. "Turn her head now."

Ivy gave the horse its orders through the reins. Rosie picked up her feet. The old horse knew she was heading for home and a warm stable.

"I telephoned Ann Marie while you were hitching up

the horse." Ivy didn't take her eyes off the horse's rump. She missed her friend. It felt as if she'd lost Ann Marie at the same time as they'd lost Emmy. Ann Marie had returned from Galway and gone directly to her Dalkey estate. The O'Connors were her guests. "I don't think our Emmy is happy." She wasn't given the chance to speak to the child but something in Ann Marie's voice had warned her that things were not running smoothly.

"There is nothing you or I can do about that, Ivy." Jem too kept his eyes on the horse's rump. He hated to see the heartbreak in his wife's eyes. The loss of Emmy was a constant ache in his own heart. He had to keep reminding himself that O'Connor was Emmy's father, her family. He, Jem Ryan, a farm hand from Sligo, had no right to the child.

"We have a lot to be thankful for." She nudged his shoulder with hers. They both enjoyed the privacy offered without a child constantly underfoot.

"I'm not in gaol." Jem turned to look at her. "That's a blessing." The horse was approaching the tunnel leading from Stephen's Lane into The Lane. "You want to be careful here. The entrance is narrow."

"Yes, sir!" She concentrated on guiding the horse home.

Truth be told, Rosie knew the way but Ivy was learning to drive the horse and needed to pay attention.

"Looks like the postman's here," Jem said as the horse and carriage cleared the tunnel.

"Wonder if he has anything from Shay?" She wanted to hop off and demand to know if the man had post for her. She had been receiving orders for her baby dolls through the post since the end of June. That business development had come as a pleasant surprise to her. Hannah Solmon had kept in touch by post too. The sight of the postman never failed to give her spirits a bit of a lift. She'd have to wait to talk to the postman though until she'd tended to the animal in the traces. Jem insisted on the horse coming first.

"Go on." Jem took the reins from her hands. "I know you won't settle until you see if he has anything for you. I'll see to the horse."

"The blessings of God on yeh!" She jumped off almost before the carriage had come to a complete stop. "I won't be long." She ran away, long legs eating up the space between the livery and the postman.

Tim Allen the postman saw her coming. He stopped and began to search through his big postbag. He knew he had something for Ivy. He sighed, knowing what the blue-pencil-crossed white envelope meant. He'd never known registered letters to bring good news.

"I've a big brown-paper-wrapped package for you from America." Tim grinned when Ivy reached his side. He might as well give the good news first. "This one is from New York though, not Hollywood." He knew all about Ivy's brother in California. The man was set to make a name for himself in the fillums, if you wouldn't be minding. He passed Ivy the brown-paper package. It was tied around with twine and well decorated with melted red wax. He continued to search in his bag for his clipboard. He needed Ivy's signature for the registered post. He gave her the white, blue-crossed envelope with one hand and a bent head while pulling the clipboard from his bag.

Ivy examined the piece of registered mail with a

sinking heart. She'd never received one before but everyone knew they were generally bad news.

"I need you to sign here, please." He pointed with his pencil at the correct line on his form.

Ivy signed her name then carried her post over and sat on the steps leading up into the house that sat over her basement rooms. She sat there like a statue for what felt like ages, the package on the steps beside her. She was afraid to open the white envelope. She paid no attention to the people walking around her to go in and out of the house. She didn't hear their words of greeting.

"What's up, love?" Jem came to sit beside her. He'd been watching her, wondering what on earth she was doing sitting on the granite steps.

"Look." She showed him the blue-crossed envelope.

"Well, you don't know it's bad news until you open it," Jem said pragmatically.

"You open it." She shoved the envelope into his hands. "I can't bear to look."

"Come on," he took her elbow, put the fingers of his free hand under the twine on the parcel and pulled her to her feet, "we'll open it in our own place." He was aware of the neighbours' curiosity and would prefer privacy for whatever was coming. He took his key from his pocket and with Ivy in tow walked down the steel stairs to the front door.

"What could it be?" she asked over her shoulder, walking towards the back room while Jem locked the door behind them.

"We'll know soon enough, love."

With the dreaded envelope and the gaily decorated parcel in hand he followed Ivy into the back room – their living space.

He pulled out one of their two kitchen chairs and waited until Ivy sat. He took the second chair and with a glance in her direction tore open the tough white fabric-imbued envelope. He pulled out a sheet of paper and quickly read the message typed on the page.

"That . . ." He bit back the curse. "It seems we are being evicted, love." The silence in the room after his words had an almost physical presence.

"Oh God, Jem." Ivy actually felt the colour drain from her face.

"Father Leary has a long reach." There wasn't a doubt in his mind that the parish priest was behind this notice. The man had been too quiet lately – the calm before the storm. He passed her the typed page.

Ivy read the words on the page. "We have a week from Sunday to get out. That's bloody generous of them." She knew she could contest this eviction notice. She was a good tenant and had never missed a week's rent. She caused problems for no one. It would cost money to fight this notice though and only delay the inevitable. What was the point? In a face-off the priest would always win. But no-one knew she had an ace in the hole when it came to this house. She couldn't think about that right now. She had dreaded this moment but now that it was actually here she was numb.

"Come here." Jem stood and pulled Ivy from her seat. He almost dragged her over to the large bed and with his arms wrapped tight around her fell onto the horsehair mattress. He was expecting her to weep and wail but Ivy surprised him. She lay silently in his arms. Her very stillness frightened him.

"It's only the two of us," he whispered into her hair.

He waited to see if she would say something but Ivy remained frozen. "You won't be homeless, love. We have my place."

"I don't want to think about anything." Ivy's voice sounded husky. "I just want to go to sleep." She snuggled into his arms. She wanted to escape the problems of her life – just for a while – was that so wrong?

Jem lay on the bed, holding her suddenly shivering body close. He rubbed his hand up and down her back. He was worried. It wasn't like his Ivy to give in without a fight. Was this the straw that would break the camel's back? He lay on the wide bed, looking around at the space Ivy had turned into a home. There had to be something he could do. His mind whirled in ever-decreasing circles. He couldn't just lie here. He had to move, to do something. He waited to move until her even breathing told him she was asleep. He moved slowly, sliding himself from the bed without waking her. He removed her shoes before pulling the covers over her. He almost tiptoed out of the basement rooms.

He crossed the cobbled space between the tenements and his livery, his blood boiling, his hands gripped in tight fists. He wished there was someone he could punch.

"Jem." John Lawless put his head around the office door.

"Later!" Jem shouted. He didn't want to stop. He didn't want to deal with more problems. Not at this moment. He climbed the ladder to his room in the eaves and slammed the door at his back. He stood staring around the room he'd called home for years. This was not what he wanted to offer his bride. Ivy deserved better. The entire place echoed painfully with Emmy's absence. How could one little girl take over his world in a little over a year? What was he going to do? He fell into the single armchair in the room and dropped his head into his hands.

"Mr Wilson, do you have a minute?" Jem looked at the old man. "I'd like to talk to you."

"Come in." Frank Wilson opened his door wide then turned and walked back into his living room, leaving Jem to follow at his heels.

"I wanted to ask you about them rooms at the back." Jem stood inside the open living-room door.

"Shut the door," Frank Wilson growled. "I haven't had time to fill those rooms since Mrs Rattigan and her boys moved out. I've been fixing the place up. The Rattigans were good tenants but a little spit and polish, a dash of white paint and the place will be good as new. I like to have the place nice before I rent it out."

"I want to rent those back rooms." Jem said.

"You and Ivy, you mean?" Wilson stared. "I thought the pair of you were well set up in that basement of hers. The rent on the back rooms here is a lot more than you've been paying."

"Ivy is being evicted," Jem said simply.

"That aul' bastard Leary has a long reach. I wonder how the man sleeps at night."

"So, about those rooms?" Jem didn't want to get into a long-drawn-out discussion on the evils of Father Leary. He wanted to have everything in place before his Ivy woke up. He knew she loved the back rooms in this house. She'd talked of them often enough after her visits to the place. Jem stood staring at the fantasy land carved into the cupboards and wondered about them.

"You're looking at my carvings." Wilson went to put the kettle on. They could talk money over a cup of tea. "I carved them for my lads."

"I didn't know you had children." Jem didn't know what to do with himself. He and Frank Wilson had never exactly held a conversation before. If he was going to be his landlord it would fit him better to get to know the man.

"Twin boys." He stood watching the kettle, his back to Jem. His lads had loved running their fingers over those carvings. "They were never right." He took a deep breath and turned to take mugs from one of his cupboards.

"I'm sorry." What could he say?

"They died long before you ever came to The Lane." Wilson made the tea. "The consumption took them. The missus died not long after my boys. I've been living here with my memories for a very long time." He looked around the familiar room, the glitter of tears in his eyes. "I suppose I should have changed the doors but I could never bring myself to get rid of them."

"They're beautiful," Jem said truthfully.

"I've ne'er a biscuit to offer you, I'm afraid." Wilson didn't want to talk about his carvings any more.

Jem watched while the man pulled his cleverly concealed table out from the wall units. The entire room was a work of art in his opinion.

"So, lad," Wilson gestured to one of the two stools he'd pulled to the table, "let's talk money and rules. I have rules for the people who live in my house, you know."

"I'd never have guessed." Jem joined the man at the table. "I want to have a look at the rooms. Ivy talked a lot about them. She thought they were grand."

"And so they are."

"I'm worried about her business." Jem didn't think Wilson would want Ivy dragging her pram through his spotlessly clean house. His Ivy was used to coming and going at her own pace. She wouldn't want anyone keeping an eye on her or passing comment.

"If we put our heads together we can come up with something." He'd be glad to have those rooms rented out. The lack of that rent was a big cut in his money.

"Can we look now?" Jem stood. "Ivy is asleep – I don't want her to wake up alone. She's only just heard the news."

The two men stood and Frank Wilson showed Jem around what he was hoping would be the home he could be proud to bring his Ivy to. His heart beat hard in his chest as the rooms and all that came with them were shown to him. His mind spun with ideas of how he could turn this place into a little palace. Yes, the rent was high in comparison to what Ivy paid now but they could afford it.

"Have you any objection to me and Ivy renting these rooms, Mr Wilson?"

"Not a one."

"Then let's talk money," Jem said. "I'll pay you a month's rent now." He knew Ivy wanted the security of renting monthly. He didn't think Old Man Wilson would ever evict them. Look how the man had treated the Rattigans when they fell on hard times. Nevertheless, he wanted to rent by the month. "If it's no problem to you we can start moving our stuff in immediately." That would make the moving easier on everyone.

"I'll get you a rent book."

"Ivy." Jem sat on the side of the bed and shook her gently.

He was surprised when he returned to find her still asleep. The track of fresh tears on her cheeks broke his heart.

"Jem, where were you?" She sat up in bed, pushing her hair out of her face. "I woke up and you were gone."

"I went to see Old Man Wilson." He bent forward and pressed a kiss into her forehead. "I told him we would take the back rooms. The ones you liked so much." He'd also talked the man into helping him install a gas cooker for Ivy. No more lighting the range when the heat outside could peel the skin from your body.

"The rent on that place must be sky high." Ivy shook her head, trying to wake herself up completely. "That place has indoor plumbing, a garden, outbuildings and a private toilet. We can't afford something like that."

"We can and we will." Jem wouldn't tell her the rent. He knew she'd dig in her heels. "Old Man Wilson has the place shining white. He's even limed and whitewashed the outhouse."

"What about me round?" She moved to sit beside him on the side of the bed. "Old Man Wilson would have a fit if I dragged me pram through his house ninety times a day," she exaggerated.

"Wilson has ideas about that as well – I'll tell you later." Jem was delighted with the surprises he was going to put in place for his wife. If ever a woman deserved a treat now and again it was his Ivy.

"I hope old Leary," she nudged her shoulder against his, "chokes when he finds out he did a favour for all of us." She'd been thinking about suggesting moving into those rooms ever since the Rattigans left. She'd work harder than ever to make the rent.

"Do you want to go over and see the place," Jem

wanted to keep the light in her eyes, "now that you know it's going to be yours?"

"Ours," Ivy said, having to remind herself yet again that she was a married woman. It wouldn't be only her making sure the rent was paid. "I went to sleep in the depths of despair . . ."

"That sounds like something Emmy would say, Ivy – 'the depths of despair' indeed."

"Like her, I heard it at story night and liked it. I was waiting for a chance to use it."

"Well, come out of the depths, woman, and walk over to the Wilson place with me."

"Honest to God, Jem, I won't know meself with running water and me own private toilet. I'll be getting too big for me boots."

"You deserve to hold your head up, love." He'd be glad to get out of these two rooms. There was something depressing about living in a basement. The sun never seemed to light the place. "I won't know what to do with myself when I have a lawn. We wouldn't want to keep animals so I'll turn the enclosure into a place to grow a few flowers and veg."

"How do people pack up their home and move?" She looked around the space that suddenly seemed to echo with so many memories of her life. How did you walk out and leave all that behind you? Still, she'd be glad to leave the ghosts of Eamo and Petey here. The pain of their betrayal stung. "I've never moved in me life. You have." She nudged his shoulder again. "How's the thing done?"

"Not the same thing, love." He put his arm around her shoulders and pulled her in close to his body. "I arrived in Dublin from Sligo with the clothes I stood up in. There was nothing to bring but me big ugly self. It was the same when I moved in here with you. I carried the stuff we wanted over when the mood struck me."

"How can they expect people to pack up and move in a week?" She collapsed into his body, glad of the support.

"We'll do it, love, because we have to."

"I'll be the talk of The Lane." Ivy stood suddenly. She couldn't collapse. She didn't have that luxury. "The rent man will be telling everyone about my eviction on Monday. The place will be buzzing with that tasty bit of gossip."

"Put your shoes on, love." Jem stood and took her by the shoulders. "Wash your face, put your head in the air and come on over to Wilson's." He shook her gently. "I want to walk around those rooms with you and plan our future."

"The rooms look much bigger without the furniture." She was determined to make the most of this forced move. She might never have had the nerve to leave her basement rooms if she wasn't pushed. "It's lovely and bright in here." She walked around the kitchen space. "We'll need more than them two kitchen chairs now, Jem." She could see it in her mind's eye.

"I can fix up six of those old wooden chairs I've seen you throw out onto the courtyard, Jem Ryan." Frank Wilson was following along behind his new tenants. Jem had paid the rent. The rooms and back garden were now theirs. "If you can find six that match all the better."

Ivy almost danced around the space. She could see it all. She'd put her kitchen table in the back yard of the tenement and scrub it within an inch of its life before bringing it over here. Her two old easy chairs would fit in front of the range in here. "Where am I going to put all that stuff from my front room, Jem?" She didn't want to have that mess in their new home. She needed somewhere for a work room. Perhaps she should think about using that room of Jem's over the livery? She walked around, the two men at her heels.

"This could be our bedroom." Two windows stood open to catch the little wind that stirred. She wanted to cry but they were tears of joy. She'd kill herself to earn the rent on this place. The air that came in the windows smelled different from the hot human smell of her old rooms.

"Why don't you move your bed over now?" Frank Wilson suggested. "This heat is bringing people out in prickly rash." Dublin had been suffering through the worst lightning storms the capital had ever known, according to his crystal radio. "I'll leave you to show your wife around, Jem." He backed out of the room. He'd go into his own place and make a pot of tea. He'd carry it out into the back garden. There was a first time for everything.

"There is another room here." Jem took her hand and led her away from her fascination with the two open windows. "It's a bit dark. Maybe we should use it as our bedroom and the light airy room could be your work space. You'd have the light and fresh air while you worked. Then in the winter you could light the fire in there."

"All of this space, what will we do with it?" She didn't expect an answer but kept walking about, shifting things around in her mind. "I don't want to fill these rooms with me bits and bobs, Jem."

"Then step outside, Missus." He took her hand and pulled her out into the back garden. "You know the Rattigans kept animals out here." He waved around at the stone sheds lining one of the walls that closed in the garden. "Wilson sold them for the back rent the Rattigans owed him. The man has limed and whitewashed all the sheds. Look!" He pulled open wooden doors to reveal stone walls and floors sparkling white in the light. "I thought you could use one of these sheds for storage. The doors are sturdy enough. We can buy locks from the locksmith."

Ivy wasn't capable of speaking. She was sure her heart was somewhere in her mouth. Was she still lying on her bed dreaming?

"Look." He took her hand, pulling her along at his side, delighted with her reaction. He'd rendered his Ivy speechless. "There's a back lane here that runs along these houses. This door opens onto that lane." He pulled open the heavy door set into a stone wall. "You'll be able to pull your pram along that area of scrub." He stood staring at the area the people of The Lane used to pick blackberries and rosehips. "I'll widen the path that Mrs Rattigan used. You won't know yourself, love."

"Pinch me, Jem." Ivy stared around, her violet eyes hurting they were open so wide. "I want to know if I'm dreaming – *ouch*!" She yelped when he took her literally.

"You'll be able to walk around the outside of the house and into this yard." Jem shoved his hands into his pockets and rocked back and forth on his heels, a big smile on his face. "The rear door has a good heavy lock on it." He pointed it out to her. "You can wheel your pram into one of the sheds and park it. We have to figure out a way of lighting the sheds but it's doable, don't you think?"

"Don't ask me to think right now, love – it's beyond me."

"Lend a hand here, Jem!" Frank yelled out the open back door. He had a tray with mugs, milk and sugar in his hands. He'd even managed to put his hand on a packet of biscuits. "I have to go back and get the teapot. I've never served tea in a garden before."

"I'll be back in a minute." Jem didn't think Ivy even noticed him leaving. She was standing staring around her with sparkling eyes. That was good enough for him. With light steps he walked over the grass to give Old Man Wilson a hand serving his Ivy her first cup of tea in her new home.

Ivy kicked off her canvas shoes and buried her toes in the grass. She wanted to fall to her knees and cry. She'd wanted something better than her two-room basement. Look at her now! Eat your heart out, Father Leary, she thought, and after a quick glance around to check she was alone she spat into the grass. The bloody man had done her a favour. She'd be sure to thank him.

Chapter 45

"Jem said to bring these over." Conn Connelly pushed a hand trolley along the back yard of the tenement block. Six matching wooden chairs were sitting high on the trolley. "Where do you want them?"

"Leave them here." Ivy pointed with the scrubbing brush she held in her hand. She'd dragged her kitchen table out into the back yard. Jem was over at the livery looking for tools to pull their big brass bed apart. She'd scrub every inch of that too as soon as it had been broken down into its parts.

"In the name of God, Ivy." Marcella Wiggins hurried over, a gaggle of women following her. They'd been watching the goings-on from their place in line at the outdoor tap. "Have you lost the run of yourself? What is going on?"

"I'm moving." Ivy dipped the brush into the soapy water sitting in an enamel bowl at her feet. "I want me things clean before we shift them."

"You're leaving us, Ivy," Lily Connelly said. "Conn never said a word." She glared at her son. Imagine leaving her to find out this juicy morsel of gossip like this.

"My Jem wants his own place." Ivy kept her head down as she uttered that bit of nonsense. "I only just found out meself."

"But where are you going?" came from several women.

"I'm only moving across the way into Wilson's place."

"Right." Marcella Wiggins pushed at her arms. She wasn't wearing a jumper but the move was instinctive now. "Have you another bowl and brush? I'll carry in the water and come back out and help you." She knew those rooms the Rattigans had rented. They were a big step up from these two basement rooms – more power to Jem Ryan, she thought.

"I'd be very grateful." Ivy stood, pushing the hair out of her eyes with the hand holding the scrubbing brush. "Jem and me are going out to Dalkey tomorrow for Sunday lunch." She offered that bit of news casually. The news would be around The Lane in minutes. "I've been thanking God for the long evenings. I'll have time to get a lot done before it turns dark."

"If we carry your mattress out here," Marcella pointed at the weedy, cracked, dusty cobbles under their feet, "we can beat it and air it out. Come on, ladies, let's be havin' yez! Who has a few minutes to help an old neighbour?" The woman had her work force organised before she left to carry the buckets of water up to her own rooms. Some of the neighbours offered to help out of curiosity, wanting to know what Ivy had, but most genuinely wanted to help.

"Ivy, there's a brown-paper packet here from America not even opened." Lily Connelly held the parcel in her hands. "What do you want me to do with it?" The women working in the back yard stopped moving. The women sweltering in the back basement room stared. A parcel from America and it not even opened yet – imagine that.

"Conn." Ivy wanted to sit down and never move again. She didn't think she'd ever worked so hard in her life. Marcella Wiggins was a slave driver – and they hadn't even touched the front room – that was for her to do. "Grab a bicycle and get us a block of ice from the ice man."

"Won't be long." Conn was glad to escape the women. He took off around the tenement block. Jem would give him the money he needed.

"He didn't wait for me to get me purse." Ivy stared after the fleeing lad.

"You've got a husband now, Ivy," Marcella said. "Let him pay for it."

"Right." She still sometimes forgot she was married. "I haven't enough mugs but there are jars of barley water in the bottom of me cupboard and a big pot of it on the back of the stove. We'll have iced barley water like the nobs." She smiled a little at the women's reaction. Iced anything was a rare treat. "We've been drinking our sweat scrubbing. I'm about ready to collapse." There was a murmer of agreement.

"We could put them sheets on to boil, Ivy." A woman pointed to the heap of bedding sitting outside. "They wouldn't take long drying in this weather."

"I'm going to make me bed with the sheets Mrs Wiggins gave me for a wedding present," Ivy decided at that moment. Normally such presents were never opened but instead used as currency in The Lane. The pawn shops paid good money for an unopened package. But Ivy hadn't needed to go to the pawn for years. She would use the sheets – she meant to start out in her new home as she meant to go on, God willing.

"You never!" That started a storm of protest and exclamations of astonishment. She didn't care.

"Jem said you might be needing a load of mugs." Jimmy Johnson appeared with a basket filled to the brim with enamel mugs.

"Right, ladies," Ivy yelled. "Everyone outside! Conn won't be long getting back from the ice man."

Ivy gave a deep sigh of contentment. Her Jem had turned a nightmare into a dream and there was still that package from America to open. Ivy Murphy's moving day would be talked about for a long time.

Chapter 46

"Uncle Jem, Aunty Ivy!" Emmy ran across the green lawn towards the driveway at breakneck speed.

"Jesus!" Jem slammed on the brakes, afraid the little one was going to run out in front of the car. He jumped out and caught the racing child up into his arms. "Emmy, you should be more careful around moving vehicles." He hugged her tight.

"I missed you," Emmy leaned back to say. "Did you miss me?"

"Ivy!" Ann Marie walked at a clipped pace from the open doors of her Dalkey home. Her feet seemed to fly over the grass. "I feel I haven't seen you in ages."

"That's because you haven't," Ivy said. She thought there was a light in her friend's eyes she'd never seen before. She wasn't sure she liked it.

"Jem!" Ann Marie smiled when she reached the couple. "Edward is reading the Sunday papers in the lounge if you would care to join him."

"I'll take this little one for a walk along the strand first, if that's okay with you," Jem replied.

"Don't I get a hello?" Ivy held out her hands and took

a giggling Emmy from Jem.

"I missed you, Aunty Ivy," Emmy whispered into Ivy's neck.

"Let me look at you." Ivy stood the child on the grass.

Emmy was dressed in a white lace dress that was starched and stood out from her body due to the many petticoats. She wore long blindingly white stockings and little black patent-leather shoes. The outfit was beautiful but it didn't look like the kind of clothes for running around in the nearby sand. The sea water would ruin those shoes in no time. She pulled her own cotton dress out of the way before dropping to her knees on the grass. It was easier to ask pardon than permission, she thought.

"Jem, put your own shoes and socks in the back of the automobile," she ordered. The driveway was so wide the automobile could sit there and not cause an obstruction.

Ann Marie said nothing but watched her friends and the child. They seemed so natural together. A family group – she and Edward were so stiff with the little girl, struggling to find a way of communicating. She hated that she couldn't behave as naturally with Emerald as these two.

"You won't let your Uncle Jem go in the water, will you?" Ivy was removing Emmy's shoes and socks. She reached under the stiff dress and removed layers of petticoats. "He gets all silly when he goes to the seaside." She smiled before pressing a kiss onto Emmy's nose. "Away with the pair of you! Ann Marie and me want a bit of peace and quiet." She stood, the cast-off clothing in her hands.

"I asked Edward to give us some time alone together, Ivy," Ann Marie said as the two women stood watching

Jem and a skipping chattering Emmy make their way towards the sea and sand nearby. "I've missed you, Ivy."

She put her arm through Ivy's and they began slowly walking towards a nearby gazebo. They would be able to watch Jem and Emmy from the open-sided building.

"How's married life treating you?" Ann Marie asked when they stepped up into the gazebo.

"It's strange." Ivy dropped the clothes onto a padded bench that ran around the inside of the gazebo. She watched Ann Marie remove the top from a well-stocked silver ice bucket that was sitting on an iron table. Without asking, her friend began to fill two of the nearby tall glasses with ice and what looked like freshly squeezed lemon juice. It seemed to be Ivy's week for drinking out of doors. "Nobody ever mentions how strange it is to learn to live with someone else." She looked around before adding, "I forget sometimes that I'm married."

Ann Marie passed Ivy the chilled glass with a smile. She walked over to sit on the padded bench, ignoring the chairs pulled up to the table.

"What's wrong?" Ivy joined Ann Marie on the bench. Her friend didn't seem like her usual self to her. Something wasn't right. She could sense it. She looked out to sea. It was beautiful here. The sound of Emmy's delighted laughter and Jem's deeper laugh floated up to them.

"I don't know what I'm doing." Ann Marie stared into Ivy's concerned eyes. She had missed this woman more than she could have imagined.

Ivy waited without speaking. Ann Marie stood, stepped away and practically banged her glass onto the table-top. She whirled around and put her knee on the bench beside Ivy. She stared out to sea.

320

"What's wrong?" Ivy repeated.

"I don't know." Ann Marie didn't look around. "I like Edward. I like him very much." She thought she had found the man she could share her life with. Edward too seemed to be seeking a life change. He had invited her to join him in Galway. They had spent every spare moment together, investigating and finalising the matter of Mary Rose Donnelly. She had been invigorated by the visit. "I don't like the woman I'm becoming," she almost shouted to the sea. "I'm stiff and formal when I want to be relaxed and amusing. I second-think everything I say or do." She turned to look down at her friend. "Ivy, I'm driving myself mad."

"Perhaps it is this house."

"What do you mean?"

"Look!" Ivy stood and turned slowly around. "This place is magnificent. I can see that. I can't imagine living somewhere like this."

"And?" Ann Marie knew there was more.

"You are very much the lady of the manor living here." Ivy waved a hand between them. "You lived here with your parents. From what you've told me you were instructed in your duty to this house and your heritage when you were growing up." She'd been fascinated by the stories Ann Marie shared with her. Their lives had been so very different. "Look at us. I knew I was coming here to this estate. It never entered my head to dress formally. I was coming to see my friend Ann Marie. You have to be dying of the heat in that get-up." She pointed at Ann Marie's beige silk three-piece suit and her own lightweight cotton drop-waist dress. "You are wearing strings of pearls, for goodness' sake. You look beautiful, there's no two ways about that – but stiff and formal. It's just like

Emmy's clothes, not practical for running barefoot along the sand. And where is your camera?"

"Dear Lord . . ." Ann Marie stared, Ivy's words echoing in her head.

"I'm not the one you should be having this conversation with," Ivy said. "You need to sit Edward down and ask him what he wants. He seemed to like the Ann Marie he met who always had a camera in her hand and a thousand questions on her lips." Ann Marie was ten years older than her. Shouldn't that mean she had much more experience of life? "If you promise not to hit me I'll tell you straight out. You look like your aunt and her cronies."

"Oh, the unkindest cut of all!" Ann Marie clasped her hands dramatically to her chest. "Seriously, thank you, Ivy. I've been trying to be someone I'm not. Someone I don't even like."

"I think," Ivy had been giving a great deal of thought to this very subject, "it is having a man in your life. A man you admire and respect. Suddenly you question everything about yourself. You second-guess things, wondering if the man will like this or that. It can drive you crazy."

"The very thing." Ann Marie stared out to sea, not seeing anything but her own actions of the last weeks. "I've been trying to form myself into the perfect female for Edward without ever asking him his opinion." She wanted to kick herself.

"From what you've told me you had a better example of a good marriage than I did. My parents were all fire and flash. Your parents respected each other. But do you really want a marriage like your parents or your uncle? Times are changing. It seems to me that Edward O'Connor with his flying machine and adventuring wouldn't want to be tied

322

down with a woman that looks like she sucks lemons and talks about her charity work every evening."

"I'll be right back!" Ann Marie ran out of the gazebo, shouting over her shoulder. "Don't move!"

"I'm going nowhere." Ivy looked down the slight incline to where Jem and Emmy were building sandcastles. "Well, maybe just a short distance to join in the fun." She kicked off her shoes and stockings and with a rebel yell ran down the sand dunes to join her man and the child they both loved.

"What did Ann Marie say when you told her we were moving?" Jem drove slowly along the roads packed with families returning from a day out at the seaside.

"I forgot." Ivy slapped her hand to her mouth.

"I can't say I'm surprised." Jem kept his eyes on the road. "I didn't really enjoy the visit." He didn't want to criticise their friend but the day had been strange. It seemed to him that O'Connor and Ann Marie were very wrapped up in listening to each other speak. They were distracted. He was worried about Emmy. The little girl didn't seem to enjoy living out in the middle of nowhere – even if it was in the lap of luxury.

"That might have been my fault," Ivy said.

Ann Marie had joined them on the beach, dragging a confused Edward after her. She'd changed into a cotton dress and seemed to be acting like someone with a fever. Ivy got the impression that they were in the way. The other couple seemed to have a lot they wanted to say to each other but couldn't because she and Jem were there. It was a very odd visit, to say the least.

They drove along, lost in their own thoughts.

Chapter 47

"Are yeh off?"

"Go back to sleep." Jem eased his body out of the big bed. "It's early yet."

"I'll make a pot of tea."

"I'll get some across the way."

"I'll never get back to sleep." Ivy stretched, her naked flesh still feeling strange to her. "I've a lot to get done today."

"Are you going to go around the Tuesday markets?"

"No, I've too much to do."

She pulled on the dress she'd left over the end of the bed, not bothering with underwear. She almost skipped out of the bedroom and outside to the toilet. She would never get accustomed to having a private toilet and running water inside. She rinsed her hands, admiring the water running from her very own tap. She put the kettle on the Primus stove. She'd plenty of bread and cracked eggs on hand. She'd make a pot of scrambled eggs for breakfast. It was her duty to feed her man before he left for work.

When they were both washed, dressed and fed, Jem

crossed the short space between their new home and his work. Ivy hurried around the tenement block. She had so much to do.

"How do other people do this?" She stared around at the mess surrounding her. She'd paid her last week's rent on these rooms yesterday. The contents of the front room would be easier to shift through the empty back room and out the door. Since she used tea chests and orange boxes for storage she'd a great deal of the packing done already. The stacks of wool and rolls of fabric would need to be covered back up.

Someone knocked on her front door. She wasn't surprised, thinking it was Mr Wilson coming to check out how much stuff she had to move. He'd said he'd be by this morning. He was only getting three days work down the docks at the moment. Ivy wanted to talk to him about building special shelves and cupboards for the shed she'd use for storage. She could make note of everything she had as she packed it into the shed.

"Patty Grant, what are you doing at my front door?" Ivy didn't have time for this visitor.

"I know you went by the rent office yesterday." The woman didn't look at Ivy but was busy checking out everything she could see over her shoulder. "I heard all about you moving to a fancier place but I know you've been ordered to shift. Father Leary promised me he'd get you out and he's not a man to give his word lightly. I thought you should know that me and mine are moving in here. I want to measure up, see what needs doing." She sniffed, still refusing to look at Ivy. "You might have a few things I'd be willing to buy." She put her hand in her skirt pocket and, in a manner that set Ivy's teeth on edge, rattled the coins she'd put in there before leaving her own room. "I want to examine everything."

"Pity about yeh." Ivy longed to slam the door in the woman's face. "I'm afraid I'm too busy for you to visit right now." She closed the door quickly.

"I want to measure up, Ivy Murphy!" Patty Grant roared through the letterbox cut into the door.

"Want may be your master," Ivy yelled back, "and that's Mrs Ryan to you!"

There was a knock on the back door.

"What now?" Ivy hurried to answer. Patty Grant was still shouting and banging at her front door. Well, she could knock to her heart's content. "Mr Wilson, come in quick." She practically pulled the man over her backdoor step.

"What's all that banging?"

"Ignore it." Ivy wouldn't give Patty Grant breath. "I wanted to show you my front room. It's in a terrible mess. I need to discuss special cupboards and whatnot with you. I thought you would have more of an idea of what I'll need. I'll pay you of course for the work."

"There will be no talk of paying me for my work." Frank was glad of having something to occupy his time. "You just buy the wood."

"Nonsense, Mr Wilson. Me da always said 'a labourer is worthy of his hire', which was a bit of a cheek since he never laboured a day in his life to my knowledge. Still, the sentiment's right." She grinned.

"You weren't joking when you said the place was a mess." Frank hoped to God she wouldn't keep his back rooms in this state. "Show me what you have to put away and if you explain to me a little bit about what you plan to do with . . ." he turned in a circle, "all this stuff, it will give me a better idea of what's needed."

"Are yeh looking, Da?" Ivy stood in her empty rooms, the place echoing around her. "Granny Grunt, are you up there on a cloud passing comment on all of these goings-on? I know you'd be glad for me." She'd asked Jem and the lads to give her a chance to say goodbye to the place. She had the front and back doors open, allowing the air to circulate and remove the smell of the whitewash the lads had used. "I remembered so many things when I was packing up this place." She walked between the two rooms, checking that everything was spic and span. The big black range was polished and gleaming, the shine from the copper fittings almost blinding.

"You in there, Ivy?" Marcella Wiggins shouted from the back door.

"Just saying goodbye to the old place." Ivy walked from the front into the back room.

"You won't know yourself with the luxury of Frank Wilson's place." Marcella stepped into the back room. "You've left the place lovely for Patty Grant and her family I must say."

Marcella started to say more but Patty Grant shouted from the front door. The woman refused to come around to the back door. She'd let it be known that she'd be using her own front door now.

"Can I do me measuring now, Ivy Murphy, or are yeh going to slam the door in me face again?"

Marcella raised her eyes to heaven and, with a finger to her lips for silence, slipped out the back door.

"Come on in, Mrs Grant," Ivy called sweetly, walking forward. There was no sense of making an enemy of the woman. Not if she had the ear of Father Leary. "I was just giving the place a final polish." She would put the keys to the place through the letterbox when she left. The changeover of tenants would be handled by the rent man. She'd hoped for time alone to say goodbye but it didn't look like she was going to get it. Perhaps that was for the best. It was better to look forward after all.

Chapter 48

"Ivy," Jem shouted. "Ivy, are you about?"

"Over here," a voice answered.

"In the name of God, Ivy, what are you up to now?" Jem walked around to the bramble patch that infested the area between the back walls of the houses on Stephen's Lane and Old Man Wilson's place.

"I'm picking the last of the blackberries."

She wasn't the only one – a whole bunch of women and children were busily picking.

"Well, come out of there, Missus." Jem shook his head. His Ivy was never still. He waited and watched while his wife pulled away from the brambles that stuck to her long black skirt. Her face and hands were covered in blackberry juice. She'd been eating as many as she put in the bucket in her hand.

"What's up?" Ivy used the toe of her boys' boots to hold down the nettles.

"You are about to have a visitor." Jem took her elbow and almost pulled her away from the other curious blackberry-pickers.

"What!"

"Billy Flint telephoned the livery." Jem walked Ivy along the path he'd cut in the brambles to make a walkway around the side of Wilson's house, along the outside wall of their yard. The path was almost bald now, Ivy used it so much.

"In the name of God," Ivy stopped walking to stare at Jem, "what does he want?"

"He's coming here to see you." Jem started her walking again. She'd be mortified if she had to greet the man in her old clothes and covered in blackberry juice.

"When?"

"I told him to wait an hour."

"That should give you time to roll out the red carpet."

"It won't, no," Jem teased, "but it'll give you time to wash your face and change your clothes."

"He can take me as he finds me. I didn't invite him."

"Well, I've passed the message along." He turned to leave. "I'll get back to my work."

"What, you're going to leave me here alone to meet him?" she shouted at his back.

"He's your uncle," he answered over his shoulder. "Nothing to do with me."

"Jem!"

"If you need me," he walked back to say softly, "give us a shout, okay?"

"Right, I better get myself organised for His Majesty." She lifted her hand to touch his face but stopped when she saw the state of her fingers. "Get you about your business, Mr Ryan." She hurried away.

"This is a nice place," It would be easy for him to visit her here, he thought, with not a house between her and the

Stephen's Lane entry tunnel and only the blind side of the livery on the other. He'd pulled his cap down low and the collar of his donkey jacket up around his face when he'd seen the gang of people picking blackberries of all things. He wouldn't have thought anything could grow in this place.

"Glad you like it," Ivy answered sarcastically.

The man sitting at her brightly coloured oilcloth-covered kitchen table was Billy Flint. He was dressed like the rest of the men who toiled down the docks. There was no sign of William Armstrong about this man.

"Do you have an ashtray?" He pulled a cigar from his breast pocket. "You better put the kettle on." She turned away, probably to find a chipped saucer or something he could use. "I hear you're a devil for the tea." He bit the end off his cigar.

"Don't dare spit that on my clean floor." She passed him the heavy glass ashtray she kept to hand. She wouldn't be surprised if she'd been given the thing at this man's back door. Wouldn't that be a joke?

She wondered if the man could have any idea of the thrill she got every single time she filled the kettle from her very own inside tap. She turned from the tap to put the kettle on her lovely new gas cooker. A surprise gift from her husband. She had to pinch herself sometimes – she couldn't believe how easy Jem had made her life.

"You even have a bit of a garden." Billy stood and walked over to open the back door and blow puffs of smoke out into the well-tended little garden. He'd used the back gate to enter this property. It was a good solid little place. Jem Ryan was doing well by his niece – although he didn't like to think of them renting.

"You didn't come here to discuss me garden."

"I'll wait until you have your tea and are sitting down." He watched as she set the table with a yellow flowered milk jug and sugar bowl. She set out matching cups, plates and saucers. His eyes narrowed when she bent to the oven and removed a Victorian sponge. He supposed it was as good a place to keep a cake as any. She put the cake on its fancy plate in the middle of the table.

"Sit down and tell me what's brought you here." She carried her teapot to the table. She covered the pot with a knitted tea cosy.

"You asked me to find out about your brothers."

She'd telephoned his house and asked him to see what he could discover. It was the first time she'd ever asked him for anything. He wished he had better news to give her. She didn't say anything.

"I'm finding this amazingly difficult to say." He wanted to punch something. "Your brothers are no longer Eamonn and Peter Murphy but I believe you knew or suspected that."

"Shay told me."

"Well, your mother has remarried." Billy almost bit the end of his cigar. "She has married my father's legitimate son. He claims the boys as his. They are now Richard and George. They plan to remain in Ireland, supposedly because of my father's illness. I've been bumping into them everywhere I go."

"My brothers are Armstrongs now?"

"Armstrong is my mother's name. We're the bastard branch of the family. Your mother and brothers now go by the name Williams."

"She married me da's brother." Ivy didn't comment on his own name.

"The woman's nobody's fool. She has married the legal heir and in one stroke made your two brothers my old man's legitimate grandsons. He'll accept them – they are his blood after all."

"Well," she held up her cup, waiting until he mirrored the gesture, "you have to admit we come from a delightful family." She toasted and tapped her cup against his. "Here, have a slice of me cake before the cream goes off." She got a knife from the drawer in the kitchen table. She was glad to be able to put her hand on it. She was having a hard time finding things since she moved. She didn't know where the lads put half her things.

"I thought you'd be more upset." He was bloody furious. That that weak-chinned little shite should claim everything that belonged to Eamonn – he looked at the young woman sitting across the table from him – well, almost everything.

"You didn't see the way Eamo looked at me before he jumped into his fancy car," Ivy said. "I don't want to know anyone who would look at someone else like that. Our Shay tried to tell me but I suppose seeing is believing."

"I'm glad you feel that way." He bit into the cake. "This is good." He grunted in surprise.

"Of course it is – made with me own lily-white hands."

"Betty sent my wife a load of fancy creams. She said in her letter that she'd sent you a package."

"She did that." When she had finally got around to opening the package from America it had contained fancy glass jars of cream. "I was delighted to see she had used some of Granny's recipes." The women of The Lane had been impressed that Granny Grunt's familiar 'cures' were coming from America in fancy packaging.

"Betty has asked me to invest in her company," Billy was surprised to hear himself say. He didn't normally discuss business sitting in someone's kitchen eating cake. He found he wanted to hear what this young woman thought. She'd driven a hard bargain with the sale of Nanny Grace and her goods. She'd done him a good turn there – old Granny was worth her weight in gold.

"I'd do it if I were you," Ivy said. "If the business brings in even a portion of what that woman talks about, you'd be a fool not to jump on the bandwagon."

"I'm heading towards New York myself soon." He didn't feel it was his place to tell her that he was going in the company of O'Connor and her friend Miss Gannon. "I'll be able to check everything out for myself."

"More power to you."

The house almost shook and a dreadful bang rattled the door that led from the rooms to the main house.

"What in the name of God is that?"

"I don't know," Ivy jumped to her feet, "but I'll find out." She pulled open the door that led into the long main hallway.

"That fuckin' Leary has a long reach!" Frank Wilson practically screamed. He was red in the face, standing inside the door he'd slammed, his tools scattered around the floor at his feet. "I've been sacked. After fifty-five years they handed me me cards!"

Billy Flint slipped out the back door. He'd enjoyed this visit with his niece more than he had thought possible. He'd come again but right now he needed to disappear.

Chapter 49

"I'll be away now, Miss Emerald." April Stevenson didn't look at the child sitting in the window seat. She was busy arranging her new hat over her dark hair. "I'll not be back this evening." Sunday was her afternoon and evening off. She was leaving a bit early but no one would ever know. She wanted to spend time with her young man and her family. The job of nanny to Miss Emerald O'Connor was only for a short time. She was glad to get the work and the little girl was no bother. The child seemed happy as a lark sitting quietly playing with her dolls or reading. No trouble at all really.

"You be good now, Miss Emerald." April spun on her heel, anxious to get out and enjoy herself. It was hard to stay closed up in these rooms all the time, no matter how luxurious they were. Without another word the young woman almost skipped out of the nursery.

"I'm not Emerald." The almost silent whisper echoed around the cavernous space, a silent space tucked away at the top of the house. The rooms seemed to be occupied by the ghosts of children long gone. "I'm Emmy," silent tears rolled down the sad little face, "and I'm hungry."

When no one came to feed her Emmy decided she'd have to take things into her own hands. She'd been good. She'd waited patiently. Her papa had promised if she was a good girl for one month they would move close to her Uncle Jem and Aunty Ivy. The month was up. She'd been keeping count. She'd kept her promise but papa had broken his. That was wrong.

She jumped off the window seat, the stiff material of the dress and petticoats she was wearing ripping at her delicate skin. She pulled at the neckline scratching her skin raw. She hated these clothes. The clothes Aunty Ivy made for her had never itched and scratched. She made her way out of the nursery and down the long servant's staircase to the kitchen. She needed something to eat. Her tummy was grumbling.

She pushed open the door to the kitchen. Mrs Skelly was nice. She always greeted Emmy with a smile. She never had time to talk with her though. She had a very important job keeping Papa and Ann Marie fed, that's what she'd told Emmy.

There was no one in the kitchen but there were lovely smells that made her tummy rumble even more. She stood looking around. Everything was set so high up. She pulled one of the wooden chairs out from under the work table and stood on it to see what she could find to eat. She didn't go looking for someone to feed her. She knew her papa and Ann Marie had gone to Ann Marie's church. She'd seen them go out in the car from her window.

She found a loaf of bread sitting under a damp tea towel. She pulled it towards her and started stuffing the dry bread into her mouth. She remembered her Uncle Jem giving her bread with fat on it. Maybe there was something in the big oven. She jumped off the chair and with great difficulty pulled open the oven door. There was a dish of meat cooking in fat, sitting on a shelf in the oven. She dipped the piece of bread she held in her hand into the fat, careful not to burn her fingers. She blew on the bread before she popped the fat-soaked piece into her hungry mouth. It wasn't as good as Uncle Jem's but it was better than dry bread. She returned to get the loaf, pulling it off the work surface.

She decided to look around see what else she could find to eat. She found the cold cupboard. There were eggs, a great big ham and a wheel of cheese as well as milk and cream sitting in the cupboard. She stared at the food for a long time, tears running down her face. A sharp nod of her head signalled she'd reached a decision. She closed the cupboard door and rubbed her greasy hands on the beautiful dress she hated.

"I don't like it here," the little girl stated aloud. "Everyone has gone out and forgotten all about me." She knew the Skellys were in their cottage – she could go there – there were men working in the orchard, but she wanted her Uncle Jem. "Well, I'm going out too, so there." She stuck her tongue out at the empty room.

Emmy ran through the house. She'd take the main staircase this time. She ran up the stairs and into her papa's bedroom. She knew her papa emptied his pockets every night. She began to search the room for coins. She found what she needed spread over the dressing table. She pulled the skirt of the dress out and with her arm emptied all of the coins from the top of the dresser into her skirt. She carefully clutched the bundle to her and left the room.

When she was back in the nursery Emmy tried to

remove the stiff dress but without a servant to help her she couldn't reach the buttons at the back of her neck. She stamped her little feet in frustration before crossing to her desk and getting a pair of scissors. She cut the neck of the dress open and tore the annoying thing from her. She gave the stiff fabric a kick when she finally got it off. She fell to her knees in front of the wardrobe, searching for the white sailor dress Ivy had made for her. She'd been wearing it when they brought her to this house. She knew it had to be here somewhere.

Emmy was at the back door of the house, her hand on the doorknob, when she remembered the cheese and ham. Ivy would like those. She had the coins tied up in one of the handkerchiefs Ivy had made for her. She'd tried to restore order to her hair but she didn't care if it was messy.

She went back to get the cheese and ham. She pulled the items from the cold cupboard with difficulty. She struggled over to a nearby table and dropped each item down on it. She was breathless. Those things were heavy. She'd never be able to carry them. She smiled suddenly and ran to a cupboard hidden under the stairs. She pulled out the big doll's pram stored there for her use. With a happy laugh she pushed the pram, almost an exact copy of Ivy's, over to where she'd left the ham and cheese. With a grunt she upended both items into the bed of the pram. She ran back up the servant's stairs to fetch one of the porcelain dolls that you could look at but not play with. She didn't want the doll. She had her rag dolls waiting for her in The Lane. But Ivy, she thought, should be able to get money down the market for the doll. She put it in the pram and covered it and her other treasures with the doll's blankets. She opened the back door and pushed her pram out into the yard.

She pushed her well-filled pram along the driveway. There was no one to stop the little girl. Everyone was tending to his or her own business. Emmy knew where the charabanc stop was in the village. She hoped she had enough money to pay the fare.

The area set aside for the charabanc was busy. No one took any notice of the child. If anyone did think about the pretty little girl, each person thought she was with someone else. A kind gentleman helped Emmy get her pram up onto the step of the charabanc. The man grinned down at her when he felt the weight. He asked if she was smuggling rocks home from the seaside. She gave him a wide smile and sat down to enjoy the journey, the first she'd ever taken on a charabanc.

"Fares, please, fares!" The conductor walked down the aisle of the charabanc taking coins from everyone.

Emmy watched carefully, making careful note of the price of a trip 'all the way' that the people around her requested.

"Where to, Miss?" the conductor asked when he reached the place where Emmy sat. The man didn't think anything of a child paying her own fare. It wasn't unusual for parents to allow their children to do that. It made them feel grown up and helped them appreciate the value of money.

"Dublin," Emmy chirped, "city centre, please." She knew The Lane was in the city centre – Aunty Ivy often remarked that she loved living in the centre of the city.

In this fashion Miss Emerald O'Connor made her break for freedom. She sat on the high seat of the charabanc, a big smile on her face. She didn't think she was doing anything wrong. Papa was always busy. He and Ann Marie talked and walked and talked some more. In the evening they got all dressed up and went out again. They wouldn't miss her. She sat watching the scenery go by and listening to the families around her talk about their day out at the seaside.

"Last stop, everybody off, last stop!" The conductor's voice was almost drowned out by the noise of the bell the driver was clanging. "Last stop!"

Emmy was again assisted with her pram, this time by a youth. He smiled at her before running away. She stood alone in the street for a moment, looking around her. She knew this place. This was where Aunty Ivy did her banking. She wasn't far from home. With a smile fit to break her face, she took hold of the handle of the pram and pushed it in the direction of The Lane.

Emmy felt as if there were wings on her heels as she almost ran along the busy streets of Dublin. She knew exactly how to get from where she was to where she longed to be.

Chapter 50

"Do you think Emerald will mind that we married without inviting her?" Ann Marie was feeling giddy as a young girl. She glanced over at the handsome man at her side in the car – her husband.

"I don't think Emerald will give our marriage a moment's thought when we tell her we are moving back to your house in Dublin." Edward smiled over at his new bride. They had spent the last weeks talking and making plans for their life together. "You really believe Emerald will be safe running between two households?"

"I haven't spoken with Jem and Ivy yet." Ann Marie had fought long and hard to make Edward see the advantage to Emerald that staying with Jem and Ivy would bring. "We have talked of travelling. It is not fair to Emerald to leave her with staff all the time. Jem and Ivy love your little girl. They are more natural parents than either you or I. We can learn a lot from them. Times are changing, darling. We both want to change with them."

"I have a feeling being married to you is going to be one long adventure." Edward didn't take his eyes off the road. They were coming up to the entrance to Ann

Marie's Dalkey estate. It would soon be time to close and lock the main gates. The house could go back to sleep for winter. He and his little family were moving into the city. He smiled at the thought.

"Something is wrong." Ann Marie looked around at the people running around the grounds. Eleanor Skelly, when she saw the car, charged towards them, tears running down her face.

"We can't find Emerald," she shouted.

"What do you mean you can't find Emerald?" Edward jumped out of the car, his heart almost stopping. He couldn't lose his little girl again. "How can you lose a child? Where is she?"

"Edward . . ." Ann Marie put her hand gently on his arm. It was no good shouting at the help. Poor Mrs Skelly was distraught. "Where is the nursemaid, Mrs Skelly? Where is Nanny April?" Ann Marie had asked the nanny to wait with Emerald until she returned. The woman had agreed to do so. What on earth could have happened?

"I don't know. I'm sorry. There was no-one here when we arrived at the house." Eleanor Skelly was sick with nerves. They would lose their jobs over this. "I went up to the nursery first thing to check on Nanny April and the child. There was no sign of them but Emerald's white dress was torn and thrown on the floor. And there are things missing from the kitchen." Eleanor didn't feel it was her place to wonder why Miss Gannon had asked them to change their hours around. They were to take the morning off and work the afternoon. She'd arrived to find her cupboards open and items missing. She'd run up the stairs to confront the nursemaid.

"Call the Garda," Edward ordered. They could figure

342

out the ins and outs later. His little girl was missing and he wanted her found.

"Howayeh, Emmy," one of the young lads that hung around The Lane shouted as he ran to retrieve his paper-and-twine ball. "Haven't seen yeh in ages."

"Hello, Eric," Emmy replied. "I'm going to see my Uncle Jem."

"He's gone home." Eric gave a gap-toothed grin. "Saw him meself."

"Thank you." Emmy turned her pram in the direction of her Aunty Ivy's. She left the pram at the top of the steps as she'd seen Aunty Ivy do. She'd need help getting the heavy pram down the steel steps. She knocked on the familiar front door and waited, almost dancing in her excitement.

The door opened.

"Who are you?" Emmy demanded of the stranger who stood in the open door. "Where is my Aunty Ivy?" She was shocked at finding someone she didn't know in her aunt's home.

"She moved." The door slammed. Eve Grant, Patty's eldest daughter, had enough to put up with without answering questions from rude little girls.

Emmy stood stunned for a moment. She didn't know what to do. Her Aunty Ivy had moved away and now she didn't know where she was. She went up the steel steps like an old woman. It was all too much for her. She sat on the steps leading up to the tenement house and sobbed as if her heart was breaking.

"Emmy!" Maisie Reynolds ran down the steps and dropped down beside the little girl. She put her arm around the child's shaking figure and pulled her in close to her side. "Emmy, love, tell me what's wrong."

"I can't find my Aunty Ivy," Emmy wailed, tears running down her face, her entire body shaking with sobs. "I don't know where she's gone. My Aunty Ivy is gone."

"Silly little girl!" Maisie used her apron to wipe the little girl's face. "She's only across the way." She stood up, shouting for her husband. As soon as he appeared in the open door of the house, she said, "I'm going to take this little one across to Ivy and Jem." She gave him a look that said she didn't know what was going on but she was going to find out. She picked the child up off the steps and put her on her hip.

"My pram!" Emmy reached down to grab at the handle of her doll's pram still sitting at the gate leading down to the two basement rooms. "I can't leave my pram. I have presents for my Aunty Ivy."

"Give the child to me." Peter Reynolds came down the steps to take the child. "You get the pram, love." The pair set out together to take Emmy home.

"This is Old Man Wilson's house," Emmy whispered when she saw where they had stopped. "He doesn't like to be bothered by little girls." She'd been warned to stay away from this door.

"I think he changed his mind," Peter said simply. He rapped on the door and waited.

"Peter Reynolds," Frank Wilson opened his front door and stared at the people in front of him, "what brings you to my door?"

"I want my Uncle Jem and my Aunty Ivy, please, sir," Emmy pushed her head away from the big man's shoulder to say.

"Name of Jesus," Frank Wilson gaped, "what's going on?"

"That's what we'd like to know," Maisie Reynolds said with a frown.

"Jem," Frank shouted down the hall. "Ivy, get out here! Jem Ryan! Ivy!"

The pair almost exploded from the door leading to the back rooms.

They stopped suddenly, staring at the sight in front of them.

"Emmy!" they screamed as one, charging down the long hallway.

Jem pulled the little girl into his arms, his green eyes wild.

"Uncle Jem!" Emmy wrapped her arms around Jem's neck and almost choked the life out of him. She never wanted to let go ever again. "I couldn't find you."

"Oh, love!" Ivy petted the child's back and stared at the other adults. No one knew what to say or do. Ivy did what she always did in an emergency. "Come along in, everyone," she said. "I'll put the kettle on and we'll find out what's going on." She knew her neighbours wouldn't budge until they'd heard the whole story.

"Jem!" Conn Connelly almost exploded out of the livery. He shouted when he saw the door to the very house he wanted was about to close. "Jem Ryan, don't close that door! Jem!" He ran forward and slammed his hand on the door. "Emmy is missing!" he shouted through the gap in the door. "Ann Marie is on the telephone in an awful state. The Garda have been called. Did you hear me, man? Emmy is missing!"

"I'm not missing, silly," Emmy giggled as soon as Jem pulled the front door open. "I'm right here."

"I'm either too old or too young for this." Conn stared at the grinning girl in disbelief. His heart had almost stopped when he'd been told she was missing. Now look at her – happy as a lark.

"I'll go." Ivy pushed Jem out of her way. "You put the kettle on, Jem, and find out from Emmy what's going on. In the meantime I'll tell Ann Marie that Emmy is with us." She didn't even take the time to remove her apron but ran back across to the livery with Conn at her side.

"Ivy . . ." John Lawless was ashen-faced. He couldn't imagine how he would feel if one of his children went missing.

"It's all right, John," Ivy put her hand on his shoulder and picked up the telephone he indicated. "Emmy is safe across the way with Jem."

"Ivy, did I hear you say Emmy is with you?" Ann Marie's voice shouted down the telephone. "Did Jem come and pick her up? What is going on?"

"Ann Marie," Ivy said, "I haven't a clue what's going on. We opened our door to find Emmy on the doorstep. Conn was only seconds behind the child telling us you were on the telephone and Emmy was missing. She's safe and sound at the moment with Jem."

"Dear Lord, Ivy!" There was a pause and then Ivy heard her say, "Emerald is with Jem and Ivy, Edward."

"Ivy?" Edward was on the line.

"Edward, Emmy is here with us. She has only this minute arrived. I don't know any more than that, I'm afraid. She seemed to be fine from the little I saw. If you'll give me a little time I'll find out what happened and telephone you. Is that alright?"

"Thank you, Ivy." The man's voice was laden with relief. "We will wait to hear from you."

"Jesus, Ivy," John said as soon as Ivy put the telephone down, "what's going on?"

"I haven't a clue, John." Ivy turned to return to her own home and get to the bottom of this. "You heard me tell them – Emmy turned up at our door. We haven't a notion how she got there. She's with Jem – he'll get the full story." She patted Conn's shoulder as she passed him. "Thanks, Conn."

She ran across to her own place and through the open front door. She closed the door at her back, ran down the hall and almost fell into her own kitchen. The visitors were sitting at the table while Jem sat in one of her old easy chairs with Emmy on his lap.

"Have you the ingredients for a bit of goody on hand, Ivy?" Maisie said as soon as Ivy came through the door. She had watched with envy while Jem filled a familiar black kettle from a water tap right in their very own room – and a sink! "The wonder of it," she gasped, when Jem set the kettle to boil on a brand spanking-new gas stove that was tucked into the alcove on one side of the big gleaming black range. She'd have plenty to tell the neighbours about Ivy Murphy and her new rooms. Evicted indeed – the girl was coming up in the world as far as she could see. "I could run across to my place and fetch the stuff if you haven't it on hand." Maisie couldn't wait to tell all she'd seen.

"I've everything at hand," Ivy said. "Give us a minute to gather me thoughts." A bowl of goody might be the very thing for Emmy just now. The child looked pale and clammy to her. The rich goody, bread soaked in warm milk with a knob of butter and sugar, might settle well in the little one's stomach.

"Mr Wilson!" Jem rubbed the little girl's back constantly. He'd made and served the tea. That was all he was capable of doing. He knew he should be up and helping Ivy but he couldn't bear to turn loose the shivering child in his arms. "Mr Wilson," he called again, "would you mind opening the window over the sink and perhaps the back door as well? We need a bit more air in here."

"Take Emmy into the garden for a minute, Jem," Ivy suggested. They needed to know how Emmy had arrived here. The child didn't look well. She knew the little girl would tell Jem everything when they were alone. He could decide what he wanted to share with the people in this room. She'd find out the whole story for herself later.

"You served the tea in enamel mugs, Jem," she said, looking at the table in horror.

"Sorry, love." Jem stepped through the back door with Emmy in his arms. He'd more important things to be thinking about than setting a pretty table.

"You won't know yerself in this place, Ivy." Maisie and her husband were seated with Mr Wilson at the kitchen table. She looked around, trying to take everything in. The tall dresser Ivy had inherited was pushed against the wall that stretched from one of the range alcoves to the hall door that opened to the front of the house. Maisie wanted to get up and touch everything. She'd never seen anything like the lovely big cupboards under the wide long window that looked out over a garden. She recognised the two old chairs sitting in front of the cold range. The kitchen table and chairs sat out, not quite in the middle of the room. The tall cupboard bed Jem had built for Emmy sat proudly in an area of wall between the door that led out of the kitchen into the back garden and towards the second of their rooms.

"I'm still finding me way around." Ivy looked at her old kitchen table covered in its floral-design oilcloth. It looked very festive to her eyes. Mr Wilson had fixed the six matching kitchen chairs. Her two old kitchen chairs were only fit for the fire. The new gas stove was a sheer delight. Mr Wilson and Jem had plumbed it in as a surprise for her. She wanted to show off her new place. She was only human after all. She'd take the time to invite some of the neighbours when she was settled but right now her mind was filled with little Emmy. She sighed over the sight of the enamel mugs on her lovely table. Still, she had biscuits she'd picked up from Jacob's factory and a Victoria sponge she'd made, she thought with pleasure.

She'd take care of this lot while Jem was outside sorting out poor little Emmy.

"I don't feel so good, Uncle Jem." Emmy hadn't raised her head to look around the garden.

"Here, love." Jem pulled open the door of the outside toilet. He stood the little girl on the ground in front of the toilet bowl and squatted down beside her. He rubbed her little back in gentle circles. "I'm here, love, if you need to throw up. You go right ahead." He practically felt his heart crack as the little girl dry-heaved. She had nothing in her stomach to throw up. He wanted to punch someone. What had they done to the child?

"Jem." Ivy had seen some of what was going on from

the kitchen window. She'd guessed the rest. She stood in the open back door, torn between the needs of the child and her guests. "I've a warm washcloth here."

"Don't leave me." Emmy grabbed onto Jem's hand.

"Bring it here, love," Jem shouted to Ivy out the open door of the toilet.

"Are you alright, Emmy?" Ivy passed Jem the cloth. She stared into his eyes, a silent question in her raised eyebrows.

He took the cloth from her hand with a headshake. He was none the wiser.

"Okay," Ivy turned to go back inside, "the food will be ready whenever you are." She wanted to kick something.

"I'm still hungry, Aunty Ivy – but don't say 'Duck under the table!'" Emmy giggled, looking around her.

"Let the food settle in your stomach for a minute, love. If you're still hungry I'll make you something else, okay?"

"Okay. Where is my pram?" With the resilience of youth she was sitting at the kitchen table, an empty plate in front of her. "I brought you a present, Aunty Ivy."

"Did you, love?" Ivy wasn't sure what she was feeling. Emmy had delighted in telling the people sitting around the table the story of her journey from Dalkey to Dublin. She'd had the best of audiences, everyone hanging on her every word. She didn't seem to be aware of the horrified glances being exchanged over her head. The clenched fists of the men on the table went unnoticed by her.

"I put the pram in the front hall." Frank Wilson felt strange sitting here like a member of a family. He'd forgotten that sensation – it was nice.

Jem held out his hand to Emmy. "Come on, love, I'll

show you where your pram is." He didn't want to let Emmy out of his sight.

"In the name of Jesus, Ivy, can yeh credit it?" Maisie said when the door into the hallway was closed behind Jem and the child. "Do you think they really left that little love on her own in that great big house? It doesn't sound right to me."

"I know nothing." Ivy stood to replenish the teapot. She had the kettle simmering on the gas stove. She was going to have to look for a bigger pot down the market if she was going to entertain guests. Her little teapot wasn't up to the job.

"They must have been worried sick." Peter Reynolds, the father of two strong sons, couldn't imagine losing either one of them.

"That little girl is smart as sixpence." Frank Wilson thought of his dead sons and wondered at any parent who could neglect their young.

"Did you see how she laughed when she told us about the charabanc conductor telling her the fare was only half price for her since she was half-sized?" Maisie shook her head.

"I have it." Emmy pushed her pram before her into the room. "I saw Biddy – can I go out and play? Where's my rubber balls?" The little girl seemed back to her old self. "May I have a jamjar of tea, Aunty Ivy?" Emmy grinned to see Ivy serve more tea. She had missed her Aunty Ivy's tea. Mrs Skelly didn't know how to make it.

"You had better empty your pram first," Frank Wilson suggested. He'd thought the thing was darn heavy when he pushed it inside. He was expecting the child to unload a lot of pretty pebbles from the seaside. They'd be wet and if they sat much longer in the pram the toy would be ruined.

"Here!" Under the adults' amused eyes Emmy passed an exquisitely gowned porcelain doll to Ivy without a second glance.

She removed the doll's blankets and revealed the bowels of the pram. The room exploded with laughter when the ham and cheese were revealed in all their glory.

"I couldn't carry it all." Emmy didn't understand the laughter.

"You've someone to follow in your footsteps there, Ivy Murphy," Peter Reynolds grinned.

"I ask your sacred pardon!" Ivy gasped at the size of the ham and cheese. She'd never seen anything that big outside a shop. "Where did this stuff come from?"

"It was in the cupboard." Emmy shrugged. "I knew you'd like it. May I give some to Biddy?"

"Of course you can, love," Ivy answered absentmindedly. "Jem, take that stuff out of there, although where we'll store it I've no idea." She looked around at the adults who were trying to hide their broad grins. "Here!" She tried to pass the doll back to Emmy.

"I don't want that one, Aunty Ivy." Emmy refused to take the doll. "Where's my rag doll?" She looked around the room as if expecting the doll to be in plain view. "I want my own doll."

"Jem, show her." Ivy put the doll back in the pram, all the while staring at the food on her kitchen table.

"Your dolls and your balls and anything else you can think of are in the drawer under your bed." Jem pointed to her cupboard. The words were hardly out of his mouth before Emmy was dropping to her knees to pull the big double drawer out of the cupboard that hid her bed.

"I don't know where me big knife is." Ivy had her hands to her face. She was accustomed to keeping all of her cutlery in the drawers of her kitchen table. With the oilcloth covering the table she had decided to change their location.

"The lads most likely put them in the drawers beside the sink." Jem had had the lads help them move into these rooms. They were still searching out their belongings in this much bigger space. "What do you need a knife for?"

"I want to cut some of that ham and cheese. I'll pass some to Biddy to take home and I'm sure the Reynolds would enjoy a bite," Ivy said. "They can have it for their tea."

"Much obliged." Maisie felt her mouth watering at the thought of the treat.

"We should be getting along, love," Peter Reynolds said. "We didn't tell the lads where we were going." That wasn't a problem since everyone in The Lane would be aware of what was going on. But it was time for them to shift. This little family had things to do.

"Do I need to change out of my good sailor dress?" Emmy stood staring at the adults, two colourful rubber balls in her hands. "I want to go out and play with my friends."

"Leave that on." Ivy looked at the white dress that needed to be bleached and starched. It wouldn't do the thing any more harm to play outside in it.

"If you are going to be running in and out of the place," Frank Wilson stood, "you better use the back way. I don't want a gang of childer running past my door." He put his hand on Emmy's shoulder and turned her towards the back door. "Come on, I'll show you."

"I'll bring over a plate for that ham and cheese, Ivy." Maisie and Peter stood. She didn't want to take Ivy's plate. You never sent back a plate empty that you had received full. Lord alone knew when she'd have the means to send back a full plate. Best if she used her own plate to shift the promised treat – there would be no obligation.

"Give us time to find me knives," Ivy said. "Or better yet, bring a knife with you when you bring the plate."

"I'll do that."

The Reynolds left. The news would be all over The Lane in next to no time.

"Jesus, Jem," Ivy wasn't capable of saying more.

"I know, love," Jem pulled Ivy into his arms, "but she's here and alright. That's the main thing."

Chapter 51

Ann Marie's fists were clenched on the steering wheel. She had to consciously remind herself not to speed. These country roads were not safe.

Edward O'Connor sat in the passenger seat, sick with the knowledge he had once again failed to keep his daughter safe. He would be eternally grateful for the telephone call informing them of his daughter's safety.

"The responsibility for this fiasco is not yours alone." She could practically see him kicking himself. She pushed her glasses up her nose.

"I am her father." He was almost ashamed to state that aloud. What kind of father lost his child by his own negligence not once but twice?

"It is considered the done thing, is it not, to allow servants full responsibility for our children's upbringing? I believed myself to be more enlightened. Yet, I too passed responsibility for Emerald onto staff." Ann Marie wanted to slap herself.

They drove in silence, each lost in their thoughts of what might have happened. The knowledge that Emerald had been so unhappy with them that she would run away was eating at both of them. They had failed the child.

Emmy saw them first. She was playing chase with Biddy in the courtyard of The Lane and by chance saw Ann Marie's automobile as it drove past the old entrance from Mount Street. She shouted goodbye to her friends and ran into the livery. It had been explained to her that what she had done was naughty but she didn't care.

"What's wrong?" Jem asked when Emmy threw herself at him, her two arms wrapped around one of his legs. He'd been instructing his jarveys leaving to pick up passengers.

"They're here!" She almost climbed up his body.

"Are they indeed?" He settled the child on his hip and continued to issue instructions. They could bloody wait until he was ready to talk to them. There was work to be done. He stood back and watched carefully as whips were cracked over horses' heads and wheels turned. His men drove out of the new opening in his livery to take up their work.

"Right, lads," he shouted when the aisle was clear of carriages. "I want these floors swept, stalls cleaned and fresh straw put out." He watched the young lads he employed jump to obey. "Conn, you're in charge out here. John's in the office. I'm away home on business. I'll be back as soon as I can."

Jem and Ivy had tried to plan what they would say, what they could do when Emmy's parent turned up. They were constrained by the fact that they were not related in any way to Emmy.

"Right, petal, let's go say hello to your papa." Jem was resisting the temptation to simply run away with the child on his hip. A ridiculous notion since he had nowhere to run. "You can go back to playing with your friends after you've shown the man that you are in fine fettle," he promised the solemn-eyed little girl on his hip.

He walked out of the livery into the cobbled courtyard of The Lane. He turned right in the direction of his new home.

"Emerald!" Edward O'Connor walked swiftly down the courtyard, avoiding the shabbily dressed children playing loudly all around.

Ann Marie stood alone looking on. She felt disorientated. She knew Ivy had moved from her two basement rooms but was unsure which house held her new lodgings.

"Papa." Emmy stared at her parent with accusing green eyes.

"You can see she's fine." Jem dropped Emmy to her feet. "You go play, your papa and I need to talk." He gave the little girl's bottom a pat.

"Grown-up talk," Emmy didn't run away but stood for a moment staring back and forth at the two tall green-eyed men, "about me?"

"That's right, so scram." Jem waited while Emmy rejoined her friends. "Come along, Edward."

He walked away, rooting in his pocket for the key to the front door. He would not walk with this aristocratic man through the back garden and into his kitchen. They would use the front entrance.

"Hello, Ann Marie," Jem said when they reached her side. "I'm afraid you'll have to take us as you find us."

He opened the front door and led the way down the long hallway to the door leading into the back rooms. There was no sign of Ivy. He thought she was probably in one of her sheds taking out her anger and fear on the goods she had stored. He'd been doing much the same at the livery.

"Jem, I am heartily ashamed of myself." Ann Marie wanted to look at everything. She wanted to exclaim aloud at her friends' improved circumstance but she rather thought Edward believed Jem owned the entire house. She was not going to say anything to disabuse him of that notion.

"Thankfully Emmy arrived here safe and sound." Jem washed his hands, filled the kettle and put it on top of the gas stove. "However, no one had thought to tell the child that Ivy moved – she was extremely distressed when a stranger opened what she believed was Ivy's door."

"Well, well, the dead arose and appeared to many!" Ivy stepped into the kitchen.

"Ivy." Ann Marie stood to greet her friend.

Jem hid a grin. Edward stared at the female glaring daggers at him.

"We're good enough to visit when we have something you want, it seems." Ivy stepped around Ann Marie. She wasn't ready to kiss and make up. "I want to slap you both senseless for what you've done to that child."

The two elegantly dressed people sat at her kitchen table and didn't try to defend themselves.

"Jem Ryan, are you out of your mind?" She'd noticed the enamel mugs on her lovely oilcloth. "I won't let you shame me in front of this shower." She grabbed the mugs from the table and began setting the table with her china.

"It's of no matter, Mrs Ryan," Edward said.

"Don't you talk to me, Your Highness, until I've calmed down," Ivy snapped.

"But –"

"But me no buts, yeh stuck-up *amadán*!"

"Sit down, love." Jem almost pushed Ivy into a chair with his hands on her shoulders. "I'll make a fresh pot of tea." He pressed a finger to her lips. "These people are guests and they feel bad enough."

"I didn't invite them in," Ivy fumed.

"I did." Jem turned to take care of making tea.

"There was a reason I never told you for my removing Edward and Emerald to Dalkey," Ann Marie said when Ivy had her first cup of tea in her hands.

"Getting them away from unsavoury sorts like us?"

"Ivy Murphy Ryan, that is uncalled for," Ann Marie snapped. "I am not a snob, nor is Edward."

"Sorry," Ivy said when Jem poked her shoulder.

"And so you should be," Ann Marie snapped. "I was reliably informed that Father Leary had people investigating Emmy and her appearance in your life. I could not risk that man sticking his nose into this business."

Edward took Ann Marie's hand in his. "To our knowledge the matter of Mary Rose Donnelly and Bishop Troy has been settled, and indeed buried, but Ann Marie wasn't willing to allow any danger to come to your door, Mrs Ryan."

"The name's Ivy." She didn't want to let go of her anger.

"Ann Marie and I are married," Edward said.

"So." Ivy leaned back and stared. "It's okay for you two to get married on the quiet but me and Jem had to be done up like the dog's dinner and trotted around the place?"

"You are such a hard head, Ivy," Ann Marie said. "It was important that you should be seen to marry. You know that as well as I."

"We wish you every happiness." Jem shook his head, standing to cross and press a kiss into Ann Marie's cheek. He held out his hand to Edward. "I know you will both be very happy,"

"Ditto," Ivy said.

"You are close enough to my feet for me to kick you, Mrs Ryan." Ann Marie shoved her glasses up her nose. Enough was enough.

The two men exchanged glances and silently decided to ignore the women for the moment.

"I will continue to travel for business and pleasure," Edward said into the silence that had fallen over the room. "Ann Marie will travel with me. We intend to make the house on the Grand Canal our main residence."

"And your daughter?" Ivy asked the question Jem longed to ask.

"I have thought long and hard about what is best for Emerald. Ann Marie and I have discussed the matter in great detail." He looked directly at Jem. "I believe we could easily claim to be related." He waited a moment before saying, "I would not claim to be your father although the Lord knows some days I feel old enough."

"I've had one of those, thanks." Jem didn't know where he was going with this.

"We have reached a decision that we think will work best for all." Edward took a sip of tea. "My wife has the most amazing mind."

"I know and I'm fortunate enough to be married to another such." Jem waited.

"The superficial physical resemblance between us is the reason I thought of this. I think if we claimed to be related through your mother it would suffice."

"Suffice for what?"

"I desire to make you and your wife the legal guardians of my daughter." Edward sat back and waited.

"In the name of God." Ivy looked to Ann Marie to see if she knew about this. Her friend gave a nod but remained silent.

"What would that mean?" Jem had a white-knuckled grip on Ivy's hand.

"As I've stated, I will continue to travel. I must for my business and truthfully I enjoy it. I want you to be her parents when Ann Marie and I are not available. We wish to learn from you two how to be good parents to Emerald and any other children we may be blessed with. Emerald would be as much your child as mine. She already is if the truth were told. I am not willing to give up all rights to my child. However, recent events have forced me to consider what my position in her life should be."

"If I'm understanding you correctly," Jem could feel the grin almost splitting his face, "I," he turned at Ivy's nudge, "I mean we, would be honoured."

"We will need to make it official." Edward was relieved to have got that out of the way. He admired Jem Ryan. The man was honest as the day was long. He'd insisted on giving an accounting of every pound of the money he had used from the stash Miss Donnelly had been carrying when she died. He insisted he would pay the money back in spite of Edward's statement that the money was owed to him for the care he'd taken of Emerald – Emmy, he really would have to remember to call his child

Emmy or be the only one calling her Emerald. "I have to fly back to Galway." Edward would prefer to place this matter in the hands of his family lawyer. "I thought to offer you a flight. Didn't you say your family lived in Sligo?"

"Dear Lord!" The idea of taking an airplane to see his family! It had been a very long time since he'd visited. The livery didn't allow time for pleasure trips.

"That sounds like a fine idea to me, Jem Ryan." Ivy knew he would be in heaven to get a chance to travel in one of those flying machines. "John can handle the business. Ann Marie and I between us will sit on little Miss Runaway."

"Ivy –"

"Jem, talk to the man." She waved her hand in the direction of the livery. He felt most at home there. "Go on, me and Ann Marie have things to talk about. You two go away and talk. Go on."

"Ann Marie?" Edward asked.

"You have your orders, darling. You'll find it doesn't do to disobey Ivy."

Chapter 52

"Tell me again why I'm putting a knocker on me back gate," Frank Wilson said.

"Father Leary." Ivy stood in the open doorway of one of her huts watching the old man on his knees, his tools around him. He was a very handy man to have around the place. "He has my work force terrified. They don't want him to see me going in and out of their places." She needed these women to prepare the dolls for her. She couldn't do everything herself. Well, she could but it would interfere with her profit margin.

"So the knocker is for them to use." Frank tightened the screw he was putting into the heavy brass knocker.

"They want to pick up and collect the dolls and whatnot from here. I won't invite them into my home. I'll handle my business from one of these sheds." Ivy walked over to join him. "They need the money and I need the work done. Still, it saves me time and shoe leather, I suppose." She watched for a while before asking the question that really bothered her. "How are you managing for work?"

"I'm getting a bit about the place." He pushed himself

to his feet. "I make more money but it's not steady."

"I'm sorry I brought this trouble to your door."

"Nonsense." Frank carefully repacked his tools. "Don't you be taking Leary's sins on yourself! He's a dictator with delusions of grandeur. He always has been."

"He still managed to bring a great deal of trouble to our door."

"I saw your brothers at the last place I worked." He hadn't been sure if he should say anything. "I was working on a broken staircase." He wanted to shuffle his feet like a nervous boy at the look she gave him.

"Come up in the world, haven't they?" She'd seen them about town herself but she made sure they never saw her. She had practice at remaining unseen.

"Would you think so?" Frank checked the knocker was secure. "I thought they looked like two kicked pups meself."

"Here's where you are. I tried knocking on the front door." The postman stood behind them. "One of the lads told me to try the back." He was rooting in his postbag while trying to get a look inside the gate. He pulled an envelope that struck fear into his audience and his clipboard from his bag. "I'll need your signature." Tim passed the blue-crossed envelope to Frank Wilson. Ivy watched with her heart in her mouth. She waited till the postman took his leave before taking Frank by the elbow and almost pulling him back into the garden. She locked the gate – shutting out the world.

"It might not be bad news." Frank raised worried eyes.

"That's what we all say." Ivy left him to stand there while she shut down her work. They had gas light in the huts now. She had a free-standing paraffin heater she wouldn't leave standing around her work. It was too dangerous.

Frank watched Ivy hurry around the place, the envelope clenched in his trembling hand. He didn't think he was ready for another shock.

"Come on, I'll put the kettle on and fix us a bite to eat." Ivy led the way into her kitchen. "You can read your letter in peace."

"That aul' bastard," Frank couldn't stay seated. He stood and shook the letter in his hand. "This is from the bank." He swallowed nosily. "They are calling in the loan on this house. I have one month to come up with the remainder of the money I owe them or they'll put this house on the market."

"Can they do that?" Ivy thought you were safe from eviction when you owned your own house.

"They can do anything they bloody like." Frank took the mug she gave him without noticing. "I haven't any way of getting the money to pay back the outstanding balance on that loan. Not in the time they've given me. The bank are going to force me to sell this house. There's no two ways about it." He dropped back into the easy chair by the range. He took a gulp of tea and almost choked. There was a lump in his throat.

Ivy left the man to his thoughts while she prepared a pot of rabbit stew to sit on the back of the range. The days were getting cooler and the heat from the range was a welcome addition to the kitchen. She chopped and diced vegetables while keeping Frank's mug filled. She put a cheese sandwich in his hand. He ate it without comment. The poor man was in shock. She wasn't feeling much better herself. They had spent time and money on getting these rooms and her work area up to a standard that still took her breath away. She was not willing to allow Father Leary to force her out of her home again. She'd be damned before she'd give the aul' goat the satisfaction. He was making her working life difficult but she had found a way around that. She'd handle this too. She wished to God Jem hadn't gone flying around the country just now.

"Mr Wilson." Ivy had the stew on the stove. The old man was still sitting with his feet in the range surround. She didn't think he even remembered she was there. "I know how you feel about people sticking their nose in your business but I have a reason for asking." Now she had his attention. She straightened her shoulders. Nothing ventured, nothing gained. "I have a reason for asking." She gulped air before blurting out: "How much money do you owe the bank?"

"What?"

"Just tell me."

Ivy wished Jem was here. She should talk to him about this first but he was away with Edward O'Connor and wouldn't be back for three more days. She didn't want to wait. She'd chicken out if she gave too much thought to this.

Frank Wilson named a figure that had Ivy gasping. She fell into the chair across the range from him.

"Mr Wilson, I have money in the bank." The thought of handing all of that money over made her sick. She wanted to put her head between her knees, but this needed saying. "You and I are going to go to the bank and I am going to give you the money to repay your loan. It would give me great pleasure to see you hit the bank manager

366

around the chops with that money." There was a lot more to her idea but she needed advice.

"My God girl, you're away with the fairies!" Frank Wilson gasped.

"I'm not really, Mr Wilson." Ivy said. "I've been pushed to my limits I will admit. We would have to consult experts to keep everything legal and above board but we have a bit of time on our hands."

"You can't do something like this without talking to your husband." Frank Wilson stared at her as if she were a candidate for Bedlam.

Chapter 53

"Mr Wilson," Ann Marie addressed the man seated at one end of Ivy's kitchen table, "what I want to speak to you about could be considered extremely personal and indeed nosy and I ask your pardon in advance."

Edward O'Connor looked at his wife with a small smile. His life was certainly interesting since he'd married Ann Marie Gannon. If someone had told him he'd be holding a serious business meeting seated at an oilcloth-covered kitchen table he'd have laughed in their face yet here he sat being served seemingly endless cups of tea while they talked of 'real' money. His daughter was running around outside playing ball and shouting. He could hear her voice echo into the room from time to time.

"I consider the people here my friends." Ann Marie pushed her gold-rimmed glasses up her nose. She had an open folder of papers on the table. "However, if you so desire we can have this conversation in your own room." She held her hand up before the man could say anything. "I feel it only fair to tell you however that I will inform the people here present of whatever we discuss."

"In the name of God, Ann Marie," Ivy dropped into a chair beside Jem. "You sound like you swallowed a plum."

"Go on." Frank Wilson wondered if he'd have stepped forward to help Ivy Murphy if he'd known it would lead to the disruption of his life like this.

"Ivy wishes to advance you a large sum of money," Ann Marie had to get this matter sorted before she and Edward left for America.

"I'll pay it back."

"No one seated around this table doubts that for a moment," Jem put in quickly.

"Please," Ann Marie leaned forward to stare into the man's furious eyes, "bear with me. I truly think I have come up with a plan that suits everyone involved. To know if my plan will work I must ask rude questions. I'm sorry but there is no other way."

"Think a lot of yourself, don't you?" Frank said.

"Steady." Edward would not allow anyone to insult his wife. She'd worked long and hard on this plan.

"I think a lot of Ivy."

"I'd never take advantage."

"Please, Mr Wilson."

"If you're going to be rude and nosy you may as well call me Frank."

The other three at the table looked back and forth between the two as if they were seated at a boxing match.

"Thank you – Frank." Ann Marie pushed her glasses up her nose – took firm control of her nerves and jumped in. "I believe you own this house."

"I do." He sat back in his chair and crossed his arms.

"The money Ivy loans you will pay off the last of your

mortgage, is that correct?" When Frank simply nodded she asked softly, "What do you plan to do with this house when you die?" He wasn't a young man; he must have thought of this.

"You think I should leave a house worth," he named a sum she knew to be fair, "to your friend Ivy, do you?"

"No, that is not what I'm thinking," Ann Marie said. "I have heard of the loss of your family, sir, and I am heartily sorry for the pain you suffered. However, what I need to know from you is if you have close family ties that you believe would dispute what you might do with this house."

"If that's your way of asking if I have anyone to leave the house to when I die then the answer is no."

"Good." She waved her hands in the air, silently apologising for the way that sounded. They hadn't time to tiptoe around hurt feelings. "What I am suggesting is that you offer to sell this house to Ivy at a reduced rate."

"I'm not selling me home and living in the streets for no-one," Frank snapped.

"Please listen." Ann Marie had consulted a lawyer about this matter. It would work if this man was agreeable. "I think you know that if you needed care or assistance you couldn't have a better pair of friends than Ivy and Jem Ryan." She looked towards the pair silently watching. "I'm suggesting that we have papers drawn up selling this house to Ivy for a reduced rate. It will be written into the documents that your rooms are yours for as long as you live. Should you become feeble and need care, Jem and Ivy will be on hand to take care of you."

"Ivy's a married woman. The papers should be drawn up in her husband's name." Frank had worried about what might happen to him in his old age.

"I have business plans coming up," Jem said. They were only talking about their big plans for the moment. He'd know more when Edward and Armstrong returned from America. He wanted the roof over Ivy's head to be secure. He wouldn't do anything that would jeopardise that. "I don't want to endanger Ivy's savings."

"Can you really do all you say you can?" Frank had never heard of the like.

"Edward and his lawyers assure me that I can," Ann Marie said while Edward nodded. "I don't think you will find anything to disagree with, Frank. Ivy and Jem would have looked after you no matter what. I think you know that. However, if you agree to this you would have a large sum of cash in the bank for your own use. You would be free to work or not as you pleased."

"I like to work," Frank said. "I'm good with me hands."

"You would be free to do only the work you wanted. No more jumping to for a boss."

"No more walking out in the cold and dark." Frank had been looking for steady work ever since he was laid off. He didn't enjoy taking orders but a man had to do what a man had to do. He needed to pay his way.

"The money and the worry of the tenants would of course pass to Ivy." Ann Marie could see the man wanted to agree. She felt like jumping up and dancing. It was ideal. Ivy would be a homeowner. She need never again fear eviction.

"I'll need to talk more about this but, from what you've said here, it looks like I'll have to agree." Frank looked at the men to see what they thought of the situation.

"I think it might be the best thing you have ever done, Frank," Jem said. "I don't see anything in this that would bring harm to you."

"It is an excellent solution for all concerned," Edward said. "I've sat in on the talks my wife had with the lawyers. I believe this is a brilliant solution to a variety of problems. Truthfully, I can see no injury to your good person at all. I do however advise you to consult your own lawyer if you know such a man."

"I promise not to be as grumpy a landlord as you've been, Mr Wilson," Ivy said.

"Ivy Ryan," Frank looked at her and shook his head in wonder at the changes she was bringing to his life, "it's all up here for thinking," he pointed at his head, "and down there for dancing," he pointed at his feet, "with you." He was seeing a rosy old age for himself. He looked at the people gathered around the table and said, "The woman wants me to build a shed to the side of this house and start repairing furniture for resale. She even has the name of me first apprentice on her lips."

"Would that be something you would enjoy?" Jem knew that if his Ivy wanted a work shed then she'd have one.

"It's worth thinking about," Frank had a great deal to think about. Things just might be looking up for him.

"We need to set up an appointment to visit the lawyers and sign papers." Edward knew his wife was determined this matter be settled before they left the country.

"I'll sort out me best suit," Frank Wilson said simply.

Chapter 54

"Ivy," Frank Wilson put his head around the hall door after rapping his knuckles on the wood, "is Emmy around?"

"No, she's out playing." Ivy sat back in her chair, glad of the break from her ever-increasing bookwork. "Jem is out and about with Edward." Since the O'Connors' return from America the two men had become thick as thieves. She put the top back on the bottle of ink she'd been using. "Jem spends more time dressed up in his fancy suits than his work clothes these days," she remarked absently.

"I wanted to have a word with you about the little one's Christmas present." Emmy had decided that, since she didn't have a grandfather living near, Mr Wilson would become her grandfather. Emmy lived with Jem and Ivy. Her father and Ann Marie shared in her care but more as beloved aunt and uncle than parents. The child didn't seem to care as she ran between both homes happily.

"I can't believe it's nearly that time of year again." Ivy stood waving her hand to invite him in. The pantomime this year was *Aladdin* so she hadn't made a doll to sell in the street. The Alice dolls were a steady seller and the demand for baby dolls never seemed to diminish. Her doll business was thriving. The Lawless family were kept busy with the demands. "I'll put the kettle on."

"No," Frank said, "if you'll step into my place I'll put the kettle on. I've something I want to show you."

"I'll take you up on that offer." Ivy pulled off her apron and washed the ink off her hands. She was glad to get out of this room. She'd been working on her accounts all morning and her eyes were ready to cross. She followed Frank to his room.

"Oh dear God above!" She clapped her hands to her mouth and stared. "That is the most beautiful doll's house I've ever seen in my life." She walked around the table the doll's house was standing on. The late Victorian style house had three floors with bay windows at the front – it even had dormer windows under the roof. She looked at Frank for permission to pull the front of the house open so she could see the interior. At his nod she carefully pulled the front of the house away and gasped at the beautifully carved staircase in the centre – at the four rooms, two on each side of the stairs. "You know . . ." she started slowly.

"Don't start telling me we could make money off this, Ivy Ryan." Frank knew that look by now. The woman never stopped thinking of ways to make money. "I made this for the only grandchild I have," he stared at her, "at least until you and Jem get busy making me some more."

"Mind your manners." She was used to comments about her lack of a baby. She didn't care. She'd have a baby when she was ready and not before.

"I need help with the soft furnishings." Frank had the

374

kettle on and was back watching Ivy stand staring at the doll's house.

"Emmy is not touching this until Ann Marie has photographed every inch of it," Ivy stated firmly. The doll's house was furnished with the most beautiful hand-carved furniture she had ever seen. She reached out slowly, almost afraid to touch the tiny objects. "You, Mr Frank Wilson, are a true artist."

He ignored her comment. "It needs carpets and cushions and such like. I can't make those."

"It would be a labour of love and an honour for me to make them, Frank," Ivy wanted the doll's house for herself. It was astonishing.

"Good." Frank had been hoping she would offer. "I've time yet but I want to get it finished to put under the tree." He got busy serving the tea that seemed to fuel this dynamo of a woman.

"There's money to be made from houses like that, Frank." Ivy could see something similar in the window of Geraldine's shop in Grafton Street.

"Don't start." He shook his finger in her face. "I want to get this one done first," he said with a grin. "Then we'll talk."

They sat drinking their tea, admiring the doll's house and talking about soft furnishings.

"Ivy!"

"I'm with Frank, Jem," she shouted back.

"It comes to something when a man comes home to find his wife with another man!" Jem's voice echoed along the hallway.

"I'm hungry, Aunty Ivy!"

Emmy's voice had them both jumping to their feet. The

little girl couldn't see the doll house.

"When are you not?" Ivy whispered "We'll talk later" to Frank and hurried to step out into the hallway. She pulled the door closed at her back before the other two could look inside.

Jem, with Emmy on his back, raised his eyebrows but said nothing when Ivy shook her head.

"What are we having to eat?" Emmy demanded, not noticing the byplay between the adults.

"Duck."

"Don't say duck under the table, Aunty Ivy!" Emmy said. "I'm really hungry."

"I'll have to see if I've any stale bread." Ivy led the way back to their rooms. She had a pork roast with carrots and potatoes in the oven of her gas cooker.

"I met the postman coming in, Ivy," Jem said.

"Anything for us?" She opened the door as she asked. There was a large brown-paper-wrapped package sitting on the table beside her account books. That wasn't what had the breath trapped in her throat however. A familiar white blue-crossed envelope sat on top of the package.

"Sweet Jesus," Ivy prayed, falling into one of her kitchen chairs, "what now?"

"It may not be bad news." Jem slid Emmy off his back.

"Where have I heard that before?"

"What's wrong?" Emmy looked between the two adults.

"Wait just a minute, Emmy." Jem began to remove the books and bottles from the table. He placed everything carefully in the cupboard Ivy kept for her work items. "We won't know what's in that until you open it, Ivy." He sat on the kitchen chair alongside Ivy. When she made no move he opened the table drawer and drew out a knife. Those cursed envelopes were hard to tear. He cut through the fabric-imbued envelope and removed the contents. He scanned the note briefly. "Looks like it's third time lucky, Ivy. Look."

Ivy took the paper from his hands, wondering at the big grin on his face. She glanced down at the two pieces of paper she held, unable to understand what she was seeing.

"That can't be right," she gasped.

"What is it?" Emmy asked.

"A cheque." Jem knew they'd get no peace if he didn't answer. "A great big fat cheque."

"Oh." Emmy wasn't interested in cheques – they weren't exciting. "May I open the package?"

"Here . . ." Jem pushed the package towards the curious child. He used the knife in his hand to cut the twine off.

"Jem, are me eyes deceiving me?" Ivy whispered under the noise of Emmy's excited cries as she emptied the package of bottles of lotions and potions. "Is that dollars? How much is that worth?"

"It's not dollars." He took the paper from her hand. He looked again, having a hard time believing what he was seeing, "See, it says here that Betty lodged the money in her Irish bank account. They've cut a banker's cheque at her request. That's pounds, shillings and pence, Ivy."

"It can't be." Ivy couldn't believe it. "All of that money, Jem. It can't be right." Tears began to leak from her eyes. Granny Grunt. That old woman was still looking after her.

"I'm married to a wealthy woman." Jem stood and

pulled her into his arms. He rocked her gently back and forth while watching Emmy unpack the package of goodies from America. He was doubly glad Ann Marie had protected Ivy's money from him. The O'Connors and Armstrongs had returned from America full of ideas. They had invited him to be part of their business dealings. He had taken out a mortgage on the livery and entered into what many would call a risky business venture. Ann Marie, her husband Edward, Jem and William Armstrong had gone into business together to buy a theatre. They were convinced that talking pictures were the way of the future. Their theatre was the only one in Ireland equipped to play talking pictures. He believed in what they were doing but if they failed – well, his Ivy was protected.

Chapter 55

"You look gorgeous, Ivy," Sadie said. Her daughters and an eagle-eyed Emmy stood at her side. "Honest to God, you look like a fillum star yerself." The women were gathered in one of the spare bedrooms in Ann Marie's house. The bed had been removed to allow room for the experts to work.

"These products you received from America are wonderful," Carmela, the number one beautician in Dublin, said.

Ann Marie came to stand at her friend's shoulder. "We both look wonderful. I want to thank you ladies very much for all your hard work." She had already passed Carmela a generous cheque.

Ivy wore a heavily beaded silver dress that left her shoulders and upper chest bare before falling like water down to her silver shoes. Her hair was completely hidden by one of the new-fashioned beaded caps. A fringe of beads dancing on her forehead made her violet eyes surrounded by their thick dark lashes stand out like jewels.

"Here!" Sadie bent to remove a white fur from a familiar box on the floor at her feet.

"I borrowed my aunt's winter-wolf fur," Ann Marie explained while Sadie stood behind Ivy holding the coat open. "None of my coats would be long enough for you Ivy."

"Aunty Ivy," Emmy said, staring, "you look like the Snow Queen out of my fairytale book."

"Does that make me the Wicked Stepmother in *Snow White*?" Ann Marie, in crystal-encrusted black, asked.

"You both look like film stars," Emmy said.

"Who is going to take the photographs?" Sadie couldn't believe Ann Marie hadn't been taking pictures of every moment of this day.

"I employed Milo for this evening." Ann Marie was unwilling to let this important occasion pass without a pictorial record.

"We better get downstairs soon or you won't have any men in your photographs, Ann Marie. I keep half expecting Jem to run down the street and check on things."

"We'll go down first." Sadie took Emmy's hand in hers. "I'll tell Milo you're ready,"

"Are we ready, Ivy?" Ann Marie felt slightly breathless. Edward had planned every stage of this development with military precision.

"Look out, Dublin," Ivy grinned, "here we come!"

"Hold it," Milo Norton shouted from the bottom of the staircase. "I want you to walk down the stairs one at a time. Then I'll take one of the two women together."

"I don't think my knees will keep me upright if that fella doesn't stop sending us up and down stairs like a yo-yo." Ivy stood by Jem's side, admiring the picture presented by

Ann Marie and Edward O'Connor. The couple were standing on the staircase being photographed. She examined the tuxedo Edward was wearing, comparing it to Jem's. To her eyes there was little difference between the Saville Row suit Edward wore and Mr Solomon's creation for Jem. The two men looked breathtakingly handsome.

"I have to say, love, your brother knows what suits you." Ivy's brother Shay had insisted the garment she was wearing be included on the flights that carried the films they were showing this evening. "I don't know what creams and potions Betty sent along but your skin is like ice cream. I want to bite it." Betty Armstrong had moved to Hollywood, leaving Hannah Solomon to manage the New York branch of her business. Betty believed there was a fortune to be made in Hollywood.

Edward had set up a flight relay with friends from his army days. One man had flown from California to New York. A second man and plane had travelled from New York to Galway before Edward's brother had flown the film and packages to Dublin. It had taken days instead of months. Edward believed the delivery would put their business ahead of everyone else. The showing tonight was an invitation-only Gala opening. The demand for tickets would fill their theatre for months.

"It's time for us to leave." Jem consulted his gold fob watch.

"I'd rather be one of the people watching us," Ivy admitted.

There was a flurry of movement as the couples checked to see if they had everything they would need.

They stepped outside where a Rolls Royce was sitting

in the driveway, its engine purring.

"Your man Armstrong doesn't believe in doing anything by halves, does he?" Ivy gasped. The area around the theatre was floodlit. Lights lit up the sky and a red carpet was rolled out into the street.

"He is copying that theatre in New York that played the first talking film back in August," Jem said. "The crowds in New York stopped traffic."

William Armstrong was standing on the first-floor carpeted hallway. He might be in partnership with others but his name and face would lead the company. His eyes glanced over Ivy before snapping back. The bloody woman looked like something out of a magazine.

"I'm going to kill him," Ivy whispered to Jem sitting alongside her.

She and everyone else were enthralled by the talking, singing, moving pictures. It was magical to see Shay open his mouth and words she could actually hear come out. He'd taken her breath away. In this second short film featuring Shay, he was singing to a young woman wearing the exact outfit Ivy was wearing. The bloody man had set her up for attention.

"It's almost time for intermission," Jem whispered. A long feature film with sound was not available yet but it was coming. He expected to make a fortune from this marvel.

Edward O'Connor sipped from his glass of champagne. They were standing in a group drinking champagne while the men congratulated each other on being the first to venture into this brand-new world of talking pictures.

"Ivy," said Edward, "you look more beautiful than the woman on screen who had the temerity to wear your gown."

William Armstrong and his wife Thelma were standing with them. "I saw some gentlemen of the press running out of here to publish their story," said William. "Ivy, I must say you look a wonder. That brother of yours has a good head on his shoulders. Your wearing that outfit will set the tongues wagging which can only be good for our enterprise, gentlemen." He hadn't seen this outfit under the fur she'd been wearing.

"Truly stunning, Ivy," Thelma Armstrong said.

"William, won't you introduce my family to these people?" Cedric Williams called aloud as he approached the group. "After all, it is my son up there on the big screen, is it not?" He was aware of people turning to stare. He enjoyed the attention. "I'm sure everyone has noticed the male star's startling resemblance to my lady wife."

Ivy was frozen in place. She had her back turned to the people who had joined their group, her hand on Jem's arm in a death grip.

"Allow me to introduce my friends." William delighted in the shock he offered to his snobby half-brother as he introduced Ann Marie and her husband to him. Cedric made it his business to know all of the current Dublin gossip. Ann Marie Gannon's marriage was a nine-day wonder amongst their social set.

Then he introduced Jem but Jem refused to acknowledge the introduction.

"Ivy," William turned her to face her mother and

brothers, "I believe these people are known to you."

The beaded cap hid Ivy's dark hair completely. The resemblance between Ivy and her mother was striking.

"You are mistaken, I believe," said Ivy. "These people are strangers to me."

She was aware of her friends closing in around her. Jem put his arm around her waist. Ann Marie took her hand and Edward stood behind the two women.

Ivy allowed her eyes to examine the people standing in front of her. She noticed her brothers had the grace to drop their eyes but her mother stared, the expression on her face almost malicious.

"We should return to our seats." She turned to take Jem's arm in hers. "I'd hate to miss my brother's performance. He is, after all, the star of the show." She turned her back and walked away.

"Ivy, love," Jem knew her knees must be knocking, "I think you just put your mother and brothers in the ha'penny place."

Now that you're hooked why not try
Through Streets Broad and Narrow?
also published by Poolbeg

Here's a sneak preview of
chapters one and two.

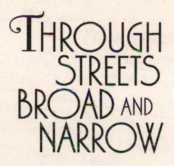

Chapter 1

The sound of her own teeth chattering woke Ivy Murphy from her uneasy sleep. She had a crick in her neck and every bone in her body wanted to complain. Ivy didn't know if the aches she felt were the result of her uncomfortable position in her battered fireside chair or her shenanigans in the street earlier. The Lane had celebrated the brand-new year with a lively street party.

Ivy didn't drink alcohol but she'd been the first to start dancing and singing. To someone unused to celebration it had been a wonderful way to greet the year 1925. She'd been giddy with happiness until she'd returned home.

Ivy stared in the general direction of the battered clock ticking away on her mantelpiece. She had no idea how long she'd slept. She'd been waiting for her da to come home, praying he had a few coppers left in his pocket.

"Stupid woman," Ivy muttered, trying to stand.

It was pitch-black and cold, the fire in the grate having died completely. She couldn't see her hand in front of her face. By feel and familiarity she found a couple of matches and pulled the chain on one of the glass-covered lamps situated on the side of the mantel. She struck the match off the mantelpiece and held the tiny flame to the gas jet. The light flickered weakly. The gas supply coughed and sputtered. A sure sign indicating the need for more money in the gas meter.

"Da, are you home?" She kicked the black knitted shawl she'd used to cover her knees away from her. The darn thing was wrapped around her ankles. She stumbled, shivering in the cold predawn air. "Da, where are you?" She held her arms in front of her as she made her way to

387

the second of the two rooms they called home. She pushed the heavy wood door ajar.

"Da, it's black as pitch in here." She sniffed the air like a hound. Her da smelt like the bottom of a barrel after a night on the tiles. "Da!" she shouted again even though she knew the back room was empty of life. "Where in the name of God did yeh get to, Da?"

Ivy longed to collapse on the floor and scream like a banshee.

"It's past four in the morning. Where can he be? The pubs are all closed," she sobbed.

Last night, not for the first time, Éamonn Murphy had cleaned out the jar she kept her housekeeping money in – the rent-money jar was empty too. Thanks to her da's two-finger habit, Ivy always checked her cash before she went to bed. There wasn't a penny piece to be found in the place. Her da had waited until Ivy joined the street party before stealing the money and disappearing with his drinking cronies.

The sound of footsteps coming down the entry steps had Ivy spinning around towards the window of their basement flat. It wasn't her father: the footsteps were steady. Ivy froze for a moment. Should she blow out the gas lamp and pretend she was asleep?

"Miss Murphy! It's Officer Collins, Miss Murphy." The soft words were accompanied by the rap of knuckles on the entry door. The Murphys were fortunate in that their basement rooms had a private entrance, a luxury in the tenements. "Miss Murphy!"

"Officer Collins!" Ivy opened the door, trying to make out the features of the man standing in the concrete cage that framed the iron steps leading down to the doorway. Officer Collins was a familiar face to the residents of these tenements. "What in the name of God are you doing at my door?"

"Could I come inside, Miss Murphy?"

Barney Collins wished he was anywhere but here. He'd walked the streets of this tenement block known locally as "The Lane" for years. Ivy Murphy was a well-known local figure. She'd pushed a pram around the high-class streets that existed only yards away from the squalor of The Lane from the time she was knee-high to a grasshopper.

Ivy stepped back and watched the tall police officer remove his hat and bend his head to enter the tiny hallway. "I can't offer yeh a cup of tea," she said, leading him into the front room. "It's a bit early for visitors."

"I wonder if we could have a bit more light on the subject?" Barney Collins couldn't see a thing in the flickering gaslight. With Ivy's pride in mind he held out a copper penny and offered it to her with the words: "Saves you searching in the dark." Barney well knew everyone in these tenements squeezed every penny until it screamed but right now he needed to be able to see the woman.

"Give me a minute." Ivy was glad the dim light hid her burning cheeks.

She hurried into the hallway and quickly pulled the door of the cupboard that hid the gas meter open. The strength went from her legs when she noticed the broken seal on the money-box of the meter. Her da had nicked the gas money as well. Ivy passed the penny through. Might as well be hung for a sheep as a lamb, she thought, catching the penny in her open palm and passing it through the meter again.

"Thank you, Officer," Ivy said, returning the coin to the policeman. "I had several coins on top of the meter."

She lied without a blush but she was mortified at being forced to play penny tag with a police officer.

She quickly lit the second gas lamp on the mantel. With very little fuss she raked the fire and in minutes had a blaze climbing up the chimney. When you came in freezing from the winter conditions you needed to get the fire going, fast. Paper, sticks and small nuggets of coal were kept close to hand.

Ivy wiped her black-stained hands on a damp rag hanging by the grate, before turning back around to face Officer Collins. To give her father his due, he was a dab hand at finding nuggets of coal spilled around the docks. He sold some for drink money but always made sure there was enough at home for his own comfort.

"What's going on?" Ivy sank down into one of the chairs flanking the fireplace. She gestured towards the chair on the opposite side of the fireplace.

"I'm afraid I have bad news." Barney Collins perched on the edge of the chair, staring at the woman opposite.

Ivy Murphy was a good-looking young woman. In the proper clothes she would stand out in any company. Her blue-black hair pulled back into an old-fashioned bun suited her face. The starvation diet of the tenements gave her face a high-boned patrician appearance. Eyes of brilliant blue framed by thick black lashes stared across the space between them.

"Just get it out quick, please." Ivy forced the words out. Her lips felt frozen and her teeth wanted to rattle, but she sat stiffly upright. "What has me da been up to now?"

"There's no easy way to tell you this, Miss Murphy." Barney Collins swallowed audibly. "Sometime during the early hours of this morning, in what we believe was a drunken stupor, your father Éamonn Murphy fell into the cement horse trough outside Brennan's public house and drowned."

"Me da is dead?" Ivy fell back against the chair, her hand going to her incredibly narrow neck, almost as if she needed help holding up her head. "That's not possible. I'm expecting me da home any minute."

"I'm very sorry for your loss." Barney Collins wondered if he was going to have a hysterical woman on his hands.

"He's really dead?" Ivy whispered. "You're sure? It's not some kind of mistake?"

"I'm sure, Miss Murphy. I know your father well enough to make a positive identification."

"Yes, I suppose you do." Ivy wanted to float away, disappear. What on earth was she supposed to do now?

"Ivy, Miss Murphy, is there anyone I could call to be with you?" Barney Collins couldn't just leave the poor young woman here alone.

"There's only me and me da," Ivy whispered. "All the others left." Her three younger brothers had taken the mail-boat to England as soon as each turned sixteen. Ivy hadn't seen or heard from them since.

"I could knock on Father Leary's door if you like," Barney offered. "I pass his house on my way home."

"He'd only be round here with his hand out!" Ivy blurted out before slapping her hand across her mouth. It didn't do to badmouth the clergy in Holy Catholic Ireland.

"I see." Barney Collins was astonished to hear anyone dare to voice a negative comment on the clergy. The poverty-stricken families living in this slum were devoted Catholics. The people of The Lane accepted the decisions of the priest before the law of the land. Every family gave pennies they couldn't afford to the Church each Sunday and every Saint's Day. It was a wonder the local church didn't burn down with the number of candles these people lit.

"I'm sure you don't see." Ivy grinned in spite of herself. "I have a problem . . ." she paused, wondering how much to say, "with the Church. It's a well-known fact in these parts."

"I'll have to leave you to it then," Barney Collins was unsure what to make of this situation. "The death certificate and your father's body will be waiting for you at the morgue in the basement of Kevin's Hospital. Because of the time of year," he shook his head – it was a rotten start to 1925 for this woman, "it will be a few days before the body is released into your care."

"Thank you for coming in person to tell me." Ivy stood waiting for Officer Collins to push himself upright, then slowly walked the police officer to the door. She wanted a cup of tea and time alone to think.

"I'll keep in touch if you don't mind," he said.

"Thank you." Ivy held out one pale, cold, shaking hand, offering a handshake as a token of her gratitude. It was all she could afford.

"Let me know if I can help in any way." Barney Collins stepped through the open door and replaced his uniform hat on his head. "It seems almost insulting to wish you a Happy New Year," he shrugged, "but I don't know what else to say." He began to climb the iron stairs leading up to the street. When he reached street level he turned with his hand on the iron railings to look down. The door was closed tight, the gas lamps extinguished.

Ivy wasn't even aware of turning off the gas lamps – the habit of saving money by any means possible was bred into her bones. She dropped back into her chair, staring without seeing into the fire.

"What in the name of all that's good and holy am I going to do now?" she croaked aloud, tears running down her cheeks unnoticed. Her da had left her without a brass farthing to her name. There was no way she could give him the send-off he would want, the kind of send-off his friends and drinking cronies would expect. Her body began to shake as she tried to grasp the situation she found herself in. What would she do? Where could she go?

Ivy finally gave in to the sobs she'd been forcing back since she heard the news. Her big, tough, rascal of a da was gone. She'd never see him again. She'd never again scream at him for the trouble he never failed to bring to her door.

"Tea, I need a river of tea." Ivy wiped her hands across her wet cheeks, her eyes sore from the ocean of tears that had poured from her shaking heart.

She grabbed the heavy black kettle from the grate and without conscious thought picked up the galvanised water bucket. She hoped she could get down the back of the tenement building to the communal outdoor tap without anyone seeing her. She didn't want to talk to anyone. All she was capable of thinking of at this moment was her desperate need for a cup of tea. She wanted to think, plan, try and find some way out of this nightmare.

While the heavy stream of water slapped against the bucket a smoky rasp issued from the half-open door of the outside toilet.

"Jesus, would yeh have some mercy for the suffering of others!"

Ivy raised her eyes to heaven, praying she'd have all the water she needed before Nelly Kelly came storming out to see who was out and about at this hour. Nelly made no secret of her admiration for Ivy's da. She'd try to barge her way in to see him. Ivy knew enough about the mating of animals to know what the noises coming from her da's room meant whenever Nelly closed the door that separated the two rooms. Nelly was the last thing she needed this morning.

The kettle and bucket filled at last, she scurried away and back to the basement.

There she sat for hours at the table under the window of their front room, moving only occasionally to tend the fire and add hot water to the tea she sipped through pale lips. She held the chipped enamel mug to her mouth with two hands, trying to force her mind to settle into some useful train of thought. She listened to children scream in the street and barely flinched when the steel rim the boys were playing with fell down the basement steps with an unmerciful clatter. Even Nelly Kelly's screamed curses and shouted abuse failed to penetrate the daze she'd fallen into. She had to think.

She'd visit her da. That was the Christian thing to do. Her head almost wagged off her shoulders as she nodded frantically at the first solid idea that had come to her. She'd go and see her da – then she'd be able to think.

She stood and stared around the sparsely furnished room, wondering what she should do first. She banked the fire with wet newspaper, causing clouds of grey smoke to fill the chimney breast.

Without thought she picked up the threadbare old army overcoat one of her brothers left behind. She pulled the coat over her shaking body. Throwing the black knitted shawl over her head and shoulders, she wrapped the belt of the coat around her waist to hold the long ends of the shawl in place. Without a backward glance she let herself out of the only home she'd ever known.

Ivy ignored the shouts of the children playing in the square cobblestoned courtyard. She was aware of the women leaning in the open doors of the block of twelve Georgian tenements at her back but didn't respond to their shouted greetings. She stared without seeing across the courtyard at the local livery, a long barn-like building that snaked along one complete side of this hidden square. Mothers yelled at their children from the row of two-storey, double-fronted houses that marched across the furthest end of the square but Ivy didn't hear them.

She bowed her head, covered her face with her shawl and walked quickly across the cobbles towards the tunnel that was the only entry and exit point to this hidden enclave. The square sported the official name of Verschoyle Place but the inhabitants, for no apparent reason, never called it anything but The Lane.

Ivy wrinkled her finely formed nose at the stench that seemed to reach out of the tunnel and choke her. The wide tunnel was cut into a high wall that formed the fourth section of the square. The wall protected the rear entrances of the prosperous Mount Street houses from their impoverished neighbours.

One wall of the tunnel stretched along the side of the last house on Mount Street. The wall on the opposite side formed the side wall of the public house that occupied the rest of Mount Street and backed onto the livery. The drunks who fell out of the pub daily used the tunnel as a public toilet. The women of The Lane battled constantly with the odour of stale urine, but no matter how many times they scrubbed the tunnel out, it still stank.

Ivy stood for a moment with the rank-smelling tunnel

at her back. She ignored the shouted comments of the drunks standing outside the public house as she gazed around at a world that had suddenly become alien to her. She knew this area like the back of her hand. How could she suddenly feel so lost?

The Georgian mansions that marched along both sides of Mount Street blazed and sparkled in the sharp icy-cold air. Snow-white steps leading up to impressive doors with polished brass fittings lined both sides of the street. One row of Mount Street mansions elegantly hid most of the poverty-stricken world mere steps from their rear gardens. Mount Street was a different world entirely from the world Ivy and her friends inhabited.

Which way should she go? If she had a ha'penny for the charabanc she could walk through Merrion Square towards Grafton Street and public transport, but it would be Shank's mare all the way for her. The biting cold of the stones under her feet ate through the paper covering the holes in the soles of her shoes.

Ivy turned towards the Grand Canal. She'd follow the canal, walking along the pathways worn bald by the constant passage of the horses that pulled the barges travelling from Dublin to Kildare daily. Following the canal would take at least twenty minutes off the hour-long walk. The bare earth should be warmer and softer than the stone pavements.

Ivy felt invisible, a lost soul no-one could see, moving along the river path without friend or family to comfort or console her. Her da was gone. The big noisy laughing rogue that broke her heart once a day and twice on Sunday was dead. What was she going to do without him?

Ivy had been looking after her da since her ninth birthday. Ever since her ma had taken the mail-boat to

England leaving her da alone with four kids under nine to raise. Ivy covered her mouth with her hand, pushing back the laugh that seemed disrespectful under the circumstances. Her da raise the kids? That was a joke. Ivy had become the mother and chief earner of the family from that day to this. It was Ivy who walked the streets pushing a pram, begging clothes and unwanted items from the wealthy houses that encaged her world. It was Ivy who sat up all night cutting and stitching at the discarded clothing, turning rags into money-making serviceable items she'd sold back to the servants of the houses she frequented.

She stepped off the path to let a horse-drawn barge pass her by. She waved to the people on board, wondering what life would be like living on one of those floating homes. Was it any better than the life she led? She shrugged and turned to walk on.

A sudden thought almost brought her to her knees. The rent book – had her da changed the title-holder like he'd promised? Sweet Lord, was she about to lose her home as well as everything else? She thought back frantically to her twenty-first birthday – hadn't her da boasted to his cronies about being a modern man and changing the rent book to her name now she was a woman grown? Whose name was on the rent book? If it was still in her da's name she'd be evicted. Her ma had shouted often enough, "You can eat in the street but you can't sleep in the street!" Dear God, was she about to become homeless? She could end up in the poorhouse.

Ivy tried to think back – late last year, when she turned twenty-one, had the name on the rent book been changed? She'd check as soon as she returned home. It would be the first thing she did. Ivy shook herself like a wet dog. She couldn't think about that, not now that she was at the back end of Kevin's Hospital. Garda Collins said the morgue was in the basement. She'd visit her da and pray for a miracle, some kind of a sign.

Ivy stared at the large signs with pointing arrows in despair. How she longed to be able to read the words! She could follow the arrows with her head held high then. A sigh that seemed to start at her feet shook her slender frame. It wasn't to be. She was ignorant, stupid. The pretty squiggles meant nothing to her.

Ivy ignored the tuts of disgust she received from the people she asked directions from. She was used to that. She just wanted to see her da. Make sure it was really him. Maybe the police had made a mistake. Her big laughing da couldn't be dead. Not her da, the larger-than-life Éamonn Murphy.

It took a lot of time and effort but finally Ivy was outside the cold grey doors that led to the morgue. She was shaking, unaware of the tears that soaked into the part of the woollen shawl she'd wrapped around her face. Her hands were blue, frozen, but she forced herself to apply pressure and push the heavy doors apart.

Chapter 2

Ann Marie Gannon watched the wide double doors of the morgue open slowly. She wondered who else was on duty this New Year's Day. Ann Marie had drawn the short straw yet again. Everyone knew she lived with her uncle and was a soft touch. Every holiday or feast day, here she sat filing reports and shivering in the badly heated small office attached to the morgue, her only company the dead.

"Can I help you?" Ann Marie came out of her office and into the frozen stillness of the morgue. She walked slowly over to the visitor. She didn't judge the strangely dressed figure standing frozen with her back to the double doors of the entryway. Death didn't distinguish between social classes. She saw all sorts down here.

"Me da," Ivy croaked, pushing the shawl away from her face, being careful to leave her head decently covered. "They said me da was down here."

"What's your da's name?" Ann Marie asked gently. There were corpses in here with more colour in their faces than this poor woman.

"He's me da." Ivy stared at the woman, seeing only the white coat. She couldn't be a doctor – everyone knew that was impossible.

"What's his name?" Ann Marie repeated.

"Éamonn Murphy," Ivy forced out through chattering teeth. "They told me me da would be in here."

"Ah yes . . ." Ann Marie turned her head towards the sheet-shrouded tables that lined the cavernous space, then turned back in time to see the woman sink gracefully to the floor.

Ann Marie wasn't surprised. This happened a great deal in here but normally there were more people around to lend a hand. She didn't try to catch the woman. She was taller than Ann Marie. It was difficult to judge her size in the bulky clothes she wore but at a quick glance she outweighed Ann Marie by several stone.

"My goodness!" Ann Marie put her hands under Ivy's arms and began to pull her along the floor out of the path of the slowly opening door.

"Another one overcome by your stunning beauty, Ann Marie?" Austin Quigley, one of the hospital porters, stuck his face through the opening gap.

"Give me a hand here Austin, please." Ann Marie ignored his lame remark. The man was a joker but now was not the time. "She must have bird bones because in spite of her size she's light as a feather."

"It's all bulky clothes I imagine," Austin grunted as he picked Ivy's unconscious form up from the floor. He stood holding the inert body, waiting for his instructions. "I'm surprised you didn't recognise the signs of slow starvation in her face. The Good Lord knows it's a common enough sight where I live."

"How in the name of goodness would I be able to see anything under all those rags? Bring her into my office please, Austin." Ann Marie hurried back in the direction of her private kingdom. She held the office door open for Austin to pass through with his burden. "Listen, Austin – could you sneak a bowl of soup and a couple of buttered rolls from the doctors' kitchen?"

400

"Her table manners will probably upset your stomach." Austin wasn't joking. Ann Marie had a heart of gold but her weak stomach was a standing joke. Bad table manners had been known to cause her stomach to revolt.

"Austin, you would try the patience of a saint! Would you please put her down here?" She indicated the visitor's chair in front of her desk. "If you could bring this poor woman a bowl of soup I'd appreciate it." Ann Marie knew the porters helped themselves to the food in the doctors' kitchen. She didn't see why this poor creature couldn't have a little something. No-one would miss it.

"If I get caught stealing I'm blaming you, Ann Marie Gannon!" Austin put the woman in the chair and turned to leave. He walked swiftly back out through the office door, pulling the door closed quickly to keep the heat inside where it was needed. The poor sods in the main part of the morgue didn't need heating. Austin pulled the morgue's main doors open and hurried away to see what he could finagle from the well-stocked doctor's kitchen.

"Oh me aching head, what happened?" Ivy held a shaking hand to her head. Her stomach felt sick. "Where am I?"

"Just sit still a moment, dear." Ann Marie walked over to sit behind her desk. "You fainted."

"I've never fainted in me life!" Ivy snapped, struggling to find an inner balance. "Oh, I remember . . ." she sighed. "I prayed it was a dream."

Ivy made a concentrated effort to force her eyes to focus on the woman sitting behind the desk. The pretty face, with its peaches-and-cream complexion, was framed by hair the colour of toffee and pale-blue eyes beamed goodwill from behind wire-framed glasses. To Ivy's befuddled eyes the woman looked as if she hadn't a care in the world. Working in a place of death, how could she look so at peace?

"I'm sorry," Ivy said. "I didn't mean to snap at you."

"No need to apologise to me," Ann Marie said and smiled. Before she could add anything else the phone on her desk rang. To her complete amazement the young woman almost jumped out of her skin. Ann Marie grabbed the phone, wanting to stop its strident demand before the woman fainted again.

Ivy watched, her eyes hurting they were open so wide. This must be one of them telephone things she'd been hearing about. Wasn't that a wonder? Without a pause the woman put something against her ear and spoke aloud into the black thing she was holding up to her face. As Ivy watched in stunned admiration, the woman took a paper out of a nearby huge grey drawer and read from it into the phone, unaware of the genuine awe and envy of her audience. The woman was obviously well educated, Ivy thought and sighed. What would that be like?

Ann Marie completed her phone call and returned the file to its drawer. "I'm sorry about that," she said, smiling at Ivy. "I don't know your name." She waited, the smile still curving her pale lips.

"Ivy," Ivy croaked, unable to believe this superior being was actually speaking to her, asking her name. "Me name is Ivy Murphy."

Ann Marie's little office had a long glass window to allow her to see into the morgue at all times. Now she spotted Austin pushing open the main mortuary doors with his back, while carrying a tray in his hands. "Well, Ivy Murphy, here's Austin with the soup I asked him to bring for you."

Ivy wanted to refuse but the smell coming from the

bowl on the tray had her mouth watering. She couldn't remember the last time she'd eaten. She definitely couldn't remember the last time she'd been served and never by a man.

Without a word being spoken Austin placed the tray on the desk, then with a quick nod of his head towards the two women he left the office.

Ivy waited until the man had left the office before allowing herself to examine the tray. It held a bowl of soup, a plate with two buttered rolls and, holiest of holiest as far as Ivy was concerned, a pot of tea steaming gently, surrounded by two cups and saucers, a milk jug and a sugar bowl. A feast fit for a king.

"Would it bother you to answer some questions while you eat?" Ann Marie had expected Ivy to attack the food in front of her but Ivy surprised her by eating slowly and elegantly. She was fascinated by this young woman who appeared, to her eyes, like a creature from a fable. The total and complete shock Ivy had experienced when the phone rang could not be feigned. Obviously she had never seen a phone before. In this day and age how was that possible?

"What do you need to know?" Ivy wanted to close her eyes and groan at the first taste of the food in her mouth. The rolls had actual butter on them. She vaguely remembered her mother buying butter but it had been years since she'd tasted it. She, like everyone else she knew, used the drippin' from any meat she was lucky enough to fry. She bought drippin' from the butcher when she had the pennies, drippin' from the meat the butcher roasted – that was the stuff of legend.

"I don't mean to appear indelicate," Ann Marie shrugged, "but why are you here alone? Surely your mother or some other member of your family could have accompanied you?"

"There's only me." Ivy couldn't believe the richness of the soup she'd been served. She'd never tasted soup with so much meat in it before. It was delicious.

"You don't want your parish priest or perhaps a nun from one of the local convents to come?" Ann Marie saw the figure in front of her stiffen. The reaction surprised her. She was of the Quaker faith herself but generally the people of Dublin were Catholic. "Have you no-one to share this burden?"

"Like I said, there's only me." Ivy savoured her soup and rolls with a blissful sigh. She was conscious of the ticking of a clock somewhere but she refused to rush. Who knew when she'd get to eat again? She wanted to lift the bowl up in her two hands and slurp, but she remembered enough of the lessons on manners her mother had drummed into her to know that was unacceptable.

"Do you have a local funeral home I could telephone for you?" Ann Marie offered. She really wanted to help.

"Lady, I don't mean to be rude or ungrateful but you have no idea, do you?" Ivy hoped she hadn't sounded too sharp – she didn't want to repay this woman's kindness with rudeness.

"Please, explain to me while I pour us both a cup of tea." Ann Marie busied herself setting out the cups and saucers and pouring from the pot of tea.

"I don't have a brown penny to me name." Ivy was tired of always being the strong one. She didn't have to protect her da any more. Her da was dead and nothing on this earth could hurt him now. And she'd never see this woman with the kind eyes after today.

"Me da, the man who fell into a horse trough and

drowned, the man out there on one of your tables, he took the last bit of food in the house and shared it with his drinking pals. Not satisfied with that, he cleaned out every penny of my hard-earned money and blew it celebrating the New Year with his cronies." Ivy bit back a sob. She was damned forever now for speaking ill of the dead.

"Oh, my goodness!" Ann Marie had no experience at all of something like this.

"If I fail to give me da the send-off his drinking cronies and all of the neighbours think he deserves I'll be shunned," Ivy continued. "People will cross the road to avoid me." Her sigh came from her tired soul. She'd carried the weight of her family for so long. "I don't know if I have a home to return to. I can't remember if me da put my name on the rent book or not. I have no money for the rent anyway – me da took that too and the rent man isn't exactly understanding."

"Today is the first day of a brand-new year." Ann Marie believed every word out of this young woman's mouth. Those blue eyes clouded by tears could not lie. Ann Marie believed in fate. This woman, this Ivy Murphy, was the answer to her prayers. She believed Ivy had been sent by a higher power – she was a lost soul in desperate need of her help. She would do everything in her power to aid this woman in her hour of need. "We are two women who find ourselves in a very unusual situation." Ann Marie refilled Ivy's teacup. "Will you allow me to assist – to help – you?"

"I know what 'assist' means." Ivy was bone-weary now. How could anyone help her?

"Ivy, without taking anything away from the pain and loss you are suffering," Ann Marie spoke softly, afraid of offending "would you agree your greatest problem at the moment is a lack of funds, of money?"

"The story of me life," Ivy sighed.

"Then let us put our two heads together and figure something out." Ann Marie slapped her two hands on her desk, shoved her chair away and stood up. "First let us visit your father. Then, with a fresh pot of tea, we will begin to try and find a solution to your problem."

Ann Marie had an idea but she didn't wish to share it with Ivy just yet. First she needed to see Ivy's father. She wasn't sure which body belonged to Éamonn Murphy. If it was the emaciated, wizened old man she'd seen earlier in the day her idea would not be feasible.

"You'll come with me?" Ivy had seen dead bodies lying in the street or laid out in the tenements but she'd never seen the dead body of someone she loved.

"Of course. We're in this together now."

Ann Marie quickly checked Éamonn Murphy's details and with the slab-number fresh in her head, she led the way out of her office.

"This is it." Ann Marie stopped before the third table from her office. "Are you ready?" She waited for Ivy's nod before pulling the sheet away from the rigid form.

"Ah, Da!" Ivy stroked her fingers through her father's mane of rich auburn hair. Someone had washed it recently and it felt like silk under her fingers. "Da, look what you've done to yourself! Yeh auld eejit!" Ivy's tears dropped onto the waxen features.

Ann Marie stood with her arm around the sobbing woman's shoulders. She was shocked and appalled by this man's appearance. He was young, his heavily muscled chest and full-featured face showing no sign of the starvation that was written so clearly on his daughter's face.

Ann Marie promised herself she'd pull the sheet back later just to check but it appeared to her the man was taller than average with all the hallmarks of a rich life written into his skin and bone. She was honest enough to admit that if she'd seen this man on the street she'd have turned around to get a second look.

"Da, what am I going to do without you?" Ivy pressed her trembling lips against the ice-cold skin. There was no reaction. Her da didn't open his laughing blue eyes and grin at her. He was really dead – not here – gone away without her. She should be used to it by now – all of her family left her behind one way and another.

"Would you like some time alone with your father?" Ann Marie was familiar with the crippling grief the death of a loved one brought.

"No, thank you." Ivy pulled her shoulders back and straightened. "This is his body but me da is not here. He always told me the body we wear is just an old overall, nothing special. He was religious me da, never doubt it, and he always said that when we died we left our old worn-out overall behind and went on to a better place." Ivy wiped her shaking hands over her tear-stained cheeks. "His overall is not that old but he's left it here anyway."

"Come away then, Ivy." Ann Marie slowly covered Éamonn Murphy's handsome face. "I have the makings of tea in my office. I'll make us a fresh pot and we'll talk."

"I'll be grateful for any advice you can offer." Ivy was so tired, so emotionally bankrupt she didn't seem to be capable of making a decision for herself. It was seldom anyone offered her help. She'd listen to what this woman had to say.

She sat silently, grieving, while the tea was being made.

"Believe it or not, Ivy, there are several options open to

407

you," Ann Marie said as she poured the tea.

"I'm glad you think so."

Ann Marie sipped her tea with a grateful sigh. "If I understand correctly, in order for you personally to survive you need to find money for food and rent, urgently." She waited for Ivy's nod. "A big send-off for your father is out of the question. I don't for a moment mean to be disrespectful to the deceased but wouldn't you agree that by taking the last of your food and all of your money your father has already had his big splash?"

"I hadn't thought of it like that!" Ivy laughed. Her da would be tickled pink to think he'd danced at his own wake.

"I know of a way your father can earn a few pounds." Ann Marie grinned, delighted to have some way of helping Ivy.

"Would yeh go way!" Ivy gasped. "Me da never earned a pound in his life!"